REIGN

of the
FALLEN

REIGN
of the
FALLEN

SARAH GLENN MARSH

RAZORBILL®

RAZORBILL®

An Imprint of Penguin Random House LLC
Penguin.com

RAZORBILL & colophon is a registered trademark
of Penguin Random House LLC.

First published in the United States of America by Razorbill,
an imprint of Penguin Random House LLC, 2018

Copyright © 2018 by Sarah Glenn Marsh

LIBRARY OF CONGRESS CATALOGING-IN-PUBLICATION DATA IS AVAILABLE

ISBN: 9780448494395

Printed in the United States of America

1 3 5 7 9 10 8 6 4 2

Interior design by Eric Ford

For my parents,

who always encourage me to follow my dreams.

And for Chris,

who never lets me give up, even when those
dreams seem impossibly distant. You're
the best part of my story.

I

Today, for the second time in my life, I killed King Wylding. Killing's the easy part of the job, though. He never even bleeds when a sword runs through him. It's what comes after that gets messy.

When Evander and I finally stride through the wide palace doors, shouldering the burden of the king's corpse between us, the sun is a gash on the horizon. It stains the jagged clouds, the palace's marble walls, and every blade of grass with red as we trudge downhill toward the sea. King Wylding always likes a sea view when we necromancers bring him back to life.

I wonder how much of the rolling waves he can even glimpse through his mask and death shroud, but maybe it's the sound of the crashing surf or the smell of the salt air he craves. Either way, I don't question the man. And not just because he's been ruling

Karthia for two whole centuries. I can't stand the rasp of his voice, dry as the wind rattling bare branches.

"Here we are." Evander sets the king's feet down before stretching to his full height. He reminds me of a crow in his fitted black necromancer's clothes and long dark cloak, which covers his gloriously broad shoulders and the hard lines of muscle in his arms as he makes a sweeping gesture. "The best view in Grenwyr Province, Majesty." His lips twitch as he catches my eye roll. "What?"

I grin and ease His Majesty's head onto a bed of grass. Evander knows as well as I do that the king can't hear us. Not yet. I just hope his spirit hasn't gone too deep into the Deadlands, the spirits' world.

I glance back toward the palace on the hill, but the path there is empty. None of the royal residents—living or Dead—have yet emerged. And we can't raise the king, or anyone else, without one of their kin.

"I don't remember a Wylding heir ever being late for a raising," I say. "Even the nervous ones show up on time. Think something's wrong?"

"I'm not worried." Evander winks, then scans the overgrown field at our backs. Slipping an arm around my waist, he draws me against his side. "If you're interested, I know a way to make the wait fly by, my lady—I mean, *Master* Odessa."

I cringe and shove him away as irritation flutters in my chest. He's been relentless with using our titles since we woke up today. "How many times do I have to punch you before you'll stop calling me 'Master'?"

"I'm sorry," he says, a shiver of amusement in his voice. "Forgive me, Sparrow." He presses a light kiss to my forehead, brushing his fingers over each of the birds tattooed above my elbows.

I meet his eyes. Then his lips. The heat of our kiss is almost enough to make me forget the dead king at our feet, who looks like someone's lost, forgotten shadow in his dark shroud.

"I'm just proud of you," he amends against my mouth. "Of us. We might be Grenwyr's newest necromancers, but we're definitely the best-looking." He twines his ivory fingers through my brown ones. I've always loved the way they looked together, a tangle of dark and light. I shoot him a look that demands seriousness, and when he speaks again, all traces of merriment have fled. "We're finally *mages*, Sparrow. That's more than most people can say. We should shout it to all of Karthia!"

He's right, of course. We've been training for this since I was a ten-year-old pest, and he, twelve. This job is all I've ever wanted—at least, it was all I wanted until two years ago, when Evander and I first kissed at the Festival of the Face of Cloud. If only being with him were as simple as moving between our world and the Deadlands.

"Careful," I warn, only half joking. "Doesn't your mother forbid such talk?"

Evander rests a hand on my back and gives me the look he's perfected over time, the one that always wins me over, where his midnight-blue eyes soften like he's letting me see inside him. All necromancers have blue eyes, but I'd never seen a hue that dark until I met Evander.

He drops his voice to a whisper, the kind that makes things clench low in my stomach. "Since when do you care about what's forbidden by anyone?"

"Ha," I say weakly, remembering a supper just a few nights ago when Evander's mother spoke of her hopes for her only son to marry above his station. A countess, a duchess, someone with a fortune. But really, I think any girl would do—a baroness, or perhaps even a royal chambermaid—as long as she's not a necromancer. Unlike the rest of Karthia, I think she'd rather die than allow another necromancer into her family, especially after she's fought so hard against Evander's chosen career these past seven years.

If it weren't for the fact that we need his mother's blessing for any Karthian priest to marry us, Evander and I would be wearing each other's rings by now.

Pushing Baroness Crowther to the blackest corners of my mind, I run a hand through Evander's close-cropped dark hair, making him smile. I won't let her ruin a moment that she's not part of. I kiss him breathless, filled with a longing and a recklessness that seem to be growing stronger every time we're together.

A faint noise jolts us apart.

There's no telling how long we've been standing here entwined, except that the sky is pure lavender now—but then, time always seems fluid when we're together like this, as strange and unpredictable as the way hours pass in the Deadlands.

"Stop, Van," I murmur, forcing the word out as cold grips me from head to toe. High on the palace ramparts, a black-shrouded figure turns to face us. My face warms, banishing some of the cold. "They're finally here."

Evander's cheek presses against mine, scratching me with the stubble on his jaw. "Another day, another raising." He keeps his voice low as he watches the distant figures.

Another shadow flits onto the ramparts, then another. I count perhaps twenty masked and shrouded nobles, all impossible to tell apart by height alone. Dead princes and princesses, deceased dukes and their wives, and of course, Her Majesty. All brought back by necromancers so that those who know Karthia best can continue to run it the way they always have, each one wearing a dark shroud for the protection of living and Dead alike. If a living person were to see even a sliver of a Dead one's flesh, the Dead person would become a Shade—a monster notoriously difficult to kill.

"Wonder who's making the sacrifice this time," Evander mutters, shaking me from my thoughts. "Remember Prince Myk?"

I wrinkle my nose, tearing my gaze away from the Dead royals to look at him. "The one who started crying before we'd even reached the gate?"

Evander's roguish grin returns. "Indeed. You'd think that for all the time they spend around the Dead, the Wylding descendants would be a little . . ."

"Braver?" I supply, narrowing my eyes at the palace's wrought-iron gates. They slowly swing open to reveal a girl almost as tall as me, dressed in flowing red silk. A golden diadem set with a single teardrop-shaped opal rests at the peak of her forehead, flashing in the low light, marking her status as one of the king's living heirs. As she strides toward us, the wind lifts her long blond hair behind her like a banner.

"I hope you've got a handkerchief ready," I whisper to Evander. But as the princess glides nearer and I meet her brown eyes, bright with determination, I doubt we'll be reliving the crying prince incident today.

"You must forgive my lateness," she gushes as she reaches us. Even when standing still, she has an air of constant motion that makes me dizzy. "I was working. I'm afraid I lost track of the time."

Evander and I exchange a look. Since when do any of the palace's living occupants apologize for anything? For that matter, when do any of them *work*? All they do is sit around eating fancy cheeses and planning parties and art festivals. Maybe that's what royalty calls "work," though.

Up close, the ashen pallor of her skin and the smudges beneath her eyes are unmissable. Twin red lines on her cheeks suggest she wears glasses, but she seems to have forgotten them in her rush to meet us. Stranger still, she's paler than Evander, and that's saying something. Either she's sick, or she doesn't spend much time outside.

"It's no trouble at all, Highness," Evander assures her, smiling politely. With a glance at the shadowy figures watching from the palace walls in the distance, he gives the princess a deep bow. "I'm—"

"Evander Crowther. And this is your partner, Odessa of Grenwyr," the princess chimes in, smiling as though pleased with herself. "I've heard all about you from my brother."

"We'll be helping you raise the king tonight," Evander continues, sounding slightly amused. "Or rather, you'll be helping us."

The princess nods in answer, watching me with a keen gaze as I roll up my sleeves. She's probably waiting for me to greet her properly, too.

I make a much quicker version of Evander's bow, mostly because I can get away with it. Everyone expects fine manners from Baron Crowther's only son, but from an orphan dumped in a convent's garden, they're usually amazed I don't eat with my hands.

"Remind me of your name," I say as I straighten. I've seen the princess around, of course, but she makes herself scarce enough that we've never been properly introduced. She's the oldest living princess at the palace, one of two, and while it's on the tip of my tongue—Vala? Vandra?—I can't dredge it up just now.

She rubs her temples, gazing out over the water like she didn't hear me. "Oh!" she says at last, turning back to us and blinking. "I'm Princess Valoria Juline Wylding. It's an honor to meet you, both of you."

I steal a quick look at Evander, who seems to be thinking along the same lines as I am: We shouldn't take this dreamy-eyed girl to the perilous Deadlands.

"Highness?" Evander clears his throat. "Are you sure you're feeling up to this? I could run to the palace and fetch someone to take your place. It'd be no trouble. You look—"

"Dead on your feet," I finish for him, grinning at Princess Valoria while Evander groans at my joke. "Here." I fish a few of my beloved coffee beans from my pocket and offer them to her. "Eat these. They should wake you up."

"Don't touch them!" Evander says sharply as the princess reaches out a hand. She hesitates, and Evander blinks at me in disbelief. "I mean, she could be allergic," he says, a telltale flush creeping up his neck as he tries to avoid the princess's questioning glance. "What were you thinking?"

"I'm thinking anyone who's going into the Deadlands for the first time needs their wits about them," I say firmly. But Evander's just worried the princess will tell her however-many-times-great-grandfather the king that I offered her illegally imported goods. Evander's trying to protect me, because he must not see what I do in Princess Valoria's keen eyes.

Curiosity.

"What are they?" Princess Valoria closes her pale hand over the coffee beans, surprising me with callused fingers that scrape my skin as she pulls away. She brings the beans to her nose and inhales. "They don't smell poisonous." For the first time, she smiles. "I'll try anything to help me stay awake while I finish my project."

"Project?" I kneel beside the king's shrouded body and tie back my wavy dark brown hair, ready to get to work—and not the party-planning kind.

Evander relaxes his shoulders, seeming to realize that the princess isn't about to run screaming to her kin over my dirty little coffee habit.

"An invention. I've been tinkering with it all summer. I'm so close to finishing that I've not been sleeping much. I'm hoping..." Princess Valoria pauses, popping a coffee bean into her mouth and crunching it. She makes a face at the bitterness. "I'm hoping Eldest Grandfather comes back to us in good spirits. I thought if I went to the Deadlands to fetch him this time, he might be grateful enough to let me share this one with the people of Karthia."

Evander glances up midway through crouching beside me to help prepare the king's body and almost topples onto the dead man. He falls to the side at the last moment, knocking the king's left arm askew. "You're an inventor?" he growls, brushing off bits of grass. "I never thought I'd see one in the flesh. I mean, I heard a story about a man who invented a new recipe for a duke once. It didn't end well, though . . ."

As we learn from birth, the slightest change from the old ways is forbidden in Karthia. No leaving the country. No new recipes, no new forms of art, no new fashions, and especially no inventions. "Progress," the king always says when he gives his twice-yearly public address, "is a slow-acting poison that will ensure Karthia's eventual death."

Princess Valoria's expression is defiant. "He's not happy about it." She points to the king, but doesn't look at him. "But so long as I hide everything in my room and don't show anyone, he doesn't complain about it anymore. Not much, anyway." She glances away, toward the sea again. "I spend most of my time alone, working."

Now I know why I've never seen her at parties. Pity. I have the feeling her stubborn streak matches mine. We could have fun together.

"I thought you might understand," she adds, nodding to the contraband coffee beans tucked in my pocket, "as you don't seem to mind bending rules."

"You could say that." I break the stare, fiddling with the double-sapphire pin on my tunic. The pin is a gift given to every mage when they become a master, the gems representing our blue eyes that mark us as necromancers. Mine is still new enough that it feels oddly heavy at times. "Now let's get this over with so you can return to your inventing, Highness."

I pull up the hem of my long shirt and study the three glass vials on my necromancer's belt. Milk. Honey. Blood. All three are full, two of them waiting to be called upon once we've traveled through one of the Deadlands' constantly roaming gates.

But first, as always, comes the milk.

It gives strength to dead flesh, making it easier for a spirit to slip back into its shell. As I pour my vial of milk over the king's body, the princess's hushed voice rings in my ear. "He hates waking up all damp and sticky."

"Well, then it's a bad day to be him," I mutter, stashing away the empty vial.

"What's the honey for?" Princess Valoria's coffee breath washes over me as she peers over my shoulder to study my belt.

I arch a brow at her. Most of the royal family members know all about raising the dead, especially since we necromancers live among them, and because so many of them are Dead themselves. But Valoria clearly keeps to herself more than most.

"The honey's for us. So we aren't tempted to eat anything in the Deadlands. Do that, and you'll be trapped there forever." Seeing the next question forming on her lips, I hurry to add, "The blood is for His Majesty's spirit, when we find him. The spirits all crave it. It reminds them of the life they had and makes it easier to guide them back to their bodies."

Beside me, Evander works quietly to make sure the king is completely covered by his shroud. One small slip once he wakes, one roaming pair of living eyes, and we'd have a Shade on our hands.

And I really don't feel like fighting a monster tonight. There are enough of them lurking in the Deadlands without adding one more.

"We won't have far to walk, at least." Evander points west, toward the sea.

There, suspended in the air above a not-too-distant rocky tree-strewn cliff, a round blue gate shimmers as clearly as the moon and stars. The gates are easiest to spot at dusk. At least, for anyone with blue eyes. To everyone else, they're forever invisible, and my stomach clenches as I imagine what walking through this particular gate will look like for Princess Valoria.

Like leaping into the far-below sea.

"What do you see over there?" the princess demands.

"The way forward," I answer, and her eyes widen. Sometimes I wish I'd been born with brown eyes like hers, so my Sight would show me how the parts of something worked together. I could've been a potioneer then, and worked in an apothecary like an ordinary Karthian. Of course, if King Wylding didn't forbid change, I bet brown-eyed citizens would be anything but ordinary—putting their talents to work at new ideas.

Standing and stuffing a few coffee beans in my mouth, I offer a hand to Princess Valoria. "Hold tight. If we get separated, you're doomed."

The princess nods, but her face is pinched like she's about to vomit.

"Relax." I squeeze her hand. "We'll be in and out of there in no time. You'll see."

The princess takes a shaky breath. "You can't promise that."

"Of course I can." Grinning, I point out one of the birds etched in indigo on my arm.

"Forgive me." Valoria rubs her eyes and blinks. "Of *course* I have absolute faith in you—you're the Sparrow!"

My grin widens. "The one and only." I got the nickname because I'm the best guide through the ever-shifting Deadlands. It's good to know my reputation is alive and well. "Now let's grab the king before he wanders somewhere we won't want to follow."

We begin the march toward the cliff nearest the gate, leaving the king's body in the grass to await our return. Evander leads the way. Normally, I'd enjoy the view of his tight backside as he strides toward our destination, but the princess's fingers are so icy in mine that I can think of nothing but her dread.

"Did your family explain the price of walking into the Deadlands, Highness?" I whisper. I still don't like how pale she is. Or, I realize for the first time, how young. She can't be quite as old as my seventeen years.

"Fertility," she whispers back.

I nod. Entering the realm of death demands life, at least for those without blue eyes. Necromancers like Evander and me can walk through the Deadlands without a cost, but not many realize the price we must pay later. When we die, our spirits never reach the Deadlands. We can raise the dead time and again, but no one will be able to give us a second chance at life.

Valoria squeezes my hand tighter. "Will it hurt? Losing my—ah—?" She looks queasier than ever, pressing her free hand against her stomach.

I hold back a smile with practiced ease. Our clients always ask that. "No. And fertility means a lot of things to Death, Highness."

The princess smiles. "Call me Valoria, if you please."

Clearing my throat, I continue, "Death's touch might mean you won't bear children. Or it might mean that any seed planted by your hand will never grow. Or that blight will strike your fields. Or you might never be able to heal from sickness, or wounds."

"I see." Valoria's voice grows smaller as we near the cliff, where it was deemed too jagged and steep to build any houses. Dotted with stubborn, twisted cypress trees, the layers of weathered white and gray rock plunge sharply into the deep blue waters below. Valoria looks between me and Evander, pressing her chapped lips together. "So what now? We just . . . fling ourselves into the ocean and wake up in the Deadlands?"

Evander opens his mouth to answer, but the princess squares her shoulders and raises her chin as the wind whips her blond hair across her eyes. "Whatever happens, I'm not afraid."

I grip her cold hand a little more carefully. I'm starting to like Princess Valoria a lot more than most of the royals I've danced with at the palace. Maybe I'll convince her to come to a party someday.

Just a short walk away from the edge of the cliff, which juts out from the others around it, Evander begins explaining to Valoria how we'll get through a gate she can't see.

As his voice washes over me, I tip my head back for a final glimpse of the stars, so numerous tonight that they glisten like diamond powder blown across a cloak of darkest velvet. Lowering my gaze, I take in the houses studding the other seaside cliffs, with their warm stone walls and jewel-bright roofs and gardens of olive and lemon trees. And on the second highest hill in Grenwyr, overlooking all that beauty, the distant palace. I open my mouth, sipping salt air and savoring the taste like I always do before entering the Deadlands. Just in case I don't return.

After a moment, I close my eyes to focus on the cries of the gulls. But a low groan coming from the gate at the cliff's edge, followed by a thump, interrupts their chatter.

At almost the same time, Evander shouts, a sound that clutches at my heart. My eyes snap open. As we draw our swords, my mind struggles to make sense of the grisly sight just in front of the glowing blue gate, separated from us by a distance of a hundred feet or less.

Valoria clings to my arm as a misshapen figure fresh from the Deadlands struggles to push itself upright, clearly having fallen out of the gate. Swallowing hard, I force myself to focus on any details that might point to the identity of the unfortunate mess of blood and mangled flesh as it crawls toward us.

There's a tattered necromancer's black uniform hanging in strips over a shattered leg. A hand clutching at a spill of guts. A bald head crowned with crimson. A torn and gushing throat. And just about the only part of him still wholly intact, a single brightblue eye.

A familiar eye. One that looked into mine mere nights ago, full of warmth and understanding—orphan to orphan—as I accepted my master necromancer's pin.

"Master Nicanor!" As his name tears from Evander's lips, the horror of this reality hits me in a dizzying rush.

"What happened?" I cry, my heart beating an erratic melody against my ribs. "Where's Master Cymbre?" Nicanor shouldn't have been in the Deadlands without his partner. It's against the rules.

I want to run to the edge of the cliff, to close the distance between us and be with him in his final moments. But like Evander and Valoria, I'm frozen in my tracks by a mixture of fear and revulsion as the battered and bloody figure crawls toward us with painstaking slowness, an arm outstretched.

This can't be happening. Not tonight. Not ever. Not to someone as good and wise as Master Nicanor. I wish I could tell myself I'm dreaming, but Valoria's screams assure me I'm painfully awake.

Nicanor opens his mouth. I tense, ready to hear the name of his attacker, but the raw, guttural sound that emerges is less than human.

Not halfway between the gate and where we stand, his broken body cradled by the roots of an old cypress, he collapses and gasps out his last breath.

II

I close my eyes, drowning out the horrible scene before me, and allow my mind to carry me back to the beach below these very cliffs, where Evander and I stood with Master Nicanor only a week ago.

There was a bonfire that night, stretching toward the indigo sky, calling for dancing and the kind of celebration we Karthians love best: one that rages late into the night, long after the moon and stars have gone to bed.

And though there were only four of us gathered on the beach on that sweltering summer's night, we ate and drank enough for a crowd.

"More elderflower wine, anyone?" Master Cymbre asked, holding up a blue glass bottle and glancing at each of us in turn. The firelight melted years off our teacher's face, and I had a sudden urge to throw my arms around her waist and hold on the way I did when I was ten. The year she took me in and began my training.

"I think it's time we present your students with their pins, Cymbre." Master Nicanor, her partner, drew out her name with the lyrical accent of a southern province. *Sim-bree*. He rose, the flames glinting off his bald head, and held up a velvet pouch.

The sight of that little bag made my breath hitch in my throat.

Cymbre leapt to her feet, accidentally whipping Master Nicanor in the face with one of her long cinnamon braids. I disguised my snort of laughter as a cough while Nicanor rubbed his cheek. In my seven years of training at Cymbre's side, watching her every move as she worked with her partner, I'd seen this happen more than once.

"Ready?" Master Cymbre's steel-blue eyes sought mine.

Squaring my shoulders, I nodded. She knew as well as I did that I'd been ready from almost the moment I began shadowing her steps seven years ago.

Cymbre then turned to Evander. He grinned at her as he dug his toes into the sand, restless, more than ready for this next big adventure.

Clearing her throat, Cymbre intoned in a solemn voice far from her usual drawl, "Odessa of Grenwyr. Evander Crowther. Please rise." Evander winked and grabbed my hands, and we supported each other in standing as Cymbre continued, "The pins you are about to receive will signify your status as master necromancers to all of Karthia."

I raised my chin a fraction as my teacher—my former teacher now—stepped forward to fasten a gleaming gold and sapphire pin to my crisp new necromancer's tunic.

"Wear it with honor," Master Nicanor murmured, though there was no need for such formality.

There were no spectators that night, after all. The pin ceremony called for at least one member of a mage's family to bear witness, but Evander's mother—the only family either of us had—refused to come. Ignoring the ceremony was her way of protesting that Evander and I had chosen this path when she was dead set against it.

I wondered if she knew how much it wounded him, or if she was too oblivious to see through the mask of pleasantries he put on for her. After all, she couldn't see how Evander felt about me.

At least we had Master Nicanor, ready in a pinch to be our fill-in family for the ceremony.

"Nervous about next week's raising?" he asked me as Cymbre turned to fasten Evander's pin. My teacher's partner was so tall, he had to bend his knees to converse with most people. "King Wylding requested you specifically," Nicanor said quietly. "Requested *the Sparrow*," he corrected himself, smiling at my nickname.

"You know I don't get nervous. It's just . . ." I toyed with the twin eye-shaped sapphires on my new pin. None of the other mages I knew had ever bothered to tell me how *heavy* the little pin felt as it rested against their hearts. "Without this pin . . . without this title, I'm just . . ."

"Just an orphan?"

Startled by his understanding, I blinked up at Master Nicanor. His bright-blue eyes turned dark like the depths of the sea, unreadable for a moment.

"How did you know—?"

"Before I was Master Nicanor, I was just Nicanor of Dargany

Province." He smiled, and my heart skipped as understanding passed between us, orphan to orphan. I'd never thought to ask about his life before coming to Grenwyr City, and he'd never offered to share. "When I was a trainee, earning that title was everything. I thought that without it, I'd be just another poor boy condemned to a life in the Ashes. Insignificant."

Unable to speak around a lump in my throat, I nodded and glanced at Evander, who tossed me a wink as Cymbre admired his new pin in the firelight. Without *his* title, he would still be nobility. Still be someone's son. Still be a brother. A mapmaker. An adventurer. Without my title, I'd be just a poor girl lucky enough to have been raised by the Sisters of Death. I'd be nothing more than a charity case.

I clutched my new pin, the cold metal digging into my sweaty palm.

This is a job to Evander, and one he loves, but to me, it's everything.

"I won't pretend it's not a daunting task, living up to the title of master," Nicanor continued, cutting into my thoughts. "Counting you and Evander, there are only a handful of us in Grenwyr Province. But you're more than just a necromancer. More than an orphan."

He turned, as if he meant to walk down to the shoreline, but I grabbed his wrist. I'd seen him and Cymbre at work for years. He had two trainees of his own, my friends, and we all agreed he was the wise man to Master Cymbre's warrior.

"What am I, then?" I demanded.

Nicanor shook his head, a smile lingering at the corners of his eyes. "That's for you to decide." He strode to the water, dipping his toes into the frigid sea foam. A moment later, Cymbre followed with the remnants of the elderflower wine in hand, leaving me alone at the fireside with Evander.

"See that?" I murmured, slipping an arm around his waist and pointing to the two masters by the seaside. "That's our future."

Evander's hand on my shoulder tears me from the peace of the memory, back to a future now forever changed, to a reality where Princess Valoria is on her knees mere paces from the fallen Nicanor, shaking like a leaf in a storm. She's probably never seen so much blood before.

Nor have I. This goes well beyond a spilled vial from my necromancer's belt. It seeps into the pale rocks, a gruesome river. Vaguely, Evander's shouts pierce through the fog in my brain, but the sound is a faint hum compared to the roaring of blood in my ears as I try and fail to rip my gaze away from the crimson ground.

"Odessa!" Evander shakes my shoulders, snapping me from my daze.

Hot, nasty bile rises in my throat and forces me to swallow hard or be sick on my boots. My chest heaves with the effort, and Evander puts a steadying hand on my back.

Far up on the high hill at our backs, the palace's iron gates spring open. Several guards stream down toward us, brandishing spears and blades. "Who's hurt?" a sharp-eyed woman at the front of the group demands as they finally draw near. She frowns at the sight of Evander's ashen face and my tear-streaked one. Or perhaps at the princess cowering among rocks and tree roots. "Where's the attacker? Did you—?"

Her voice dies the instant she spots the body at the base of the tree, and she lowers her weapon. "By Vaia's grace . . ." She invokes the name of the Five-Faced God, clutching a tiny pendant of the Face of Death she wears on a silver chain.

"By Vaia's grace," another guard echoes.

Murmurs ripple through the guards, but the blade-wielding woman nearest us drowns out the rest as she demands, "Who could do such a thing?"

A Shade, I'm betting. Something with teeth that can tear flesh as easily as a hawk's wing slices the air.

And as my eyes meet Evander's, he gives a slight nod, confirming my suspicion. "I saw it," he mutters hoarsely. "Just a glimpse before it retreated, when Master . . . Nicanor . . ." He falters, and I grab his hand. As I squeeze his cold fingers, he finishes, "When he fell out of the gate. It was the biggest Shade I've ever seen."

Which means it's been feasting on countless spirits in the Deadlands, growing stronger. It's a necromancer's nightmare come to life. Evander and I can perform a raising in no time with me leading the way, but we've yet to kill a Shade on our own, and this one has to be powerful if it killed a seasoned necromancer like Nicanor.

The shrouded nobles and several of their living descendants watch from on high, distant black specks hardly discernable from the night sky, as more guards surround us, followed by a hazel-eyed young man in robes. A healer. He rushes to Princess Valoria's side, breezing past Evander and me like we're a couple of statues.

"You need something for shock." He presses a vial of smoking gray liquid into the princess's hands. He has to hold the vial to her lips in order for her to drink it down, and after a moment's hesitation, he drags her across the hard ground away from Master Nicanor.

From the body.

Someone's covered it—or rather, what's left of it—with a cloak.

"As soon as you drink some of that potion, you'll need to tell us everything," a tall guard says, his voice hushed but his tone clipped.

I nod. Everything seems to be moving in slow motion, reminding me of the few nights when I've had too much wine.

"Here you are." The healer approaches Evander and me with two more vials of smoking liquid. We accept them with barely uttered thanks, waiting for him to turn away. But he narrows his eyes at us and crosses his arms expectantly.

Sighing, I lift the vial to my lips. Evander does the same. I let the liquid fill my mouth, its taste sour like overripe berries, and pretend to swallow.

The healer gives a satisfied nod, then turns back to Valoria. After exchanging a quick glance, Evander and I cough the potions into our hands, then wipe the remnants on the rocks, where they smolder gently as they seep into the pale earth. We still have a job to do tonight, and we both know how important it is to have our wits about us in the Deadlands, where anything can happen.

Evander wipes his mouth on his sleeve, then starts relating Master Nicanor's final moments to the guards. There isn't much to tell, and knowing it won't be long until we'll need to head through the gate bathing us in its ethereal light, I hurry to where the princess sits and crouch beside her.

"I'm sorry to say this," I say in a steady voice, squashing down my own pain for the sake of the younger girl's shimmering eyes, "but we still have to find King Wylding. I hate to think of how far his spirit's traveled while we've been delayed."

Valoria takes a deep breath, then pulls back her hair, seemingly trying to steel herself for what's to come.

"And I hate to think what would happen if the giant Shade in there catches a whiff of us. I don't feel good about going in there tonight, even with this . . ." Evander murmurs, touching a hand to his sword hilt. "Fire is the only thing that destroys a Shade, but blades can slow them down," he adds at the princess's curious look. "I'm no Nicanor, and if even *he* couldn't . . ." He lowers his gaze to the ground, blinking hard.

"You're right," I say briskly, hoping to cover the cracks in my voice. "There's a chance we may never return." I inhale deeply. There's always that chance, even without a giant Shade skulking around. "Still, it's our duty to raise the king, and if we die trying to finish what we started . . ." Shrugging helplessly, I add, "But we can't ask you to risk your life, Valoria. If you'd like to trade places with a relative, if someone's willing—"

"No. I knew the risks when I signed up for this." The princess reaches for my hand and pulls herself to her feet with my help.

Keeping hold of me, she looks toward the cliff's edge. "Let's go," she says, standing taller, her brown eyes hard as stone. Most of the royals would be a blubbering mess by now, but not this one. "We have a job to finish."

After a final word to the guards, Evander takes my free hand.

It's just a dead body, I tell myself as I force my legs to move. I'm around them all the time. Why should this one be any different? An image of Nicanor's smiling eyes flashes to mind, giving me the answer: *because they aren't usually necromancers.*

The king's routine slayings are usually peaceful. We swiftly kill him when he's showing signs of becoming a Shade, having been in our world too long. Then we fetch his spirit, and soon, he's able to walk and talk and think as he did in life.

But Nicanor's one chance at life is over. It makes my chest ache as I think of the breaths he should be drawing at this very moment. Yet, as Valoria said, we have a job to finish. And right now, doing our job seems a lot easier than trying to understand that the man I sat with on the beach last week is in pieces on the ground.

Hand in hand, the three of us stride into the glowing blue light, no one looking back at the body. As we near the edge of the cliff, Valoria closes her eyes and sucks in a breath.

The gate's chill washes over us, something even the princess can feel. She seems to faint right after making the leap with us, her hand turning limp in mine. Our toes skim the air above the ocean for the briefest moment before we fall onto the hard dirt floor of the tunnel concealed behind the gate.

"I'll check her pulse," I whisper as Evander climbs to his feet and draws his sword.

As I press my fingers to the princess's wrist, feeling for a heart-beat, she shudders and pulls back. "I'm all right. That awful potion's made my head all fuzzy, though." She absently rubs her nose, per-haps trying to push up the glasses that normally rest there. "Let's finish this. I have so much work waiting for me back in my cham-bers, I'll be up past sunrise at this rate. Lead the way."

III

We march toward the tunnel's end, wrapped in the kind of silence that takes hold deep in my bones and makes me want to jump at the slightest noise. Shades crave the permanent twilight and shadows of this place, which means Master Nicanor's killer is surely prowling nearby.

The tunnel spits us out in a Deadlands forest, its trees tall and ancient, more like the pines in northerly Lorness than the oaks and cypresses found throughout Grenwyr. But when I breathe deeply, there's none of the clean, crisp scent the trees in our world give off. Walking through the Deadlands is an eerie experience, like I've lost half my senses. Between the pale trunks, there are glimpses of distant mountaintops where no sun ever shines. No sun, no wind, no rain. No scents of anything growing here.

As we crest a rise in the land, I spin around, leading Valoria with me. Turning slowly, I point out the endless confusion of meadows, rivers, and lakes spread out below us that make up this strange landscape.

"There are no homes," Valoria murmurs curiously.

"The spirits don't need them."

"And the air—it's chilly here."

Evander nods patiently. "It's always like that. Spirits don't feel cold like we do." He whips off his cloak and offers it to her. "Take this."

Our walk through the forest is just as quiet as the tunnel, and so is the meadow that welcomes us where the trees end. Our footsteps make lonely echoes down the narrow dirt paths that cut through a misty field of marigolds and moonflowers, a field that's usually teeming with filmy figures. After all, this is where every spirit in the world comes when they leave their bodies. Eventually, after they've been here long enough, the spirits move on—to what, not even the oldest and wisest necromancer can say.

"This way," I whisper. My voice slithers through the silver leaves of the gnarled old trees that form a canopy over us at the edge of the marigold field. On the other side of this grove, there's usually a sprawling garden with overgrown trees, glossy plum-colored flowers, and lilies as big as my head. It's a place King Wylding's spirit frequents, along with many others, a place where elderflower wine bubbles from marble fountains and no one ever weeps.

Those finished with life crave it less over time. And the spirits who linger here longest, the ones whose memories have faded to a single point of laughter, or a pretty face whose name they can't remember, hardly ever come to the gardens like King Wylding does. Instead, they wade in the rivers or bathe in the lakes, letting

SARAH GLENN MARSH

the flowing water strip them of every last bit of themselves as they wait for whatever's next to claim them.

"Fascinating," Valoria breathes as we pass a statue of a man holding a bar of gold. Her earlier tears of shock have dried, leaving faint trails down her cheeks. "How do you suppose the spirits build things? Can they *touch*?"

Turning my head slightly, I roll my eyes at the question. Only Evander notices.

"Of course, Highness," he says, lifting a branch so we can walk beneath it. "This is their realm, not ours. They have power here, like we do in the living world."

As I walk past Evander into a swirl of mist as thick as cream, I brush my fingertips over his and mouth a silent thank you. The princess hasn't stopped talking since we got here, and my patience for questions evaporated right around the time Master Nicanor died at our feet.

No matter how many times I repeat it over in my mind, I can't seem to grasp its completeness. Master Nicanor is *dead*. I press a hand to my writhing stomach, still sickened by the memory of the corpse.

The princess clears her throat. "Speaking of powerful things . . . what are the chances we'll run into that Shade?"

"I don't know, but I'd like to cut off its ugly head." Evander's voice is jagged, like he's swallowed too much grief. He pauses with his back against an enormous tree, one hand on his sword, the other clutching the vial of human blood he sprinkles along our path to try to draw the king's spirit near.

28

"Lucky for us, the Deadlands are vast. We probably won't see a thing," I grit out in a tone that doesn't invite more questions. I hate how each word is magnified in the immense emptiness of the grove. The Shade that killed Master Nicanor must have scared any nearby spirits into some deeper part of the Deadlands where we don't often travel. I've never walked this long down here without seeing a soul, and I don't like it one bit.

As if sensing my thoughts, Valoria shivers against me.

"It has to be a really nasty Shade to have gotten the better of Nicanor," Evander says after a while, putting away his vial of blood to scrub a hand over his shadowed jaw.

I wonder if he's also thinking of what happened to his father, Baron Crowther, and wish I could wrap him in my arms.

"What gives Shades their strength?" the princess whispers as we push through the deepest shadows of the grove.

I rub my aching temples. I wish there was some way of telling time here, but the permanently twilit sky gives away nothing, so I can't say whether the soothing potion Valoria drank is starting to wear off.

"For that matter," she adds thoughtfully, "what do they look like?"

"If you've never seen a Shade, you're lucky. I'm not going to describe one for you." I frown as Valoria shoots me an affronted look.

The Shades that haunt the Deadlands dislike sunlight and usually keep to the darkest shadows, occasionally finding a spirit to devour. They're rarely bold enough to attack a necromancer. Still, they're a big part of the reason why we always work in pairs. And why we kill any Dead—like King Wylding—at the first signs that they've been in their old bodies for too long: increased aggression, snarling at their families, and generally acting strange. Lucky for the Dead, the transformation from person to monster is much slower when they're shrouded, giving us necromancers time to intervene with a mercy killing and another raising. Once some-one's turned into a Shade, there's no reversing it.

A soft humming fills the misty grove, drawing my attention back to the princess.

Valoria clutches a pendant around her neck, a wooden token etched with swirling lines that make the rough shape of a face. "Dear Vaia, show us mercy and grant us safe passage," she mutters under her breath. "Help us find the king, and guide us safely home."

She's praying, I realize, to the brown-eyed Face of Change. The only one of Vaia the Five-Faced God's faces whose temples have been abandoned for over two hundred years, since King Wylding was first raised from the dead and outlawed the worship of Change.

"No music," Evander says gently, turning back to us. "Apologies, Highness, but the sound might attract more than just the king. Many spirits miss being able to laugh and sing. Get too many of them hungry at once, and we'll have to fight them off with our swords like a pack of wild dogs."

As we emerge from the silver tree grove and approach the edge of the massive garden, something stirs in the shadows at the corner of my vision. I whirl around, staring hard at the spot. My heart thuds dully in my ears, and though Valoria says my name in a far-away voice, I'm too focused to answer.

At first, all I can see is blackness between the trees that looks thick enough to swim in. Then I glance lower, and I spot it. The outline of a rotting arm or leg, a piece of mottled gray flesh stretching toward me through the darkness, changing the shape of the mists.

The sight squeezes all the air out of my chest.

"Odessa?" Evander grabs my shoulder. The spark of his touch breaks the spell the grisly sight cast on me, and I suck in a breath. "What is it?"

I blink, and it's gone.

Shades always move faster than humans, but the speed with which this one disappeared makes me feel like bolting for the nearest gate. Only my legs have turned to jelly, and there's no way I can go anywhere just now.

Meeting Evander's worried gaze, I shake my head. It isn't until Valoria's back is turned that I mouth, "Shade. It's gone now." The blood drains from Evander's face, and he meets my eyes as we exchange a wordless agreement: There's no point unsettling Valoria any further by mentioning this.

Still, Evander guards our backs with his blade. Just in case the Shade decides to return.

Valoria tugs on my hand, drawing my gaze to the garden. It's empty. No spirits stand around the giant marble fountain at its center, though the elderflower wine splashes merrily over the stone as always. My heart sinks at the sight.

Maybe all the spirits are gone because the giant Shade devoured them—the king included. But it's such a terrible thought, I can't bring myself to voice it.

"I thought you said he'd be here," the princess whispers. Her tone isn't accusing, but she shrinks against me.

"Maybe we need to spill more blood," Evander ventures, taking a few steps into the silent garden. "Fresher blood, so they can smell it from farther away." He holds up his left arm and lays the sharp edge of his sword against his pale skin.

Valoria sucks in a breath as I cry, "Don't!"

Evander lowers his blade at the sound of my protest, having made only a shallow cut along his forearm.

I can't stand to see a living thing in pain, least of all Evander. The nuns who raised me said I'd been that way since birth. Trying to put the wings back on a trampled butterfly. Tending the weakest plants in their garden. That's what made me so well suited for walking in the Deadlands, they said. My love of life.

"I'll do it," I say quickly, raising my arm and my sword. "Valoria, take my vial of honey. If you start feeling dizzy, eat as much as you need."

"Odessa, don't you dare!" Evander growls as I grit my teeth and pull the blade across my skin. One quick slice, and I'm bleeding on the ferns and the big white lilies.

Normally the sight wouldn't bother me, but today it makes me think of Master Nicanor's ribbons of flesh. I fight to keep breathing steadily as Evander rushes to my side, covering the wound with a scrap of his torn shirt.

"That's more than enough," he says sharply, probably thinking we'll attract that giant Shade with the mess I'm making. To my relief, the blood leaking from the shallow cut on his arm is already clotting.

"Just trying to help," I gasp out as my knees buckle. I must've lost a bit too much blood. Valoria steadies me. I glance back over my shoulder and offer her a weak smile as Evander finishes tying my bandage. "You're stronger than you look."

Valoria's lips twitch. "I know."

"Death be damned." Evander draws his sword again, a motion as fluid and natural as breathing. The few times I've seen someone best Evander in a sword fight, it was because he was too sick to know which end was the pointy one. "Looks like we'll be taking the long way home tonight," he grumbles, gazing at something behind us.

A hot prickle of fear stings the back of my neck as I whirl around, remembering the glimpse of rotten gray flesh in the shadows of the grove.

But the tightness in my chest dissolves. There's nothing in the darkness. In fact, there aren't any shadows at all. Instead, the silvery trees have been quietly replaced by a field of marigolds, just like the ones we crossed to get to the garden.

"How does an entire grove disappear like that?" Valoria asks.

"That's how it is here." I shrug. "Things are always changing. Moving themselves when you least expect it, just like the gates that let us in."

"It's why you're lucky to be here with the Sparrow." Evander shoots me an admiring glance. "Why *we're* lucky," he amends.

Already, a slight tug around my navel tells me that despite appearances, the gate isn't so far away anymore. Since the grove shifted off to some other part of the Deadlands, more of the landscape has moved, too, and we're suddenly much closer to an exit.

"There's a gate at the back of the garden now," I say, looking out across its wide expanse. There are dozens of fountains, bridges, and pathways to walk before we reach the new gate. "But we have to find the king first."

"In that case, ladies . . ." Evander puts on a smile, but it wavers. "Fancy a nighttime stroll through this beautiful garden?"

We wind our way slowly past the fountain, pacing ourselves so Evander and I can gaze around tall statues and flowers in search of the king. The marble fountain and even some of the plants give off a muted glow that serves as our only source of light, and it's a good thing, as no man-made lantern works down here.

"King Wylding," I call softly, pointlessly. "Majesty?"

I don't say it, not wanting to alarm Valoria, but I've never spilled that much of my own blood and not had at least a dozen spirits come out to fight over who gets to lap it up.

"This is beyond incredible." Valoria plucks a stem of purple flowers and brings it to her nose—lavender, the symbol of serenity. The language of flowers is the same in this world as in ours, the only way the spirits can communicate with the living from here.

"Strange—it doesn't smell like anything!" Valoria says, blinking at the lavender.

I tug on her hand, pulling her forward before she can spot the luscious-looking plums and apples hanging from the nearest tree. My injured arm throbs in response.

"Someday I'm going to figure it all out, you know." Valoria's eyes are bright and shining as she tucks the lavender stem in her hair. "The science behind our magic."

I arch my brows. "I don't think King Wylding would appreciate that kind of talk."

"But *I* do. I've been studying the correlation between eye color and different forms of magic, like how everyone with blue-eyed Sight sees gateways to the Deadlands and can learn to raise the dead." Valoria peers thoughtfully through the wooden slats of the bridge beneath our feet as we march over a small stream. "Someday I'm going to unlock the way magic works, and then I'll be able to explain all sorts of things. Don't you want to know why the Dead come back with their Sight but not their magic when you raise them?"

I wince, pausing just after the bridge and sheathing my sword. I don't want to answer any more questions. I just want to think about Nicanor as I remember him in life, uninterrupted, so he can stay real to me. Not like that bloody mess on the ground.

As the princess stops beside me, I take both her hands in mine. "There's nothing to study, or understand, or explain. It just *is*. It's not science. Our Sight is Vaia's gift to us. The sooner you accept that, the sooner you can start enjoying life."

"But I *do* enjoy it!" Valoria frowns. "Learning is what makes things fun."

"Hey, you two, hurry up!" Evander waves us over from beside a neat line of hedges, the garden border. "Look who I found," Evander says as we approach, the calm in his voice straining.

On the dark horizon is the reassuring blue glow of a gate. The way home. But Evander points down, just on the other side of the hedge.

Following his gaze, I lean over the prickly bushes. The sight that greets me makes me feel sick all over again, remembering the fear in Master Nicanor's remaining eye. And not just because it's surely an old pool of Nicanor's blood staining the ground beyond the hedge.

What chills me to the core is the way King Wylding's filmy spirit kneels beside the pool, scooping up tacky blood and smearing gobs of it into and around his mouth.

"Keep holding my hand, and grab on to His Majesty with your other one," I tell Valoria in what I hope is a soothing voice. When she blanches and shakes her head, I give her a nudge with my shoulder. "You're his connection to the world. No one else can do it. That's why you're here." But she remains frozen in fear. "You only have to hold him until we're through the gate. Then he'll wake up where we left him, safe in his shroud."

"Odessa's right." Evander frowns at the bloody grass. "Unless, Highness, you'd rather stay down here with whatever did that . . ."

Valoria groans and shakily climbs over the hedge, holding tight to my hand. The king looks up, unable to utter a sound in his spirit form. Free of his shroud in this world, he's a translucent version of himself in life, still a great bear of a man with arms built for chopping trees, but no longer darkly tanned and raven-haired like he is in many of the portraits decorating the palace walls. Now his skin and shoulder-length hair are as pale and fine as gossamer. Perhaps some would find him handsome, if he weren't lapping up blood and sporting the sword wound in his chest from when I killed him earlier.

Disgusting a sight as he is, I'm struck by a sudden rush of appreciation for King Wylding. He may be terrifying sometimes, and hand out threats freely, but most days I'm proud to be his necromancer. He can be as kind as he is harsh. He tries his hardest to prevent things from changing. And he loves Karthia enough to endure so many slayings and raisings, always returning ready to be our guardian. No one knows the hearts and minds of Karthians better than him after all these years, and I doubt anyone loves us as fiercely. Master Nicanor's death will hit him hard when he learns of it.

Summoning her strength, Valoria finally reaches out a hand.

The king's red lips form a gentle smile as the princess grabs hold of his wispy arm and pulls him toward the gate.

IV

Midnight has come and gone by the time we sit down for supper at Evander's house. The leftover rooster pie is mercifully warm, thanks to Baroness Crowther's servants keeping it on the stove. Someone's opened most of the downstairs windows, and a cool sea breeze tickles our ankles as we take our seats in the larger of the two dining rooms.

The baroness herself joins us, sliding into her customary spot at one end of the long table. As usual, she avoids looking too long at Baron Crowther's seat that will be forever empty.

I lift my fork, waiting to see if the baroness will say a prayer, but there's not much point since Evander's already tucking in noisily beside me.

"Eat," the baroness encourages, smiling softly in a way that makes her pale blue eyes crinkle at the corners. She pushes a basket of sliced fig-and-ginger bread toward me like nothing's changed since I saw her last, like it's no big deal that she failed to turn up for our title ceremony last week. "You look exhausted, Sparrow."

When I was younger, I used to think Lyda Crowther should have been born a duke's daughter, not a lowly miller's—especially on nights like tonight, when the gems she's pinned in her light brown hair sparkle like they're trying to outshine her. But of course, they can't. She's that beautiful, at least on the outside. I would've said *inside* once, back when I first became Evander's partner and she invited me here for every meal, offered me a bed, and fussed over me like a mother. Back when I didn't understand that she only kept me close because she hoped she could mold me into someone other than the necromancer I was born to be. And perhaps, because she saw how Evander and I shared every confidence, she hoped she could change his mind through changing me.

But last week's ceremony marked the day she finally gave up.

Lyda's voice, thick with concern, cuts into my thoughts once again. "Whatever's upset you and Evander this evening, I can't help but feel it's at least partly my fault . . ."

I've never really felt at home here, in the stiff, high-backed chairs that decorate the Crowthers' imposing manor, but Lyda has always encouraged me to call it home. And I guess I *should* call it that, since it's where I sleep most nights after fooling around with Evander, in a spare room where all my belongings fit in one dresser drawer.

"If I'd just done a better job at talking you two out of studying Death's magic! I haven't slept all week, I've been so worried . . ." Lyda wrings her hands in her lap, faint lines creasing her forehead as we all continue to eat our fill of a meal I can barely taste.

After several long moments, a pretty serving girl arrives to collect our plates. I wink at her as she takes up mine, then shift my attention to Evander.

"Speaking of death," he says hesitantly, as if he can't bear to relive the night's events, "I'm glad you're sitting down for this, Mother." He takes my hand under the table, after a practiced hasty glance over his shoulder to make sure no servants are watching from the shadowed halls. He sounds older than his nineteen years as he declares, "We were delayed tonight because Master Nicanor was murdered. It looked like he was torn apart by some wild animal. But it was a Shade. I saw it, just for a moment."

Lyda's hand flutters at her throat. All the nobles and necromancers know each other at least in passing, and Lyda knew Master Nicanor better than most. He's the one who stepped in to help when Baron Crowther himself became a Shade many years ago.

He's also the one who offered to train Lyda as a necromancer when she was a girl, according to Evander. But Lyda was never interested.

"Yana!" The baroness rises, crossing the room to ring a silver bell as she calls for one of her maids. "Bring some cold water, please. And hurry! I'm so distressed." She sets the bell down and turns back to us. Our gazes lock for the briefest moment.

Her eyes are perfectly dry, and her smooth face is expressionless. Whatever grief she's feeling, she buried it in a hurry. Maybe she's always blamed Nicanor for not reaching her manor in time to spare her from what she had to do to her husband, but it's hard to feel too sorry for her just now.

"This is yet another example of what I've been trying to tell you both all these years," she says slowly, in her soft, disarming way. "Without anyone to raise the dead, there would be no Shades." Her face is sorrowful again as she focuses on her son. "No Shades, and far fewer senseless tragedies."

I'm suddenly reminded of the time I overheard her telling Evander that if she could, she'd pay someone to change her eye color from blue to anything else. A dangerous thing to discuss—change—even if it's in whispers in one's own home.

"If there's one thing I wish you'd learned from your father's death," Lyda continues, blossoms of color appearing on her cheeks, "it's that if we love the Dead, we should leave them in their own world, where they belong."

The summoned maid, Yana, arrives with a pitcher of cold water and has to stifle a gasp at her mistress's words.

Evander clenches his jaw. "All I learned from Father's death is that the Dead need gifted necromancers to keep them and everyone else safe." His voice rises, and the maid scurries from the room. "Father *wanted* to be raised. He was there to see me grow up thanks to *necromancers*! I doubt I'd remember him otherwise."

Lyda opens her mouth, but Evander keeps talking, building steam. "If there were no necromancers, what would become of the Dead already here? Would you have them all slain just to return them to the Deadlands? Would anyone ever deserve that?"

Wincing, Lyda covers her face with her hands. A moment later, a whisper of her usual voice issues from between her fingers. "Of course not. What a horrible thing to say."

"If we love the Dead, we should honor their wishes and protect them, same as the living. And that's the last I'll hear of it." Evander leans back in his seat, breathing hard.

When they both glance in my direction, I spot a crumb of bread on the table and pop it in my mouth to avoid speaking my mind, because I actually think they *both* have a point. The Dead do pose a threat. I've seen the danger, just today, in the Shade that tore Master Nicanor to pieces. But the Dead need me far more than the living, and I, them. Without Dead to raise, I'd be nothing but an orphan. As long as the Dead are around, I'm their Sparrow, and I won't give that up for anything—not even for Lyda's blessing to marry Evander.

"We should pay for Master Nicanor's funeral," Lyda says timidly a moment later, her cheeks still ruddy with color. "He was a dear family friend, after all."

It's a peace offering, and Evander, seeming too tired to argue anymore, seizes it. He nods, and they start discussing plans. I try to listen, but my attention keeps wandering to Baron Crowther's empty chair at the far end of the table. No one's ever told me the whole story, not even Evander. But from what I've gathered, the baron died of a plague when Evander was small, and a necromancer brought him back. Then Lyda got a glimpse of him beneath his shroud, a terrible accident, and he became a Shade. He tried to kill Evander's little sister and broke Evander's arm when he stepped in to save her. Lyda killed the monster she'd once loved so dearly, setting it ablaze just before Master Nicanor and his apprentice arrived at the manor.

There's still a scorch mark in the smaller dining room. No one goes in there, but I peeked once. The story's true.

"Odessa?" Evander frowns like he knows I wasn't listening.

I fake a yawn, stalling for time as I try to figure out a vague answer to whatever question I missed. But I'm saved from answering at all by a rustling of skirts coming down the hallway, followed by the clicking of claws on the wooden floor.

The eldest of Evander's two siblings, Elibeth, appears in the doorway. Three of her greyhounds, blinking their liquid amber eyes, poke their heads into the room by pushing past their owner's billowing skirts.

"We've been sent a raven," Elibeth announces, casting a quick smile my way. I like everything about the future baroness, who as eldest will inherit the manor, from her sparkling green eyes, to the claw scars all over her hands and arms, to her bobbed, feathery brown hair. And I absolutely adore the pack of long-legged, skinny hounds that follow her everywhere. Like a matched set, all have white fur with large blue patches, but I know she has several other dogs here in the manor. I'd expect no less from a beast mage who maintains the royal family's fox-hunting kennels for a living.

Elibeth unfurls a piece of parchment, clears her throat, and reads, "Evander. And Odessa, if you're there: We must discuss what happened tonight. Get some rest, and meet me at the graveyard behind Noble Park tomorrow before noon." She sets the parchment on the dining table and adds, though we already know who it's from, "Signed, Master Cymbre."

Cymbre and Nicanor retired as of last week, having seen our training through to the end. But Cymbre seems to want to keep guiding us even now that we've come of age.

"She probably wants us to help her hunt down the Shade that did this," Evander mutters, picking up the parchment and crumpling it in his fist.

Elibeth's delicate brows shoot upward, and she grips the back of her mother's chair. "The Shade that did *what*?"

One of her greyhounds whines softly, as sensitive to her mistress's every shift in mood as Elibeth is to theirs. Another curls up on my feet under the table. I take comfort in the rhythm of its beating heart and the warmth of its fur as Evander sighs and repeats the night's events for his elder sister.

Once Lyda and Elibeth and her many hounds are fast asleep, I join Evander on the back end of the manor's roof. It's a quick climb from the balcony off Evander's bedroom to the rooftop, and the chairs he keeps out there are the perfect boost for getting onto the shingles. We can make it to the top in near silence thanks to years of practice.

I don't even flinch when the bandage on my aching arm snags on a patch of roof. Evander quickly helps me free it with a gentleness that's surprising from such strong, rough hands. I can always count on him to untangle me.

Once we're seated, we dangle our legs and kick at the brisk night air, thick with the familiar, comforting scents of bergamot and lemons, the restless sea at our backs. Around us, the stately homes of Noble Park are bathed in moonlight, all trying to outshine one another with the grandest balconies and the prettiest rose gardens. I never tire of the splendid houses, at least not at night, when their occupants are how I like them best: asleep.

"I don't know how I'm going to get any rest at all tonight." Evander takes my hand in his, rubbing his thumb over my palm. "I can't stop thinking about it, Sparrow. Every time I close my eyes, I see him. What was left of him."

I hate the roughness in his voice, those tiny cracks of fear and hurt. I hate the monster that took Master Nicanor and burned the horrible image of his final moments into both our minds. "We'll fix this, Van. We'll get revenge when we kill the Shade."

I'm reminded of the flash of the bony, rotting figure I saw in the Deadlands grove. Of how fast it moved. Faster than the other Shades we've glimpsed in the past. Of how hard we'll have to train if we want to fight it. But Evander doesn't need anything else troubling his thoughts tonight.

I wrap my arms around him, and for a long time, we just breathe.

It isn't until the sky lightens to a pearly gray that Evander lays a hand on my back and clears his throat. "I'm sending a raven to Kasmira after breakfast. As soon as we find and kill this Shade, we're booking passage out of here on the *Paradise*."

I draw back to give him a sharp look, suddenly alert despite my lack of sleep. He knows as well as I do that it's illegal for any Karthian to sail away from our rocky shores. Of course, that doesn't stop people like Kasmira and her smugglers from exploring under cover of darkness when they should be running routine supply ships up and down the coast. But if the king somehow got wind of our escape attempt before we set sail, he wouldn't hesitate to bind me in chains for the rest of my life. Just to keep me, his most prized necromancer, at his side. And when I think of it that way, leaving never seems worth the risk, even though staying means having to sneak around Evander's overbearing mother.

"We've talked about this before, Van," I say at last. "First of all, we have a home here, and now a job that brings the kind of riches most people only dream about."

Evander grins, undaunted. "So we'll build a new house and raise the dead somewhere different. People are always dying, and the gates into the Deadlands are always moving. Mages with our talent must be needed elsewhere, too." He lowers his gaze to my now-empty right pocket, where my coffee beans are usually hidden. "Kasmira and her crew get your treats from someplace outside Karthia. Another island."

"That's what she says." I shake my head, unable to hold back a slight smile as I think of her. "But people who trust Kasmira's word tend to wind up broke, lost, or dead."

"My point is, if she's telling the truth, we already know of one island where we could settle after exploring," Evander presses, his eyes gleaming as he pictures it. "Imagine—a shore full of coffee beans! And best of all . . . a place where we can marry."

I start to say something, but Evander beats me to it, taking both my hands in his. "Just think about it. There's nothing for us here. We can't get married without my mother's blessing, and Elibeth will inherit the manor and title besides. All I'll inherit—all I've ever been given—are my father's dreams."

I never met Baron Crowther, but he lives on through Evander's stories. He used to captain his brother's trading ship after his brother was crippled in an accident. And once, when he got knocked off course during a storm, he swore he saw a strange island. He became a Shade before he ever got a chance to retrace his path, to learn what was out there.

"The island, you mean?" I tentatively ask.

"Exactly. We can find it for him, together." Evander presses a kiss to my cheek. "That is, if you'll still come with me."

I shake my head to clear the cobwebs of exhaustion. "You'd go without me?"

Evander loosens his grip, drawing back to look at me with shining eyes. "I—I didn't mean I'd just take off—"

"Save it, Van," I snap, trying to cover my hurt with anger. "You meant what you said."

He tries to grab my hand, but I pull away too quickly. "Don't you want to see what's beyond our walls and our harbors without being afraid of losing our jobs? Or swinging from the hangman's noose?" His voice strains with the effort of keeping it steady. "Don't you want to get married?"

"I do." The words stick in my throat along with the tears I'm holding back. Even if our leaving went unnoticed until we were far from shore, I wouldn't know who I am if I'm not the Sparrow. I'm afraid I'd just be some girl on a boat. But keeping Evander in Karthia when he's dreamed forever of mapping out rivers and lakes and sleeping under new skies seems almost cruel. Even if I need him here. Even if the one dream I've never told anyone—of finally having a family of my own—would die the moment he left.

After a while, Evander says softly, "Tell me what you want most."

What I want is an end to these arguments. They only wind up hurting us both, never solving anything, because I never meant to fall for someone so in love with the unknown that it would threaten to take me away from the things that make me the Sparrow and the job it took seven years to learn. I doubt he meant to fall for me either, but now I'm caught up in his dreams of maps and distant shores, complicating everything.

"Maybe I don't know what I want anymore." I push a lock of hair out of my face with a shaking hand. With Nicanor's death fresh in my mind, a vivid reminder that we necromancers only get one chance at life, every little decision feels like an anchor holding me underwater. "This life is all we get, Van. There's no room for mistakes. No second chances, no do-overs. I just want to make sure we consider all the consequences before rushing off."

Evader grips my shoulders like I'm scaring him. The realization makes anger flare in my chest, because without it, I'd be scared, too, and there's no room for fear in Karthia. Not with the Dead among us, and with the possibility of a Shade being created at any moment.

"I know what *I* want. To be with you—*really* be with you. Out in the open." Evander's voice deepens with longing. "That's why we have to go."

I say the same thing I always do when he brings up leaving. "If it's me you want, then tell Lyda we're in love and demand her blessing. She'll come around eventually. We don't have to go anywhere to really be together."

"If she knew we were in love, she'd never let you stay here again. She'll never let me marry a necromancer."

"She doesn't want you to *be* a necromancer," I correct, clenching my hands at my sides. "Or me. It scares her, because of your father. But we can go live at the palace whether we're married or not. We have rooms there, thanks to His Majesty. It would mean no more sneaking, even if your mother never accepts what's been in front of her for years."

"That'll crush her, and you know it. She'll have no one then, with Meredy studying so far away, and Elibeth working all the time." He lowers his gaze. "We may not agree on, well, anything, but she's the only parent I've got. I can't hurt her like that."

"If you think moving to the palace would hurt her, how do you think it'll be when you vanish completely?" My voice comes out sharper than I intended. "You want to leave Karthia. *That's* what you really want. Stop pretending leaving is all about being with me!"

Stung, Evander drops his hands from my shoulders. "You're right. About everything." He takes a deep breath. "Leaving will destroy her, but at least I won't have to see her face."

"Coward." I wince, partly at the hurt on his face, and partly because I'm ashamed to admit I'm glad I said it.

"I could say the same of you." Evander leans close, breathing fast. "Even if you won't admit it, you're just like everyone else. Scared of what's out there." He sweeps his arm toward the sea. "Scared of change."

"If that's what you think, then you don't know me at all."

I leap to my feet.

"Odessa—"

Dodging his outstretched hand, I slide down the roof, taking care to not make a sound in case Lyda or Elibeth are sleeping restlessly. The patter of Evander's hurried steps pursues me as I dash toward the guest room where I stay—seven years, and I'll always be a guest. I change course at the last minute, ducking into Meredy's room two doors away instead.

I sink onto the edge of her bed as I struggle to get control of my breathing, coming in ragged gasps. The faint scent of the clean, sparse room always calms my nerves, though I can't explain why. It's a mixture of cedar chips, vanilla, and something I can't name. All I know is, it helps me clear my mind. I don't want to think right now, about Evander, Nicanor, or sailing ships or anything else.

I haven't seen Evander's younger sister Meredy since she was ten, starting her mage training a year after Evander and I began ours. She'd be sixteen now, training to be a beast master like her sister.

Burying my damp face in Meredy's quilt, I wonder if she's freezing to death in one of the northernmost provinces, Lorness or Oslea, learning to understand and control the seals and winter-white foxes. Or maybe she's down in Dargany Province, riding on a camel's back. I've only ever seen camels in paintings, but I wouldn't mind going somewhere like Dargany to experience new things. No matter what Evander thinks, I'm *not* scared of change—even if I don't always like it. I'm scared of going someplace where I might not be the Sparrow, of not knowing who or what I'd be then.

Yet I wonder if some small part of me is afraid, too, that Evander is right about leaving. We only get one chance at life—what if staying isn't keeping us safe, but holding us back? I wonder if I'd ever be brave enough to admit that aloud, much less to him.

After a while, I fall asleep and images blur together in my dreams: a bloodied Master Nicanor staggering through the icy tundra.

V

The last person I want to see this morning is Kasmira. But after waking with my face buried in Meredy's quilt to find two of the Crowther maids gawking at me from the doorway, I remember I gave the last of my coffee beans to Princess Valoria yesterday. So I don't have much of a choice.

I throw on a clean shirt, breeze down the stairs without looking to see if Evander is watching me from the parlor, and manage to dash outside before Elibeth's hounds cover me in drool.

There's not a cloud in the blazing blue sky this morning, yet there's a bite to the wind that says it will soon be time for the Festival of the Face of Cloud, signaling the start of autumn.

My stomach growls as I hurry through the wide, cobbled lanes of Noble Park. Servants airing out their masters' linens on sun-drenched balconies wave, bow, or curtsy as I pass. I wave back half-heartedly, unable to fully appreciate their enthusiastic greetings with Evander's heated words from last night still echoing in my mind. The stricken look on his face when I fled the rooftop makes me wonder if I should apologize. But an apology won't change the fact that we're at an impasse when it comes to our future.

I pass a market on a lower hill where most of the royal family's errand boys and girls do the shopping for the palace kitchens. The smells of saffron and sage make my stomach groan again, and I quicken my pace. Hopefully Kasmira has something edible on board the *Paradise* besides stale bread.

The way to the harbor takes me past warm yellow and pink stone buildings, their fronts wrapped with flowering vines, where shopkeepers live and work. Farther on, I pass a boarded-up temple for the Face of Change, its once-proud columns cracked and sagging. Someone has drawn Change's likeness in black ink on one of the building's vine-choked sides. It must be freshly done, as vandalism of this sort is promptly painted over or scrubbed away at the king's behest. The image reminds me of Valoria's necklace, and I wonder how she's holding up since her trip to the Deadlands.

Next I pass the convent for the blue-eyed Face of Death, a cheerful white building with a sapphire-hued domed roof flanked on either side by an ancient, hunched cypress tree. Within its generous courtyard is a sprawling garden, larger than the convent itself, where a few of the sapphire-robed Sisters pick rosemary and prune their potted shrubs. It's also where I grew up. If I wasn't in a hurry to get my coffee before I have to meet Master Cymbre, I'd stop in for one of the Sisters' famed fig-and-raspberry tarts.

I pull up the hood of my cloak to take a shortcut through the Ashes. The cramped, tumbledown houses are where the city's poor reside, those too sick or weak to go work on one of the farms outside Grenwyr City, and those too addicted to their favorite potions to do anything but sit on the filthy street and beg for coins.

No matter how many charities King Wylding organizes for the poor, this place never seems to get any richer.

"Blessed day to you!" a little girl's voice says as I step into the shadows of the battered homes. I push back my hood enough to see her and try not to cringe as my lungs fill with air that reeks of spilled ale, sweat, and rotten meat.

The raven-haired, copper-skinned girl can't be more than six. She sucks her thumb as she watches me from her crumbling front step. There's a doll tucked under her arm, an ugly thing as big as her head, made of cloth scraps and bits of colorful thread. Judging by the doll's long curly hair and pink robes, it must be a woman.

"How long has your mother or sister been gone, sweetheart?" I ask, nodding to the doll.

She pulls her thumb out of her mouth long enough to say, "My mom. Last spring. She had the black fever."

The black fever. A sickness so foul, even the healers can't cure it without killing themselves. It's been ravaging the people of the Ashes for years.

"And where's your father?"

"Scrubbing boats." The girl pops her thumb back into her mouth and looks in the direction of the harbor, though tall, old houses block it from view. As she returns her gaze to me, her brown eyes widen as if seeing me for the first time. "Your clothes . . ." she says slowly. "You're a mage, aren't you? The kind that brings people back to life?" She grins.

All this girl will ever have of her mother is that doll, sloppily made by some friend or relative to look like the loved one she's lost. I'll bet every child in these rickety houses has at least one doll like that, a poor substitute for what they dream about but will never be able to afford: a raising by a necromancer. *My* services.

"Take care of yourself, all right?" I say, but the girl doesn't seem to hear. She's busy crooning a lullaby to her doll.

"May he reign eternal," she says moments later, a farewell so faint I almost miss it.

The people of the Ashes adore King Wylding for never forgetting them, for not looking past them the way merchants and many nobles do. He comes down here sometimes, to serve them soup and bread, but I think they'd be a lot better off if he served them gold from his coffers or gave them jobs. Of course, that would be a change, so instead he'll keep doing what he's done decade after decade, wondering and worrying why his subjects are still suffering.

"May he reign eternal," I echo hollowly.

Pulling up my hood, I practically fly to the harbor, where the sun in my hair, the stench of fresh-caught fish, and the green-and-yellow banners of the *Paradise* snapping in the breeze push the little girl from my thoughts. The worn dock creaks under my weight as I tread the familiar path to where the *Paradise* is anchored.

There are crates stacked all over the ship's main deck. Barrels of elderflower wine from Ethria Province. Tart green apples from Adia Province. Bananas from Idrany Province, the islands that make up Karthia's southernmost point. But the good stuff is down below, behind a false wall in the back of the cargo hold. Coffee beans. A bitter thing called cacao. Spices with delicious names like cardamom and anise.

I'm about to jump on board when a tangle of salt-crusted raven hair catches my eye, gleaming blue-black in the morning light as Kasmira bends to inspect a crate. Her cool brown skin is several shades darker than mine, and knowing she's from Idrany's largest island makes me think one of my parents must've been from Idrany, too.

"Well, well," she drawls, turning to face me with a gleam in her deep gray eyes, "someone must be needing another fix." She grins, her teeth bright white against her skin, and beckons me closer. "You're in luck. I haven't eaten them all myself yet."

"Good. I'm desperate." I hurry onto the ship and join her by a stack of crates. "After the night I had, I'd do anything to get my hands on some."

She arches one perfect brow. "Anything?" She draws the word out, giving me an appraising look that makes heat rush to my face.

I wouldn't be opposed to the idea of kissing her, except that my heart chose Evander long before I even realized it.

And since Kasmira is the only one who can take Evander out of Karthia, she's partly to blame for last night's stupid fight. Today, I just want to get my coffee beans and leave.

I cross my arms and step back. "I'm in a hurry."

Kasmira frowns. "What's wrong, Sparrow? You're not your cheerful self today." She studies the bandage on my arm, a scrap of one of Evander's many black tunics. "Something happen I should know about?"

The concern in her voice melts my anger faster than a flame on wax. I stretch out my injured arm, holding very still while she peeks under the bandage.

"Doesn't take a healer's Sight to tell this isn't infected." She releases me, brushing away a strand of dark hair that's fallen across her forehead. "What's really hurting you?"

I reach for Kasmira's hand, telling her everything that happened last night, starting with Master Nicanor's death.

I've barely finished describing how I cut my arm too deep when Kasmira winces, pressing a hand to her forehead. She sways a little, so I steady her with an arm around her shoulders.

"What is it?" I whisper. She wouldn't want any of her crew overhearing that she's not feeling well. They'd give her more lip than usual, and they're hard enough to control as it is. "Do you need me to fetch a healer?"

But as Kasmira rubs her temples, I realize what's ailing her. "You've been changing the winds again." I try to keep the worry from my voice, but I can't help it.

She nods, and the slight motion makes her grimace. "There was hardly a breeze to speak of on our latest run. I had to shift things in our favor to get home before His Majesty could miss us, if you get my drift."

"Kas, you should rest more often. Hire another weather mage to do half the work or something."

A shadow crosses her face at my suggestion. "Another weather mage? There are only three in Grenwyr, so far as I know. Besides me," she adds, a hint of pride in her tone. "And they all have jobs that pay better than anything I could offer. Maybe I could train someone. But let's be honest. How many blue-eyed people actually bother with all the training needed to become a necromancer, assuming they're even chosen to try?"

I sigh. She's made her point. There's me and Evander, and our teacher, Master Cymbre. Then there's Jax and Simeon, who trained under Master Nicanor. As far as I know, we're the only necromancers in Grenwyr City, perhaps in the whole province. Each of Karthia's eleven provinces have a few blue-eyed mages, but that's still not many. And from what I understand, weather mages are even rarer, and harder to train into masters.

"Just take it easy for a while, all right?" I squeeze Kasmira's hand before dropping it.

She grins. "No promises."

I hesitate, then plunge ahead. "Can I ask you something strange, Kas?"

"No question's too strange for me. Go ahead." She takes a seat on a low stack of crates. Her head must still be bothering her.

"What's out there?" I nod toward the harbor.

Kasmira presses her lips together as her eyes crinkle at the corners, like she's holding back a laugh. "Water. Lots and lots of water. No place for a Sparrow to land."

I frown at her dismissal. I've never wanted to know anything about her journeys before, but after last night, I can't get Evander's plan out of my head. "This is serious." When Kasmira's amusement fades, I ask, "What about the ports where you get the coffee and spices? What are the people like there?"

"The people are just . . . people. Their skins are brown and black and white, like Karthians'. Some wear bright silks, and some wear rags. They like to eat and dance and gamble. And have a romp. It's the same everywhere." She tries to smile, but winces and rubs her temples again. "They talk in different tongues. It startled me at first, but we figured each other out pretty quick. Coins for goods."

"And the land? Are there shores full of coffee beans?"

This time, Kasmira can't contain her laughter. "Not exactly." Her expression turns thoughtful. "But why the sudden need to know?"

"I'm sure you'll find out soon enough," I grumble, thinking of Evander's raven, wondering if he sent it after all that was said—and unsaid—last night. A glance at the sun tells me it's nearly time to meet Evander and Master Cymbre. I drop my voice to a whisper in case any of the dock workers have keen ears. "Can you get me the goods now? I have to be somewhere."

She nods and disappears into the hold, leaving me alone on deck.

As I wait, I skim my gaze along the shoreline, where tangles of crimson seaweed from the ocean's depths have snagged on rocks. The seaweed's red hue makes my mind flash to Nicanor's final moments. I lean against the ship's rail and try to dredge up a happy memory to push back the darkness, but my stubborn brain is stuck on the horror of last night.

"What's the matter?" Kasmira demands when she returns with the coffee beans. "You look like you've seen a Shade."

My face hot, I stammer, "No. Not today, anyway." I force a grin, because Kasmira is giving me a deep, searching look, and she needs to be worrying about *her* health, not mine. "And neither will you, so long as you keep floating in this old bucket."

Kasmira clutches at her heart. "Old . . . bucket? Master Necromancer, you must be thinking of some other ship. Not the vessel that brings you your beloved coffee beans. Not the one that survived not two, not three, but—"

"*Six* massive storms, with hardly a scratch," I finish for her, grinning effortlessly now. Kasmira has that effect on people.

Filled with the calm only friends and coffee can provide, I dash off the ship, bound for my meeting with Master Cymbre. It's only when I'm well out of sight of the *Paradise* that unease steals over me again, and I jump at every shadowed alley and wind-tossed tree I pass.

VI

The graveyard behind Noble Park is the size of several manor homes put together, but I know exactly where to find Master Cymbre once I've leapt the wrought-iron fence and landed among the broad cypresses and oaks.

The caretaker's cottage.

Like all retired necromancers, Cymbre took up residence at a graveyard when Evander and I completed our training. Now she tends the land inside the iron fence and polishes the marble monuments of dukes' and counts' and barons' families. Those who, for whatever reason, weren't raised from the dead. Those nobles whose spirits have left the Deadlands for whatever lies beyond.

The cottage is unlocked when I arrive. Sun streams in from the many windows, yet the air turns cold as I spot them: a bouquet of wildflowers on Cymbre's dining table. Hot-pink rhododendrons.

Tiny white clusters of dogsbane. And even a few of those rare bright-red blossoms, star glories.

My pulse quickens at the sight. "Where did those come from?" I demand, unable to rip my gaze from them just yet. If they were growing over any of the graves outside, we're in trouble. Flowers only bloom over graves when the spirits have a message to send to our world. Part of a retired necromancer's duty as grave-minder is to watch for flowers, then send a raven to the right person when there's a message. "Where?" I ask again, breathless.

"They were all over. On too many graves to name," my friend Jax says from beside the hearth, as if coming out of a daze. "Simeon and I saved a few and burned the rest."

My hand instinctively creeps toward my sword. Not even the cottage seems safe now, knowing what the flowers on the table mean: Danger. Deception. Death.

"Master Cymbre was called away this morning, apparently," Simeon adds from the back of the cottage, striding to the hearth with four steaming mugs of tea clutched in his hands. "Jax and I got a raven last night, telling us to be here at noon. But when we came in, we found a note pinned under her kettle and flowers growing all over the graves—so at least she got the warning, too." He nods to a scrap of parchment on a nearby table.

I skim the note, hardly taking in a word, crinkling it in my fist as my gaze shifts from the flowers to my friends beside the hearth.

"You're late, Sparrow." Jax leans back on his elbows, gazing up at me with his crystal-blue eyes and not even a shadow of his normal grin. He's warming his bare feet near the flames, his sword balanced on his lap as he stretches across Master Cymbre's woven carpet. Dressed in his necromancer's tight black shirt and trousers, his muscles bulging, he looks completely out of place in the dainty white stone cottage. "We were getting worried. If you didn't show up soon, I'd have started looking for people to kill."

I shiver. Knowing Jax, he's not kidding.

Sitting rigidly beside him, Evander accepts a mug of tea from Simeon with a murmured thanks. The sound of his voice, though it's strained, settles around me like an embrace.

"What kept you?" Evander asks, his words careful. He stares into the dwindling fire, a crease between his brows.

"Just getting something from Kasmira." Hoping to ease the tension between us, I plop down in the narrow space between Jax and Evander, making a place for myself by forcing them to move or have their legs squished, like I've been doing for years. Jax's familiar grumble and Evander's familiar light touch on my back help the horrible events of last night seem farther away, like a bad dream, as I crunch down on a few of my ill-gotten goods. "Though even coffee beans aren't exactly helping—"

"But you always say there's nothing coffee can't cure," Simeon says in slight alarm, handing me a mug and peering into my face, scrutinizing. "Who are you, and what have you done with my sister?"

He tries to hide his pain behind a ghost of a smile, but I recognize the hollowness in his voice and eyes. Where Jax is foulmouthed and surly, Simeon is always quick to crack a joke or smile.

"That's what I used to think, too. But after last night, I'm not so sure." I yank on a lock of his sandy blond hair, one of the many telltale signs we're not really brother and sister. But after being raised together in Death's convent from the time we were toddlers, we're as good as family. "How are you holding up? I'm worried about you . . ."

"Me?" Simeon takes a seat on Jax's other side, cradling his own tea between his palms. "Whatever for?" The sparkle I'm so used to seeing in his baby-blue eyes has faded, and a knot forms in my chest as he adds softly, "*I'm* still here."

Evander blows steam off the top of his mug, gazing deep within it, and says nothing. Jax gulps his scalding tea without hesitation. His thoughts are surely with Master Nicanor, who was like a father to him, trying to understand the extent of his loss.

For a moment, as we sit together in a deep silence broken only by the occasional pop and hiss of the dwindling fire, I wish I could stay in this cottage with my friends forever. We've never received a warning from the Deadlands before, and I have no idea if it means we're up against more than a Shade, or if we can handle it. We're not exactly seasoned warriors. We're just three orphans, and one baron's son who grew up without a father. The king's ideal necromancers, with no loved ones to distract us in the Deadlands, trying to keep each other sane both in and out of the spirits' realm.

Jax spills his tea and spits a curse, breaking the silence. Simeon leaps up to help contain the mess.

While they're busy, Evander and I exchange a look. He catches my fingers in his.

Squeezing his hand, I silently let him know I don't want to fight anymore. "Where did Cymbre go, anyway?" I ask, her note still clutched in my hand. I could hardly read a word of it—the characters swam together on the page in my shock over the flowers.

"Duchess Bevan needed her help, so she went to Oslea Province," Jax grunts, wringing tea out of his tight shirt. "Seems the duke's been missing from their manor in Dyrn City for three days. Went for an afternoon stroll and never came home. If the duchess is lucky, the bastard wound up falling in a frozen lake."

Simeon shakes his head.

"What?" Jax mutters when no one agrees with him. "Have you met him? He beats his wife. Maybe a few days under the ice will help him rearrange his priorities."

"I don't see what Master Cymbre will be able to do, anyway. She's not a bloodhound." Evander frowns into his tea. "People seem to think that just because we raise the dead, we can solve all their problems when the Dead don't act exactly the way they want."

Everyone nods. It's not the first time we've complained about this.

"So what are we supposed to do about Master Nicanor's funeral? Delay it until she returns?" I wonder aloud. "And hunting down the Shade that—?"

"Sparrow. We have more to worry about than just some Shade." Simeon runs a hand through his shaggy hair. The circles under his eyes are dark as the bruises we used to give each other at sword practice.

Even Jax looks ill, almost like he did last winter after beating the black fever. "We went to Master Nicanor's cottage early this morning, to find something nice to bury him in." His voice is taut as he fights to keep it from wavering. "The place was wrecked. Papers everywhere. A smashed plate of supper on the floor. Scratch marks on the doorframe."

I shiver again. "Could it have been a vandal? A farmer's son?" I have to ask, even if it's unlikely. After all, Master Nicanor had just started tending the massive graveyard outside Grenwyr City, the one used by merchants and wealthy farmers. "A couple of boys messing around, looking for spare coins when they saw Master Nicanor had gone out for the evening?"

"Nice try, sister." Simeon leans forward. "But I don't think so. I can't think of *anything* that would cause Master Nicanor to go into the Deadlands alone. I think he was taken against his will."

"Exactly. Think about it: Who would he have needed to raise so badly that it couldn't have waited until Cymbre could come with him?" Jax demands. "Why wouldn't he have just asked us to raise the person for him?"

"Okay. Let's assume someone forced him to go to the Deadlands against his will." Evander's eyes are narrowed in thought. "Why did he come out alone, then? What happened to the person who took him there? Everyone knows Shades will devour anything in sight, so . . ." At the look on Simeon's face, he loses the thread of his words.

"You don't have to watch what you say around us. We know what the Shade did to Master Nicanor." Simeon grimaces, and I reach behind Jax to pat his shoulder. "We were in our rooms at the palace when they brought him up. We saw the—ah—"

"Mangled body," Jax finishes for him, unflinching. An outsider probably wouldn't guess he's in pain, but the way he's quietly grinding his teeth tells me he's just managed to channel it into quiet fury. "So I say we hunt this damned Shade. Today."

Between the flowers on Cymbre's table and the glimpse I had of a giant Shade in the Deadlands grove, I'm not sure we should go anywhere right now. "Does anyone have a plan, then? One that doesn't involve us all dying?"

Evander looks up, his gaze unreadable. "Me," he says simply. "I'll cut it to pieces, and then you all will burn it."

No one's better with a sword than Evander. There's no denying it.

"We both saw it. The monster that killed Nicanor." I describe what I saw in the shadows, how quickly it moved. "It won't stand a chance against *four* of us, though."

I hope I sound more confident than I feel.

"If we can catch it, that is," Evander whispers.

Simeon leaps to his feet and starts pacing. "I don't think any of us should go into the Deadlands until Master Cymbre's back. Killing the Shade won't explain why Master Nicanor's cottage was torn up. Maybe Cymbre can help us get answers."

"There's so much about this I don't like," Evander agrees. "And Cymbre said to wait in her note. She'll be back tomorrow, in time for the Festival of the Face of Cloud."

Jax catches my eye and shrugs, his powerful shoulders bunching. "I still say we kill it now. If we wait for the Festival of Cloud, what's to keep us from waiting for the Festival of Moon three days later?"

I almost grin. He's right, there's a festival in Karthia at least once a week, and not just for Vaia's five faces. The king observes all the festivals started before his reign, celebrations honoring everything from the sea to marriages to red fruits. With the Dead walking among us, reminding us of our mortality—and their very presence meaning a Shade could attack at any time—it's no wonder we need an excuse to throw a raucous party every few days.

The Festival of Olive and Tomato is actually my favorite, but Vaia's festivals are always grandest.

"Cymbre might be mad for a bit, but she'll thank us when she calms down," Jax insists, drawing me back to the present. "This monster murdered her partner, *my* mentor, damn it!" After a moment of quiet, he asks more calmly, "What do you think, Sparrow?"

"I . . ." Three pairs of blue eyes watch me as I stall, thinking furiously. Like Jax, I think slaying and burning the monster will ease a little of everyone's pain—that is, if it doesn't kill us first. But Evander and Simeon have a point: There's more to what's happening than just a Shade, and Cymbre will help us figure it out. "I say we wait for Cymbre. That way we can attend the festival." I force a grin. "One last chance to eat, drink, and generally make fools of ourselves, just in case we don't all make it back from Shade-hunting alive."

As the others talk among themselves, my gaze returns again to the flowers. The Dead don't often send warnings from their world, which means something is seriously wrong. *Danger,* I understand: The Deadlands aren't exactly safe at the moment. The message of death, of course, is obvious. But deception? That worries me most of all.

VII

The palace courtyards swarm with bodies tonight, both living and Dead. King Wylding's most beloved citizens are
all here for the Festival of Cloud—painters and sculptors, poets
and musicians—competing for attention as they show off their
autumn-themed creations in the center courtyard where I stand
with Evander. My heart changes rhythm to match the drums,
harps, and tambourines that sound from all directions as I loop
my arm through Evander's.

"Help me look for Master Cymbre!" I shout over the music
and chatter. All of Noble Park seems to be here, along with the
ever-growing Wylding family, the city's wealthiest merchants, and
almost every mage from Grenwyr Province.

Evander puts his lips to my ear. "I would, if I could keep my
eyes off you."

We're supposed to dress in our finest for festival days, which means no comfortable black uniforms. And for me, that means letting Lyda's maids pin up my wavy hair into the most popular style of the past two hundred years, and stuff me into a pretty crimson dress with flowing skirts that make it impossible to wear my sword and belt. My lips are dabbed with rouge, which I always like, though I refused the crumbly brown powder they wanted to pat on my nose and cheeks.

Evander's words should make me feel better, but they don't. Nothing has been able to ease the constant feeling of dread that's hounded me ever since I saw Master Nicanor die. Since the flowers from the graveyard spelled out a warning.

Just a few feet in front of us, two obviously drunk Wylding nobles, Valoria's cousins, throw fistfuls of cake at each other's faces. Noble girls gathered around them giggle shrilly, seeming desperate to laugh off their nerves in the wake of Master Nicanor's death. And it's not just them. Everyone seems determined to get as drunk and happy as possible until they forget their sorrow over the necromancer forever ripped from their midst.

A roaring sound and a burst of light to my left draw my gaze. The Sisters of Cloud have started the first of many bonfires, and children gather round with fistfuls of color-changing powder, all waiting their turn to make a little magic for the Face of Cloud.

With a flash, the column of flames stretching toward the sky turns blue. Another child steps forward. Another flash. The fire changes to a brilliant poppy red. Flash. Plum-colored fire pops and sizzles as onlookers cheer.

Kasmira would love this. She's likely dancing around a bonfire at one of the parties in the city below with her crew and the
rest of Grenwyr's citizens, toasting the king's eternal reign, but it
seems a shame that Karthia's best weather mage wasn't invited to
the grandest celebration.

"Odessa! Evander!"

We turn toward the voice, which seems to be coming from
somewhere near the banquet tables. That's where most of the Dead
gather, piling their plates high with roasted fish and cold cuts of
spiced wild boar imported all the way from Lorness, steaming
mounds of whipped potatoes, and blackened mushrooms.

In their shrouds, it would be nearly impossible to tell the Dead
man cracking jokes beside the punch bowl from the one taking
almost half the potatoes, if not for the ornate pins of copper or silver that denote their titles and often even show their family crests.
The Dead women sometimes wear pins, too, though many prefer
to paint their masks and don the most exquisite baubles they wore
in life. There's a duchess I call Lady Emerald because she adorns
her shroud with nothing but the biggest, shiniest emerald choker
necklace I've ever seen—I still haven't learned her real name.

As two ancient Dead marchionesses glide away with their
plates, no doubt to eat in seclusion where they can lift their masks,
Princess Valoria appears and waves us over. She must have been the
one calling our names.

The crowd parts to let us pass, some offering greetings, others
bowing or waving.

"I see you've found your glasses," Evander says when we reach
the princess, making her grin. "They look nice on you, Highness."

The delicate gold spectacles reflect the light of the bonfires as Valoria adjusts them behind her ears. They look even more polished than the opal-and-silver circlet in her hair. "I was hoping you'd be here." She meets my eyes for a brief moment before dropping her gaze, then tucks a few wisps of her blond hair back into her braided crown. "I mean, and I didn't have anything better to do."

I stare at her, more uncomfortable now than I was when I first squeezed myself into my party dress. Everyone in Grenwyr knows me, or knows *of* me, but I don't have many friends outside our circle of necromancers. Aside from Kasmira, of course.

"I finished it!" the princess adds in a whisper. "My latest *you-know-what*!" That explains the smudge of dirt on her cheek, and the black stain on the sleeve of her stunning red-and-gold beaded gown.

"Maybe you can show us the you-know-what later, when there aren't any Dead around," I venture cautiously, earning a smile from her. "How have you been holding up since we saw you last?"

"The grape vines outside my room wilted the night we got back from the Deadlands. When I saw it the next morning, I knew it had to be death's blight." Valoria frowns. "My mother planted those vines. She's so disappointed. See? That's my room, just there."

She points to a distant domed spire, and I narrow my eyes to see it clearly. Though the Dead can't reproduce, the palace gets bigger every year, with more wings added constantly to house all the Wylding relatives and their children, and their children's children. When they aren't planning parties or painting scenery to keep busy, the living Wyldings are quite fond of making babies. There's a picture of the original palace hanging in the grand entryway, and it's definitely swelled with time and demand for more space.

"You have your own tower." I grin at the princess. "Not bad. How'd you get so much space to yourself? Did you have to fight a hundred of your cousins for it?"

"Being the second living heir in line to the throne helps," Valoria murmurs, her face burning. "Not that it matters, but my parents both died in the yearly black fever outbreak when I was young. My mother was raised. My father chose not to be." She shrugs, but her eyes glisten. "Anyway, Eldest Grandfather will rule as long as I'm alive. So I don't have to worry about what a headache I'd have from wearing a heavy crown all the time. Besides, Hadrien would inherit before I did, as he's the oldest of the five living heirs."

"Oldest and best looking," a smooth male voice says from behind me.

Dislike flashes in Evander's eyes, and his lip curls, leaving no doubt as to who's just put a hand on my waist.

"Prince Hadrien," I say in the warmest voice I can muster when someone's touching me without my permission and I have no authority to snap their fingers like kindling. "Happy festival day to you."

"If you really want to make it a happy one," Hadrien says, smiling in a way that shows off all his perfect teeth and makes his dark brown eyes shine brighter than the opals in his silver crown, "you'll come dance with me, Sparrow."

"She's fine right here," Evander growls, then quickly shoots me an apologetic look. He knows I can speak for myself, but he can never stay quiet when Hadrien is around. I'd thought that after three years of the prince's shameless flirting, Evander would learn to ignore it, but Hadrien has a way of getting under people's skin.

I sidestep Hadrien's touch, positioning myself beside Valoria. "If I try to bend and twist in this dress, it'll rip. And that would give King Wylding quite a shock." My gaze darts between the golden-haired prince and Evander, who's gripping his sword hilt. I'm glad at least one of us came to this party armed. "Maybe some other time, Highness."

"One must always hold on to hope," Hadrien says good-naturedly. He gives me a sweeping bow, the kind people usually reserve for King Wylding. The mischievous gleam in his eyes softens as he straightens. "My condolences to you both"—he pauses to glance at Evander—"for Master Nicanor. Such a terrible loss. Though I suppose that's the risk of walking where only the dead should dwell."

"That's why we normally travel there in pairs," Evander murmurs darkly. "But there are some suspicious circumstances around Master Nicanor's death, which we intend to investigate. I'm sure you'll help with that."

"I had no idea . . . I was told it was an accident!" Hadrien's dark eyes are round with sincerity. "Of course I'll help. Anything and anyone within these walls"—he gestures to the palace around us, suddenly more somber than I've ever seen him—"is at your disposal, day or night. Simply say the word."

Evander looks at Hadrien a long moment, then grits out, "Thank you."

"We appreciate it, Highness," I add, giving Hadrien a gracious smile I hope will take his mind off Evander's surliness.

In the distance, someone calls Hadrien's name, and he turns toward the sound. "Ah, I've just spotted a lovely lady in dire need of a glass of wine. Can't leave anyone empty-handed on festival night, or I'm a rotten host. See you around, Sparrow." With a wink, he disappears into a sea of black-shrouded figures and ladies in flowing silks of every autumn hue.

"I think he actually *likes* you." Valoria gives me a bewildered glance, seeming torn between amusement and revulsion at her brother's behavior. "And—Evander, isn't that your mother he's talking to now?"

Hadrien reappears near the bonfire, where he's already managed to find a glass of wine. He presses it into Lyda Crowther's delicate hand, drawing her away from the group of Dead nobles with whom she was chatting. Even from a distance, her smile is unmistakable. I'm sure she has the good sense not to utter any of what she told us over our midnight supper.

Evander says nothing, but kicks a chipped piece of cobblestone toward the fire.

"Careful with that!" a gruff voice says. "You trying to blind me, Crowther?" Jax pushes through the crowd, the jagged rock Evander kicked grasped in his large fist. He's wearing his customary black, though he's swapped his necromancer's uniform for a set of silk robes that make him look so uncomfortable, he'd probably rather be naked. He glances from Evander to Prince Hadrien and Lyda. "Or are your knickers in a bunch because the prince is moving in on your mother?"

"Guilty." Evander holds up his hands, his anger fading at the sight of our friend. "Just trying to thin out the competition. Like there aren't enough dead people to raise in Grenwyr."

"Lucky for you both," Simeon's voice bursts from behind Jax's tall figure, "I've brought a healer with me."

Using his bony elbow to clear a path through the crowd, Simeon appears with a raven-haired young man on his arm. They're both dressed in tailored pants and long-sleeved tunics, far more sensible than Jax's ridiculous formal robes.

"Who remembers this handsome rogue?" Simeon's smile broadens as he adds, "Danial's just told me he's moving here from Oslea! Finally!"

"And just in time, too." Danial smiles at us all, his kohl-lined hazel eyes sparkling despite a shadow of worry lingering behind them. "Who knows what trouble Si was getting into without me around?"

"All kinds," Jax deadpans. "All the time." He glances toward the banquet tables. "Think the Dead left any of the undercooked meat for the rest of us?"

Valoria raises her brows at that, and I lay my hand on her shoulder. "Princess Valoria, I'd like you to meet my friends. This is my almost-brother, Simeon of Grenwyr." Simeon winks as I say his name. "His boyfriend, the healer mage Danial Swancott." When his name is mentioned, Danial makes a deep bow that's less flashy and somehow more sincere than Prince Hadrien's. "And the brute who prefers his meat still bleeding is Jax of Lorness."

Taking that as his cue to go fill up his plate, Jax nods to the princess before stalking toward the feast.

"Sparrow!" Danial exclaims, taking my hands. Everything he says has a musical lilt that always draws smiles from his listeners. I swear he should've been a bard. "Let me get a good look at you. It's always a treat."

I can't help but grin. Danial's a treat to look at himself, with powder perfectly applied over his creamy alabaster skin and kohl around his eyes painted on with an artist's skill. It compliments his shoulder-length hair that's as black as Idrany ink, and draws attention to his wide eyes.

"I think I've already heard what happened here." Danial's brows knit in concern as he rubs a thumb over the long gash on my forearm. It was healed enough for me to leave the bandage off for the festival, but it's scabbed and puckered and far from pretty. "May I?"

When I nod, Danial lays a hand over the cut and narrows his eyes, no doubt using his hazel Sight to check the extent of the damage beneath my skin. Evander and Simeon talk among themselves, having seen Danial at work so many times the novelty's worn off. But Valoria peers over his shoulder with interest.

Heat rushes up my arm, and when Danial drops his hand, my skin is soft and whole again, with no evidence of the cut that would have otherwise left a scar.

"You're the best." I give Danial a warm smile of thanks.

He returns to Simeon's side, clutching his right hand to his chest, his fingers looking as frozen and twisted as the dried birds' feet kept in glass jars on apothecary shelves.

"Temporary paralysis," Valoria says to herself. "The price of a healer's magic."

"What'd I miss?" Jax reappears with what looks like an entire serving platter, comically enormous compared to the plates intended for guests. As he dangles a scrap of boar meat above his lips, he spots Valoria, and a thoughtful expression crosses his face. He holds the meat out to her. "The best piece, Highness. It's yours if you want it."

Valoria blinks at the bloody scrap, then at Jax as he holds it out to her. "Oh. I—yes, thank you." Her face turns redder than the meat as she takes it from him and swallows it in one unladylike bite.

Evander makes his way to my side and offers me his hand. "Would you care for a dance?" He keeps his voice carefully neutral, saving the tenderness for the moment our eyes meet. There are few things Evander likes better than dancing.

I grab his hand in answer. Let Lyda think what she will, if she's looking on with the rest. She can't keep us from having fun tonight, when it could well be our last.

"I understand your dress might rip if you spin around too much." Evander grins, which makes his eyes shine. "But I'm willing to risk it if you are."

We hurry to an empty space on the flagstones, well away from the bonfire, but close enough to feel an occasional burst of heat when the wind blows. Danial practically sweeps Simeon off his feet in their haste to join us.

I tip my head back to the night sky. The moon and stars become a baffling whorl of lights as Evander spins me around and pulls me back to his arms again and again.

For the first time in days, the weight on my shoulders is starting to ease. Dancing with Evander is like walking on air, but with the certainty of knowing he'll be waiting to catch me when I'm ready to come back down.

"I couldn't find Duke Bevan." Master Cymbre breaks the spell, and Danial, Simeon, Evander, and I all stop dancing and turn to face her. I expected to feel braver, ready to take on anything when Master Cymbre returned. But our former teacher looks as defeated as she sounds, with circles under her eyes and strands coming loose from her waist-length braid. It's only been a week since I saw her last, yet there seems to be more gray than red in her hair now.

"If he doesn't reappear within the month," she continues as we leave the dance floor and close in around her, joined almost at once by Jax, "his living heir will inherit his fortune, home, and title."

"Not the duchess?" I ask, surprised.

Master Cymbre shakes her head. "She'd rather not be raised again, now that her husband's gone. I don't understand it." Her steel-blue eyes look faded, like whatever she's seen lately has leeched the color from them. "She finally has a chance to live the way she never could, without that brute breathing down her neck and controlling her every move, and now she'd rather stay in the Deadlands. I suppose that's one way to have peace, but—"

"What about Master Nicanor?" Simeon interrupts. "Do you know why he was in the Deadlands when he's supposed to be retired? Or why his cottage was wrecked?"

"No. That's why I wanted to talk to you all. To gather what you know." Cymbre bows her head, a familiar gesture. She doesn't want us to see her expression. "And I think it's better that I look into his death *alone*. It may not be my job to keep you all safe any-more, but I intend to try."

"Not a chance," Jax growls, his crystal eyes flashing. "That Shade is mine. I'm coming to the Deadlands with you."

"Me too." Simeon crosses his arms. "As soon as the festival ends, we hunt."

I glance at Evander, who shares my frown. Master Cymbre's always had the answers to our problems. A book, a potion, a sharp but well-intentioned word of advice. Something about knowing she feels as lost as we do unsettles me worse than the memory of Nicanor's death. I wonder if we were ready for the title of master. Or if anyone ever is.

"Evander?" Jax locks eyes with his friend, then turns to me. "Sparrow? What do you say? Five master necromancers against one Shade? I know it won't bring Master Nicanor back or help us find our missing duke, but . . ." He grins darkly. "It'll feel damn good."

"We're in," Evander and I agree at the same time. The red, pink, and white flowers spelling out a warning in Cymbre's cottage flash to mind, but I don't mention them. No one needs another reminder of the danger.

Master Cymbre twists the end of her braid around her fingers, a habit that's probably far older than me. "I still don't know." If any-thing, she looks more troubled than she did before we promised to help. "None of you are allowed to die before me, understand, unless I'm killing you myself for disobeying orders. That said . . ." She gazes at each of us in turn. "We can hunt together tomorrow, at dusk. That gives you each time to change your minds and back out if you should come to your senses. Agreed?"

I exchange a glance with Simeon, and we both nod. Then Evander does, too. Jax makes a grunting noise, his way of accepting terms he doesn't like.

As if also in answer, a scream tears through the courtyard from somewhere behind us.

"Hear that?" Jax cocks his head, grinning at Evander and elbowing him in the ribs. "That's the sound of your mother and Prince Hadrien making sweet love, Master Crowther."

Master Cymbre shakes her head, scowling at Jax, and turns toward the sound. Her expression quickly changes, her eyes widening.

Evander and I whirl around in unison. Stumbling into the courtyard by way of the garden archway is a Shade, once the size and height of an average man—or it would be, if it wasn't hunched over, its bony knuckles dragging the ground as it shambles toward the party.

Drawing his sword, Evander charges toward a group of young nobles cowering on the far side of the bonfire in the courtyard's center. They're pressed against one of the palace walls, too stunned and full of wine to flee the Shade that's alternately shuffling around and gazing off into the night, no doubt seeking a gate to the Deadlands.

Jax, Simeon, and I spring into action, guiding confused and frightened people toward the palace doors as the monster begins its hunt.

It's a new Shade, judging by the way it still looks and smells like a hunched, rotting corpse: its face, only vaguely human, is sunken and skeletal, with black holes where its eyes should be. Its skin is ashen, dangling in tatters, its limbs in various states of decay. I have to fight not to gag as it turns toward me and seems to meet my gaze with its empty eye sockets. Then it shrieks, its jaw unhinging as it reveals a mouth full of sharp yellow teeth that devour bodies and spirits alike.

The creature bounds toward me, passing Evander and the frightened nobles, giving the bonfire a wide berth. Then the wind shifts and the Shade pauses, sniffing the air in the young nobles' direction. Its cracked lips curl with what can only be thirst. Releasing a snarl, the monster changes course and stalks back toward them.

The more corpses and spirits Shades devour, the taller and stronger they become. This party will be like a buffet for the hungry creature, and then we'll have an even bigger, harder-to-kill problem on our hands.

Heart hammering, I feel instinctively for my blade, but my hand closes over layers of soft skirt in place of my weapon. I don't have time for this. Evander needs backup *now*. Glancing hurriedly around for something sharp, my gaze lands on the feast tables. I grab a knife from an empty platter just as Jax and Simeon run to Evander's side, their blades drawn.

"Get the Wyldings into the palace!" Master Cymbre shouts over the din. "We need fire!"

Someone cries out. Then, on the ground near the snarling creature, a figure crumples in the grass. Some poor soul is dead.

Raising his sword, Evander attempts to create a barrier between the stunned Wylding relatives and the Shade. It releases a low growl, like a hound relishing the moment before a kill. Its skin, cracked and oozing, reeks of decay so strongly that the stench assaults me from halfway across the courtyard.

The nobles scatter at last, momentarily confusing the Shade as they run around the roaring bonfire like a bunch of startled geese. A few trip over their own skirts while others kick spilled goblets out of their paths. A frightened boy in a gray servant's vest, running hard on their heels, collides face-first with a painting of the Face of Cloud. Leaping, the Shade snaps his neck with a quick twist, making a gleeful, gurgling sound as the boy drops to the ground.

Sometimes they like to eat corpses. And sometimes they just like killing.

A girl near my side heaves a sob, snapping me out of a daze. I throw the knife back down. Blades will slow the monster, but even hacking it into bite-sized pieces of flesh won't kill it. It'll pull itself back together and keep eating corpses until someone sets it ablaze.

As the palace guards stream into the courtyard, taking aim with crossbows, and as my friends and I struggle to keep the panicked partygoers away from the Shade, I realize that someone will have to be *me*.

I sprint toward the open door on one end of the courtyard, where Master Cymbre and Danial are shepherding nobles inside to safety. I'm about to grab a torch from the brackets beside the doorway when a sound freezes my blood: Valoria's scream.

Snatching up a torch, I turn around, dashing toward the princess.

The Shade has backed her into a corner on the opposite side of the courtyard. Valoria scratches vainly at the stone walls behind her, grinding her nails to bloody stubs as she tries to climb to safety. But there's nothing to hold on to, and the Shade is giving a telltale growl that means it's about to pounce.

Evander, reaching Valoria first, plunges his blade into the Shade's side. Simeon and Jax follow, charging it as it strikes Evander down, barely managing to nick its flesh before it casts them aside. I dodge terrified stragglers as they run for the safety of the palace walls, determined to reach that distant corner in time to help.

A gust of autumn wind whips the warmth of the festival bonfire onto my face as I bolt toward my friends. The Shade flicks its blackened tongue over dry lips, seemingly enjoying the way the princess raises her bloodied fists like she's prepared to fight to the death. It's distracted. Good. Time to make my move.

Darting between the Shade and Valoria, I brandish my torch as close to the monster's face as I dare, startling it into taking a step back, toward the bonfire. I lunge again, sparks from my torch kissing the Shade's putrid skin, and it takes another clumsy step backward.

The Shade snarls, a bony fist curled at its side. It seems to want to grab the torch from me, but it's too new and stupid to be confident in its own speed and strength. I snarl back as I shove the torch closer, sending smoke up the monster's decaying nose.

With a deafening screech, the Shade stumbles into the fire. I quickly step back, but as the monster falls, it manages to grab my free arm. I twist away, but its grip is too tight. It pulls me into the flames with the strength of several men.

Sparks fly as we roll into the heart of the blaze.

We land on top of each other, and as the Shade burns, so do I. Pain consumes me as my flesh sizzles, searing up my hands, my arms, my face. Searing *everything*. I wish to Death that I could float up out of my body, just leave this burnt shell behind.

I'm not sure which of us howls loudest.

Distantly, Evander yells my name, followed by something with a high, urgent ring to it. But the crackling fire, the Shade's furious screeches as it burns, and my thudding heart make it impossible to guess the words.

Hands grip my shoulders, tearing me away from the Shade and the flames. Evander's hands. He's going to get burned, probably already is, and I don't want him to know this pain. I try to shove him back, but he hangs on, and together, we free ourselves of the fire. I lie on my back, gasping, letting the cool flagstones of the courtyard soothe my hot skin. My skirts are blazing, and the smell of singed hair fills my nose and throat, choking me. But Evander, despite the burns on his arms and hands, beats out the flames around me first.

The Shade staggers out of the blaze a moment later on bony legs, its scrap of remaining flesh melting off like candle wax. It shrinks farther and farther into the stone floor as its legs burn to ashes on the wind. Soon it's nothing but a puddle of blackened bone and rubble.

For a moment, there's silence apart from the hissing and popping of the fire. The crowd collectively holds its breath, not yet ready to believe the monster is really gone.

"I did it," I whisper to myself, stunned. I've killed my first Shade.

When Evander pulls me against his chest and shouts for Danial, I realize I'm shaking.

"You were lucky," Danial says as he heals my singed face and arms, then turns to address Evander's burns. "Your dress took the worst of the heat. But I'm afraid it's ruined. There's no magic anyone can work on that disaster."

I nod, but don't have the energy to talk as I rest in Evander's arms in the middle of the courtyard. Palace guards rush over with buckets, first to put out the bonfire, then to douse the spot several feet away where the Shade dissolved into a pool of ash.

Gradually, once all the partygoers have been accounted for, my friends and Master Cymbre gather around me.

"That was a completely idiotic thing to do!" Simeon tells me, laying a hand on my shoulder. "Idiotic. Seriously." He gives me a shaky grin. "Wish I'd thought of it."

I grin back. "Just another day's work, right?"

"Another day's work, indeed. You were amazing, Sparrow," Master Cymbre says shakily.

My friends echo her. And when Valoria kneels beside me and wordlessly throws her arms around me, I know for certain it was worth the risk.

Moments later, a few of the Wyldings poke their heads out of doors and windows, then send their staff to begin clearing up the tremendous mess.

"Look." A fair-haired boy, one of the Wylding servants, sifts cautiously through the Shade's ashes and holds up a gleaming chunk of gold. Even from several feet away, I can tell it's a signet ring. "This belonged to Duke Bevan," the boy says slowly, his brow furrowing. "But . . ."

Simeon locks eyes with me, alarmed. "How did the duke become a Shade?"

VIII

The nobles in the courtyard stare at me and my friends with a mixture of fear and dislike. The same nobles who, an hour earlier, merrily greeted us like old friends. Only Lyda Crowther doesn't shrink from us, waving to let us know she's all right before turning to help a girl in a party dress who's limping. With a last look at Evander, she guides the child indoors.

One man whispers to a few of his companions, then steps forward. From where I sit, he looks like a giant bat, tall and gaunt in his black dress robes.

"That's Count Rykiel," Valoria whispers to me.

"Let me try to understand what's happened here," the count says, making each word loud and slow—no doubt for the benefit of those listening at the palace windows. "Duke Bevan went missing in Dyrn City. And we sent necromancers to find him. But they failed. Then the duke turns up here, many miles from home—"

"As a Shade," another man finishes from behind the count. "Almost like someone *wanted* him to become a monster." He locks his evergreen eyes on Master Cymbre, who presses her lips together like she's holding back a retort. "Like someone wanted to use him as a weapon, and planned to unleash him when the palace was busy and crowded."

Count Rykiel nods. "And let's not forget, you were late to the party, Cymbre."

The words spread a chill across my skin. The lack of emotion in the count's voice tells me he really believes the woman I've known for most of my life is capable of murder.

"You're supposed to keep control over the Dead. What happened?" A dark-haired young woman moves to the count's side, turning Duke Bevan's signet ring over in her shaking hands, making me wonder if she's one of his descendants. "Let me guess. Are our newest master necromancers starved for business?" She glares at us through streaming eyes. "Did you set up this attack so we'd hire you to raise the victims, knowing we can afford to pay a pretty fortune to have our families together again? Perhaps I'm mistaken, but then, you'll have to spell out your demands a bit more clearly."

"Here's a demand," Jax growls, sauntering toward the young woman until they're practically nose-to-nose. "Shut your mouth."

Valoria sucks in a breath, and my pulse quickens as I follow her gaze to Count Rykiel.

"Are you threatening us?" The count's eyes flash as he beckons to a group of nearby palace guards.

They march forward, shielding the count and other nobles from Jax.

The few Wyldings standing apart from the wall of guards quickly scurry away from us, to the safety of bows and blades and strength in numbers. Valoria and Hadrien's three younger siblings, two boys and a girl, are among them.

But Valoria doesn't follow. She loops her arm through mine, making it clear that she's not about to leave the six of us—me, Evander, Cymbre, Danial, Jax, and Simeon—any more alone than we already are.

"No one around here is thinking logically," Valoria mutters. "Master Cymbre is the only necromancer who went to Dyrn City." She raises her voice like she wants the rest of the palace to hear her. "Assuming the duke became a Shade, and she's to blame, she doesn't have the strength to drag him all the way here. And if she paid someone to help her—which sounds even more ridiculous—where would she have hidden the duke that no one would've heard him screeching before the party?"

"Even if Cymbre were capable of something like that, which I highly doubt she is . . ."

Prince Hadrien emerges from the palace and sweeps into the courtyard, turning to face us without a single glance at his relatives. "The other necromancers had nothing to do with it. They've been enjoying the party all night, just like the rest of you."

I never thought I'd be this glad to hear the prince's voice.

"I trust our mages. Every last one." Hadrien puts one hand on Master Cymbre's shoulder, the other on Evander's. "And so should you."

But the prince's relatives don't seem willing to take his word on the matter.

"Do you have anything to say for yourselves?" the dark-haired young woman with Duke Bevan's ring sneers. "Or will you just let the prince and princess speak for you?"

"I have a few words," Simeon shoots back. "You can all go straight—"

"I can't believe this," Evander interrupts, glowering at the many accusing faces directed our way. "Sparrow just saved your lives, damn near getting herself killed in the process. How can you think *we* had anything to do with what happened here?"

For a moment, silence hangs over us.

"If the necromancers aren't responsible," a woman's smooth voice calls, "who is?"

I'd love to know the answer to that myself. It has to be someone outside the law. A criminal, paid to disrupt this party by someone who hates the king or even the duke, who certainly had his enemies. Or the guilty person could be *above* the law, like the nobles who stand here accusing us. Some look thoughtful. Others move about restlessly, like the tension in the air is too much for them, and a few continue to stare at us with open revulsion.

Finally, as I watch Master Cymbre's eyes shift from anger to hurt, I find my voice again. "You've always trusted us before." That isn't the half of it, as they well know. Until tonight, every one of these people has held us in the same high esteem as Karthia's best bards. As the wealthiest silk traders from the southern provinces. As *royalty*. Now they're treating us like a couple of pox-ridden beggars from the Ashes.

I clench my fists at my sides, resisting the urge to shout. A glance at Evander helps me steady myself before I speak again.

"You realize none of your beloved Dead would be here without us, don't you? Not even—"

"Me," a scratchy voice finishes. "Yes. Thank you, Sparrow." King Wylding glides into view, flanked by two other masked and shrouded figures. "I've heard enough nonsense for one evening." He turns to face his subjects. His family. "These mages"—he spreads his arms, his long black sleeves hanging down like a crow's wings—"remain our beloved guests, and a vital part of my reign. You will continue to treat them with respect, if you do not wish to spend the next ten years admiring my dungeon walls."

Valoria beams at the king. "He's not so bad sometimes," she whispers. "For a cranky great-great-great . . . well, Eldest Grandfather."

"What happened to Duke Bevan is a tragedy," the king adds in a voice like dead leaves scraping across the courtyard. "And to the others who have died or been injured in this massacre," he adds. "But I did not give in to fear and speculation in life, and I won't in Death either. We will carry on as we always have," the king continues, raising his raspy voice and reclaiming my attention. "And we will look to our necromancers, now more than ever, to find answers and keep us safe from Shades. For Karthia. For us all."

"For Karthia," the young nobles echo, somewhat grudgingly in my opinion. "For us all."

The king claps his hands once. "Good. Now, everyone head to your rooms. I think we can all agree—the party is over."

As the royal procession disappears into the palace, Cymbre draws the four of us newest master necromancers close. Valoria and Danial hang back but stay near, no doubt listening, too.

"We need to get to the bottom of this threat—whatever it may be—and contain it swiftly. Not only for the safety of Karthia, but to uphold the name of necromancer. First, though"—Cymbre smiles wanly—"we must get some rest before the hunt tomorrow." She narrows her eyes. "Remember, if you try anything without me, I'll wring your necks faster than you can say *Deadlands*."

The group disperses, only Evander and Valoria remaining by my side.

"She's wise. If I don't head to bed now, I'll fall asleep right here." The princess smiles as she turns to leave. "Thanks again for what you did tonight. Maybe I'll see you again soon? Hadrien will mope around the palace for months if you miss his birthday celebration."

I shake my head. Disappointing Hadrien is the last thing on my mind right now. "Sure. I'll be there."

"And, Odessa?" the princess calls over her shoulder. "Whatever you're planning with the others tomorrow—be careful, all right?"

Touching two fingers to my brow in a salute, I call back, "Of course."

The moment Valoria disappears through the rose-embossed double doors, I grab Evander's hands and pull him to the quietest spot in the courtyard, behind the empty tables that so recently held the feast. His eyes look more violet than blue by the flickering torchlight as they gaze into mine. I run my fingertips over his cheeks, letting the roughness of his jaw graze my skin, making my heart beat at double its usual pace. I want to kiss him—whether his mother might see us and ban me from her manor, I don't care right now—but there's so much to say first.

"Something's always in our way," he says, sharing my thoughts. "Sparrow, when I saw you fall into that fire . . ." He pulls me closer, his hands steady despite everything the last few days have thrown at us. "I thought I'd lost you. Just for a moment, but that was enough for me to understand I never want to feel like that again."

Everything—the clatter of plates being stacked, the routine motions of the servants—fades away until there's nothing but Evander and me, and I'm right where I belong. When I look into his eyes, I get the same feeling I have whenever I walk into Death's convent after a long day. If a person can be a home, then he's mine.

"Tonight made me realize something," he whispers against my ear, making me shiver.

"Me too." My throat tightens at what I'm about to say, but Evander beats me to it.

"We're stronger together. I could never walk away." He strokes a hand through my hair, shaking loose bits of ash from the fire. "I'm not getting on a boat without you. Not tomorrow, not in a year. We don't get forever."

"No room for mistakes," I murmur. "All we have is now."

The necromancer's ultimate sacrifice, always in the back of our minds.

"Exactly. And it would be the worst mistake of my life not to spend every day I'm given with you and the Dead who need me."

He pulls me tightly against him, and for a moment we say nothing, united by our love of the job and so much more.

"What are you getting at?" I say at last, drawing back to look into his eyes again.

Evander smiles, grimly determined. "We're going to move to our rooms at the palace, whether my mother likes it or not. We've put off starting our lives together long enough on her account." He traces a thumb along the edge of my jaw, making me all the more impatient for his kiss.

"But what about your dream of seeing other shores? What about the island?" There's no way I could go with him now, not with everything that's been going on.

"Avenging Master Nicanor's death and finding his killer before anyone else gets hurt is far more important." He tilts his head. "You of all people should know—"

"Of course I know." For the first time tonight, my grin doesn't feel forced or unnatural. "I just wanted to hear you say it. But, Van . . ." I put a finger to his lips to keep him from interrupting. "Something doesn't feel right." I glance to the spot where the Shade burned, a dark stain on the gray flagstones, then back to Evander. "What if we're up against something we can't handle?"

"Odessa. Sparrow. I've met a few people who couldn't handle you, but never the other way around." Evander holds up his hands, and I link my fingers through his. "It's the killer who should be worried. Not you." He leans forward until our lips almost touch. "So after tomorrow evening's trip to the Deadlands, we'll head to the manor to pack our things, and then it's off to the palace. What do you say? One last job before our life together really begins?"

"One last job," I echo.

Evander smiles hungrily, and pulls me toward our palace rooms, the ones I've always wished we'd use. "Consider tonight a practice run."

* * *

The next day, the five of us wait on a hill overlooking the sea, just out of sight of the palace, watching for the last smoldering ember of sun to dip beneath the horizon. For the gates to shine their seductive blue, calling us into the Deadlands.

Jax paces restlessly over a bed of wildflowers—late-season marigolds. With no graves in sight, they aren't a warning from the Deadlands of grief to come, but perhaps a sign that nature somehow understands our sorrow and wants to acknowledge it.

Swinging his sword like he's practicing for a sparring match, Jax grumbles, "It's not fair." He turns, slicing upward at an imaginary monster. "Evander's got Sparrow, which means he'll find the Shade first. And he actually saw the blasted thing, so he'll recognize it when he sees it. The rest of us"—he pauses, gesturing to Simeon and Master Cymbre with his blade—"are about to have the most boring stroll of our lives. I don't see why we have to split up."

"To cover more ground," Master Cymbre answers, never taking her eyes from the sea. "You know how vast the Deadlands are. Now, does everyone have a whistle? And the liquid fire potions I bought us? And enough honey, in case you get hungry?"

Simeon wiggles his eyebrows and winks at me, but I know he's as grateful as I am that Master Cymbre's thought of everything.

As the sun disappears, Jax calls, "There's our ride to the Deadlands!" He points his blade toward a glimmer of blue on the crest of the next hill.

We begin to climb, a gnawing feeling in the pit of my stomach growing stronger with every step. Even once we kill the Shade, we won't have all the answers. We won't know what brought Master Nicanor into the Deadlands that night. Or whom.

No one breathes a word until we're near the gate.

"Whistle if you even *think* you sense the Shade," Master Cymbre commands, turning to Evander and me. She'll be traveling with Jax and Simeon, acting as navigator. She's not *me*, but she's better than either of them at sensing the Deadlands' subtle shifts. When we nod, she gives us a tense smile and murmurs, "Well, good luck."

She kisses my cheek, then Evander's, and strides through the gate.

"Just so you know, I'm going to find the monster and burn it before you're two steps out of the gate." Jax slaps Evander on the back, and Evander punches him in return.

They can joke around all they like, but I can't bring myself to join in. We've all watched the masters kill a Shade or two during training, and now I've fought one on my own. But the Shades that have lurked in the Deadlands longest are far stronger than newly made ones like Duke Bevan from last night. The oldest Shades are towering, terrible corpses rotted past recognition, things that stalk the deepest corners of a nightmare.

Simeon rolls his eyes at Jax and Evander's bizarre male punching ritual, then gives me a quick hug. "See you in a blink, sister."

He and Jax disappear through the gate, leaving Evander and me alone on the hill. I sense something staring at us from the berry bushes and catch sight of a creature's liquid brown eyes. They blink once, then vanish. Reminded of the way the Shade watched us from the shadows not long ago, I grab Evander's hand and pull him back before he steps into the gate.

Evander stops and follows my gaze. A mother deer and her two fawns prance out of the bushes.

His lips quirk as he studies me. "Hey. Sparrow." He wraps his arms around my waist, holding me tighter than last night's laced-up party dress. "I know you're not afraid of deer. What's really bothering you?"

I shake my head, unable to put my unease into words. Instead, I force a smile. "Just thinking about facing another Shade so soon. Especially since it's probably grown stronger while we were worrying about Duke Bevan and the festival yesterday. But . . . we've got this, right?"

After last night, I'm all the more eager to move into those palace rooms.

"We've got this." Evander presses his lips hard against mine, stealing my breath and sending heat through me. He draws back, grinning like he did the time we hiked to the top of a mountain just outside the city to catch the sunrise. "Now come on," he says, giving my hair a playful tug. "We've got to find the Shade before Jax."

I give him a look. "Did you two—?"

"Make a bet?" Evander winks, then draws his sword. "Absolutely."

We march through the gate's intense glow and emerge into a field of poppies bordered by distant mountains. The blossoms' lurid red color reminds me once again of Master Nicanor. I shake my head to clear it, then touch the whistle around my neck as I search the shadows. The liquid fire potion sits on my belt beside the usual vials of blood, milk, and honey, its presence giving me confidence in the near darkness.

Out of the corner of my eye, something white flits across the field. I tense and grab my sword, Evander's name on my lips. But it's only a woman's spirit trailed by several little ones in flowing dresses. I don't see any death wounds, which means they were probably victims of a fever. The little ones stick close to their mother, gathering flowers to pass the time.

As Evander gazes around the field, I close my eyes, feeling for malice or unrest, any stain on our otherwise calm surroundings. The pathways in the Deadlands call to me with a restlessness deep in my bones that somehow pulls me toward the spot where I'll find the spirit my client needs. And when it's time to leave, the gates reel me in with a faint tugging around my navel that guides my steps until I see the familiar glow.

But I've never been able to sense a Shade, contrary to what Jax seems to think. And tonight is no different.

A long, shrill whistle blast cuts across the field, and my pulse quickens.

Evander and I sprint toward the sound, keeping to the footpath between the poppies where there aren't any holes to fall in or tangled roots to trip over. The whistle seems to have come from the east, but I don't feel the Deadlands pulling me in any particular direction, so we slow our pace to a jog as we wait for another sound, another sign.

The mountains loom ahead of us, their rough peaks blueblack and ringed with mist in the permanent twilight. As we draw nearer, a narrow ravine takes shape, cast entirely in shadow by two high slopes. It appears to be the only way forward, unless the land-scape shifts or we find some grappling hooks for climbing the sheer mountain faces.

"What do we do now?" I pant, resting with my hands on my knees in the mountains' shadow. "I wouldn't go in there"—I point to the ravine—"for all the gold in Karthia."

Evander opens his mouth to answer just as the whistle blares again, so close it's almost on top of us.

"Master Cymbre? Simeon? Jax?" I shout into the ravine. They should be able to hear my call, given how close the whistle sounded.

But no one answers.

Maybe the landscape on the other side of the mountain has shifted from one valley to another, and our friends are suddenly miles away.

"I don't like this," Evander murmurs. But his nerves don't show. His hands are steady on his blade as he peers into the ravine. "I hate to say it, but I don't see any way around this. If they're in trouble and we don't hurry, we'll never forgive ourselves."

"Right." I nod, even though gazing into the ravine makes my stomach flip. I hate not being able to see where I'm going. "You're right, of course." I clutch the liquid fire potion in one hand, and my sword in the other.

Evander starts toward the ravine, but I gently push my shoul-der into his chest to hold him back. "Wait. Sparrows first." I give him the best smile I can manage. There's no way I'm letting him head into the uncertain darkness and danger before me when I'm the stronger pathfinder.

Slowly, I begin the descent, keeping a hand on the nearest cold rock wall for support. Tiny bits of stone tumble down ahead of me, jarred loose by my first tentative step. I try to listen for the moment the stones stop skittering, to gauge the distance to the bottom, but the darkness swallows up the sound of their fall much too quickly for my liking.

I count my steps, ten total, before Evander's voice reaches me.

"Try to feel your way along the walls," he calls as the blackness presses closer around me. "And remember to *breathe*, Sparrow. I'm right behind—"

His words are cut short by a jagged, guttural scream.

I whirl around, gazing upward to the ravine's entrance.

Silhouetted against the twilight, Evander dangles in the air, a large, bony hand plunged right through his middle. Scarlet seeps from the wound, and as my head spins, as I fight not to fall to my knees at the sight, something makes the shrill whistle we heard before.

Now I understand. The giant Shade was baiting us. Hunting us, when we thought we were hunting it.

Somehow, I cram my whistle into my mouth with a shaking hand and blow into it with as much breath as I can muster. My stomach drops to the ravine floor far below as Evander's eyes turn glassy and the creature pulls its hand free, carelessly dropping him and then picking him up again as if he's a toy that doesn't quite hold its interest.

He's so still, I'm afraid he's not breathing.

Please, by Vaia's grace, let him be breathing.

I force my shaking legs to run back up the short stretch of rocky path I descended, closing the distance between the Shade and me. The monster lifts Evander's limp arm to tear it off, and I take aim, throwing my vial of liquid fire right at its chest. But it easily swats the potion away like a bug. A cloud of blue flames explodes in a patch of white flowers.

The Shade is momentarily distracted, so I try again. Drawing my blade, gazing into the pitch-dark holes where its eyes should be, I slice clean through one of the monster's arms, freeing Evander from its grip. Black liquid spatters my face and chest. It reeks like spoiled fish and burns my skin.

The Shade's growl echoes through the mountains as it picks me up with its remaining arm and squeezes me so hard my sword drops from my limp hand. I twist in the monster's grasp, trying to get a look at Evander, but the Shade's strength is overpowering, squashing what little air is left in my lungs. It easily stands twice my height—the largest Shade I've ever seen.

The monster carries me toward a field, angling me so I'm able to turn my head and see him. Evander. Or what was Evander. My heart rattles sickly in my chest as his broken body shimmers beneath my gaze. His open, staring eyes reflect the twilight, and it's then I realize there's nothing of the one I love left in there. No hope for a healer's magic. Nothing I can say, no one I can bribe, or punch, or kill to get him back.

The monster flexes its bony hands, tearing into my skin. White-hot lightning flashes behind my eyes, and blood—my blood—sprays a crimson arc on a bed of lilies. They shouldn't be here. They mean beauty, in a world where nothing will ever be beautiful again.

I collapse, watching my blood pool around me as the Shade crouches near my face. The few tendrils of greasy black hair still clinging to its skull brush my cheek as it sniffs my head. I don't struggle. I don't care. My life, it doesn't matter anymore. Not now. Not without Evander.

The Shade unhinges its jaw wide enough to fit my head in its mouth, revealing its pointed teeth and blackened tongue. But before those teeth can snap my head from my neck, the monster snarls almost reluctantly at something in the distance, and bounds off into the darkness.

IX

Voices circle above me. Beside me. Over and under and around again, a baffling current of sound I can't trace.

"Danial's on his way!" Simeon declares breathlessly.

Footsteps pound down a corridor.

"She's dying. We should've stayed together!" Jax roars, followed by a sound like wood splintering. I don't have to open my eyes to know he's put his fist through a wall.

A door bangs open, and suddenly someone's touching my head, my waist. Their fingers are sticky. Warmth rushes over me like someone's dunked me in a bucket of hot water.

"She's going to make it," Danial says, his voice taut as a bowstring.

"How do you know?" Simeon sniffles and draws a shaky, wet breath.

Another wave of heat crashes into me.

Then comes pain all over, like a thousand knives being plunged into my skin at once without mercy.

Finally comes surrender. Welcome nothingness.

"I can't do it. I'm not going."

I'm ten years old again, and Evander and Master Cymbre watch with mingled surprise and worry as I flop down in the cool summer grass, bathed in the bluish light of a gate to the Deadlands. This will be our first time entering the spirit world, and I'm more afraid than I've ever been. I don't want to let go of the firm ground that cradles me, the wind that combs my hair, or the stars that make silver freckles on Evander's cheeks as he kneels beside me. I don't know what the Deadlands hold, and I don't care, because this is the world I love.

"Come on. I'll race you." Evander shoots me a grin, then nods to the gate. "Loser buys the winner sweets for a month." When I don't move, he adds in a whisper, "You're faster than me. I'd take the wager."

I shake my head and look away, not wanting him to see my tears.

"All right, then."

Evander springs to his feet. He dashes toward the gate, his face pinched with concentration, his unruly dark bangs obscuring his jewel-blue eyes. I can't help but watch, holding my breath as he sticks one foot through the low gate. Master Cymbre hides her expression behind her hand, but I spot a flicker of a smile.

Evander's leg disappears up to the ankle, then the knee. "It doesn't hurt! I'm all right!" he shouts, grinning.

He starts to pull back, to return to us, but leaning into the gate threw him off-balance. He flails his arms as he disappears into the blue light completely, stealing my breath.

I leap up. Three swift bounds and I'm through the gate, landing right on top of Evander on the other side. We're in a damp tunnel that's not so different from the tunnels in our world.

"Did it hurt?" he whispers through the dark. "Is this place as awful as you imagined?"

I shrug. All I knew in the moment Evander disappeared was that I had to go after him, no matter the cost.

Not even the Deadlands could be awful with him by my side. My partner.

"Evander?" I mumble, surprising myself with how groggy I sound.

"No, sweet sister," Simeon answers, a hitch in his voice, as I open my eyes and blink the grit from them. His face becomes clearer, from his messy hair to his waxy skin and his eyes rimmed with red.

There's an open book in his lap, its pages crumpled, the ink running in places.

"You look like shit," I blurt, putting a hand to my aching head without bothering to try sitting up. My whole body aches, and I don't think it's up for the challenge. "Rough night?" My mouth is dry, and I have to pause to lick my lips. "Where are we?"

I gaze around the plain but soothing room. The afternoon sun streams through the window, bathing bland portraits of lemon blossoms and cypress trees on all four walls and a wilting vase of flowers on the table opposite the bed in warm light.

We're in the palace, in the healers' wing.

"Where is he? Where's Evander?"

I grip Simeon by his tunic and shake him so hard, his book slips to the floor. He gently pries away my shaking fingers. "I'm so sorry, Sparrow," he says, his voice hoarse. "We couldn't save him."

The noise that escapes me is like the last breath of the dying. Pain burns through me, swallowing me up, like the yawning blackness of the Deadlands ravine.

Evander's dying scream rings in my ears as the healer's room shimmers before my eyes, becoming darker, sunless as the place where I last saw Evander's body. The stink of the Shade's flesh fills my nostrils. Its breath washes over me, ready to devour me as I lie helpless, watching the shell that was Evander, foolishly begging it to move.

My scream startles a bird from the windowsill.

"Shhhh, Sparrow." Simeon touches my shoulder, and I fight to stop screaming. "I'm sorry. I'm sorry. I'm sorry." He stretches out beside me, the way we used to sleep in our shared bed at the convent, and repeats the words until my scream becomes a whimper.

Danial sweeps into the room carrying a tray. His eyes are more bloodshot than Simeon's. "We're going to make you better," he says, "which is what Evander would want." He sounds defeated. "That's all we can do."

"Don't talk about him like he's dead!" I shout, my voice breaking over the words.

Danial bows his head. "Of course. My mistake." He sets his tray down on a high table and begins pouring a dazzling blue liquid into a glass.

Simeon holds me against him, and I put my hands over his, clinging to them.

"I hurt, Si." I sound like a child, but I can't make myself stop any more than I can stop my body from shaking. "I can't take it. I can't."

Danial strides to my bedside, smoothing back my hair and holding the glass of blue drink to my lips. "I've healed all your wounds, Sparrow. The only pain you feel is in here." He taps his head, his kohl-lined eyes glistening. "I can't heal the mind—no mage can. But this should help. Drink up."

"What is it?" I manage.

"A tonic to soothe the nerves."

Even through the haze of pain, I remember that the usual calming tonic is gray and smokes at the surface. "Are you sure?"

Danial almost smiles at that. "This one is stronger than those we normally give. It'll help. Trust me."

Somehow, between sobbing breaths, I drain the glass. It tastes like the small, hard green apples the Sisters of Death sometimes use in their pies. I close my eyes when Danial takes away the glass, suddenly exhausted.

I don't want to scream anymore. I don't want to do much of anything. I can only think of Evander, the Deadlands, and the Shade, but almost like an outsider. I know I should be hurting, but the pain can't sink its hooks as deep into me as it did moments before I drank the potion.

"How is she?" someone asks from out of sight.

My head is too muddled to place her voice right away, but I recognize her long red braid when it swishes past the door. Master

Cymbre doesn't come in. Instead, she draws Danial into the hallway, and I don't have the strength to wonder why.

With Simeon's arms around me, I lie back and listen to his heartbeat, to the vibrant rhythm of life, until I slide into the nothingness of a dreamless sleep.

The sun still rises and sets, like it always has. It seems cruel that it wouldn't stop, just for a little while, to show how much darker the world is without Evander in it.

I stop looking at the sun.

Without it, one day blurs into the next, until two or three or five have gone by.

Walking alone down the palace corridor that leads to Jax's room, to my room, and a few doors beyond that, to Evander's former room, I have no destination in mind. Nothing to fill my days.

I'm always alone now, even when someone is right beside me.

Footsteps jar me out of my drug-induced daze long enough to recognize Danial striding toward me, wearing his sturdy cotton healer's whites and the gold pin with double turquoise gems that signifies his master status. He opens his mouth to say something, but my head spins violently and the polished marble corridor becomes a blur as I sink to my knees.

The sixth dizzy spell in as many days.

Cool, gentle hands smooth my hair back from my forehead.

"Evander?" My heart skips as I gaze into the bluest eyes in all of Karthia.

"No," he says, frowning, but I'd know that voice, that face, those eyes anywhere. He kneels beside me, his forehead lined with concern, trying to get a better look at me. But I fling my arms around him, frantic, knocking the breath from him.

"How is this possible?" I laugh. "It's *you* . . ."

"Odessa." Evander frowns harder still, leaning away from me.

I pull him near, surprised by his resistance. "I thought you were dead!" I whisper fiercely into his neck.

"Odessa!"

Evander gives my shoulders a sharp shake, and suddenly in his place is Danial. He's kneeling on the floor beside me, gazing into my face with so much worry. "I'm not him, Odessa. You're having delusions."

I cross my arms and shake my head. I know he's right, but I don't want to believe him. If delusions are the only way to see Evander, then so be it. I'll take what I can get.

"I can heal your body again and again," Danial says distantly, like he's talking to someone else even though he's looking right at me, "but I don't know what else to try for your mind—you look dead on your feet, Sparrow!"

Tears slide down my face, seeping onto Danial's fingers. The look he's giving me shifts from one of worry to something worse: pity.

Lost girl, his eyes say. *Broken girl.*

He bows his head like everyone else does when they see me lately. It's like they're scared that if they hold my gaze too long, if they look too deep, they'll lose something that matters to them, too.

"Danial." I don't recognize the cracked voice coming out of my mouth as I tug on his shirtsleeve. "I need more of that calming potion. To keep the nightmares at bay." They aren't just happening at night, but Danial doesn't need to know that. He also doesn't need to know how much they dull my mind, or he might take them away, and then I can't say what I'll do with myself.

Danial nods reluctantly. "I'm glad it's helping." He hauls me to my feet, keeping an arm securely around my waist. "But if you have any more of these . . . delusions . . . let me know, will you, and we'll find you a different tonic."

"Right. Sure." I shrug him off. "I can still stand on my own, see?" There's that stranger's voice again.

"Okay," Danial says softly. He gazes down the hall, like he was headed somewhere, then looks at me again. "Let me help you back to your room, at least."

I shake my head. "I'm actually going for a walk."

"Sparrow, please tell me how you're really—"

Turning my back on him, I continue down the hall, slower than normal but moving just fine without anyone's help. I pass my room, taking my time as I head toward Evander's, until I hear Danial's boots clicking down the hall in the opposite direction.

One twist of the cold doorknob and I'm inside Evander's empty palace quarters. There's a wardrobe, a desk and chair, a tall painted vase full of fake and very dusty black poplar branches—their flowers are his favorite, a symbol of courage—and a bed with a basic blue quilt on it. There's not even a hint of his sandalwood, cut-grass, and leather smell in here. None of his silly drawings or maps scrawled on the bare walls. In all our years together, I think we've used this room maybe a handful of times, including after the recent festival.

As my fingers touch the quilt, a memory springs to mind: Me, sitting on this very bed. Evander, facing me, armed with what seemed like an entire closet full of bandages. Patching me up after sparring practice, mending a small cut beneath my eye as I tried to rub ointment on his bruises. We were both too proud to see a healer after Master Cymbre showed us how a real warrior fights.

Shaking my head to clear it, I stagger to the desk and pull open the single drawer there, searching for a distraction.

There's nothing inside but a dead fly. I don't know what I thought I'd find. Letters, maybe, which Evander had written to help me through this difficult time. But no one expected this, least of all him.

I sink into the rough wooden chair by the desk. I shouldn't have come here. This room is as Evander-less as the rest of the world, a world I'm stuck in without him.

So when I turn to face the bed, a tremor of cold runs through me as I meet the midnight-blue eyes of the young man sitting on it. He looks more polished than the Evander I knew, not one dark hair out of place or a hint of stubble on his jaw. He doesn't say anything, but he appears real enough.

Real or not, I need him.

"Since you've been gone, I don't even feel right in my own skin anymore," I tell him, breaking the silence. I wonder if he can speak. After a long silence, I go on, "It's like I'm missing a part, a lung or a kidney, and the rest of me can't figure out how to work together without that one piece."

My throat tightens, but I force more words out somehow. "I finally spent the whole night lying beside you, without having to run back to some other bed before sunup so your mother wouldn't know. It wasn't like I imagined it would be, though. You were just a cold shell, but I guarded you until it was time to prepare for . . ."

The fist of grief wrapping around my neck silences me for a moment, and the shadow of Evander on the bed flickers beneath my gaze.

"They're having your funeral tomorrow," I continue shakily, "and I'm sorry, but I'll have to close my eyes when they put your coffin in the ground. It's too much like saying goodbye. And I can't do that. I won't."

Evander was a necromancer, a cruel little voice in the back of my mind points out. *He's gone, no matter what you* think *you're seeing.*

I wonder if it's like Master Cymbre says—that our spirits travel on to whatever comes next, the place beyond the Deadlands where all spirits eventually go. But for all I know, Evander blinked out of existence when the Shade sliced through him.

The shadow Evander on the bed flickers again and disappears.

A low groan escapes my throat.

"You know what else isn't fair about all this?" I say, my voice hollow in the empty room. "You left Karthia without me, right after you'd decided to stay."

And I can never follow, on foot or by ship.

I run my hands through my hair, clawing at my scalp, trying to silence the wretched voice in my mind that keeps getting louder.

For the rest of my life, I could journey into the unknown world, small or vast or whatever it may be, and not find a trace of Evander anywhere but in my head.

But the only place I want to go now is the Deadlands, where I like walking the paths. Where I have unfinished business.

"And here's what hurts worst of all," I whisper to the empty bed where just nights ago, Evander kissed me until our lips were warm and swollen. "You'll never hear any of this, because you've vanished and I have to carry on alone."

Without my best friend. Without half of my heart.

"I wish you could tell me where to go from here, Evander." I slump in the chair. My head feels too heavy to be supported by my body any longer. "Or how to get my heart to stop repeating your name."

I touch the two gold pins on my worn black tunic, two sets of Vaia's blue eyes, the eyes of Death immortalized in sapphires. My own necromancer's pin and Evander's. I can't remember who gave it to me, but I'm never taking his pin off so long as I wear mine.

Everything I do is for both of us now.

X

The night of Evander's funeral, as those finished paying their respects are leaving the graveyard for Lyda's manor, I climb to the highest point in Grenwyr City. Partly because I can't stand the thought of ever setting foot in the Crowthers' home again, even to collect the few belongings from my drawer, and partly because the steep walk reminds me of how much Evander loved to hike. Besides, I can't go back to my palace room to sleep. Not until Danial delivers more of the bittersweet potions that lull me into a dreamless haze where I float for hours, high above the nightmares' grasping fingers, sometimes watched over by that silent shadow of Evander that only seems to appear when there's potion in my veins.

Fastening my cloak tighter to guard against the bitter night's wind, I sweep left out of the graveyard's main gate, away from the fading murmurs and sobs of the mourners. There's a single hill that peeks up above the palace and offers a bird's-eye view of the sea and the entire city, and that's where I'm headed.

King Wylding hates the unnamed hill, because he doesn't believe anything should be taller or more imposing than his family's ruling seat. I'm not sure I like it either. It makes me think nature wanted to remind the king that there will always be some things outside his control, just as some things are maddeningly outside mine.

Jax and Simeon follow me up the hill at a distance, trailed by Danial, who's still in his healer's whites and who gasps for breath like he's never hiked before. He comes from the flattest part of Oslea, where there aren't many hills to speak of.

Behind Danial, so far down the path that the babble of their voices is barely noticeable, Kasmira and her crew make a slow ascent to join us. I was surprised to see them at the funeral, as I never got the impression any of them were close with Evander. But Kasmira, who sat right beside me despite a lot of grumbling and muttering from the nobles, tugged a lock of my hair and whispered, "It's not the dead we came for, lovey."

The moment I reach the top of the hill, I sink down on the flat, worn boulder Evander used to claim as a seat whenever we came up here, and stare at the starry sky. Jax sits far apart from the rest of us, his back rigid and his expression unreadable. He'd known Evander even longer than I did.

I roll onto my side, the boulder digging into my ribs, to watch Kasmira and her crew make a bonfire on the middle of the hilltop. A tall, stately woman named Dvora drops an armful of kindling in the space the men have cleared, and Kasmira pulls out a piece of flint and a dagger to create the first spark of flame.

"Master Cymbre should be here." Simeon watches the kindling catch fire, his face as lean and hollow as an elf's in a children's tale.

Danial puts an arm around Simeon's shoulders and draws his sandy-haired lover against his side. "I'm sure she's remembering Evander in her own way tonight," he murmurs. "I went to give her something for her headache earlier, and . . ." His voice grows so soft, I have to strain my ears to catch the last words. "She feels like his death is her fault."

"It's no one's fault." Simeon hides his face in his hands, a gesture that makes my heart ache even more.

I understand how Master Cymbre is feeling. I keep thinking, if I'd just let him go into the ravine first, the Shade would have grabbed me instead. Evander would've had time to flee, or maybe even fight—after all, he's the better swordsman. Or was.

I wipe the wetness from my cheeks and lick the salt from my lips, surprised I haven't cried my eyes dry in the last several days. The potion must be wearing off.

"Guess this means you all won't be returning to the Deadlands anytime soon." One of Kasmira's crew, a burly mate whose name I can't remember, draws my attention as he plunks himself down opposite Simeon and Danial.

"Maybe," Jax grunts without looking toward the fire. He still hasn't moved from his spot on the far side of the hill, where he's no more than a solid outline in the dark.

Simeon glances toward his partner, his brows raised, but Jax says nothing more. "There's still the matter of hunting the giant

Shade." His face is barely recognizable without his usual good-natured grin. "It'll have to be stopped, and I expect King Wylding will order Jax and me to take care of it, since he knows us best. I won't agree if he expects us to go at it alone, though." He twists one of the gold rings on his fingers, seeming lost in thought. A few moments later, he adds, "Twenty of his best archers and several vials of liquid fire potion to light their arrows ought to be enough."

Danial presses his lips together and shakes his head. Though he doesn't say anything, there's a storm brewing in his kohl-rimmed eyes. Simeon is definitely in for a long night of arguing.

I wish I could save them the trouble and heartache. But if they knew about my plans to go into the Deadlands and kill the Shade myself or die trying, they'd probably lock me in a room for all eternity and say it was for my own good.

So I'll keep my silence until I leave. Just as soon as I stop taking these calming potions and have my wits about me. Because when I return to the Deadlands, I need to make sure I stay alive long enough to watch the monster die.

"Sparrow?" Kasmira's voice cuts into my thoughts, making me wince. Her lips are pursed. When I meet her eyes, she gestures to the fire and asks, "Why don't you say a few words?"

I stagger to my feet and take an unsteady step toward the fire. My throat is too tight to allow any words to come out, but I pull a crumpled piece of parchment from my back pocket. A map of Grenwyr Province, one Evander had been working on practically since we met, detailing all our favorite places. I clench my hand around the parchment until it's little more than a tiny wrinkled ball and toss it into the flames, then fall to my knees in the grass as

Evander's dreams rise into the night sky on puffs of smoke, vanishing like the rest of him.

No one speaks again for a long while. Kasmira passes around a flask, but it's too much effort to raise my hand to take it.

Eventually, she and the crew make their way back to the *Paradise*, and Simeon douses the fire before he and Danial stumble down the hill to bed. I sit in the cold grass, watching smoke from the fire's ashes curl into the velvet black sky, until Jax climbs to his feet and offers me a hand. "Coming?"

I nod but push myself to my feet without his help. We trudge back to the palace as the sky lightens to a misty gray. And when faced with the choice of returning to my dark, empty room or following Jax into his, it doesn't take long to decide.

"Sorry about the, uh, mess." Jax kicks his spare cloak out of the narrow entryway. There's another pile of clothes on his bed—unwashed, by the sharp, spicy scent of them—that he shoves aside to make a place for me to sit. Two lanterns flicker to life, then Jax grabs the wooden chair from his desk and sinks into it, facing the bed.

Hugging my knees to my chest and pushing my back against the wall, I try to get comfortable on the lumpy mattress. The lanterns don't shine bright enough to illuminate the far corners of the room, which is just as well because it looks like Jax keeps his life's belongings stashed in careless heaps.

I blink, realizing I can't remember the last time I was in here.

Feeling Jax's gaze on me, I clear my throat and point to the wardrobe at the back of the room. "You know, they gave you that so you could put your things *inside* it."

He runs a hand through his raven hair, then shrugs. "Sorry." Reaching out with his foot, he kicks a dagger under the bed. "It's not usually this bad. I . . ." He swallows, and I brace myself for the sting of hearing Evander's name. "Well, you know."

My shoulders slump in relief. I follow Jax's gaze to the stretch of wall beside the desk and suck in a breath at the number of holes punched there. Sure enough, when I peer at his right fist, his knuckles are raw.

Shivering, I climb to my feet. I shouldn't be here, intruding on his grief. There's nothing I can offer Jax, even though he's been my friend almost my whole life. I'm all out of sympathy, and the last thing he needs is the added weight of someone else's sorrow.

As I stride to the door, Jax hurries after me and puts a hand on my arm, gazing down at me from barely an inch away. His breath is hot on my chilled face. "You just got here."

"That's right. And now I'm going." I tug my arm from his grasp. "Goodnight, Jax."

My hand is on the door when he says roughly, "Odessa. Wait."

I turn, and he drops his arms to his sides. I've never seen him like this, standing with his head bowed, his whole body shivering slightly as he struggles to raise his eyes to mine. Looking like I could wound him with a single word.

After a long and heavy moment of silence, he murmurs, "I miss him, too."

"I know." I have a strange urge to brush his hair out of his face. And maybe it's the soothing potion wearing off, but I'm shaking as I reach up. My hand gets lost on the way to his hair, sliding over the roughness of his cheek and cupping the back of his neck.

We stare at each other, frozen like that until I find my voice. "I'm sorry. I don't know what's wrong with—"

"The same thing that's wrong with me," he growls as he grabs me by the waist and pulls me against him.

Together, we fall onto the bed. He searches for my lips for a hopeful moment, nuzzling my neck, but I shake my head even as I cling to him. He wraps his arms around me, clutching me against his chest as he clumsily strokes my hair with his bloodied hand.

We douse the torchlight, and Jax groans a little as I turn and press my back against his chest. "No," I whisper as his straying fingers curl around the hem of my snug tunic. He returns his hands to holding me.

This isn't love. I know this. But in Jax's arms, I don't feel completely alone. I can breathe better with his weight pressing against my back, with my legs twined around his, our hot skin separated only by the thin layer of our necromancer's uniforms. I wrap my body in his copper skin stretched over hard muscle, wearing him like a shield against the rest of the world, and it makes the thought of living bearable again.

This isn't love. This is just two people, shaking and sobbing together in the semidark, breathing hard in each other's ears as we try to forget our worst nightmares.

This is survival.

I'm not sure how I got back to my room last night. All I know is that the noon sun hurts my eyes, and Princess Valoria looks like a fiery spirit silhouetted against the merciless blaze.

"Get up," she says cheerily, like she's talking to a child or a puppy. She pulls back my blankets and wrinkles her nose. "What's that awful smell? Oh, Sparrow. That's it. You're coming with me." She gives my hand a firm tug.

I bolt upright, suck in a breath, and wrap the sheets around me like a cloak to hide my nakedness before I realize I'm still wearing my uniform.

"What're you doing here?" I demand groggily, running a hand through my tangled hair and getting my fingers stuck halfway down.

Valoria frowns, her doe-brown eyes shining behind her glasses. "I came to see how you were faring. And as it seems you're in dire need of a bath, I'm here to escort you to the bathing house. You can use my private chamber, even."

"Thanks." I flop back down on the bed and pull the quilt over my head. "But no."

"You can't stay in here forever, Odessa," Valoria says gently. "When my father died, I thought I'd hide away for good. But everyone needs to eat and sleep and"—she pauses to cough—"bathe once in a while. It gets easier as the days pass. You'll see. One morning after he was gone, I realized the sun was still shining without him. And since I was still here, I figured I'd make myself useful to other Karthians who were missing a leg like he was. That's how I started working on my first invention."

I shake my head under the quilt. Her words make my stomach churn, so I poke an arm out of bed to feel around for the latest vial of potion Danial left me.

But Valoria grabs my hand and gives it a firm tug, surprising me again with her strength.

"Just go. Please." I roll over, putting my back to the princess. "There's nothing you can do, Valoria. I'm not one of your inventions. I'm broken, part of me is missing, and you can't fix me with copper wires or a piece of string."

For a highborn lady of fine breeding, Valoria's sigh is a lot like a growl. She strips off my quilt and grabs me by the shoulders.

"Your mother brought you into this world as a whole person," the princess huffs, pulling so hard that I slide to the edge of the bed. "And last I checked, you still are one. No matter what or who you've lost. Now get"—she jerks on my arms—"up!"

I cling to the bed, and Valoria stumbles backward alone.

"Fine." She straightens, smoothing her rose-patterned gown. "You win today. But I'm coming back, same time tomorrow. And I'll bring extra muscle if need be."

"By Vaia's grace, *why*?"

"Because that's what friends do." She turns on her heel and strides from the room.

Once she slams the door, I drain a vial of potion in a huge gulp. I don't know what the princess expected. I can't be anything to anyone right now, which she'd know if she'd bothered to listen to me. I hurl the empty potion vial at the wall and watch it shatter.

XI

The bells on the apothecary door jingle merrily, making my head throb as I step inside. Worse than the noise is the smell, which is somewhere between a musty attic and a healer's closet full of pungent herbs. Mysterious spicy fumes leak from spilled bottles.

I stride to the back counter, shoving my shaking hands in my pockets as I walk. It's been six hours since my last calming potion, six hours since I drank the blue liquid that keeps me floating just a little outside myself, outside the worst of the pain. The potion that banishes the thoughts that would destroy me, of blood and sightless creatures, of rotting flesh and a soul-shattering scream.

Danial says it's time to stop abusing the potion or risk terrible side effects, but he doesn't understand that I need this to survive, to keep seeing my silent visions of Evander, all I have left of him. And if Danial won't fetch the potion for me anymore, I'll just buy it myself. Vaia knows I've got enough gold to afford what I need, between my savings and what Evander left sitting in Grenwyr Treasury under my name.

Maybe he did see this coming, or something like it, after all.

My insides twist into hundreds of tiny knots when I think of using Evander's coins to buy a calming potion that makes me numb, makes me see his phantom so I won't forget his face. But he'll never know, so I guess it's not really hurting anyone.

As I wait for the apothecary or one of his assistants to appear, I drum my fingers on the long counter and my hand comes away caked in dust. The wall behind the counter is stacked to the ceiling with glass jars, and one in the middle is full of the bitter-apple liquid I badly need. I study the waist-high counter, trying to decide whether I can jump it, when a soft voice gasps, "Odessa!"

A jolt runs through me. I straighten and glance at the woman who's appeared behind the counter, her usually beautiful features pinched in a frown.

"What are you doing here?" Lyda Crowther demands, leaning against the other side of the counter so we're nose-to-nose.

At almost the same time, I blurt, "You shouldn't be here."

Lyda's always worked a few days a week at the city apothecary. She doesn't have a keen eye for mixing potions—hers are blue, of course, not brown—but she says she likes working much better than sitting in the manor all day arranging tea parties, and the head apothecary was in need of someone to manage the front of the shop. But Lyda shouldn't be here today. Not with Evander so recently laid in the ground.

"Odessa." Lyda's voice is low and urgent. She grips my upper arm, her fingernails pricking my skin beneath my thin shirt. "Are you all right?"

Blinking, I realize I'm leaning against the counter with a hand pressed to my forehead. "I'm a little dizzy," I confess as I take in Lyda's appearance. "But I'll be fine. The more important question is, how are you?"

Lyda purses her lips, like she's not sure how to answer. There are no smudges under her eyes, and her pale skin is flawless as ever. Her stiff, high-collared sapphire dress is neat and unwrinkled, and her hands are perfectly manicured. But I know as well as anyone that we all wear scars others can't see.

"I'm managing," Lyda says at last. "Elibeth's taking some time off from her duties at the kennels to help me sort through all of Evander's things. We'll be donating them to the Convent of Death." She draws a heavy breath. "And Meredy's on her way home as well, though I wish it was under happier—"

"You're giving away Evander's belongings? *All of them?*" My face warms, and heat creeps up the back of my neck.

Lyda reaches out to smooth my hair, and I pull away. She lowers her hand, frowning again. "I've been through this before, remember?" Her voice is just above a whisper, like she can't bear to hear the words coming from her own mouth. "With my husband. And for me, the best way to move on is to purge the manor of reminders of the deceased."

"The deceased?" I repeat the words through numb lips. "Did you ever bother asking Evander what he wanted you to do with all his things if he—if he *died*?" My vision grows hazy, as though Lyda's standing behind a cloud of smoke, but I continue. "Or how about asking me? He was mine, and no one's asked me what I thought he wanted!"

Silence settles over us as we lock eyes, the perfumed air too thick to carry sound. Lyda's eyes are round with shock or revulsion or something else I can't name.

I struggle for what feels like hours to get my tongue and throat working again. "I mean," I finally manage in a steady-enough voice, "he was my partner. And I *loved* him. He was going to tell you. We were going to move to the palace together." I pause to wipe the sweat beading on my forehead. "Right after we killed the Shade, he was going to tell you."

"I already knew," Lyda says slowly. She glances down at her hands, making it impossible to read her expression. "I've known for a year or so. Love is difficult to disguise."

"You knew," I repeat flatly. "You knew we were in love, but you reminded Van all the time that he couldn't marry a necromancer with your blessing—*why?*"

Swallowing hard, I taste the sour beginnings of anger, the realest, strongest thing I've felt in days.

"I thought it would make you both give up the job," Lyda whispers, still not meeting my eyes. Tears spill onto her cheeks. "I thought, if you wanted each other badly enough, more than you wanted the job, you'd give it up, and then you'd both live long, happy lives. I was trying to *save you!*"

At last, she looks up, her eyes gleaming. "If you keep playing with death, you'll end up just like him." Some of her sadness gives way to anger. "Is that what you want?"

Bristling, I lean toward her, gripping the counter. "I have a score to settle with Evander's killer, and unlike you, I don't run from a fight."

"Is everything all right out there?" a dry voice calls. There's a rustling from deep within the shop's back room, and slowly, a shrouded figure emerges. Lyda and I carefully avoid each other's eyes as the apothecary joins the baroness at the counter.

"Good afternoon, Sparrow," the apothecary rasps. A faint whiff of mint and rosemary wafts under my nose, no doubt because the apothecary has stuffed fresh bundles of herbs under his shroud. Most of the Dead prefer not to stink like the corpses they are, and that's fine by me. "What can we get you today?"

"I need another month's worth of your strongest calming tonic." I nod to the jar of liquid glittering a cobalt promise, then shrug and pretend to look annoyed. "Healer's orders."

"Are you sure, Sparrow?" The apothecary rests a gloved hand lightly on my forearm, making me flinch. "That's a powerful tonic. I've never heard of anyone taking it for so long without becoming . . . dependent upon it. The side effects can be rather nasty for days after a dose. Shaking fits. Dizzy spells. Even hallucinations."

Staring into his masked face, my thoughts begin to wander. I know I can't bring Evander back, but if I could, would it be what was best for him, for us? Would I ever be satisfied with staring into a mask instead of Evander's stunning eyes? Would we be able to embrace? Or would I be too repulsed by the thought of rotting skin and the stench of a corpse rising from his shroud? Surely it would all be worth it to have him at my side again, whether I could see him or not. To hear his jokes and keep his company . . . but even if I had to kill him to stop him from becoming a Shade?

Suddenly, a little of my anger at Lyda fades. She's been through this before. Her husband became a Shade, and she had to slay him. Of course she doesn't want to be constantly reminded of the son she lost. To pick up a shirt that still faintly smells of Evander, of sandalwood and fresh-cut grass—and wonder, like I am, if things could've been different this time somehow. Of course she'd want to get rid of his belongings.

As I cast an apologetic glance at the baroness, I notice the apothecary is waiting for my reply. I imagine him giving me a questioning look behind his mask and cross my arms, making it clear I'm not going anywhere until I get what I came for.

"I'm certain it's what I need," I say at last.

"She's a grown woman," Lyda tells the apothecary. "If you won't pour it for her, I will."

She catches my nod of thanks, and her lips twitch the slightest bit. The look she gives me is almost maternal, taking me back several years. This must be her way of saying she's sorry, hopefully for more than just today. I hope it's for the years of standing between me and Evander, when it all turned out to be for nothing.

The apothecary heaves a rattling sigh and gathers several empty vials from under the counter, thrusting them at the baroness. "Very well, Lyda. I'll leave you to finish up here." With a quick bow to me, he trudges toward the back room, his black shroud trailing on the floor behind him like an elongated shadow.

Lyda doesn't say a word as she fills the vials from the big glass jar. The sound of the potion sloshing in the vial helps loosen the knots in my shoulders and stomach. I curl and uncurl my fingers and gaze around the shop, desperate to occupy the little moments until the potion's burning through my veins and I'm back in control.

I'm trying to name the different herbs hanging in dried bunches overhead when a strange tingling at the back of my neck makes me whirl around.

There, blocking the shop's only exit, is a Shade as huge and hideous as the one that killed Evander. It must be the *same* one, because there's a bony stump where its arm once was. I don't know how it even fit through the narrow door, or what the blazes compelled it to come out of the Deadlands. It trains its dark eye sockets on me as it opens its yawning mouth wide, and I fumble for my sword.

"Lyda, get back!" I shout. She's still behind the counter, but that's hardly a barrier to a Shade.

At last, I brandish my blade, daring the monster to come one step closer.

"You ready to lose the other arm?" I snarl. The Shade creeps toward me, then scuttles back against the door, its skeletal fingers dragging the ground. Mocking me. It knows it can outrun me.

I charge it. I may not have a fire potion at the ready, but if I'm lucky, I can at least do some damage.

"Sparrow!" Lyda gasps. Her voice is high and harsh in my ear. She's right beside me, the foolish woman, which means she leapt the counter and headed right toward the danger. "What's gotten into you?"

I break my stare with the Shade for just a moment to gape at her. Her eyes are wide and wild.

When I glance back at the Shade, it's gone.

I lower my sword, heat rushing to my face as Lyda checks me for fever. "There . . . there wasn't anything in here with us just now?"

Lyda grips my shoulders, forcing me to look her in the eye. "Odessa. What did you see?"

I wave her and her concerns away, though I'd be lying if I said what just happened didn't get under my skin. I've got to keep it together long enough to kill the monster that took Evander. I'll be no use to anyone if I can't tell the real monsters from the ones in my head, and I'm far from doing a good job of holding on to my sanity.

Someone knocks on the door of my palace room, a sharp and purposeful sound. I bury my head in my pillow to muffle it. The doorknob rattles. More knocking follows, and a smooth male voice says, "Special delivery from Prince Hadrien Wylding, for one Odessa of Grenwyr!"

I shake my head at the familiar voice. Sitting up, I call, "I know it's you, Highness!"

"It's *Hadrien*, as I've told you countless times." The smile in his voice is unmistakable as he adds, "And if you know it's me, why aren't you opening the door, Sparrow?"

I'm pretty sure the wardrobe in the corner of my room is judging me as I try to smooth my rumpled uniform. I hurry to unlock the door, only to be greeted by—

"That's a lot of flowers, Hadrien. Surely they aren't all for me?"

The bouquet, no doubt plucked fresh from the palace greenhouse—white carnations for endearment, cheerful yellow acacia for friendship, and, unsurprisingly, lilac for new affections—tickles my nose as I peer around the blossoms for a glimpse of the smiling prince.

"They are. But never mind them." He lowers the bouquet. "Read the invitation they come with. It's far more important." As his gaze sweeps over my face, whatever he sees there steals the sunshine from his deep brown eyes.

Clearing his throat, he adds in a far more solemn tone, "My birthday festival is tonight. I came to invite you in person . . ." His fingers touch my cheek for the briefest moment, hummingbird-light. "And to see how you're holding up."

I blink and look away, lost for words. When I raise my eyes again, Shadow Evander—often my only companion these days—stands behind the prince, pretending to kick Hadrien in the rear to make me laugh. I quickly bite my lip, resisting the urge to grin.

"Sparrow, do you need to sit? Can I—? Here." Hadrien sweeps into the room, pulling out a chair and gently guiding me into it. "Do you need anything?" he asks, even as I shake my head. "Water, perhaps?"

Heat creeps back into my face as I remember yesterday's disastrous visit to the apothecary. The potion made a fool out of me, and it's threatening to do so again now, but I need it to keep the pain away. At this rate, I'm destined to become a public laughingstock.

"I'm fine." I realize my sweaty palm is soaking the invitation he handed me, and I pull the creamy piece of parchment from its envelope. It smells clean, like sage. Like Hadrien. The scent clears my head a little.

"If you're not feeling up to a party, I'll understand," Hadrien says, kneeling by my chair. "Just say the word, and we can pretend this invitation never found its way here. There'll be other parties. Other invitations I can deliver in person."

I press my lips together, lost for words. I'm only staying at the palace until I can keep my head clear long enough to know the real Shade when I see it, so I can be sure I've killed Evander's murderer. And once the Shade is dead, I assume I will be, too.

I don't know how to tell Hadrien that I'll be wherever the real Evander is soon.

"I'll be there," I blurt, surprising myself as much as Hadrien.

"Are you certain?" He tilts his head, and when he meets my eyes, my breath catches in my throat. It might just be another hallucination, but the look he gives me reminds me of one Evander and I used to share when we were alone. "It would mean a lot to me."

Behind him, Shadow Evander pretends to retch.

"Of course. It's . . ." I lower my eyes to the invitation to avoid his earnest gaze. "Perfect timing." Hadrien coughs, as though he doesn't believe that for a moment, but I rush on, "I needed an excuse to wear my favorite party dress again, and you've delivered it."

If he recognizes the false cheer in my voice, he makes no sign of it. He climbs to his feet, just to give me a deep bow.

Shadow Evander flashes me a look of betrayal. I know he's not real, but he looks it, and my stomach aches as I feel like I've hurt him all over again.

"I've been losing sleep every night since it happened," Hadrien says softly, jarring me back to reality. "I lie awake thinking of Master Crowther, and how we lost him far too soon. And Master Nicanor, too. I urged His Majesty to assign extra guards to patrol these halls and keep the rest of you safe, though they certainly didn't prove their worth against the last Shade they met." Admiration glints in his dark eyes as he adds, "*You* took care of that brilliantly on your own."

I don't know what to say to that. I never know what to say to Hadrien. I settle on, "I'd better bathe and change if I'm attending a party in a few hours. Unless you want me to show up in this."

"You look perfect in everything." The prince's smile returns as I gesture at my tired black uniform. "My only birthday wish is to see your face tonight."

I nod, once again unable to form words as my mind races.

"See you soon, sweet Sparrow," Hadrien calls as he closes the door on his way out.

Shadow Evander aims a kick at the door in response.

"I need you, and you're not here," I whisper as he flickers and disappears beneath my bleary gaze. "I miss you. We all miss you."

I think of Jax with a guilty pang. Shadow Evander's look of betrayal would be far worse if he ever appeared in Jax's darkened room to find us in the bed we now share out of desperation. "I love you. And I'm sorry."

Tonight, I'll put on the blue silk dress that drove Evander mad when we were in public and all he could do was hold my hand. And I'll dance, and drink, and fake a smile for everyone who smiles at me.

Tonight, I'm going to live. One last time.

XII

A pounding on my door nearly causes me to drop my latest dose of potion.

"Sparrow, let's go," Jax calls. "I don't want to miss the first batch of party food. We'll be lucky if the Dead leave us scraps."

I swallow the contents of the vial in one huge gulp, then try to tug my dress up to cover more of my chest even though I know it's pointless. I shake my dark brown waves loose from the butterfly pin holding them up and let my hair fall over my shoulders. I grab a second vial from my stash and splash more blue liquid down my throat. I want to make sure Evander is within reach tonight.

As if reading my thoughts, he appears from behind my wardrobe, smiling appraisingly at my dress.

When I open the door to the hall, Jax is standing off to one side, staring at a painting of King Wylding in his shroud. If not for the crown, it could be a portrait of any of the Dead.

As usual, Jax has put on his finest for the royal celebration: black silk robes, his only adornments a longsword in a golden scabbard and his master necromancer's sapphire pin.

I prop a hand on my hip. "What are you doing out here, anyway?" I assumed I'd see him at the party, hovering near the banquet tables or trying to outdrink the Dead.

Jax's copper skin gleams in the torchlight of the hall as he turns to me, his eyes uncertain. "I thought we'd go together." He shrugs. "If you'd rather go alone, I'll give you five minutes' head start." He points to the left, down the hallway. "The party's that way."

"This isn't . . ." I pause and lick my lips, struggling for words. I need Jax in a way I've never needed anyone before, but he can't fill Evander's place at my side. "This isn't like that. *We're* not like that."

Jax scowls. "Like what? You mean we're not friends anymore?"

I shake my head, relieved, and twine my arm around his. "Of course we are. Lead the way."

The palace courtyard looks much as it did on the night of the Festival of Cloud, only there are no nuns in charcoal-gray habits or any roaring bonfires. Instead, glass jars filled with water and tiny candles perched on every ledge overhead give the impression of floating lights. There's a large space for dancing, and the musicians who aren't currently performing roam among the crowd, their chests thrown out to show off the gleaming silver harp pins bestowed upon them by King Wylding, eating their fill before they take the stage.

Gathered around a magnificent display of tarts, the queen and her ladies-in-waiting are deep in conversation. The gold bangles and other gems on their shrouded figures chime softly with each gesture, the air around them thick with citrus and spice, as though they've all doused themselves in bergamot perfume.

There's no sign of King Wylding yet. He's surely busy writing out a long, rambling speech about Hadrien's accomplishments, which he'll give before he cuts the cake—honey and lavender, the same as it's been the last seven years I've attended the royal birthday parties. Jax makes a beeline for the banquet tables, leaving me adrift in a sea of flowing silks and bodies warm and cold.

"Thanks, *friend*," I mutter after him.

A servant bearing a large and heavy-looking silver tray passes by, and I swipe a glass of pale liquid and sniff it. Honeysuckle wine, I think, but there's only one way to be sure.

Two glasses of sweet wine later, I'm no longer bothered that everyone seems to be sneaking curious glances at me instead of talking to me or asking how I've been. I'm swaying slightly to the lively tunes of the evening's main band. I'm singing along, making up my own lyrics. I'm laughing as Jax bumps into Princess Valoria, knocking her glasses into a bowl of cranberry sauce and then frantically trying to clean them on his tunic. The redness of the sauce is nothing compared to the fire in Valoria's cheeks as she snatches her glasses back and adjusts them, stealing glances at Jax after putting them back on.

I don't have any time to dwell on what those glances mean, or how I feel about it, because someone shouts my name as I reach for my third or fourth glass of wine from a tray that's moving alarmingly fast.

"I've been looking everywhere for you," Prince Hadrien says as he squeezes between two dancing couples to reach me. "And I'm not the only one."

The prince's messy blond hair seems paler than usual, especially where the longest strands brush the shoulders of his midnight-blue tunic. He scans the crowd around us before focusing the full intensity of his gaze on me and spreads his hands in a helpless gesture. "I swear she was just over by the cake, talking to Mother . . ."

I have no idea what he's talking about. "Valoria?" I guess, cringing at the way I slur the name. I've had three glasses of wine before, but maybe it's not mixing well with the calming potion.

"No, my sister is always easy to pick out of a crowd." Hadrien smiles, the kind that lights his eyes from within, the kind he always gives to me in particular. "I'm afraid I don't know the young woman's name." He runs a hand through his hair, ruffling it even though the breeze was already doing that for him. Maybe he knows how perfectly imperfect he looks with pale strands falling across his eyes. "I've never seen her before, which is strange, because she seemed to be about our age. But she's very insistent on speaking with you."

I run through a list of names in my head, though it pounds with the beginnings of a headache. Master Cymbre? No, Hadrien knows her. Elibeth? But Hadrien knows her, too. One of Kasmira's crew, perhaps?

"Here, join me." Hadrien presses a glass of dark elderflower wine into my hands, chasing away the mystery of who would be asking for me tonight. "A little something to raise our spirits in these troubled times." His hands are on my waist, keeping me steady. I hadn't realized how much I was swaying.

I clink my glass against his and drain it quickly, drowning my thoughts of how Evander would've snarled to see Hadrien holding me like this. "Happy birthday, Highness." I lift my glass again, but it's nearly empty. A lone drop splashes my cheek.

"Hadrien," he corrects me again. He pulls a white handkerchief from the pocket of his leather trousers and dabs my cheek dry. "And if you really want to make it a happy one, you'll—"

"Yes." My heart's hammering a staccato beat, at odds with the gentle waltz the fiddlers have just begun to play. "I'd love to dance with you, Hadrien."

The prince blinks, closes his open mouth, and takes my hands.

I'm not sure how we wind up in the middle of the dance floor, or how I let Hadrien pull me so close that I'm forced to gaze deep into his eyes. They're the darkest brown I've ever seen, like Evander's were the darkest blue.

I want to ask him if he's ever seen his sister's inventions. Or if he creates things in secret, too. But I've never asked for secrets from a prince, and if I move my lips too much just now, they might catch on Hadrien's, and that would create a whole new mess I'm in no state to clean up.

"How have you been, Sparrow?" Hadrien whispers, his mouth near my ear.

Now I can see the many stares I expected. Even the Dead have turned their masked faces our way, and their silence is palpable, leaving only the music.

"No different than I was when you asked this afternoon in my chamber," I answer at last. Hadrien pushes me away so I can twirl in time with the chorus, then pulls me in with a force that makes my head spin. "You're the only one who's asked lately, though." I try to take a deep breath, but it's not easy with the prince's arms hugging my waist like the corsets the noblewomen wear. "Thank you—for caring."

Hadrien shakes his head, looking solemn. "You don't have to thank me for that. I care for every living person in this rich and beautiful land, Sparrow."

I twirl away from him again, meeting his eyes from the distance created by our outstretched arms. His face is the only thing I see clearly amidst a swirl of colors and shapes. "You say my name a lot."

He pulls me back to his arms, stumbling a bit on the impact of our collision. Quickly recovering his footing, he flashes a dazzling grin. "Maybe that's because I like the sound of it."

We dance for a few more minutes until someone—Hadrien, I think—presses another glass of wine into my hands. I'm losing track of how much I've had, and my stomach is churning, but the wine warms me all over, and the fiddlers' music sings through my blood.

This is it. *Living.*

If only Evander were here to do it all with me.

I blink back the sudden tears pricking my eyes and look around for another servant bearing wine.

Hadrien's hands are on my waist again. Now they're cupping my face, pulling me in for a kiss, and I clumsily take a step back.

But before I can object to his apparent habit of kissing people without their permission, Hadrien's face melts away, replaced by Jax's in a single confusing blink. The sight makes me shiver. "Is that really you?" I demand, remembering the potion's tricks even through the haze I'm in.

"You've either had too much to drink, or not enough." Jax's gruff voice and rough but steady hands assure me it's him. "So the question is, do you need me to fetch you some water? Or something stronger?"

I rest my head on his chest, inhaling the now-familiar scent of his sweat. This is my last night before I enter the Deadlands. My last night to feel truly alive. I can't stop now and head inside when the moon is paper white and young and full.

"Neither," I say finally. "Let's dance."

We take it slow, though the music's pounding beat is fast. As I catch sight of Her Majesty by the cake again, something Hadrien said comes back to me. "Jax?" I have to shout to be heard over the fiddles and pipes. "Did you notice someone looking for me earlier—a girl?"

Jax thinks for a moment, then grunts, "Dark red hair. Nice ass. I remember."

"Did you get a name? What does she want?" The thought that someone I don't know is looking for me sends a spike of cold into my chest. It must be someone with news from Kasmira, though she's never sent a messenger to me before.

"Sorry, Sparrow." Jax shrugs. "I was talking to Princess Valoria when she came by, and keeping up with her requires my full attention. I'll be damned if I understood half the things she was saying—something about flying."

"Don't worry about it." I lean against Jax, letting him support most of my weight through the next dance. My legs feel like anchors, and even dragging my feet across the flagstones takes great effort. "If someone's that determined to find me, they will."

I'd keep wondering who it might be, if not for my blasted headache. Instead, all I can think to say is, "What was Valoria talking about?" More importantly, "You're not going to breathe a word about her . . . projects, are you?"

Jax's lips twitch, but instead of answering, he twirls me around.

As one song blends seamlessly into the next, Jax shrinks down several inches, his curly dark hair turning long and sandy blond. "Simeon!" I blink several times, and from what I can tell, it's really my almost-brother guiding me through a complicated dance step.

"I've been really worried about you," he says in a somber voice unlike his own. "Danial says you've been having night terrors. If you are, you know you can talk to me about them. I'll understand."

Of course he would. Simeon was found by one of the Sisters of Death, wandering the Ashes alone at only three years old, wearing a ring on a tarnished chain around his neck that must have belonged to a wealthy family. He's held on to that ring all these years. And though he claims he doesn't remember any of his life before the convent, he used to wake me in the night with his screams at least once a week. I don't know what they were about, only that the nightmares still plague him sometimes.

But the potion I've been taking keeps most of my dreams away. "Everything's fine," I assure him. "I've got it all under—"

"Control," Simeon finishes for me, flashing a tight grin. "That's my Sparrow."

He spins me around, and somehow, Simeon becomes Danial when I turn back to him. Then Danial turns into Evander, who turns into Jax again, faces and colors flashing too quickly for my eyes to keep up. My head throbs with a sharp pain like someone's bashed me on the temple. Someone else reaches for my hands, but I jerk away. There's an archway at the back of the courtyard that leads to the palace citrus and floral gardens, the one through which Duke Bevan so recently appeared as a Shade, and I stagger toward it until I can't hear any voices calling me or see any shadows in pursuit of mine.

I gulp a greedy breath of cool air and sink to my knees beside some rosebushes, stars bursting behind my eyes. Suddenly, my stomach gives a painful lurch, but I manage to swallow the mouthful of bile before it leaves my lips. It burns all the way down.

The second time, I'm not as lucky. I just hope Prince Hadrien and the others can't hear my sweet noises over the music.

Movement in the bushes deeper in the garden draws my attention. My heart beats a little faster as I slick back my sweaty hair and narrow my eyes at the spot where I think the soft rustling of branches came from.

"Death be damned," I groan under my breath.

A rotting hand feels its way around a trellis, loose bits of mottled flesh washed with moonlight. The Shade is here. It must've crawled out of the Deadlands, though such a thing has only happened maybe once in all my years. Still, this can't be another hallucination, because its stench overpowers the roses.

I reach for my sword, but just like at the Festival of Cloud, I couldn't wear my scabbard over my dress. But I'm not completely unprepared this time. From inside my boot, I grab one of Jax's knives and push myself off the ground, charging toward the Shade.

The hunched monster screeches, unfurling itself to its full height as I lunge with the knife and slice its flesh. It's not moving at its usual lightning speed. It must not be doing so well with one of its arms missing.

Something sharp knocks the knife from my hand. I grope in the dirt, feeling for the hilt. The sharp thing sears my hand as it cuts deeper. It feels like the monster's trying to peck me to death, but I didn't think Shades had razor-sharp *beaks*.

I lash out at the Shade with both hands, one good and one bloodied, tearing at its flesh the way it tore Evander open and spilled his blood before my eyes.

The Shade squeaks piteously.

"Odessa!" a girl's voice gasps. "What the blazes are you doing?"

I shake my head to clear it, growling, "Saving the palace from this monster."

"That's my aunt's favorite peacock!" Valoria cries.

I blink, and the monster changes shape beneath my hands. Rotting flesh becomes a rich cape of blue and green feathers, bright as jewels. Beady eyes stare up at me, shining with a plea for mercy. I release the poor bird, backing away with a shudder. One of its wings is mangled, and its right side is scratched and bleeding. Still, it manages to hop to its long yellow feet and disappear into the garden, its trailing tail shedding a few feathers in its wake.

I hold up my shaking, bloody hands and turn to find Valoria staring at me with a mixture of shock and disgust, her glasses reflecting the distant glimmering party lights.

"I came to find you because I thought you could help," she stammers in a voice that's slightly off-key. "My mother's missing. Along with several other Dead who never turned up for the party. I've been looking all night, and Hadrien's too busy to . . ."

I lose the thread of Valoria's words as I sway again. This time there's no Hadrien or Jax to catch me, and when I fall to my knees, something slices through my dress. And my skin. It seems I've found my knife.

"Oh, Sparrow." Valoria wraps her arms around my waist, trying to haul me to my feet, but I shake my head in protest. "I'm taking you inside. You need rest. And quite possibly a healer."

The image of the maimed peacock feels like a gut punch. How did I get here, where I can't tell the difference between a defenseless creature and a monster? Me, the girl who once tried to put the wings back on a trampled butterfly. The girl who coaxed reluctant plants to blossom in the convent garden. The girl so in love with life, she couldn't harm a living thing.

I should be helping Valoria find the missing Dead right now, but instead, I'm shoving my head into a bush so she won't see me heave up the contents of my stomach. I should be protecting the country I love and the Dead I've always guarded. I should console the worried princess who's holding back my hair while I vomit all over the violets and marigolds.

Through the bewildering haze of too much potion and wine, the question nags at me: *How did I get here?*

For the first time, I'm glad Evander's gone. Glad he can't see how far I've fallen.

XIII

I open my eyes to a room blazing with torchlight and wide windows showing a sky as black as pitch. Pain rips through my head when I try to sit up, and someone presses a hand to the center of my chest, shoving me back down against the pillows.

"Drink this." Valoria touches a glass of water to my lips and gently tips it until I've sipped about half the contents. "It's only been a few hours. I'm surprised you're awake already." As she pulls a chair up to the bed—her bed—she opens her mouth like there's something more she wants to say.

"What is it?" I gingerly check my face for crusted bits of vomit and dirt from the garden, then touch my tender right knee where the dagger kissed it. Valoria's bandaged the wound, but even the light pressure of my fingers makes it ache.

The princess scoots to the edge of her seat, frowning. She cleans her glasses on her mint-green gown and still says nothing.

"Come on." I manage to prop myself up on my elbows. The room spins like a pinwheel, complete with mesmerizing colors. "Out with it."

"Fine." Valoria sighs, meeting my eyes. "Evander Crowther is dead and gone, and no amount of drinking anything—say, too much wine, or certain potions meant to dull the senses—can bring him back." She bends down to toy with loose threads on the rug beneath her chair. "But there are others here who need you. Two necromancers have been killed in the Deadlands. That never happens. And Duke Bevan went missing from his own province and reappeared here as a Shade." She raises her glistening eyes to mine. "And now my mother and several other Dead, the nobility that you and Evander and your friends raised, have vanished. Something in Karthia *reeks*, but I can't figure it out on my own. I need your help."

I shake my head. "Look, Valoria. I don't have the answers either. All I have is a score to settle and one nasty Shade waiting for me in the Deadlands."

"Then you're not who I thought you were."

"Seems that way."

Valoria rises to her feet, turning her back on me, and for the first time I notice the many curved shelves lining her tower room. She fusses with something I can't see from here, but around her, I take note of coils of copper wire, ropes, odd silver bits, and what look like wood-and-metal arms and legs, complete with moveable joints.

I climb off the bed and approach a shelf that holds several strange glass balls with tiny wires inside. I bump one with my hand, and it fills with an orange glow that steals my breath and freezes me on the spot.

"It's just a light," Valoria calls from across the room. "I made them for my little sister. Ever since she saw the Shade at the Festival of Cloud, she's been scared of the dark."

I nod, backing away from the glowing ball, and something brushes the top of my head. I glance up to find a long and heavy-looking sack of fabric dangling from the vaulted ceiling.

"That's my air balloon." There's a hint of amusement in Valoria's voice. "Rather, it will be. It's not finished, for obvious reasons. It's not like I can take it into the gardens and tinker with it where any of the Dead might see."

"Air balloon," I repeat.

A chill spreads up my arms the longer I gaze around the cluttered room. My feet suddenly seem to have a mind of their own, carrying me to the princess's side.

She stands by a table pushed up against the wall, gazing down at a tiny, perfect model of Grenwyr City.

"There's Noble Park!" I point to houses that are hardly bigger than my thumbnail. "And the apothecary. And the Ashes. And here's where we are now!" I tap a tower on one corner of the little palace, realizing when it wobbles that I could've knocked it over. I tuck my hands in the folds of my dress. "Valoria, this is amazing!" Unlike the metal arms or lengths of wire on the other shelves, the model city doesn't frighten me—it inspires me. "Did you make all this yourself?"

Valoria shakes her head. Without meeting my eyes, she says, "Hadrien carved some of the buildings for me. He doesn't know half of what I do up here." Her lips curve into a slight smile. "He probably thinks they're for a dollhouse or something."

"Well, whatever this is, it's perfect. Except—you made the roads too wide." For some reason, my comment makes Valoria's smile widen. Carefully, I point to some twisty painted blue lines that definitely aren't part of Grenwyr City. "And we don't have all these rivers." I motion to a large building near the palace. "Our horse stables aren't that big, either."

"That's right. I call this my Dream City. It's what I've been working on all year." She meets my gaze. "The bigger stables are so our animals can be more comfortable. They deserve more space." A hint of pink appears in her cheeks, and I nod to encourage her to go on. "The wide roads are because the ones we have now are too narrow. And the canals are to help carry sewage and muck out of the city. With the city so cramped, it's no wonder the black fever rips through Grenwyr like wildfire each year. I think . . ." She pauses for a deep breath. "I think my designs would make the city cleaner and help stop the spread of sickness, putting less strain on our healers so they can focus on other things—say, learning how to restore the mind."

"This is incredible." I stare at her, amazed King Wylding discourages her inventions when she's finding ways to combat the black fever and perhaps give people from the Ashes a chance for some paid work. "With ideas like this, you could be a real leader in Grenwyr City, or even Karthia. Have you asked about being on the king's council?"

Valoria arches her brows. "I couldn't possibly. Having someone new on the council would upset the Dead."

"But you're *brilliant*! You deserve to be there."

"Really? Well, if you say so . . ." Valoria presses a hand to her forehead, but I can tell by the glint in her eyes that she's secretly more pleased than bothered by the thought. "Think how shocked the Dead would be if they saw the Dream City!"

"But even the Dead want their loved ones to live, and your city would help keep away the black fever. It could save people. The things you've thought of!"

"I haven't added half of the finer details yet . . ." She shakes her head, wringing her hands in an obvious case of nerves. "But I'm glad you like it. I've barely shown it to anyone. Only . . . my mother."

Before I know what's come over me, I grab Valoria's callused hands. "I'm going to help you find her. I promise."

"I'm so scared she'll end up like Duke Bevan. I couldn't bear it if that happened." Valoria squeezes my hands. "But I knew I could count on you."

The way she says those words with such confidence makes my face burn. I wish she'd put her trust in someone else, even if I do *want* to help her. "We'll search the palace tomorrow, once we've gotten enough sleep to keep our wits about us."

Valoria bites her lip. "Odessa. About what happened back in the garden . . ."

I hold her gaze. "I'm seeing imaginary monsters." I don't mention Evander. For some reason, I want to keep his silent apparition a secret for me alone. "It's a side effect of the potion. There's nothing I can do about it."

"But there is. You could stop taking the potion." Valoria's eyes glisten, making me wonder if she's had a similar talk with someone else before. "Whatever feelings you're avoiding can't be as bad as what that potion's doing to you."

I want to reassure her, but the truth is, I'm dying for another dose at the mere mention of the potion.

Muttering an excuse about needing sleep, I leave Valoria's tower for my cold, empty room and the bitter blue vials waiting beneath the bed.

I push open the door to my room, anticipating the potion's bitter-apple taste, to find a girl with waves of dark red hair sitting on my bed. Her shirt and cloak are fur-trimmed, and the fang of some unfortunate creature hangs from her neck. I know even before glancing at the double-emerald pin gleaming on her collar that she's a beast master.

Pausing just inside the door, I blink hard in case this is another hallucination, a trick of the flickering torchlight.

She turns toward me, and I remember Hadrien's words about the red-haired girl who was asking after me.

"You were looking for me," I say slowly, edging toward the sword waiting for me on my table, "at the party tonight. Why?"

The girl tilts her head slightly to one side, her face cast in shadow, though I can tell by her stillness that she's studying me. She doesn't utter a word or even bat an eye as I grab my sword. I'm grateful for its comforting weight in my hand, and while I keep it pointed at the ground, I know it'll be ready at my slightest command.

"You don't remember me." She finally speaks in a silvery voice, though the words seem calculated, like she's practiced at staying in control of every sound she makes, every gesture. She raises her head and locks her intense green eyes on mine.

A shiver of surprise runs through me.

The sound of my sword hitting the floor is only a distant thud.

She has Elibeth's eyes. Lyda's swanlike neck and ivory skin, though hers is dusted with light brown freckles, and a white scar—four jagged lines like claw marks—covers much of her left cheek. And—though it's tight and wary and only lasts a second, I'd recognize it anywhere—she has Evander's smile.

Meredy.

"Your hair was brown the last time we saw each other," I murmur.

Meredy nods solemnly. "I was ten years old and had a terrible gap in my teeth the last time we saw each other, too. A lot's changed in six years."

I lick my dry lips, wanting to gaze past her in hope of glimpsing Shadow Evander, but something about this girl demands my entire focus. "Where have you been all this time?"

"The northernmost wilderness of Lorness." Meredy tips her chin up as she adds, "Learning from one of the greatest beast masters of the century. But that's finished now, and I'm a master. Like you."

My heart's hammering so hard I'm dizzy. "You finished training a year early?"

She arches a brow. "Is that so hard to believe? I've only been back in Grenwyr City for a day, and I've already heard they call you Sparrow because you seem to effortlessly fly between this world and the other. Yet you don't think I could be a great beast master?"

I don't mean to offend her, but I've never met anyone who finished training early. The apology that's on the tip of my tongue dies as she gazes coolly up at me.

"You've got a scar that says otherwise . . ." I touch the spot on my cheek where hers is scarred. "What happened there?"

"It was a training accident," she mutters. "What happened to your knee?"

"My own stupidity." The moment I say the words, I regret them. I've made her give that tiny almost-smile again, the one that's too sharp but still somehow an echo of Evander's. I can't do this. I can't have these vivid reminders of him in my room, on my bed, reminders that can walk and talk and hurt me.

Meredy hooks her hair behind her ear. When it catches the light, it reminds me of the elderflower wine I drank at the party. "I'll confess, I saw some of your trouble in the garden earlier. But I felt it best to give you time to collect yourself before I came around."

"That was generous of you," I say dryly, hoping I sound half as casual as she does. Leaning against the wall for support, I rub my temples. Surely she didn't mean to, but she's dredging up thoughts and memories I've been trying so hard to bury.

Meredy leaps to her feet, fastening her fur-trimmed burgundy cloak like she's about to leave. But she holds my gaze and squares her shoulders. "It seems we're starting off on the wrong note. I apologize for the lateness of my visit, but this can't wait. I've come to secure your services." She draws a lumpy bag from her cloak pocket, and the clinking sound it makes leaves no question as to what's inside.

"I can't raise Evander from the dead." Each word opens a new wound as it leaves my lips. Curse Meredy Crowther for making me speak them. She looks as poised as her mother while I take a step back and accidently kick my sword across the floor.

Meredy moves forward, stepping lightly over the blade. Her voice remains low and clear. "I wasn't asking you to." She tosses the bag of coins onto my bed. "I'm no fool. I know necromancers can't be raised, no matter how much we might wish otherwise."

Do I wish I could raise Evander? To never see him, to never really touch him, to constantly fear that he could become a monster—we could never be like we used to. Not even magic can bring back what we had. Days ago, I'd have wanted to pull Evander from the Deadlands in a heartbeat, but now the idea feels somehow selfish.

"Odessa?" Meredy waves a hand in front of my face, snapping me from my daze.

"Sorry. What is it, then?" My hands are shaking from the lack of potion. It's all I can do to keep from sliding under the bed and downing every last vial in front of this girl who's practically a stranger.

"My girlfriend." Meredy's face is expressionless, as still as though carved from marble. "She died in a hunting accident. I want to bring her back from the Deadlands, and I'll pay you whatever King Wylding would." She points to the coins on the bed. "Name your price, and consider that the first installment. The rest will be delivered when I have Firiel back."

Unable to fight the urge, I laugh. The kind of laughter that bubbles up from deep in the pit of my stomach and squeezes my ribs. Maybe it's the absence of the potion messing with my head, but her request seems like a clever trick someone's playing on me.

"I don't see anything funny here." Meredy crosses her arms. "I lost my brother and my love in a matter of days, and I'll do anything to steal back even a little of what death has taken from me. Even if it means giving you my family's fortune. In the few letters Evander sent me, he said you're the best at what you do. And if he says so, I trust him."

I swallow a delirious giggle. "First of all, I can't go into the Deadlands without a partner. It's forbidden, and I probably wouldn't make it out, besides." Rubbing some of the grit from my eyes, I blink at her. "Second, do I look like I'm in any shape to raise the dead just now?"

Meredy gives the slightest headshake. "For all I know, this is how you always look."

"Does Firiel want to be raised?" I usually only ask a client that after I've accepted a job, but since Meredy showed up uninvited, I don't see the harm in prying.

Frowning, Meredy says quietly, "We never discussed it. But I know her. I know she wants to be with me no matter the cost."

It's a familiar answer, one I've heard often. Sometimes, a spirit wants to come back, but not always. I want her to consider what she's asking of the dead girl. "Would *you* want to be raised?"

It's my job to protect the Dead, Evander would say, in our world and in theirs. And that means honoring their choice to be raised or not, regardless of their families' wishes.

"Would *you*?" Meredy's gaze never falters.

As I search for words, I think of thick layers of cloth having to be adjusted constantly. Of wearing sachets of herbs against my dead flesh to keep it from stinking at parties. Of the worst hunger I've ever experienced, of feeling that way constantly. Of craving food, touch, warmth. Of never sleeping, never dreaming.

Of possibly becoming a Shade and losing the very essence of who I am.

I think of all the suffering before I think of the things I'd miss about this world: Fig jam. Sunshine. The sea. Kissing. Especially kissing.

"I doubt," I say slowly, "it would be a life worth living. At least for me. But plenty of Dead are glad to make sacrifices to come back." I shrug. "Not that I'll ever have to decide."

Meredy nods, her face betraying nothing of her thoughts. "So, will you help me?"

"No. Even if I could, I'm not interested. Sorry." I pick up my sword, wincing at the stars that appear at the corners of my eyes when I straighten. "The next time I go to the Deadlands, it'll be my last." I swipe the coin purse off the bed and toss it at her. I can't bear the thought of accidentally brushing her skin.

Meredy's mouth falls open. "You were more than just his partner. Evander's." There's no question at the end of her words. Without another glance at me, she bends to retrieve the bag of coins.

I gesture at the door with my sword. "There's the exit, whenever you're ready."

She presses her lips into a thin line, the first real emotion I think I've seen from her. If I had half her self-control, maybe I could ditch my potion habit.

"Fine." She starts toward the door but pauses to glance over her shoulder. "There are other necromancers who will take my money. I intended to honor Evander's memory by coming to you first, but I see now that was a mistake."

"A huge one," I agree, jabbing my sword at the door again. "And stay out of the Deadlands!" I call after her. "Evander wouldn't want you going there, especially not now. It's more dangerous than ever."

Meredy carries herself with a dancer's grace, gliding through the door into the dim hallway. If she heard me, she shows no sign of it. "Come, Lysander," she calls to someone out of sight. As Meredy strides briskly away, a massive brown bear lumbers in her wake. I must be really out of it to have missed the beast when I came down the hall. It pauses in my open doorway, and I freeze as it sniffs the room. My knees turn to water despite the sword in my hand.

"Lysander!"

With a deep grumble, the grizzly heeds Meredy's call and vanishes.

I can't slam my door fast enough. It's rare that a beast master can keep control over such a powerful animal. And rarer still for any mage to finish training a year ahead of schedule. Meredy must be an extremely competent beast master. A mage with that much fang and muscle behind them could work security anywhere, from the gates of Noble Park to the king's personal guard.

Grabbing a vial of potion from under the bed, I raise it to the still and silent room. "Here's to your health, Meredy Crowther."

XIV

I wake drenched in sweat, Evander's dying screams echoing in my mind. Sunlight glares through my window, and every part of my body aches. Groaning, I bury my face in my pillow to hide from the sun a little longer.

This is all Meredy's fault. I don't know how, but her presence has to be the reason I'm hearing Evander's screams again. This is the first night in weeks I've relived those gut-wrenching sounds, so vivid even the potion couldn't dull them.

Tossing off the blankets, I throw on the first tunic and pair of trousers I find. Blood pounds in my ears as the events of last night come rushing back. The mangled bird. Valoria's Dream City. The missing Dead nobles. The bear named Lysander.

I secure my sword and pull back my long hair, then reach for two vials of potion to get me through the morning. I'll need its calming influence to help me keep both my promises today: First to Valoria, to help find her mother and the rest of the missing Dead. And then, to Evander.

The palace is strangely quiet as I step into the hall. I pause outside Jax's door, trailing my fingers across the wood. My breath echoes in the emptiness.

I press my ear to the door and smile at the faint snoring coming from the other side. There's no point waking him to help with the search. After all, the king's guards have probably combed the palace from top to bottom while I slept off the potion and wine. Even if the guards have already found the missing Dead, I need Valoria to know that I tried. I'm not even sure why I care, only that I do.

Hurrying in the direction of her tower, I don't take notice of the figure striding toward me from the base of the nearest stairwell until he's practically touching me.

I gasp, inhaling the scents of rosemary and rue.

"Sparrow," King Wylding says, gripping my shoulder with a gloved hand, "just the mage I was looking for. How are you faring?"

Though I can't see his face, the way he squeezes my shoulder and tilts his head seems almost paternal.

I stand taller, putting my hand over his gloved one. "I'll be all right."

"Good. That's good. I can always count on you, Sparrow, and that makes me the luckiest man in the kingdom." He clears his throat and asks, "Did you see anything strange last night? Anyone who doesn't belong here?"

I'm tempted to name Meredy and her pet grizzly. But the entire Crowther family has a permanent invitation to all palace festivities. And after meeting her, I doubt Meredy's capable of the abduction of several nobles. I shake my head.

"Most of my kin, living and Dead, are keeping to their rooms today at my request. I've stationed extra guards outside their chambers, just as I've done for yours." King Wylding was a bear of a man in life, one whose first death happened in battle too young, and his massive form is intimidating as he towers over me. Yet the rapid rattle of breath in his chest suggests that, for the first time in memory, he's afraid. "Several of my relatives never made it to the celebration, and the guards can't find a trace of any intruders."

"I'll search the Deadlands for you in case they've been killed," I say. "Master Cymbre will accompany me." I imagine a troubled look behind the king's dark mask and wish I could better reassure him. "It might help if we could figure out why anyone would do this—for a hefty ransom?"

There are certainly a number of people in the Ashes desperate enough to attempt a kidnapping, but coming to the palace is a bolder move than any of them have attempted before. And then there's what happened to Duke Bevan, though I'm not sure how the two events are related. The duke had plenty of enemies, as Jax pointed out, while I don't think anyone had a grudge against Valoria's mother or the rest of the Wyldings.

"Perhaps it *is* gold they want," King Wylding says at last. "But all these madmen will get is the noose, once we find them." He squeezes my shoulders. "I know you'll help the guards bring them to justice and return my family. You're a treasure to the Dead, my Sparrow."

"Thank you, Majesty." I bow, and heat creeps into my face. My head feels clearer than it has in days as I mull over what might have happened to the nobles. And a clear head is what I've been waiting for, which means it's time.

Time for one last trip to the Deadlands.

"I shouldn't delay any longer. I'm off to find Master Cymbre and begin the search." I give the king another bow, this one of farewell, though he doesn't know it. Now if I'm killed in the Deadlands, I'll have the perfect cover. And even though I have no intention of knocking on Master Cymbre's cottage door before I jump through the nearest gateway, I can't be punished for the transgression if I'm dead.

Since when do you care about what's forbidden by anyone? Evander teased me on the palace's windswept hillside mere weeks ago. If only he could see me now, shattering rules at every turn for the sake of revenge.

"If you would, please tell Princess Valoria where I've gone and what I'm doing," I say before continuing on.

"Sparrow!" the king calls, jarring me from my thoughts. When I turn back, he rasps, "Give Master Cymbre my best. Tell her to stay strong."

I hurry away, marveling at how much the king cares for each of his necromancers, wondering how many more losses he and I will have to endure. How many more losses it would take to push him toward madness or the sort of carelessness that leads to becoming a Shade. I shiver as an autumn breeze hugs my shoulders.

Things are changing all around me, whether the king realizes it or not, and I'm afraid neither he nor anyone else seems to have the power to stop it.

The only thing I can prevent is any more death at the hands of the powerful Shade, so I quicken my pace on the brisk jog to the apothecary. After peeking through the windows and seeing no trace of Lyda, I buy enough liquid fire to light up the night sky over Grenwyr City, then stride back into the brisk afternoon in search of a gate.

Today, the city's usually vibrant colors are muted—the pink flowering vines spilling over a shop window, the blue domed roofs of Death's temple and convent, the yellow and orange sun-washed walls of craftsmen's houses, the occasional tree full of white autumn blossoms bearing symbols of beauty and peace—they're all paler than I remember, as if I'm seeing them through a foggy window.

Gateways to the Deadlands are nearly impossible to spot in daylight, even to a trained eye. But as I walk deeper into the warren of houses and shops, away from the sea, a telltale pull around my middle draws me toward an alleyway between a tavern and a boarded-up bakery just a few blocks from the Ashes.

Not exactly where I'd hoped to end up. Especially when I peek down the alleyway and the tugging sensation grows stronger, guiding me to the faintest blue haze that I can only see when I squint and tilt my head back.

Of course the gate has to be right on top of the tavern's stinking trash heap. Pinching my nose, I place a foot on the soft, warm pile of discarded vegetables, rotting meat, and moldy black lumps that remain a mystery. The ooze at the center of the trash heap sucks at my knees as I climb higher. I'm going to sink through the middle if I'm not careful. Gripping the wall for balance, I put one foot in the gate and hoist myself up as the rubbish wobbles and rotten food rolls down the pile.

Breathing hard, I crawl into the solid tunnel opening.

There was no time to take a last look at the sky. No time to think up words of goodbye I could have said to Jax. Simeon. Valoria. Kasmira. Danial. Master Cymbre. Even Hadrien. To wonder why I feel so sick when I realize the list of names I'm leaving behind is so much longer than the list of ones I'm going to avenge.

But I made a promise. Evander's and Master Nicanor's lives will be the last this monster ever takes. Jax, Simeon, Cymbre, and all the other necromancers will be able to raise the dead again without the fear of losing the only life they get.

I can't think of any greater cause worth dying for.

Still, thinking of my promise to Evander reminds me that I made another promise, to bring back the missing Dead, and I imagine the disappointment in Valoria's eyes when she hears I didn't find her mother. That I'm never coming back.

Brushing dirt from the tunnel floor off my trousers, I let my eyes adjust to the dimness, grateful none of my fire potions exploded in the jump. I'm carrying them in a sack the apothecary gave me because they wouldn't all fit in my cloak pockets. Then I make sure the vials of blood and honey on my belt are still intact. Just in case.

Potions secure, I march on through the shadows. I still have the whistle Master Cymbre gave me the last time we came here, and I fish it out from underneath my tunic as I near the tunnel's end, running my thumb over the smooth ivory of the mouthpiece.

The Shade mimicked this whistle before. Hopefully it remembers the sound and comes straight for me.

When the tunnel leads me out into the Deadlands' twilit landscape, I wade into a knee-high field of roses as big as my fist and check for any Dead who might be lurking nearby. I don't want the spirits here getting killed, their souls destroyed just because they happened to be in the way of my battle.

A flash of white hovers at the corner of my gaze, but when I turn, all I see are the heavy heads of flowers nodding in a slow breeze.

Someone giggles, a high girlish sound.

"If anyone's out here," I call into the field, "you'd better leave now. I'm hunting the foulest Shade that's ever walked the Deadlands, and you don't want to be here when I find it. Or it finds me."

A small pale figure peeks out of the tall flowers, grinning despite the massive pox scars on her face and arms. She seems to be an ordinary spirit, not one of my hallucinations, but something about her stirs a memory and makes me take a second glance.

"I recognize you." While the spirits have no voices, she can hear mine. "We met in the Ashes. You had a doll. You'd lost your mother, is that right?" When the girl nods, I add, "I hope you've found each other again. Now please, go hide somewhere and tell any others you meet to stay hidden, too."

She nods, her expression determined. As she dashes through the field, grass whipping at her legs, my thoughts wander to Valoria's Dream City of wide roads and flowing canals that would wash away sickness even from places like the Ashes. I hope King

Wylding will find the strength to listen to her ideas someday, even if most of them are unsettling at first. I know he's happiest seeing Karthians at work, healthy and strong.

Raising the whistle, I make the first shrill blast.

All is silent. This particular Shade seems to like toying with its victims, which means when it finally arrives, it'll try to take me by surprise. I'll only have a few heartbeats to light it up in a glorious blaze.

I curl my fingers around one of the fire potions and wait, scanning the horizon. The landscape is gently shifting, bringing the distant mountains closer, and the tunnel I came through has disappeared.

I wait for what feels like hours, until my legs start to ache. I blow the whistle again, my hands shaking slightly in the absence of the calming potion. I didn't think to bring any with me, but then, I didn't expect to have to wait this long. Pulling the vial of blood from my belt, I drizzle all the contents on the ground at my feet. Yet still, nothing stirs.

"I'm right here!" I shout into the quiet, to the mountains and the trees, their bare branches stretching toward the sky like grasping fingers. "Come get me! Can't you smell this nice fresh blood?"

That gives me an idea.

Drawing my sword, I cut a horizontal slash across my arm, gritting my teeth to hold back an embarrassing groan. My head swirls as I shake drops of red onto the roses, fresher blood than what was in my vial.

If the Shade doesn't come now, I'll have to wander the Deadlands searching for it. I use my blade to cut a piece of cloth from my cloak, and I'm so focused on tying a tight bandage that the sound of flowers being ripped and trampled steals my breath.

The Shade seems to soar across the field on all fours, the few dark hairs clinging to its skull flying in its wake. I see myself reflected in the smooth expanse of its bony forehead, a shimmering speck in a vast dark sky. Abandoning my sword, I grab a handful of fire potions and hurl them at the oncoming Shade. This is what I've been waiting for.

Yet every part of me is screaming *run. Flee, and don't look back.*

A billowing cloud of flame erupts in front of the monster, but it only slows for a moment. It hisses and snaps as the fire crackles across its skin. Fighting the urge to run, I have just enough time to grab another handful of potions and throw them at the struggling Shade.

Fire eats away the stump of its missing arm, and the monster howls until my ears ache.

I reach for another potion. Hot breath on my neck makes me spin around, smacking into the grasping bony hands of another Shade. I break a glass vial on its skin, falling into the flowers to escape the blaze that follows.

Crawling backward, I realize with a shudder that the molten pain on my arm isn't from my sword. I'm *burning* like the Shades.

I didn't count on there being two of them.

Beating out the flames with my cloak, I stagger toward the edge of the field. Panic fills my head, a buzzing like a cloud of angry bees, making it hard to think. I could run for the mountains, but the part of me that wants to watch them burn to ash wins out. I freeze in my tracks and turn back toward the two smoldering figures.

Wreathed in fire, struggling for their lives, they look almost human.

Their hissing and spitting drowns out the sound of the third Shade until it's too close. But I manage to grasp a vial and throw it at the monster whose rotten breath blows my hair back from my face. My shaking hand ruins my aim, and the potion explodes at the monster's feet. The Shade leaps sideways, and I throw another potion that again smashes near its feet. Every time it darts sideways, I try to hit it with another potion, but my hands aren't obeying and I continue to miss until there are no vials left.

I could surrender now, a little voice in my head whispers. *I could stop fighting and join Evander. Maybe I'd see his face again.*

The third Shade snarls at me, rolling on the ground to snuff out a lick of flame. I frantically gaze past it, checking for an escape route, and realize we're trapped, this monster and I, inside a circle of flames as high as my head and leaping higher with each passing breath. It's just a matter of which fate will come first: burning alive or being torn apart and eaten.

The Shade lunges, and I stumble backward into the flames. A strong hand yanks me through the fire, then forces me to the ground.

Dimly, like I'm underwater, I hear the Shades' howls as someone smothers the flames that prick my skin like thousands of needles.

"Foolish girl! What in Vaia's name possessed you?" Master Cymbre's voice is harsher than I've ever heard it, but the familiar sound still floods me with relief. "When I drag you back to the palace, you're not leaving it again until I'm dead and can't watch you throw your life away!"

I raise my head as she finishes beating out the flames. My teacher's fiery hair is plastered to her face, and her eyes, hard as gemstones, reflect the monsters burning nearby. Her gaze doesn't soften, even when I mouth, "Thank you."

She's more than just my mentor, I realize as she hauls me to my feet. She's more of a mother to me than the Sisters of Death ever were. More than Lyda pretended to be. Cymbre's the one who always comes when I need someone most, the one who came just in time today.

My death would've been a poor repayment for all the years she put into keeping me, her replacement—the closest thing she has to a daughter—alive.

I deserve her anger.

"Those three Shades are as good as dead, but more could be coming as we speak. We have to go!" Master Cymbre puts a hand beneath one of my aching arms, supporting me.

"How'd you know where to find me?" I lean against her to stay standing.

Master Cymbre purses her lips. "Call it a guardian's intuition." She points to a blue glow near the foothills of the mountains. "I heard about the missing nobles and went to see you." She begins a brisk walk, the fastest pace she can manage with me stumbling alongside her. "When you weren't in your room and your sword was gone, I made a guess. Lucky for you, I heard your whistle, but the landscape kept changing as I tried to reach you."

"But I did it . . ." I manage. "I killed the Shade that murdered Evander!"

The thought should make me giddy, yet all I feel is sore and tired and shaken.

"Yes, and you nearly lost your life in the process!" Master Cymbre's voice cracks. "Does that mean nothing to you? Do *I* mean nothing? Did you ever stop to think about everything you risked leaving behind?"

"Of course! I—"

"Tell me this," Master Cymbre cuts in sharply. "Now that it's dead, do you feel any better? Do you miss him any less?"

As we hurry into the tunnel, I search past the agony of my charred skin, seeking the hole left by Evander's absence. It's still there, gaping like the Shades' hungry mouths, a darkness that threatens to devour me.

"No," I answer as the tunnel takes us home. "I don't think I ever will."

XV

Healing all my burns makes Danial's entire arm and half his face go completely numb. After I've locked myself in Valoria's private bath and scrubbed my new skin raw with fig soap, I head to the palace kitchens and convince the cooks to whip up an amazing lemon-and-rosemary cake that I deliver to Danial's chambers myself.

"Thanks, but I'm not hungry," he says, gazing down at his favorite cake with no enthusiasm. The kohl around his eyes is blurred at the corners, smudged into his alabaster skin like bruises. Or like he wiped away tears with a careless hand. "Simeon and I had a fight."

"About what?" I probably shouldn't pry, but those two hardly ever exchange an unkind word.

"About you. About him not going to the Deadlands anymore, because I can't sleep with the thought of him bleeding out some-place where I can't save him."

"Danial—"

"So if you don't mind, I'd rather be alone right now." He gently shuts his chamber door in my face.

I wander across the palace to Jax's room, not wanting to be alone, but it's empty. I notice several new holes in the wall above his bed.

My thoughts turn to the Deadlands as I stare at the shattered wall. If Master Cymbre hadn't found me, I'd probably be dead. And as I brush pieces of wall off Jax's quilt, I realize I'm glad I'm still here.

I just wish Evander were here, too.

Tucking my shaking hands into the crooks of my elbows, I hurry to my room and the promise of a calming potion's bitter-apple relief.

It now takes three vials to get to the place I want to be, the place where closing my eyes and seeing *his* face—his real face, not the perfect apparition the potion sometimes brings—doesn't make me feel like a giant fist is squeezing my heart, trying to stop it from beating.

No longer shaking, I pick myself up off the floor and put on a clean black tunic and trousers. My belt and sword hang in my wardrobe. I won't be needing them anytime soon.

I slip into the hall and climb the tightly wound stone steps that lead to the rookery, where the palace's messenger ravens are bred and kept. It appears to be empty, save for many sets of glittering dark eyes and rustling wings. The attendants who care for the birds are likely at supper, judging by the sky's deep indigo and the crescent moon that shines down through the rookery's glass ceiling.

As I poke my head inside, a rough voice calls, "Sparrow."

Jax strides down the hallway toward me. As he moves closer, I steel myself against the storm crackling in his eyes. "I went to the healers' wing, but you weren't there." His long, muscular legs close the distance between us, and his broad hands grip my shoulders hard. "And you weren't with Simeon and Danial. Or in your room." There's something accusing in his tone as he finishes, "I thought you'd gone back to the Deadlands."

"You've been talking to Cymbre," I whisper, because whispering's about all I can do with Jax's weight pressing me against the outer wall of the rookery. "How is she?"

Jax shakes his head. "Not her best. She's been drinking and pacing and drinking some more. But she's still smart enough to know we're nowhere near finding the missing nobles. And that she can't tell King Wylding or anyone else but me and Simeon that you went to the Deadlands *alone*."

"And killed three Shades," I add, putting pressure on his wrist to free myself from his grasp. I use his momentary surprise to my advantage, shoving him against the wall and pinning his arms. Leaning in until our noses almost touch, I murmur, "Including the one that killed Evander. So you're welcome. What's the matter with you?"

Jax narrows his eyes, but they don't stop searching mine. "You should've told me what you were planning. I would've gone with you. I would've helped."

My heart picks up speed as Jax tries to twist out of my hold. "And risk getting you killed? You think I need any more nightmares?"

"What about *my* nightmares?" Jax effortlessly breaks my grip, like he was just struggling out of politeness before. He wraps his arms around my waist, his broad hands searing where they touch. I don't stop him. I'll be cold again without his touch, and I don't want to be cold anymore. I've been cold for too long.

"You think I've gotten a good night's sleep since he's been gone, even with you beside me?" he growls. "You think I'd be fine and carry on like nothing had happened if someone told me *you'd* died in the Deadlands, too?"

I swallow hard. "Jax, we've been over this." Despite the potion singing through my veins, I'm shaking from my hands down to my boots. "We're just friends." He's just a friend whose lips are dangerously close to mine. Whose eyes are like the sea, wide and deep, churning with the pain of a thousand unkindnesses the world has shown him.

"Right." Jax cups my face in his hands. His breath smells of sugary, expensive mead, overpowering the crisp scent of his evergreen soap. "Then listen, *friend*, when I say some of us still need you here."

His lips collide with mine. I open my mouth, yielding to the pressure of his tongue, which he wields like a weapon to make me weak-kneed in his arms. I tangle my fingers in his dark hair as he deepens the kiss, taking us to a place where nothing exists but our mouths and the pulsing, luminous heat between us.

He tastes sweet, and a little smoky, like the honey we eat in the Deadlands. And like the honey, his kiss reminds me of how very alive I am, makes me dizzy as blood rushes from my head to lower places that are suddenly aching.

When I shove him in the chest with my shoulder, wondering if this is really happening or if I'm having my most vivid hallucination yet, he grabs my hands and twines his fingers through mine. He kisses my hands and my shoulder, then nuzzles the curve of my neck where my pulse beats an erratic rhythm against his mouth.

I tip his chin up with my fingers, then gently catch his lips with mine. I'm falling deeper into his eyes as he lifts me into his arms and carries me down the stairs to his room.

This is probably a bad idea. Someone's going to get hurt. But I don't tell Jax to stop.

It isn't until we're in his room, as he's laying me gently on the bed, that his face shimmers and blurs into Evander's and I come to whatever senses I have left.

"I'm sorry," I say in a rush, blinking hard until Jax is Jax again and my head is clear. "It's still too soon . . ." I kiss his tattooed shoulder before he pulls away to grab the tunic he'd just thrown off.

As he puts it back on and smooths his wild dark hair, my body turns cold all over. Things between us have changed so much now. It's all my fault. I didn't mean to make Jax look at me that way. All I wanted was a few moments of selfish pleasure.

Jax starts to rise from the bed, but I grab his wrist. "Where are you going?"

He answers without meeting my eyes. "I don't know. Anywhere."

"I can't kick you out of your own room. Stay." Even as I say it, he starts to pull away. I squeeze his wrist, startling him into looking at me. *"Please?"*

Jax sighs, but he turns away from the door. He settles himself behind me on the bed, like he sometimes does when neither of us can sleep, and wraps his arms around me. His breathing has slowed, but his heart's still pounding hard. Just like mine.

"What's on your mind?" I ask, glancing over my shoulder to study his sharp profile in the shadows.

"You." His breath warms my hair as he exhales heavily. "And killing things."

I quirk a brow and shake my head. "I'm so glad I can't see inside your head."

Finally, he grins a little. "I was just thinking, now that the giant Shade is gone, maybe Simeon and I can finally get back to work. Were the others you killed as strong or as fast as . . . the one we'd been hunting?"

He's gone out of his way not to mention Evander, which is fine by me. Still, this is the first time we've talked about what happened that day.

"I'm not sure. The whole thing was strange, seeing three monsters together like that. They've never hunted in packs before. And we still don't know how that one got so strong." I turn in Jax's arms to face him. "I don't want you going back to the Deadlands until we find those missing nobles and figure out what really happened to Nicanor. Then we can go in a group and make sure it's safe to do more raisings. Just . . . one trouble at a time, all right?"

Jax rubs his fingers across the tattoo on his left shoulder, now covered by his tunic: a lone black wolf like the ones that roam the cold forests of his home province, Lorness. "I can't speak for Si, but I think we should keep taking jobs. Since we don't know if the danger's passed, we could charge a little extra." He smiles, razor-sharp. "For risking life and all the good things that come with it."

I immediately think of the little girl I met in the Ashes, sitting outside a crumbling house and clutching her doll, the only reminder of her lost mother. I know she's just one of many.

"I don't need all that gold," I murmur. "Do you?"

"Of course I do." He blinks like he's surprised by my scowl. "Mages are like *gods* among men. It might kill her, but Kasmira could stop a hurricane. Danial could pull someone back from the brink of death. And you and I give life to people who have already spent theirs. That's worth our weight in gold, *at least*." His wolfish grin surfaces. "And it's easier to come by than I used to think. Some girl who came to us this morning was willing to pay her entire fortune. We turned her down, but there'll be others."

"What was her name?" I demand, aware of my voice rising. Meredy Crowther was looking for a necromancer. And she didn't seem to hear my warning about not going into the Deadlands with or without me.

"She didn't tell us, but that's not unusual." Jax shrugs. "I was about to take her money, but when Simeon pointed out that the giant Shade was still loose in the Deadlands and she could get killed, I . . ." He grimaces. It must cost him something to admit what he's about to say. "I couldn't go through with it. There's been too much death lately."

I have a sudden urge to kiss away Jax's pain. But I won't. I've done enough damage there already, and besides, I doubt even the best kiss will help ease the sting of Evander's absence for Jax any more than it would for me.

"From the look of things, though, she's not one to give up easily," Jax mutters.

My heart skips a beat. The girl he mentioned could be anyone, but I need to be sure she's not Meredy. "What do you mean, *from the look of things*? Jax, what did this girl look like?"

"It was the same girl who was searching for you at the party—I saw her again when I was trying to find you at the healing house. She was farther down the hill, coming up from the Ashes. She had dark red hair and a scar—"

"Across her cheek . . ."

Jax nods and frowns, looking puzzled by my reaction. My skin prickles with alarm for cool, calm, distant Meredy. "Yeah," he says. "And there were a couple of men with her, and an older woman, following her to the cemetery near the healers' place."

"Shade-baiters." My heart races faster at the thought of the false necromancers, blue-eyed Karthians who never receive any formal training to raise the dead, but offer cheap trips into the Deadlands to search for loved ones—trips from which the client rarely ever returns. Shade-baiters almost always take a person's money and leave them for dead where no one will ever find a body. "And you let her go with them?"

"Sparrow, who the blazes is she?"

I turn to meet Jax's gaze, and I can tell by the look he gives me that my face betrays my worry. "Meredy Crowther. Evander's little sister."

"What?" Jax groans. "How was I supposed to know? And what could I have done to stop her from going with them, anyway? I'm not her father." He sounds as guilty as I feel. I shouldn't have been so eager to see the back of Meredy, even if I didn't want to help her. I should have told her exactly why she couldn't go to the Deadlands. Scared her away from the idea for good, even.

"She gets to make her own choices, just like us," I say softly, more to ease Jax's guilt than mine. Nothing but finding Meredy safe and sound will make me feel better now.

I leap off the bed and scramble to throw on my boots. I can't believe I didn't realize how determined she was to go to the Deadlands. I was too preoccupied by my potions and my problems to see how desperate she was.

If she dies, her blood will be on my hands.

I grab one of Jax's many knives, testing its grip in my small hand. It'll do. I shove the dagger in a spare sheath and hand Jax his sword, earning a wide grin from him. Shades are a deadly threat, but I've sparred enough to know fighting humans is much easier.

"You don't have to come," I say breathlessly as Jax rushes to the door with me, already armed. "I've been to the Deadlands alone, and I came back. I can do it again." I smirk at him as I add, "Besides, I can't offer you your weight in gold for risking your life."

"No way am I missing a chance to make something *bleed*." Jax bangs his shoulder against mine, making me grin, too. "You're stuck with me, partner."

"Fine." I fling open the door. With a guilt twisting my insides as I think of Danial, I add, "We might as well grab Simeon if he's willing, too. We could use the extra help."

Meredy might be a painful reminder of Evander, but I can't let her die like this.

I just hope we aren't too late.

XVI

Standing outside the Crowther manor in the dead of night, I'm beginning to think my idea was a bad one. Jax and Simeon, flanking me on either side, are in total agreement.

"I don't see why we need to bring a grizzly bear to the Deadlands when we're packing enough steel and fire to raze an entire province," Jax growls.

He glances over his shoulder at the nearest glowing gateway, which hovers in a neighboring manor's yard. I hope the baron who lives there won't hear the commotion we're about to cause and send for a guard. This will be difficult enough without several curious nobles poking their noses in our business.

"We're wasting valuable time," Jax mutters, jarring me from my thoughts.

"Your time is valuable? I had *no idea*," Simeon drawls. It's good to know his sarcasm is alive and well after all we've been through lately. I catch his eye, and he grins as he sweeps back his sandy blond bangs. "But really, Sparrow. I think we're strong enough to take three rogue necromancers without a thousand pounds of muscle and claws backing us up."

"Three on three," Jax agrees, squaring his shoulders with an expression as hungry and wild as the wolves inked into his skin. "A fair fight."

I shake my head, then pound on the manor door. If there's ever a time I need a vial of calming potion, it's now, when I'm about to willingly plunge into the well of memories contained by these imposing walls.

"The bear isn't a weapon," I hastily explain as I wait for Lyda or Elibeth to appear. I knock again, harder. "As a beast master, Meredy's tied to the bear somehow. He can track her scent, too. Maybe he can even tell us if we're chasing a lost cause." I knock a third time, nervousness humming in my veins.

"And what's to stop him from, you know, *eating us* instead of doing all those helpful things?" Simeon demands, his teasing grin not entirely covering his apprehension. "Danial's already unhappy with me. Just think how he'll yell if I get turned into bear chow."

"From what I understand of beast masters, their animals are tamer than wild ones. They pick up some of their master's humanity in the magical bonding process, which is why they don't just attack people in the streets." I shrug, hoping I'm right. I've never had a conversation with a beast master about their magic, despite knowing Elibeth for years.

"I dated a beast master last year," Jax says in an offhand voice. "Remember Tabathy? Older, gorgeous, taller-than-me Tabathy?

Best six weeks of my life, except she insisted we keep things secret. Oh, and her beast was an owl. It liked sitting on her wardrobe and watching me while . . ."

I press my ear to the door, listening for the patter of feet inside the manor. But all I can hear is Simeon snickering and slapping Jax on the back. "No, I don't believe it," Simeon gasps between laughs. "You and Tabathy. That's about as likely as you and—"

A harassed-looking maid flings open the door. Peering over her shoulder is Elibeth, barefoot and in her nightgown, her face soft with sleep. Her eyes go round at the sight of us, staring first at Jax and Simeon armed with knives and swords, then at me and the heavy chain coiled around my shoulder.

"Your sister's in danger," I say to Elibeth, and she and her maid step aside to let us in.

There's no sign of Lyda as we follow Elibeth across the manor and down a flight of stairs to the cellar door, explaining all we know as we go. I can't imagine how the baroness is sleeping through the commotion, unless she's taking a potion to help her rest.

"Meredy shut Lysander in here before she left this afternoon." Elibeth holds a torch aloft, bathing the cellar door in warm light. "She didn't tell me where she was going. She never does. If I'd had any idea . . ." Her eyes shimmer. "She seemed fine when she left, though I did think it a bit odd she put Lysander away when he usually remains by her side."

Simeon squeezes her shoulder and murmurs something soothing. He's had years of practice, growing up as the only boy in a convent of Death's often-brooding nuns.

"Don't blame yourself, Elibeth." I slide the chain off my

shoulder, hoping we've looped the end into a collar wide enough to fit around the bear's neck. "Meredy's not exactly easy to talk to." As Elibeth's frown deepens, I hurry to add, "If there's any chance of bringing her home, we will."

As I reach for the cellar door, she calls, "Be careful! Lysander shares Meredy's moods, like my hounds share mine. She says he's never attacked anyone without her permission, but if he's upset . . . there's always a risk." Her voice is hoarse as she adds, "I'd put the chain on him for you, but it's better that you bond with him here and now before taking him to the Deadlands."

I nod, taking a deep breath to brace myself for what's waiting behind the door.

"It's a good thing Master Cymbre's not here," Simeon mutters.

I shake my head, wishing we'd woken her after all. She'd probably have fetched the bear and found Meredy in half the time it's taken us just to get here.

"She'd kill us before the Shades even had a chance," Simeon adds. "Jax would be the first to go."

Jax elbows him, and I choke back a laugh despite the hulking shadow rising up in front of me. If Evander were here, he'd be the one holding the chain, standing between me and the snarling bear.

"Lysander," I call sweetly, slowly extending my free hand. I hope the cause of my sudden shaking has everything to do with the bear's immense size and nothing to do with my need for another potion fix. There wasn't time to go back for them once I remembered, halfway up the slope to Noble Park.

"He's worried about Meredy," Elibeth says tensely, reminding me that while she's bonded to her hounds, her Sight shows her *all* animals' emotions, including the bear's. "And he's confused. Give him a moment to get used to you."

Jax and I exchange a look before I edge deeper into the cellar.

Scuffling footsteps behind me elicit a growl from Lysander that's so deep, it shakes my bones. Jax puts a hand on my back, then lights a torch, revealing the bear's open mouth and stained teeth glistening with drool inches from my face.

If this bear is semi-tame, I'd hate to meet one that's truly wild.

My vision blurs at the corners. Peeking out from behind the bear, a Shade's bony arm stretches toward me. Its fingers, all white bone and no flesh, caress the bear's fur, taunting me. Daring me to make a fool of myself by drawing my sword and slicing at a creature no one else can see.

I squeeze my eyes shut, painfully aware of each of my five fingers still stretched in offering toward the bear. If there was ever a bad time to hallucinate, it's now. I fix an image of the wounded peacock in my mind. The mangled feathers and the blood, hoping that somehow my guilt will be a talisman to ward off imaginary monsters.

"Sparrow. Look." Jax's voice is low and urgent.

I don't need to open my eyes to know the bear is sniffing my fingers. Swallowing hard, I force my tongue to work. "Remember me, Lysander?" I croak. "We sort of met the other day. Your master Meredy is, uh, a friend of mine."

I press my lips together to hold in a whimper as the bear's hot breath warms my hand. I can't believe I'm doing this, but it was my idea, so there's no turning back.

"He's calming down." Elibeth sounds hopeful. "Keep talking!"

"Meredy's in trouble," I continue at last, trying to steady my voice. "We want to save her, but we could really use your help. You don't want to lose her, surely."

Lysander roars, splattering my face with bear spit.

There's a whine as Jax draws his sword. And a muttered curse as he nearly loses his grip on the torch.

"Don't!" Elibeth cries, chilling my blood.

"Jax, don't," I add through gritted teeth. "Put it away." I wipe the bear spit off my face with my sleeve, my hands shaking. I think the bear is upset by what's happening to his master, not about Jax and me intruding in his home. I stare straight into the bear's amber-brown eyes as he tilts his head, sizing me up. "The Deadlands are vast. You can track Meredy for us, can't you?"

Lysander lunges toward me. Jax grabs my arm, but I shrug him off and stand my ground even as my heart bangs a warning against my ribs. The bear opens his mouth again, and this time, a pink tongue lolls out and swipes my outstretched hand.

It's wet and sticky and disgusting—but there's no mistaking the gesture for anything but friendly.

"You've found your second calling as a beast master," Jax declares, a smile in his voice.

I shake my head, wiping my hand on my trousers. "I'm just lucky *he* understands *me*."

"You can use the chain now. He trusts you enough," Elibeth says, no doubt peering into the cellar. Unlike the other Crowther women, she can't disguise the worry in her voice.

A long shadow darkens the floor as Simeon pokes his head in. "I can't believe this is actually happening," he mutters as I hold up the chain for Lysander to inspect. He grumbles deep in his chest, making Simeon flinch.

"This is just so we don't lose each other in the Deadlands," I whisper, leaning forward so Lysander will know my words are only for him. "But we *really* need to hurry."

With a sigh that blows the hair back from my face and reeks of dead fish, the grizzly lowers his great shaggy head before me. I slip the chain around his neck, and thinking of the wounded bird again, I slip my fingers between metal and fur to make sure it isn't too tight.

As I rub his neck, his scent tickles my nose. It's a strangely familiar combination of cedar chips and vanilla, and something I can only describe as bear musk.

"Let's go," I murmur in the bear's ear. He's quivering all over, powerful muscles bunching like he's dying to burst out of the cellar. "Soon as we're in the Deadlands, we'll let you lead the way."

I'm definitely no beast master. My last words are completely lost on Lysander, who tears out of the cellar like he's on fire, yanking me with him as I cling to the end of the chain.

Jax dashes after us, swearing. Simeon and Elibeth leap back, pressing themselves against the walls as we pass. I whisper a hasty prayer to Vaia that Meredy will stay alive long enough for us to reach her.

Two smashed urns and a ruined rug later, we're charging into the night.

XVII

I'm not sure if anyone saw three necromancers and one huge bear leap into a gateway in the middle of a baron's lawn by moonlight. Everything was a blur from the time we burst out of the Crowthers' manor to the moment we arrived in the tunnel and Lysander slowed his pace enough to allow Jax and Simeon to jog briskly alongside us.

"So, about this Tabathy person," I whisper, flashing Jax a teasing grin in the dimness of the tunnel. We won't be able to say much once we're in the Deadlands, unless we want the Shade-baiters to hear us coming. "The best six weeks of your life sounds pretty serious, even if it was secret. What happened?"

Jax shrugs. "She didn't make me laugh. And she was leaving Grenwyr anyway, once she finished her training. She went home to Elsinor so she and her owl could take a position in the personal guard of some countess." He scratches the back of his neck and looks away.

"You ever write to her?" I'm not quite sure why I'm suddenly curious, but I can't suppress the urge to pry a little.

"Once or twice. I write to a lot of girls." He winks. "I'm a man of many words. Maybe I'll write to you one day, if you're lucky."

Simeon snickers under his breath, but I keep my attention on Jax.

I wish he'd hold my gaze a little longer so I could search his eyes. Maybe this bantering means things haven't changed between us the way I thought they had. Vaia knows I've endured enough change lately to give King Wylding a fit.

Keeping a tight hold on Lysander's chain with one hand, I use my other to touch Jax's arm. "Any girl would be lucky to get a letter from you, dummy. Me included."

"That so?" He looks my way. The sea in his eyes is restless, but after Simeon tosses us a curious glance, Jax keeps his tone light. "You don't think, given recent events, that my time would be better spent writing to someone else?"

"Maybe. But your friends appreciate letters, too. We care, like it or not." I smile. I'm not ready to give up my place in his bed, my only escape, just yet. I recall his earlier words and murmur, "Remember, some of us still need you, brother . . ."

"Just like we need *you*, Sparrow," Jax whispers. Louder, he adds, "Who else would I write to about all my flaws and insecurities?" He grins, and a silent understanding passes between us. Even though we kissed, we're already slipping back into our familiar roles as family. Just the way I like it.

"I want a letter from Jax of Lorness, too!" Simeon calls, amusement in his voice. "Assuming we all leave here alive, I'm going to need to hear more about whatever you two are *really* saying here." He waves a dagger, eyeing us both. "One way or another."

I roll my eyes and fall silent as the twilit glow on the horizon grows larger, signaling the start of the Deadlands.

Time moves differently here than in our world, so if we're quick enough, there's a chance Meredy might still be alive.

Lysander continues to strain against his collar, lending an extra quickness to my steps, but making me stumble so often that Simeon offers to take the chain for a while.

Lysander's movements are sure and swift, carrying us across a stream where we have to jump from bank to bank, then through a grove of silver maples.

After some stretch of time has passed, immeasurable by the Deadlands' frozen moon, the bear's pace begins to lag. We cross the same stream again, and the same maple grove, and I thank Death that the landscape hasn't changed on us yet.

"We're going in circles," Jax grumbles as he takes the bear's chain from Simeon. "I'm starving. It's probably morning back in Karthia. And our maiden in distress is probably dead by now." He shakes his head. "If she was anyone but Evander's sister, I'd say it was time to give up."

I blink at him, stunned, but it's Simeon who voices my thoughts. "Jax, you haven't said *his* name since—"

Lysander's moan drowns out Simeon's words. The bear halts

in the middle of an overgrown flower field and hangs his head. He moans again, higher than before, and it raises the hair on my arms.

"Death be damned," I say softly. "We're too late." My heart sinks as I gaze around the field and imagine the disappointment in Evander's eyes. In Elibeth's.

I wade deeper into the field, kicking flowers out of my path. It reminds me of the field I stood in yesterday, and as I'm busy scanning the ground for the charred remains of the three Shades, I don't notice the spirit of a solemn, willowy girl until she's right in front of me.

Her hair is shoulder-length and pale, her face heart shaped and undeniably beautiful, cold and distant as a midwinter moon. But what's even more remarkable is the long arrow sticking out of her middle, as filmy as the rest of her.

"Firiel?" I call softly over Lysander's moans and the sound of my heart racing. It just might be her, Meredy's girlfriend. The ghastly wound in her stomach certainly looks like the result of a hunting accident.

"Who's she?" Simeon demands, frowning at the spirit.

I hold up a hand, telling him and Jax to wait a moment. When the spirit blinks at me, acknowledging her name, I ask, "Where's Meredy? Is she still alive?"

Firiel nods, then raises a transparent arm and points north several times, to the trees beyond the field. Her eyes are pleading, her mouth sad.

"See that? We have to hurry!" I turn to glance at the others, and to my relief, Jax, Simeon, and Lysander are already running in the direction she pointed. The bear's chain twinkles in the faint starlight as he bounds ahead, seeming to have found new reason to hope.

"Let's go save your girl," I say to Firiel, extending a hand.

Quick as a blink, Firiel plucks a perfect lily and drops it in the palm of my shaking hand, then turns as if to leave.

"Wait! Once we find Meredy, we can fetch your body and perform the ritual to bring you back."

She faces me but shakes her head, her frown as deep as Grenwyr's western river.

And suddenly, I understand. "You want to stay here. You don't want to be raised and live a second life behind a shroud." When Firiel nods, I swallow hard and make another guess. "But you don't want Meredy to die just because you're here."

Firiel gives me a sad smile, and I get the strange feeling I'm letting Meredy down. I nod a farewell to Firiel and dash after my friends. I wonder if she'll stay in the Deadlands long, or if she'll be one of those who quickly lets the river carry her away to the mysterious place beyond.

I hope Evander's found his way there, too, somehow. I hope he can see me now, doing what I think he would, so that he knows in some small way, he still lives on while I do.

Up ahead, Jax and Simeon have stopped, crouching behind a broad tree. Jax's arms strain as he struggles to keep Lysander from charging through the brush at the three figures in the clearing beyond.

Two men and one woman, just like Jax said.

And on the ground at their feet, bleeding from several stab wounds on her arms and back, is Meredy. Her eyes are open and glassy, like Evander's were the last time I ever saw him. But unlike Evander, Meredy is still breathing.

Silently as possible, Simeon draws his sword. He's going to try to get a jump on the necromancers before Jax unleashes the bear. And while Simeon isn't the swordsman Evander was, he could be deadly with a moment of surprise on his side.

Lysander rears up despite Jax's efforts, knocking him backward. The bear roars a battle cry that makes my teeth clack together.

So much for surprise.

"We have company!" the female Shade-baiter shouts, pointing to our hiding place.

The taller of the two men whips his bald head around and locks eyes with me despite the curtain of branches between us, and my breath catches in my throat. His eyes aren't like any other necromancer's I've seen. They're the palest shade of blue, misty as a riverbank on a chill autumn morning.

He's blind, yet somehow he still seems to know exactly where I'm standing. His keen awareness makes me shiver.

Lysander crashes through the trees, blazing a trail straight to Meredy's side.

Simeon, Jax, and I run after him, as Lysander nuzzles Meredy's neck and growls softly.

The female necromancer raises an age-blackened sword, and I scream a warning as I run. Lysander's too focused on Meredy to react. The necromancer lunges, her blade aimed at the bear's ribs. With a casual swipe of his massive paw, he knocks her clean across the clearing and into a tree, never taking his eyes off his fallen master.

As we reach the clearing and surround them, the male necromancers raise their daggers. The woman struggles to recover her sword with a bloody arm, breathing hard as she drags herself toward her blade.

Jax swings his sword at her, but she lifts hers with a strangled shout at the last possible moment. The screech of steel on steel cuts into my thoughts as I rush at the shorter man with my sword drawn, Simeon at my side. I hesitate to attack the taller man—it seems wrong, somehow, since he may not see me coming. But then, he can surely sense me. I get the feeling I shouldn't underestimate him.

I catch sight of Meredy out of the corner of my eye. Lysander's licking the many wounds that gape like sad red mouths on her pale skin. A thin trail of scarlet leaks from her lips and pools on the ground.

"Vane, do it now!" the female necromancer shouts as she clashes with Jax. "Call your Shade!"

I don't know what she means, but the tall Shade-baiter with the misty blue eyes—Vane—nods in understanding. Whatever he's planning, he's not going to get very far, because he's about to feel the bite of my blade. He deserves a taste of the pain he's caused, and Simeon can handle the other man on his own.

I sprint toward Vane as he rasps, "Come here, my pet!"

As if on command, a Shade staggers from the shadows on the opposite side of the clearing, its bony arms dragging on the ground, its dark eye sockets fixed on me. Drool cascades over its pointed teeth—it's hungry, always hungry—yet it doesn't charge.

A chill envelops me as I narrow my eyes at the monster that seems to be following the rogue necromancer's orders.

But necromancers can't control Shades. That's impossible.

Or so I thought.

It's a young Shade, newly made, which means it has more flesh on its bones, more wisps of hair clinging to its skull, and its mouth can't yet stretch wide enough to swallow a deer or a cow. But it could still do plenty of damage.

Vane raises a hand and cries, "Now! Time to feed!"

Grabbing a vial of liquid fire from my belt, I leap between the Shade and Meredy. I hesitate with the potion held aloft, trying to gauge which way the Shade will move when I toss it. I only have a few vials, so there's little room for mistakes.

I'm still close enough to stab Vane with my other hand. I swing my sword, but he must hear it coming. He stumbles back, daring me to move with him. To give the Shade a clear path toward Meredy, assuming it doesn't go for me instead. Shades aren't picky, just hungry. I stand my ground and snarl at the man just out of my blade's reach.

Behind me, someone shrieks a piercing death note. If I take my eyes off the Shade a second time to see who just died, it could be the last thing I do. "Everyone all right?" I shout instead, trying to control my racing heart.

Vane turns and flees into the dark woods. I spit at the spot where he stood. It's no surprise a murderous rat like him would abandon his companions the moment he knew they were losing this fight.

Simeon calls out a breathless, "They're getting away!"

"Stay and help Sparrow!" Jax growls. "This should be quick." Dead branches crack under his weight as he chases after the wounded Shade-baiter.

"Jax! Get back here!" I scream. I need my friend where I can see him, or at least hear him. Not out in the dark woods with two armed rogue necromancers who can summon a Shade on command.

If anything happens to either Jax or Si, I won't be able to live with myself.

But Jax doesn't heed my call, and the Shade across the clearing doesn't seem compelled to follow its master into the woods. It throws back its head and releases a cry loud enough to strip the leaves from the trees.

Fury at the rogue necromancers and every Shade that's ever roamed the Deadlands sizzles in my blood. I throw a vial of fire potion at the Shade right as it darts forward on all fours, and it collides with the glass vial a moment later. It must be even younger than I thought, one of the Dead turned into a monster just today, to be moving so slowly.

That means the rogue necromancers created this Shade that's burning to ash in a blaze before my eyes. They pulled a shroud from one of the Dead so he or she would become a monster and brought it here. Why else would Vane have called it his *pet*? And they were going to feed Meredy to it, to help it grow stronger. This wasn't just about killing for money and leaving the victim in the Deadlands. This was bigger.

Shivering, I watch the Shade burn until all that's left is its head and a pool of bubbling black goo, wondering if it was someone I knew.

"Sparrow!" Simeon cries, tearing my attention away from the Shade. He's crouched beside Meredy, stroking her wine-red hair. "She's been trying to talk," he says urgently, "But I can't understand her. She's looking at you."

As I hurry to her side, a crunching sound draws my gaze to the edge of the trees. Lysander's cleaning up the remains of the dead male Shade-baiter, and the bear grumbles in deep contentment as he rips off the corpse's leg and takes a huge bite.

Somehow, I find the disgusting sound reassuring, but I'm still on edge. I don't like that Jax isn't back yet. Kneeling beside Simeon, I urge, "Go look for Jax. We'll be fine here until you get back."

With a glance at the burning Shade, already reduced to cinders, he nods and heads for the trees with his blade in hand.

Meredy mumbles something I can't quite make out. I bring my ear closer to her lips.

"She didn't want to come," Meredy whispers. Even now, in her pain and her grief, her eyes are resolutely dry. "I came all this way, and she didn't want to return with me. At least now I can join her here."

I shake my head. "No. You can't, because Evander wouldn't want that. *Firiel* doesn't want that." I take her icy hand in mine and squeeze it. A faint scent of vanilla wafts toward me, like I always imagined the Deadlands flowers would smell, or perhaps sweeter. "Hang on just a little longer, Meredy. Lysander needs you. Elibeth needs you. Your mother needs you. You have to hang on."

Fumbling with my belt, I finally find the honey and tip the glass vial to her lips. A golden drop stains her mouth, but she doesn't try to eat it or wipe it off.

She just stares up at the sky, unmoving. I slap her cold cheek to startle her into taking a shallow breath. "Meredy. I know it's tempting to give up. Believe me, I *know*. But for Evander's sake, I won't let you."

Her shoulders shake as she makes a wheezing sound that might be laughter. "Too little, too late, Sparrow." More blood trickles down her chin. "If you were going to come all this way for me," she rasps, "you could've just taken my money when I offered it. You would've done us both a favor."

Dropping her hand, I shift my gaze to Lysander and the bloody mess he's making of the rogue necromancer. I can't believe Meredy's trying to make me feel even more rotten than I already do after I came all this way to save her.

"I didn't have to come at all," I say softly. "And you don't have to thank me, but how about being glad I'm here?"

"Why would I be glad?" Meredy's breaths are becoming more rapid and shallow by the moment, but she's not as far gone as I thought. If she's busy arguing, I have this wild hope she won't suddenly give up and die on me. "You can't bring Firiel back. She's made that clear. And you can't stop me from dying. You've been no help at all."

"You're right," I mutter. Part of me wants to give her a good shake despite the blood trickling out of her. "And without my help, you wasted all your money and got yourself killed for someone who didn't want to live again, even if it meant a second chance at life with you."

Meredy's next words are almost too soft to hear. It's only by watching the shape of her lips that I understand. "Go. Please, go away. I didn't need you before, and I certainly don't need you now."

Heat rushes to my face. "Way to overestimate yourself, sweetheart."

I expect another biting remark. But the spark of life is leeching from her eyes, swift as the sun once it touches the horizon. I scoop her into my arms, careful to avoid the deep gash in her side that will be her death wound if we don't get to a healer soon.

Swallowing hard, I tear my gaze from the constellations of freckles dusting her cheeks and pray to Vaia yet again. This time, I beg that I won't have to watch this girl, this echo of Evander, die in my arms.

I wish Jax and Simeon would hurry up. If they're not back soon, I'm leaving without them. Meredy's life depends on it.

I carry her over to Lysander, who's still grinding the dead necromancer's bones, and gingerly lay the now-unconscious girl over the bear's back. Hopefully he'll be willing to carry both of us to a healer if I ask politely.

As I grab hold of the bear's loose chain, Simeon and Jax crash into the clearing, sweaty and winded and covered in scratches.

"We need to go. *Now*," I shout. "What kept you?"

"The one called Vane. He got away," Jax pants. "But the woman wasn't as lucky. She was bleeding badly, so it was easy to pick up her trail."

"And is she—?"

"I killed her." Simeon's face is eerily solemn, and I realize this is the first time he's taken the life of a living person. "The whole way back, we've been trying to work out the meaning of what she said before she died."

I frown at them. "Which was?"

Simeon and Jax exchange a glance, and Jax answers, "There will be others."

XVIII

Three vials of calming potion first thing in the morning are all it takes for me to feel comfortably numb about yesterday's rescue. To stop my hands from shaking, so I look almost normal when I make my way to the palace's dining hall.

I haven't even reached the marble stairs when I bump into Jax and Simeon, both wearing their swords and necromancer's belts. "What are you two—?"

"Looking for you," Simeon chimes in quickly, grinning at his own timing. "We ran into each other after breakfast and decided now's the time to go looking for the rogue necromancer, Vane. We'll start in the Ashes, since that's where Meredy met him. If we wait too much longer, he might leave the city."

"If he knows what's good for him, he's already gone," Jax adds, his crystal-blue eyes flashing. There's a stain on his tunic, something that dried sticky and shiny just beneath his master necromancer's pin. He rubs it absently.

"What happened there?" I ask.

"Your friend Valoria spilled her breakfast on me." He grins, shaking his head. "I've never seen someone jump that much at a simple hello."

"And in other news," Simeon cuts in, his voice rough from lack of sleep, "Danial might be moving back to Oslea thanks to our recent foray into the Deadlands."

"What?" I put an arm around his shoulders.

"After all that's happened, he thinks it's too dangerous." Simeon rolls his eyes, but the gesture does nothing to hide his pain. "I told him about rescuing Evander's sister, and he told me to leave the Shade-baiter to you and Jax. He said if I don't, I might lose him for good."

Jax spits on the polished tile floor, showing exactly what he thinks of that.

"I shouldn't have asked you to come," I say quickly. "I knew Danial was scared for you. I knew he didn't want you going to the Deadlands, but—"

"You did the right thing. I won't abandon my family, not even for the handsomest face in Karthia." With a great shuddering breath, he seems to bury his misery deep and return to his usual good-natured self. "So, are we going to stand around discussing our feelings all day, or do you want to go get your sword and join us, sister?"

"You both realize Vane is probably hiding in the Deadlands somewhere, right?" As I say it, both Jax and Simeon frown slightly, and I relent. "We can check the Ashes first, though. I'll be quick," I promise as I spin around and run back to my room.

I grab my sword off the desk, and right as I pull it from its scabbard to check it over from yesterday's fight, someone knocks briskly at the door.

"Simeon! I said I'd be right back."

But the knock comes again.

Meredy Crowther is in my doorway, wearing Evander's smile, holding out a bunch of fiery poppies whose bright petals mean consolation. "Thank you," she says tersely as she steps past me, entering my room again without invitation, "for saving my life."

She thrusts the flowers at me, and I take them with my free hand, studying her over the poppies. She looks almost as pale as she did when she was bleeding from the Shade-baiters' attack, but her wounds are healed and her hair is braided into a neat crown.

"These are nice," I mutter, bringing the flowers to my nose. "Really. Thanks." It took courage to come here after the things we said to each other. I'll give her that. But I have no idea why she's still standing here, looking at me expectantly. "So . . . are you staying in Grenwyr City for—?"

I feel something scurry over my hand. Several somethings. A shiny black bug drops from the bouquet onto my boot, and I stifle the urge to shout as I stamp on it. But when another bug crawls up my arm, I curse and throw the flowers across the room.

A stalk of deep purple foxglove, the symbol of insincerity, falls from the middle of the bouquet.

"Death be damned, these are *infested*! Where'd you find them? A dung heap?"

Meredy's face flushes as she stamps on every bug she spots. "So burn them," she mutters. "I wouldn't have come here at all if my mother hadn't dragged me the whole way and insisted I thank you. If you ask me, you don't deserve any thanks. I wish you'd left me there to die . . ." She squishes the last bug, then frowns at me.

For some reason, the sight makes my temples throb.

Meredy's pale skin turns mottled gray. Her arms grow long and skeletal. Peeling, decaying flesh bubbles on her cheeks, and her mouth, opening in surprise, is full of sharp teeth.

I shut my eyes and lean against the wall of my room, willing the hallucination to stop. But when I crack an eye open, Shade Meredy is still standing there, watching me with dark holes for eyes, snarling with her jaw unhinged and her pointy teeth exposed. Looking hungry.

"Odessa?" Her usually cool voice is tinged with concern despite her vicious appearance. "What's going on?"

"M-monster," I grit out, keeping my eyes shut tight. My whole skull hurts worse than it did the time Simeon and I rolled down a giant hill and he accidentally kicked me in the back of the head.

"What did you just call me?" Meredy's too-sharp voice crashes into my aching head.

"No, I mean—because—" I won't tell her about the potions. I can't.

"You don't get to judge me for trying to bring Firiel back when I didn't know she'd refuse to come. How could I have known that, after all the things we promised each other?" A sob escapes her. "I never should have come here!"

She slams the door behind her, and the moment her rapid footsteps in the hallway fade, I crawl toward the stash of calming potions under my bed. With the bitter liquid trickling down my throat, the pain in my head starts to recede, and I can see the trampled flowers on the floor clearly again.

I doubt Meredy will ever come back here. And I'm glad. I don't want anyone to see me like this, especially not her, a girl who's lost more than I have. Evander wouldn't recognize me right now, and that alone makes me wish I could stop needing the potion—but I'm even more afraid of what I'll feel without it.

I'm afraid of so many things.

Like a rogue necromancer who can control Shades.

After what I witnessed when I rescued Meredy, I wonder if Evander's death or Master Nicanor's were the random violent acts of a Shade. I wonder if their killer had a master and was following orders. A rogue necromancer guiding the giant Shade and feeding it corpses would explain why it was so much stronger than the usual monsters lurking in the Deadlands.

"Sparrow?" Simeon's voice cuts into my thoughts, carrying from the hallway through the closed door. "We just saw Meredy come out of your room, and she looked madder than a wet cat. Is everything all right?"

I push myself up off the floor and run my fingers through my hair, trying to look more like myself. I don't need anyone realizing I haven't stopped taking the calming potions.

"Everything's fine," I lie. "Let's get this over with."

*   *   *

The morning after our unsuccessful search in the Ashes, the faint sound of smashing glass draws me from a restless sleep. I open my eyes to a misty autumn morning and gaze around my empty room, where the piles of clothes and my sword are exactly as I left them. I must've imagined the noise. After closing my eyes for another moment and realizing sleep won't return, I wonder whether I'll need three or four potions to help me out of bed this morning.

But when I try to push back my blankets, my hands won't cooperate, and I glance down to see they're bound in iron. I blink, struggling to make sense of things. The heavy shackles on my wrists look like the ones reserved for the most violent lawbreakers.

My mind jumps to Vane, the powerful rogue necromancer, but I can't imagine how he got through the palace guards and figured out which room was mine. And if he wanted to tie me up and hurt me, he wouldn't have left me cozily tucked in bed.

There's only one thing I know for certain right now: I've got to get to the hallway and call for help before whoever did this returns.

Heart tapping out a mad beat, I stagger from my bed with the sheets wrapped around my ankles and trip as I reach the edge of my tether—I'm chained to my own bedpost. I try to catch myself, but I'm not quick enough. I land hard on my back, knocking the breath out of me. Still, whatever bruises I've just given myself don't sting nearly as badly as the sight beneath my bed.

All my calming potions are *gone*. The once-sticky floorboards where they sat are clean and dry, as though the potions were never there at all.

My scream of frustration doesn't feel as good as I hoped it might.

"Oh good," says a cool, slightly bored voice I never thought I'd hear again. My door creaks open, and the voice grows louder. "You're awake. How's your head today?"

As Meredy sweeps into the room, my face burns. I struggle to push myself up from the floor, not wanting to give her the satisfaction of towering over me while I'm sprawled on my back, helpless as a fish out of water.

"What is this? Some kind of revenge?" I growl, holding up my shackled hands. The chain binding me to the bed rattles as I push myself to my feet and glare at Meredy. "You realize I can still hurt you with my hands chained, right?"

Her lips twitch, but she quickly forces her face into its usual smooth mask. "I don't see why you'd want to, when I'm here to help you. Besides, your hands aren't bound for my protection." Meredy takes a deep breath. "Your potions are gone, and you'll be tied up and locked in this room for the next seven days, with the exception of necessities." She pauses, her eyes searching my stunned face. "That's how long the healers say it takes for the potion to leave your blood entirely and stop the cravings."

"Do you . . . do you have any idea how much those tonics cost?" I'm so furious, I can barely form words. "Or how much I need them?"

I may not want to kill her, but I would like to slap her. Really, really hard.

"Look, you know what Evander meant to me. So you should understand better than anyone why I need this one thing." I edge as close to Meredy as my blasted tether allows. "Without the potion, I'll be—"

"Alive and miserable," Meredy finishes. A flash of triumph lights her eyes. "Like me. I realized it when I got home yesterday. There's no better way to repay what you did than by giving you exactly what you gave me. *Life*, when I wanted to die. Did you know that if you were to keep taking that potion, it would eventually kill you?"

I press my lips together, a trickle of cold snaking down my back. I didn't know that, but even if she's telling the truth, it's none of her business. "If you really wanted to die," I mutter out of spite, "you wouldn't be here talking to me."

To my satisfaction, her lips open, but no sound comes out. She gives a terse nod.

"I could say the same of you," she murmurs at last, her voice crisp as winter's first frost. "You're drinking far too much of that potion for someone who plainly isn't ready to give up on life, no matter what wretched things it's forced on you lately."

My voice, unlike hers, crackles with heat. "Why do you care, anyway?"

Meredy's face reveals nothing, even when it's so close her nose is almost touching mine. "Misery loves company. And Evander would turn over in his grave if I let you keep destroying yourself."

"How did you even *know* about the potions?"

She glances away, toward the window. "Your friend is really worried about you. And after your bizarre episode yesterday, I was curious." She shrugs. "Wondering about you beats dwelling on my own problems."

Valoria.

"I'll pay you." I hate the whine in my voice, but a feeling like hundreds of tiny insects crawling around in my stomach means it's past time for my next fix. "You can have anything of mine you want. My uniforms. My party gowns. My sword. My sapphire pin. Just bring my potions back."

"Not a chance." Meredy perches on the bed, leaving the path to the door wide open.

But there's no point even trying to sprint to freedom. I can't drag the whole bed with me. As I glare at the open door, Valoria breezes into the room, looking completely unsurprised by my livid stare.

"Good morning!" she says cheerfully, pushing her glasses up her nose and kicking the door shut. Turning back, she offers me a hesitant smile I don't return. "How are you feeling? It's a good thing your potion makes you sleep so soundly, or I'd never have gotten those shackles on without you knowing. Are they too tight? I designed them with your comfort in mind . . ."

I press my lips together to hold in a groan. "Of course this was your idea."

The princess shakes her head. "Meredy's. But I wish I'd thought of it days ago."

I can't believe this is happening. I'd pinch myself to see if I'm dreaming, but I can't move my hands. And with each passing moment, what little patience I have is fading.

"Valoria. Take these off right now," I demand through gritted teeth. "I have no chance of finding your mother if I'm locked up." When she doesn't show any sign of relenting, I lower my voice to a hushed calm. "Fine. You win. I'll never touch a drop of that potion again. But Jax and Simeon need my help tracking down the missing Dead and a very dangerous man who's already tried to feed at least one person to a Shade." A man who's apparently quite good at hiding, if yesterday's search is any indication.

"Jax and Simeon know what we're doing here. And we have their support." Valoria leans closer, frowning down her nose at me. "They don't want you going back to the Deadlands, or anywhere else, until you have a clear head and aren't a few potions away from death."

I try to ball my hands into fists, but of course I can't. Instead, I give Valoria my widest, most pleading eyes. Of my two captors, she's the one I'm sure has a heart. The one I know how to wound with words. "Please, *Highness*. There's no time for this now!"

"Oh, but there is, Master Necromancer." Valoria squares her shoulders and stands taller, looking every bit like the leader I know she could be. I just wish she wasn't directing her fiercest stare at me, forcing me to glower back. "Do you have any idea what this is doing to us—your friends? You'll be more of a danger than a help to Jax and Simeon if you keep drinking that potion. Grenwyr needs you." Her gaze and voice soften as she adds, "*I* need you. The real you, not the one who's been spending half her time in an imaginary world of monsters."

Meredy's words are so quiet, I almost miss them. "There are enough real monsters in Karthia to keep you busy, if you'd just look around."

I exchange a glance with her, wondering if she's thinking of yesterday's rogue necromancers. She smiles wanly, and a flickering image of Evander hits me like a knife in the gut. I turn my back on her, focusing all my attention on the princess.

"Meredy obviously wants to see me suffer." The shaking in my hands spreads to my knees, but I'd rather fight to keep standing than sit on the bed beside *her*. "That much I understand. But, Valoria, why are *you* doing this to me?"

"You brought me out of my tower. You helped me realize I have a voice, however small, that deserves to be heard." The princess puts her arms around me, hugging my rigid back and filling me with unexpected warmth. "And now I want to lead you out of the darkness."

"What if the darkness is where I belong?" I fight to keep my voice steady as I think of all the times I walked the palace halls with Evander, when my biggest worry was how to convince him we should move there. "What if I spend every potion-free day wishing I'd died in the Deadlands with him? What if the pain of being alone is too much?"

An image of Master Cymbre's face as she pulled me from the flames in a faraway field flashes to mind, knotting my stomach with guilt.

"You won't wish that." Valoria squeezes my shoulder. "Because you won't be alone. You'll have me, and we'll fight the pain and the darkness together."

I open my mouth to ask her how I can fight anything with my hands chained, but my knees buckle and I sway. Frowning, Valoria steadies me, then pushes me gently down onto the bed. Resigned to my fate, I sink onto my unmade sheets.

When I wake up some time later, Meredy is gone. For a while, as the sun makes its ascent in a clear blue sky, I watch Valoria as she sits by my feet, scribbling in a leather-bound notebook of yellowed parchment.

"What are you working on?" I manage to ask. Beads of sweat collect on my forehead, but when Valoria pours me a glass of water, I'm too nauseated to drink.

Valoria makes a soft disapproving sound, but she doesn't force the issue. Instead, she holds up her notebook. "This is my air balloon." She taps the drawing at the center of the spread pages, a giant loopy thing with strings coming out of the bottom and what looks like a large basket dangling from the strings. "Fire should make the balloon rise, but I've got to figure out how to contain the flames so they won't burn the people sitting in the basket. A flying balloon could be a new way to travel."

I lick sweat from my lips and surprise myself by laughing. The image of several Dead looking on in awe and fear as Valoria ascends into the sky in a flaming balloon is just too much. "Where do you come up with these things? What is it your Sight shows you that inspires you to want to, well, *fly*?"

Valoria's cheeks turn rosy pink. "They're not all my ideas. I found the air balloon and several other designs for flying machines in a book. There's a section of the palace library that used to hold books from before Eldest Grandfather's second reign began, books full of all sorts of ideas people started but never got a chance to finish." She tries to push her glasses up the bridge of her nose, though they're already in place. "*He* thinks all those books were burned, but I saved as many as I could in my tower. When I read them, I see ways to improve the designs. There's just the matter of getting a chance to try . . ."

I smile, leaning back against my pillows and wondering what Evander would think of a flying balloon. He'd probably volunteer to be Valoria's first victim—er, passenger. I bet he'd consider it an exciting way to see what lies beyond Karthia's borders.

Maybe someday, I can sail the skies for him. Even if the thought terrifies me.

"Why don't we take your air balloon down to the beach one night?" I gasp between shaky breaths. I'm sweating so hard now, my blankets cling to me like a second skin. "Where the Dead won't see it. Maybe we can get it working."

Valoria's expression shifts from one of shock and gratitude to complete horror as I start to convulse.

"Have some water," Valoria says meekly, dropping her book to dab my sweaty face with a cool, damp cloth.

"Evander," I gasp as I writhe, unable to keep my traitorous body still. Without the potion, I won't see my perfect illusion of him anymore. And if I can't see him, over time, I'll forget what he looked like. Without the potion, I'll truly lose him. "I can't see him," I sob as Valoria presses the cloth to my forehead. "I can't—I can't . . ."

Moments later, my screams echo off the walls.

XIX

I don't know how much time has passed since I last opened my eyes, if it's been days or just a few hours, but the moon hangs low in my window like a curious spectator, and Valoria is nowhere to be seen.

My throat is dry, my lips rough as old parchment. "I'm thirsty," I croak to no one in particular.

"Would you like some goat's milk?" Meredy asks, emerging from the shadows dragging a chair toward my bedside. "I've brought sage water as well. If you'd like, I could make coriander water instead. It's popular in Lorness."

Every sound, from her voice to the chair scraping the wooden floor before it catches on my rug, hurts like someone is jabbing tiny knives into my ears.

"Stop talking," I beg as she holds a slender glass bottle to my lips.

I try to pretend she's not there as I drink down the sage water, but it's nearly impossible to avoid gazing into her eyes when she's so close. I focus on the scar across her cheek, the four jagged lines that must have come from a large paw.

When I've finished with the water, my head is throbbing a little less. "Why a grizzly bear?" I ask.

Meredy settles into the chair she brought over. "What?"

"Beast masters choose the animal they study and bond with, don't they?"

"They do. It helps to have a choice, because you wind up spending years in the wilderness with that animal." A rare smile lights Meredy's face, and for the first time, the resemblance to Evander doesn't hit me like a blow. Perhaps because my body's too exhausted to ache any more than it already does.

"I grew up watching Elibeth and her greyhounds. She was always bragging about how amazing their connection was, and what majestic animals they were," Meredy continues, slipping further from her usual calm as her face darkens. "It's not easy being the youngest of three siblings. Being the smallest often meant being overlooked. So when I learned I'd been selected to train as a beast master, I chose the most fearsome animal I could think of. Life hasn't been the same since I met Lysander." She bows her head. Hiding something, I'm sure. "He's the one thing I've never regretted."

"Not even when he gave you that scar?"

Meredy raises her eyes to mine again as she touches her scarred cheek. "Not even then. It's a good reminder that wild things can never truly be tamed. Only respected."

I wiggle my fingers as they start tingling, but my gaze keeps wandering back to her curtain of dark red hair.

"Are you hungry?" she asks, apparently mistaking my listless stare for something else. "I can send for something from the kitchens." When I shake my head, she pulls a small sack from inside her cloak and tosses it toward me. Her face is unreadable, but I have the strangest feeling that she's pleased with herself. "You'll at least want these. Kasmira sends her regards."

The sack hits my leg and rattles as it falls onto the bed. I blink at Meredy. "I haven't given you enough credit, young beast master," I grit out. She purses her lips as I raise my bound hands. "But how am I supposed to open them?"

"Oh." She leaps up and grabs the bag. "Right." Maybe it's a trick of the moonlight, but for a moment a hint of flush appears beneath her freckles.

As the bag falls open, the wonderful aroma of coffee beans fills the room. Oh, how I've missed them. The calming potion had put my former addiction well out of mind, but now that they're being held to my lips by Meredy's long, slender fingers, I don't know how I've gone without for so long.

Her eyes hold mine. Their rich green is flecked with amber. She blinks slowly. I lean in and catch a coffee bean with my lips. Her breath hitches, and a slight flush rises in her face.

"This doesn't mean I like you all of a sudden," I tell her. "Or that I ever will, after you've made me a prisoner in my own room."

Her cheeks are still bright, but she says, "All right," in her usual serene manner. "I'll learn to live with myself, somehow."

My lower lip brushes her thumb as I take another coffee bean, and a shiver races through me.

"You . . . you should try one," I offer.

Meredy arches a brow. "Me, eating illegal goods?" She sounds slightly out of breath at the thought. Figures she'd be that virtuous. A moment later, she pops one in her mouth and crunches down. Her eyes widen, and she smiles.

A tremor suddenly grips me as my body clamors for something stronger.

Something blue in a glass vial that left me comfortably numb.

Something that could keep me floating above this swift, searing pain.

"How do you do it?" I ask as Meredy sponges my forehead with the cloth Valoria left. "How do you handle thinking about Van and Firiel without falling apart?"

Her movements with the cloth are careful, her fingers never once grazing my skin. "I don't," she says after a while. "I try not to think of them at all."

My smile is tight with pain. "What do you think my potions were for?" I try to laugh, but it sounds more like a groan. "I wish I could be numb like you without them. I'll deny I ever said this when I'm better, *if* I get better, but: You're strong. Stronger than me."

A wave of pain makes me arch my back, my hands curling in their shackles.

Meredy's eyes narrow in concern. She dabs fresh, cool water across my brow. "Thanks. But you're the stronger one. I wish I could let myself feel as much as you do without falling apart."

I shake my head. "What do you call what I'm doing now?"

Her fingers slip over the edge of the cloth as her eyes meet mine, and clumsily, as if she's not quite aware of what she's doing, she smooths back my hair. "Surviving."

Her touch is the best thing I've felt in days—cool against my burning skin. I close my eyes, not wanting to startle her into realizing what she's doing for fear that she'll stop. But when a vicious tremor grips me, my body screaming for the potion, there's nothing that can ease the pain.

"Tell me a story," I beg as I writhe on my sweat-dampened quilt. After all, whatever dignity I once possessed is long gone. "The happiest one you can think of."

Meredy's eyes widen. For an agonizingly long moment, the only sound is my ragged breathing. At last, she says stiffly, "When I was nine, Evander squished my pet caterpillar by accident. I suppose he must've told you about it, because the first time I met you, you brought me a whole jar full of them—green ones, black-and-yellow ones, and a huge white one. You named it Pearl, remember?"

Some expression flickers across her face—amusement?—but fades as her voice becomes a whisper. "You looked like a princess that day, standing on the manor step with mud on your boots and leaves in your hair and all those caterpillars you'd found for me. I remember thinking I'd never met anyone as in love with the world around us as I was, until you."

I can't answer, not with the pain stealing my breath, but I'm sure I return her smile for a moment before the darkness pulls me under.

I'm losing track of the days. Or I was, until earlier this morning when Valoria gave me a piece of charcoal to make a slash on the wall for each potion-free night I survive. Now I draw my sixth mark above the bed, then munch on a piece of dry bread as Valoria frantically scribbles something in another notebook.

"Working on the air balloon?" I rasp. Aside from my dry throat and a dull headache, the potion's absence hasn't made me want to leap off a cliff or brought any fresh nightmares of Evander's final moments in the last few days—much to my surprise.

"Mmmm, no," Valoria murmurs. It's a wonder she's talking to me at all, after the names I called her and Meredy during the worst of my potion withdrawals.

Even yesterday, my body faintly shook through most of the day and night. But this morning, as I curl and uncurl my hands, checking for any hint of trembling, I mostly feel tired. Worn, like the leather of my necromancer's belt. And restless. I'm ready to rejoin the world beyond my window, but Valoria insists we wait the full seven days, which means one more day at her mercy.

At least they finally removed the shackles so that I can feed myself again, although it's clear that if I try to make a run for the apothecary, Lysander will stop me cold.

The sun slowly climbs higher in the sky as Valoria's quill scratches the page.

"Have Jax and Simeon been by again?" I ask, interrupting her scrawling. They've come to see me every day, and each time I've had Meredy and Lysander turn them away. I don't want anyone else witnessing my humiliation, but now I'm feeling ready to face them.

According to Valoria, they still haven't found any trace of Vane, but people in the Ashes certainly know him by reputation. It's only a matter of time before Jax finds someone he can bribe or intimidate into giving up the rogue's whereabouts. But if he hasn't made progress by tomorrow, I'm taking over.

I'd use Lysander to track the man's scent, which should still be on Meredy's bloody cloak. Jax and Simeon didn't want to borrow the bear on their own, knowing the damage he could cause if he got loose in the Ashes. He may be the most civil bear in existence, but there's wildness in his blood.

Valoria rubs her eyes, drawing my gaze back to her. She always looks tired, her stare vacant, like she's been up all night working on something or other. But I've never seen her like this, fighting back a yawn every few moments and staring at the same page in her notebook for an hour at a time.

Her mother is still missing. Every search for the nobles who vanished on the night of Hadrien's party has ended the same way. There's no sign of what happened to any of them, though everyone agrees they were dressed for the celebration when they disappeared. All King Wylding has done is increase security. Even Valoria and I are out of ideas as to where to look or who would've kidnapped a random assortment of Dead nobles and dignitaries without demanding a ransom.

"Here," she says suddenly, holding out a torn page from her notebook. Her voice quivers slightly. "So you can see him whenever you like."

I struggle to form words as I run my fingers delicately over the page, careful not to smudge the likeness of Evander grinning up at me. She even remembered the little scar above his eyebrow. "This is incredible, Valoria. Thank you."

"It was nothing," Valoria insists, her cheeks coloring. But we both know that's not true.

By the time I finish tacking the drawing on the wall above my bed, the princess is already immersed in another work of art. Waving doesn't get her attention, so I cross to her chair by the window. She doesn't seem to notice until I lean forward, blocking the light.

Gasping, she closes the notebook with a snap.

But not before I see the painstakingly detailed illustration on the back page.

"That's a very handsome drawing." I try and fail to hide a grin as I plop down on the rug by her feet. "Jax will be thrilled when you show him."

Valoria shakes her head, her face turning tomato red. "I'm not going to show him," she squeaks. "I just—I draw people whenever I need a break from my work."

"Oh? Who else?" I make a grab for the notebook. I know it's not nice, and I know she only locked me in here for the past six days for my own good, but I can't resist the urge. I want to see her squirm a little. "Come on," I beg as Valoria clutches the notebook to her chest. "We're friends. You can show me!"

The princess purses her lips and grips the notebook tighter than ever. "Try to touch this book again, and I'll feed it to Lysander. I swear I will."

"Fine. *Fine.*" I hold up my hands, wincing as something tightens in my chest. "But when it comes to Jax, there are a few things you'll want to know. Ask him what his tattoos mean. All twelve of them." Valoria opens her mouth to say something, but I continue softly, "Ask him about how he believes he's going to die, all because of some dream about ice. Ask him why he's afraid of the sea. Cook him the spiciest dish you can find, and when he starts to panic that you're getting under his skin, be patient with him."

"Odessa," Valoria says slowly, the color fading from her cheeks, "how close are you and Jax, exactly?"

"He's like a brother to me," I say firmly as Meredy bursts into the room, bringing the scents of wood smoke, crisp leaves, and cider.

"Morning, all," she says coolly.

"Meredy," Valoria murmurs, trying to recover herself. "You're just in time. I was about to see if Sparrow wanted a bath. Why don't you accompany her—?"

The princess doesn't even get her last words out as Meredy and I both say, "No!"

Valoria arches her brows, looking between us.

My face burns, though I've no idea why. Meredy gazes out the window, avoiding us both.

"Sparrow?" A call through the door breaks the heavy silence. The speaker sounds far away, like someone doesn't want to get too close to Lysander. "Prince Hadrien requests your presence in the throne room."

Meredy turns her intense eyes to the door. "Tell him she'll come find him tomorrow, when she's feeling completely better!" she shouts in answer.

"It's an *order*," the speaker says sternly. "All the necromancers are being summoned." There's a pause, a sigh, and then, "King Wylding is missing."

XX

The guard who delivered Hadrien's summons accompanies me down the hall to the throne room at the heart of the palace. He has a round, young face I don't recognize, and perhaps his youth and inexperience are to blame for the way he keeps a hand on my forearm like I'm some common criminal being brought for sentencing.

Still, I'm not in the mood for this. Not after the past six days.

I twist out of his grasp. Startled, he mutters an apology that I ignore.

Valoria, Meredy, and Lysander follow a short distance behind us. I'm sure they're wondering, like I am, how the king could vanish with all the extra guards stationed outside the palace's every door. Even if he left on his own—which is about as unlikely as the Dead wanting to fly in an air balloon—someone would've seen him.

Unless someone *inside* the palace is to blame for his disappearance. King Wylding loves his sprawling family almost as much as he loves Karthia, but Vaia knows the living and the Dead alike can hold on to the smallest of grudges.

As we trudge onward, Lysander's claws clicking against the bright tiled floor, guards press themselves against the wall to get out of his way. I turn the final corner to find the throne room doors besieged by a dark and restless sea of shrouded figures. It looks like a hundred nobles or more, every Dead person in the palace. They step to either side of the hall, clearing a path for me. Some say hello or wave, but one woman growls over the greetings, "We want you gone! Find a new home!"

"That's incredibly short-sighted of you, isn't it?" Meredy says coolly from somewhere behind me. "How do you think you'll keep coming back to your jewels and power and titles without her magic?"

Stunned, I turn to thank her, but she isn't looking my way.

"The necromancers can't be trusted!" the angry Dead woman shouts. Despite the other Dead trying to silence her, she raises her scratchy voice to add, "They bring us back to life, but they make us *weak*. Why can't they learn to raise us with our magic so we can defend ourselves from these attacks?"

Swallowing hard, I shout back, "That's not how *our* magic works! You'll have to take that up with Vaia!"

It's only one unhappy woman out of a huge crowd, but her words cut me to the core.

In the past seven years, I've speared many of these nobles on the end of my blade to save them from becoming monsters and losing their souls. I've anointed their bodies with milk, held their loved ones' hands as I guided them through the Deadlands, offered their hungry spirits my blood, and brought them back to Karthia. To life. As an orphan, I've never had a spirit waiting in the Deadlands for me, unless I count the very nobles now surrounding me.

Not for the first time, I see why so few blue-eyed Karthians want my job.

"You're not going anywhere." The angry Dead woman steps in front of the closed throne room doors and spreads her arms, blocking my way forward. "If you want what's best for us, as you always say you do, you should leave now and never return."

"Move!" Some of the other Dead shout at her, but no one dares attempt to touch her. One wrong motion, one accidental tug on her shroud or gloves, and we'll have a Shade loose in the palace for a second time.

"What's going on?" The princess sounds slightly out of breath as she catches up to me, having paused a ways back to say something to a guard Lysander startled. She pulls her glasses off, polishes them on her gown, then takes a fresh look at the gathering like she can't believe her eyes. "Why is that woman blocking the door? Uncle Ty?" She turns to one of the shrouded figures for an explanation. "Aunt Arossa?"

"She wants us gone from the palace. By us, I mean all the necromancers," I explain as the guard who brought us here tries to reason with the Dead protester. He pats the sword at his side, but green as he is, even he should know better than to draw it. "The rest of the Dead are waiting for answers, I think, just like us. But how we're going to get them with *her* in the way . . ."

"Stand back," Meredy says to the crowd of worried Dead, calmly surveying the woman. "We'll clear the way."

She gazes deep into Lysander's eyes, and something unspoken passes between them. The bear's eyes glow emerald green as he walks steadily toward the throne room doors, careful not to step too near any of the other Dead.

I wince and reach instinctively for the blade that's usually at my side, thinking he's going to collide with the Dead woman at the doors, but she darts away from him at the last moment like a startled crow.

Meredy and I almost exchange a smile.

Then Valoria grabs our hands and pulls us in Lysander's wake, leaving the young guard to address the angry Dead woman now shouting at him.

As soon as we're in the throne room, two heavily armored guards bar the doors behind us, muffling the noise outside. Meredy and Lysander hang back, but Valoria runs straight to Hadrien, who sits on the polished steps leading up to the massive throne piled high with bronze and blue velvet cushions.

"Oh, Hadrien." The princess kneels beside him, throwing her arms around his neck. "This is a nightmare. I know Eldest Grandfather isn't perfect, but he's our *king*! And we don't have a chance of finding him. We couldn't even find our own mother."

As Hadrien embraces his sister, I drag my feet toward them, trying to give them a moment alone despite my burning questions.

A shadow stirs behind the throne. The queen, recognizable only by the delicate crown of gold perched atop her shroud, surveys the cavernous room. Aside from Her Majesty, Hadrien, and several guards, we're alone in here.

Jax and Simeon must be away, hunting that Shade-baiter Vane, or they'd have answered Hadrien's summons. I wonder where Master Cymbre is. Hopefully with them and not still hiding from the world in her cottage.

"At least one of the Dead is angry already," I say softly, climbing the steps to where Hadrien and Valoria sit. "She wants the necromancers to leave the palace, and while I hope she'll be the last to suggest it, I somehow doubt that." Pausing a few steps below Hadrien, I face the queen and bow my head. "Forgive me, Majesty."

Her voice is bone-dry and little more than a whisper. "Whatever for, Sparrow?"

"King Wylding." Heat rushes to my face as everyone looks my way. "I haven't been feeling like myself lately. I should have done something more to find those missing people. As a guardian to the Dead, I should have stayed by His Majesty at all—"

"That's not your job!" Valoria says, her eyes flashing. "You're not a soldier, and you're not a shepherd to the king. You can't blame yourself for any of this!" She leaps to her feet and stands beside me, linking her arm through mine. "It's out of your control, Sparrow."

I swallow hard. The shouts of the Dead woman still ring in my ears.

"There has to be something I can do." I clench my hands at my sides, gazing up at the queen. "Please tell me how I can help, Majesty."

Her feeble voice is even harder to hear this time. "I don't know, Sparrow. It's difficult to say who's to blame, and until we know that, search parties are our only course of action."

"I might know of someone, actually." Vane and his pet Shade flash to mind. Careful to leave Meredy's name out of it, I describe my encounter with the Shade-baiter as Her Majesty, Valoria, and Hadrien listen raptly. "I think he's been creating Shades on purpose, which means he could be the one stealing our Dead. Jax and Simeon are out looking for him. Of course, someone probably would've noticed him sneaking around the palace, so . . ."

I shrug, letting the words die. The idea sounded better in my head.

"If this Vane person *is* behind the kidnappings, he has no idea what's coming for him." Hadrien rises, scrubbing a hand over his face. There's a shadow along his jaw, dark gold stubble that suggests he hasn't had time for his usual grooming routine. "Believe me, when we find whoever's behind this, we'll cut our problem off at the head. Quite literally."

He strides down the few steps between us, and for the first time I notice a small red gash and a slight bruise beneath his eye.

Reaching out with my free hand, I trace his swollen skin around the cut. "What happened there?" I murmur.

Hadrien gently takes my hand and folds his fingers over mine. "It's nothing. I fell out of bed." He bites his lip. "Rather embarrassing, isn't it? But Valoria is right, Sparrow. You can't blame yourself for what's happened to His Majesty. And rest assured, our best guards are scouring the area for him even as we speak. I'll have them search at once for the man you described, too, in case Jax and

Simeon have yet to find him." He nods to one of the guards at the back of the room, who hurries away.

Glancing from Hadrien to the queen, I search carefully for words. I can't just sit by while Karthia crumbles without its leader. "I should join the search right away, too. I wasn't . . ." I pause, as it pains me to admit it. "I wasn't well enough before, but I'm up to it now. Where would I be most useful, Majesty?"

"Actually, I need your help with another equally important matter." Hadrien squeezes my hand, drawing my attention back to him. "It's the reason I called you here, and while I regret that Jax and Simeon haven't arrived yet, we really can't delay any further."

My palm is slick with sweat in the prince's firm grip. I try to pull away, but he holds fast, refocusing his intense gaze on me. To my surprise—and everyone else's, judging by Valoria's soft intake of breath—Hadrien kneels before me.

"Odessa of Grenwyr, I ask you now: Will you be my Serpent?"

I barely hear him over the sound of my racing heart. "Your . . . what?"

With his free hand, Hadrien pulls something from his pocket. A tiny gold pin shaped like a sword with two hissing snakes wrapped around the blade, facing each other. "Every king declares a Serpent. A special soldier who answers only to him, who carries out matters of the greatest importance for the Crown—even if following orders sometimes means doing things outside the law. King Wylding's Serpent was Duke Nevet, but he went missing with my mother and the rest." He bows his head, dropping his gaze to the floor in his grief and taking a breath before raising his shining eyes to mine. "In the absence of Duke Nevet, I'm asking if you'll take on the role. It's the highest honor I can bestow, but I'll understand completely if, after all you've endured lately, you aren't up to the task."

"My husband would approve," the queen adds softly. "Young as you are, you're the best at what you do. You've been his favorite mage for some time, Sparrow."

With Valoria looking expectantly at me and the queen's mask turned my way, I can hardly refuse. I wish I could peek over my shoulder for a glance at Meredy, but she's probably wearing her usual look of indifference.

My mouth is so dry, all I can do is nod. As Hadrien fixes the gold pin to my tunic, just beneath my two necromancer's pins, my stomach churns. I haven't done anything to earn this honor, and no matter what the queen says, I doubt King Wylding would approve. Given how I've failed to protect him and Karthia, he'd probably rip the pin off my chest for pretending to be a hero I'm not.

I look down at the pin and remind myself it's only temporary. Just until we find Duke Nevet. And we *will*.

"Now that that's settled," Hadrien says, stepping back to admire my decorated tunic, "I need your help, as I mentioned. The last time I saw His Majesty, very early this morning, we had received a raven from a baroness in Elsinor Province." He pulls a piece of parchment from the pocket of his gold-trimmed doublet and hands it to me. "There are reports of Shade attacks in the area, and for some reason, the monsters aren't retreating to the Deadlands as they usually would. With all my men currently committed to the search for King Wylding, I need *you* to go to Elsinor and put the Shade to rest before any more Karthians lose their lives."

"What?" As the word leaves my lips, Hadrien frowns. I cross my arms. "Forgive me. But by my count, there are more necromancers in Elsinor than there are in Grenwyr. Why can't they handle their own Shades? I'm needed here. I have to help Jax and Simeon search for the Shade-baiter and His Majesty."

Even as I speak, my thoughts circle around the idea of a Shade coming out of the Deadlands to attack a province. They hate daylight. They wouldn't have a reason, except . . . Vane once again creeps into my thoughts.

"If the Shade-baiter I mentioned can control the monsters, he might be responsible for the attacks in Elsinor, too," I say slowly, thinking aloud. "Whether he's the one who took the king or not, he has to be stopped."

"I agree," Hadrien says at last. "And the guards *will* find him, eventually. But helping the people of Elsinor must come first, as they have no more necromancers of their own. They need someone with training to slay the monsters before they get any stronger."

"No more necromancers?" I blurt. "What are you—?"

"They're dead." The queen's chill voice raises gooseflesh on my arms. Valoria shivers beside me. "All eight of Elsinor's necromancers were slain by a Shade. I wish we'd known sooner—not that we've been in much position to help—but it seems to have happened as quickly as the raven flies."

"And so, my Serpent, please say you'll do this for me." Hadrien's voice simmers with barely controlled sorrow. "Don't make me beg. My Eldest Grandfather is missing. I can't worry about the people of Elsinor dying on my watch, too, and they have no one to deal with Shades now." He lowers his voice, leaning toward me. "I'll feel so much better if you see to it. *Please*, Sparrow. You're the best, as His Majesty knew, and you're the only one I trust."

He draws back, his eyes glistening, and takes both my hands in his.

I open my mouth. But as I look from Valoria's pale face to the queen clutching the arm of the throne for support, the words get stuck in my throat. Something doesn't feel right. King Wylding never once ordered me away from his side no matter what was happening in the other provinces, and leaving Grenwyr City with him missing seems wrong. Maybe Elsinor does need me, but Grenwyr needs me more than ever, too.

Her Majesty echoes my thoughts. "Find my husband for me, Sparrow," the queen pleads, sinking onto the throne. "I trust you more than any of the guards. I know you can do it. Then, of course, head to Elsinor afterward, by all means."

I bow to her. "Yes, Majesty." After all, with King Wylding gone, the queen is the one in charge, not Hadrien.

"Overruled," Hadrien says, frowning apologetically. "Sparrow, please pack your things and head to Elsinor at once, to Abethell Castle. Since Baroness Abethell is the one who wrote to us, she should direct you to where you're needed most. And hurry." His expression is grim. "When word of the king's disappearance gets out, we'll have panic in the streets, and it could cost you precious hours."

"Didn't you hear what Eldest Grandmother said?" Valoria demands.

Hadrien nods, still frowning. "I did. And as acting regent, I'm overruling Eldest Grandmother's wishes, with all due respect."

He runs a hand through his blond hair. "I'm sorry. I'm just doing what I think is right." Looking pleadingly at me, he adds, "Tell me, Sparrow: If it came to saving him or his people, which would His Majesty have you choose?"

I don't need to think about the answer. "His people." He's always sacrificing himself for us, after all.

"Then you understand why I think he'd want you to go to Elsinor."

I nod, resigned to the task, but something is still bothering me. I ask in a whisper, "Why did Her Majesty appoint you regent, Highness? Is she unwell?"

"It's the law," Valoria says quickly, like she's just remembered. "The laws of inheritance haven't changed in Karthia in well over two hundred years. Like everything else. And the law in place before his reign said that if the current ruler could no longer sit on the throne for any reason, the crown would pass to the next living heir who'd come of age." She blinks at Hadrien, her voice getting softer as she continues. "And since our father is dead, and Mother's Dead, and Hadrien's just turned eighteen . . ."

"The burden of the crown will pass to me if King Wylding isn't found in the next thirty days," Hadrien finishes.

He seems to have aged several years since I saw him last, at his birthday. If he had been born just a few weeks later, the queen would be the one giving orders now.

But it seems I have no choice other than to follow Hadrien's command.

"I spoke too rashly before. Forgive me. I'll leave it to you to decide," he adds softly, as though reading my thoughts. "I trust Jax and Simeon will do a fine job leading the search for the king, but if you really think you should stay, I'll respect your choice."

"I'm glad to hear you aren't letting all that power go to your head, big brother." Valoria chews on her lower lip as she studies the prince. "If it ever does, I'll have to put you in your place, understand?" Her tone is light, but her eyes are somber.

Hadrien gives her a deep bow. "You have my word, Your Highness." He straightens, grinning. "And should I fail, I shall throw myself upon the mercy of your blade."

Shaking my head at their banter, I think of King Wylding's shrouded figure lying prone in the grass, waiting for me to fetch his spirit. I think of the peace of the Deadlands he never gets for long, all for the sake of his people.

"I'll go to Elsinor," I announce. "He'd want that, as you said." Twisting the newest pin on my tunic, I add, "I'll need a partner for the journey. A fellow necromancer, in case I need to enter the Deadlands while I'm away."

"Name your choice," Hadrien says at once, his face relaxing somewhat now that I've agreed to his plan. "And Sparrow—" A note of longing breaks his voice, surprising me. "Choose wisely. It would *kill* me if anything happened to you."

I don't have to think long. "Master Cymbre."

Now, more than ever, I need her guidance.

"Miss Crowther," Hadrien calls. "You asked His Majesty about security jobs at the palace yesterday. You're still in need of work?"

Meredy nods, a hint of pink appearing beneath her freckles. She marches to the bottom of the steps to face Hadrien, Lysander prowling alongside her.

I look a question at her, but she ignores me. I thought she'd be returning to Lorness any day now, once she'd convinced herself I wasn't going to touch another drop of potion.

"I'll pay you and your beast twice what you'd make as guards if you'll accompany my Serpent to Elsinor," Hadrien says evenly. "Will you protect her as she defends my people?"

"I don't need any—" I protest, but Meredy interrupts.

"Accepted." She props a hand on her hip, taking a long look at Hadrien. "But—forgive me, Highness—weren't you one of the last people to see King Wylding before he went missing? I saw you two wandering the corridors this morning. You waved to me, remember?"

"Of course." Hadrien's expression doesn't change. "But His Majesty and I parted ways just moments after we passed you. King Wylding was hungry, as the Dead often are, and headed for the kitchen to get a honey cake. I've no idea what happened after that . . . though I'm sure you weren't trying to accuse me of anything." He smiles a little stiffly as Meredy gazes placidly back at him, her feelings and thoughts well-hidden.

"I was simply suggesting that there may be some detail in your memory that's been overlooked. Something that could help explain who took the king," she says coolly. "A shadowy figure down the hall, an odd sound . . ."

"Rest assured, I take no offense," Hadrien says swiftly. "We're *all* on edge in the king's absence." He leans forward, the steps allowing him to tower over Meredy when there normally wouldn't be much difference in height. "Still, I'm sure you'll take excellent care of my Serpent. I have every confidence."

The doors to the throne room rattle.

"For Vaia's sake, let us in!" Simeon yells.

Hadrien nods, and the guards pull up the bar, allowing Jax and Simeon to rush inside. Before the guards slam the doors again, I get a brief glimpse of the Dead still gathered in the hall, likely awaiting an audience with Her Majesty.

"Any luck with the Shade-baiter?" Hadrien asks as Jax and Simeon approach. "Sparrow has just finished filling us in."

"Afraid not." Jax's eyes find me as he answers, and I'm struck by how much I've missed his gruff voice and roguish grin. I run down the steps without another thought and crash into his open arms. Suddenly thinking of Valoria's drawing of him, I break away quickly.

"What's this?" He touches the new pin on my chest and frowns.

"Ooh." Simeon grins as he realizes what the pin means. "Can you really be a Sparrow *and* a Serpent? What if you get the urge to eat yourself for breakfast?"

Hadrien clears his throat, and Simeon falls silent as the prince begins to repeat much of what he's just told me.

The news from Elsinor quickly wipes the smile from Simeon's face, and I wonder how much longer he'll be able to keep making jokes when so much is going wrong. Always, I hope. Everyone in the palace could use a bit of laughter.

Meredy blinks at me with an unreadable expression, then strides to the doors. Now that my head is clear and I can think without the potion's influence, I still don't want her in the palace, or anywhere else I happen to be. What if she accidentally says or does something that reminds me of Evander, something that sends me right back to the calming potion?

Yet I'm stuck with her. Hadrien is relying on me, and I won't let the people of Elsinor down, or King Wylding by association. The last thing I need are more dead Karthians on my conscience.

And the longer I stand here, more people might be dying.

"Look after Valoria for me," I whisper to my friends. I know she'd protest if she could hear me. They nod solemnly, and Jax looks thoughtfully at the princess just a beat longer than normal.

"I'll be back as soon as I've killed the Shades in Elsinor. And you," I add to Simeon, "be good to Jax while I'm away. Don't tease him too much. I don't want to return from one massacre to find another."

I ruffle Simeon's hair as he makes a face, and try to ignore the twinge in my chest as his eyes search mine like he's looking for any lingering traces of potion addiction. The sadness in his gaze when he looks at me—which the blue tonic never let me see—is just one more reason I'll fight to never touch another drop.

"Be safe." Jax presses his lips into a hard line, like he's holding back so much more.

"You too," I mutter, shoving my hands in my pockets. He and Simeon are the ones who'll need to be on their guard, staying this close to the deaths and disappearances. I just hope Valoria and Danial will stand by them while I can't.

I take a last look at my friends before following Meredy and Lysander back through the crowd of masked figures, knowing at least a few of the Dead will be relieved or even glad to see me gone.

XXI

There's an old saying that sparrows always find their way home. I hope my tattoos or my name make me truly one of them, as this is the farthest I've ever been from everything I know. The moment our wagon wheels touch the base of the mountain pass marking the border of Grenwyr and Elsinor Provinces, my stomach does a flip.

Maybe because the land here is unfamiliar and wild, the ancient pines taller and fuller than those in Grenwyr, the air a touch colder, the few houses we pass made of drab wood or dark gray stone, no jewel-bright roofs or potted citrus gardens to speak of. Or maybe it's because no matter where I go, I'm afraid I have no chance of living up to the new serpent pin on my tunic.

It's Evander who should be taking jobs like this, not me. He'd have been thrilled to climb these wild, lonely mountains, would've gazed around with wide eyes and explored off the trail with an

236

adventurer's heart, much like Lysander does as he follows our wagon east and upward.

I drink in every new sight for Evander, aided by the fading light of a blood-red sky seeping through the opening in the canvas-covered wagon. I know he'd be proud I've come this far.

I clutch the pin tighter, closing my fist over it, and suck in a breath as the gold needle pricks my palm. I hold on through the pain, hoping somehow the little pin will infect me with the courage and strength of one worthy of wearing it—as opposed to the addict and poor friend I've been since Evander died.

"Odessa." Meredy waves a hand near my face, drawing my gaze. "You look ill. What's on your mind?"

I blink at her in the dimness of the wagon hold for a moment before turning away, toward the front of the wagon where Master Cymbre commands a team of sleek brown horses.

Cymbre had jumped at the chance to leave Grenwyr when we knocked on her cottage door, even as tears were drying on her weathered face. She couldn't protect her prodigy, Evander, and she couldn't protect her king. Escaping to Elsinor on a dangerous and potentially deadly mission probably seemed like the only option left to her, the way the potion seemed like my only choice to distance myself from my nightmares.

I see so much of myself in her, she might as well be my mother.

Meredy shifts her weight, pulling me back to the present again as the wagon boards creak beneath her. "Thinking about that rogue necromancer again? Vane?" she guesses.

It's a safe bet. He's all I can think of since we left the throne room many hours ago. "Have you ever heard of anyone like him?"

"Maybe," she answers thoughtfully. "I'm willing to bet he has a different Sight than we do. Which would mean he has a different power."

I blink at her. "But Vaia only has five faces. So there are only five Sights, five powers—"

"That we know of," Meredy interrupts. "But when I was in Lorness, in one of the smallest villages buying supplies, I heard a rumor about a wild man with *amber* eyes, who could change his shape at will. It was terribly painful for him, they said, and his cries in the forest near their village were often mistaken for a Shade's." She pauses, fixing me with a thoughtful look. "I don't know if it was true. I stayed near that village for weeks, camping and foraging with Lysander, and I never heard any sort of screaming. Still, there are many things we can't explain, aren't there?"

Her face falls into shadow as she bows her head, searching through her bag for something. "Things that perhaps no one can."

I rub my gooseflesh-covered arms, hoping she's wrong about that last part.

A loud, familiar crack rings in my ears as Meredy bites into a handful of coffee beans. "You're on to something with these," she mutters thickly. "Kasmira could make a fortune selling them at harbors all over Karthia. I'll have to tell her."

With the heat of annoyance prickling the back of my neck, I snatch the bag of coffee beans from her grasp. "She already does."

I toss a handful in my mouth, settling the bag on my lap. Casually, like we've been friends forever, Meredy leans over and reaches into the bag.

She gasps as my fingers close over her wrist and I say through gritted teeth, "Quit taking things that aren't yours."

"I bought these!" Meredy snarls, tugging herself free with none of her usual composure.

"Well, you can't buy Kasmira's friendship. Or Valoria's. Or *mine*." I throw the bag back at Meredy, who doesn't even attempt to catch it. She's too busy trying to keep a scowl off her face.

I close my eyes and lean against the wagon boards, thinking of the carefully folded drawing I found in my cloak pocket as we pulled away from Grenwyr. Three ink girls smiled up at me from the parchment, three perfect likenesses of me, Valoria, and Meredy. I don't know what the princess was thinking when she drew it, but had it been a gift from anyone else, I'd have fed it to Lysander instead of shoving it back in my pocket.

"Do you know why I agreed to this job?" Meredy says suddenly, cutting into my thoughts once again. "I certainly don't need the money." She waits until I've cracked open one eye, giving her a reluctant stare, before continuing, "Lysander likes you."

I look past her, through the canvas opening, to see the grizzly lumbering in the wagon's wake. "Good. I like him, too."

Meredy gives me an expectant gaze, like I'm supposed to say something more. She tilts her head in the silence. "You really don't understand the depth of the bond between beast and master, do you?"

I shrug.

She leans toward me, and I instinctively draw back. "Lysander doesn't like most people," she murmurs. "But when he looks at you, he practically *glows*. I suppose you'd have to see it to really picture it, but the feelings he shows when you're around are the brightest shades of yellow and pink that tint the air around his fur."

I smile, trying to imagine it. "What about when he's unhappy?"

"If he's sad, I see a lot of dark blues and greens. And if he's angry, reds. Or if he notices someone he really doesn't like, I see black all around him, like a stain or a silhouette of a second bear blurring with his . . ." Meredy pauses, frowning. "Like today in the throne room, for instance."

I sit taller, gooseflesh rising on my arms. "Someone there was upsetting him?"

She nods. "Could've been anyone, for any reason. It happens often, and it would be impossible to know who unless we tested each person alone with him. I've just seen that he likes you. And he thinks Valoria is a bear cub."

I can't help it. I smile. Meredy nudges my side a moment later, and I glance back. She's put the bag of coffee beans on the floor between us. When we both reach in at the same time, the back of my hand brushes hers, and a shiver runs up my arm. It startles my heart into beating double.

Her fingers curl around mine for a moment, warm and steady, before she jerks her hand away as though she's been stung. Shaking her head as though to clear it, she seems to recover herself.

"Here." Meredy's lips twitch as she holds up a coffee bean. "Catch!"

I open my mouth, but the bean hits me on the nose and skitters out of sight. Meredy tries to disguise her derisive snort as a cough, making me hot all over. "Oh, like you can do better," I growl, reaching into the bag.

I throw three beans at once, and the last one lands on her out-stretched tongue.

"You've probably been practicing," I mutter, trying not to look impressed. "Let me try again."

"Certainly." Meredy's eyes gleam. "I'll go easy on you. One at a time."

The first one hits my forehead. The second lands in my hair. The third sails over my head. Meredy's tosses are terrible. After the fifth attempt, she stops.

"Try again! The wagon keeps hitting bumps." I frown. "It's throwing off your aim."

"The wagon was rattling when I caught mine, too," Meredy says evenly, with no hint of a smirk in her voice or otherwise. "Some things are out of your control. Like the path of the wagon and who's riding in it with you. Find a way to accept it, or give up."

"You're one to talk." I lean toward her, wincing as the wagon wheels bang against a loose rock. "You act like *you* have everything under control, but you don't, and it drives you mad."

She purses her lips, then folds her hands neatly in her lap. Every small action she makes seems so carefully planned.

"*You* drive me mad," she says quietly. Blushing, she adds quickly, louder, "At least I'm in control of my own actions. At least I'm not so caught up in my own problems that I fail to see what's going on around me."

"There's nothing wrong with my eyes, thanks. Now toss me another coffee bean."

Meredy tilts her head, frowning as she grabs the coffee bag. "Are you always this stubborn?"

"Since the day I was born." I cross my arms. "So get used to it or go back to Grenwyr."

Her eyes shining like hard stones, she says, "Evander must've really loved you to put up with this every day."

My fist seems to have a mind of its own as it crashes into the wagon siding near Meredy's perfect face. She's breathing hard, her eyes closed in the aftermath of the blow. Maybe she thought I was actually aiming to hit her.

"Don't talk to me about him," I growl.

"Is everything all right back there?" Master Cymbre shouts.

"Fine!" Meredy and I answer at the same time, gazing steadily at one another. Our breathing is hot and rapid and almost stifling in the confines of the wagon's hold. The dampness of her breath collects on my lips, and I impatiently lick it away.

Glaring at her, I wish she'd take a swing back at me. "Look, we might as well be honest. For some strange, twisted reason, you don't like me because I loved your brother."

"That's not it." Meredy scowls back, but her hands remain folded in her lap. "What I don't like is that you're so selfish you don't notice anyone's pain but your own." When she speaks again, her voice is softer, more controlled. "But because it's what my brother would've wanted, I'm going to stay with you and guard you until the danger has passed. Then we can go our separate ways."

"What are you talking about, anyone's pain but mine?"

"Valoria really likes your necromancer friend Jax, but she's afraid you do, too. So she doesn't say anything to him, because she's more afraid of making you unhappy than she is of forever being unhappy herself." Meredy shakes her head, and a sudden wave of shame pummels me. "Or Master Cymbre. I bet you have no idea she's been drinking from a flask whenever she thinks no one's looking. You two aren't that different. And you certainly haven't bothered to notice—" She pauses, biting her lip. "Forget it. Really. I'm raving."

I take a long look at her. Unshed tears cling to the corners of her eyes like dewdrops. If I'm barely keeping a grip on my sanity, it's a wonder she has any wits left about her after losing both Evander and Firiel. I should probably ask how she's holding up.

Before I can get the words out, her long, cold fingers touch my shoulder. "There's something else I need to tell you. It's about Prince Hadrien. Something he said in the throne room has been bothering me." I still don't say anything, but she's got my attention. "He said King Wylding went to the kitchen for a honey cake just after we passed each other. But I was in the kitchen for well over an hour, eating and making breakfast for Lysander, and the king never arrived. There was some sort of commotion in the hall, though."

"You didn't go see what it was?"

Meredy frowns. "I had my hands in a bowl of fish guts, and the cooks were busy preparing breakfast for the rest of the palace, but I definitely heard shouting."

"Maybe a server burned themselves while carrying a hot dish." I shrug.

"Or the prince was lying for some reason." Meredy's eyes search my face, so I drop my gaze. "You don't believe me, do you?"

"Maybe. I don't know what to think anymore." I rub my temples.

I only knew Meredy for one brief year before she disappeared to Lorness and came back as someone else entirely. But I've known Hadrien since I started my necromancer training seven years ago. Seven years of attending parties together and raising his relatives. In all that time, he's never given me a reason to doubt him.

"Even if you're right," I say slowly, "and Hadrien was lying, that doesn't mean he would ever hurt King Wylding any more than he'd hurt me." Remembering how close those two have always been, I add, "Maybe Hadrien was covering something up for the king. Maybe His Majesty was on some secret errand, and he was attacked on his way to . . . wherever."

Meredy arches her brows. They're dark brown, not red like her long hair. I wonder why I hadn't noticed before, and why in Vaia's name I'm noticing now.

"Seeing as you know more about the Wyldings than I do," she murmurs, "I'll leave the worrying to you."

Taking a deep breath, I try to silence the new, nagging unease in the pit of my stomach. Whether or not Meredy's right about Hadrien, she's raised a frightening point: Given the events of the last few weeks, I can't trust anyone anymore. I lean back against the wagon, the night falling softly around me, complete with chirping crickets and a steady autumn breeze.

Meredy sighs. "I bet we couldn't go a full day without arguing."

After the coffee bean trick, the idea of beating her at something sounds rather appealing. "I'll take that bet. If we argue, you win. And if we don't, *I* win. But what should we declare as the prize?"

She taps the scar on her cheek as she thinks. "If I win, you have to promise never to insult me again. And if you win . . ."

"I get enough coffee to last a lifetime. Paid for by you."

Meredy's eyes flash with excitement. "Deal."

We shake on it. Her hesitant smile reminds me of Evander, but for the first time in a long while, remembering him doesn't make me feel like crumbling.

"Evander didn't like coffee. He said it tasted like burnt pan scrapings."

Meredy arches her brows. Slowly, a grin appears. "He didn't like hills either, after the time he ran down that big one at Grenwyr Pond—"

"The one with the sign at the top that said 'Danger. Don't run'?" I grin back.

"The very same!" Her laugh is like the rustle of bird's wings, soft and sweet, and I realize this is the first time I've heard it. "He broke his arm, and Mother told him it was a good lesson in reading before running."

"How about the time he broke his ankle playing some ball game with Simeon? I never understood how that happened, but you were there, weren't you?"

I wish I'd known sooner how easy it would be, talking about Evander together. Dredging up these memories doesn't sting nearly as much when sharing them with someone who knows exactly what I've been through. Someone who lost their love, too. Jax and I spent most of our time in bed trying *not* to mention Evander, but it feels right here, now, with Meredy.

"Oh! His ankle? That's a funny story." Meredy's voice draws me back to her. "The healers mended the break, but he woke up thinking he was still in the field with the ball, and tried to—"

Meredy's words are cut off when a shriek splits the night air. Sharp. Unrestrained. *Eager*.

Meredy and I exchange a glance. I'd recognize that sound anywhere.

A Shade is on the hunt, and we're the prey.

XXII

As the wagon comes to a sudden halt, I reach for my sword and strain my ears to detect what's happening over the horses' frightened whinnies and Lysander's hair-raising roar. Master Cymbre yells something I can't quite make out. Her cry is abruptly cut short, and a cold weight settles in my chest as I imagine why.

Something crashes into the wagon hold, making Meredy and me jump as the wagon rocks violently from side to side.

I dive toward the crate where we've carefully nestled several glass vials of liquid fire potion for the journey to Elsinor. Without those precious vials, we can't kill any Shades. The crate's lid is ajar, and I hurry to push it back into place. Meredy puts a hand on the crate's side to steady it as the wagon continues to shake.

Another shriek nearly deafens me. The monster must be right on top of us.

I draw my sword and stagger to my feet as a long, bony arm shreds the wagon's canvas covering and smashes the crate of fire potions. The wood splinters under Meredy's hands, and she cries out. The vials scatter everywhere, some shattering, others rolling across the floor. The ones that break erupt into flames, and just like that, the wagon is done for.

I drop my blade, trying to save as many of the potions as I can before the blaze in the wagon forces me out. The Shade knocks the few vials I managed to gather out of my hands; its sharp, bare-boned fingers tangle in my hair as the vials hit the ground and burst into flames. Quick as lightning, the Shade pulls me toward the huge hole it's created in the canvas. I dig my nails into its flesh, hoping it'll drop me. Instead, its grip tightens, its free hand closing around my neck.

I can't breathe. My body shakes, and I start to panic as my vision blurs.

"Let her go!" Meredy shrieks, jabbing my sword into the fleshi-est part of the monster's rotting arm, looking pale but not the least bit afraid despite the flames licking at her feet and the shimmering curtain of smoke filling the wagon.

The Shade's howl deafens me as it drops me. I push myself upright in time to see Lysander attack the monster from behind in a fury of claws and teeth.

Quickly, I scan the mess of glass and tar-like potion burning on the wagon floor. All the vials are shattered, but we can still stop this Shade. I've pushed one into a bonfire before, which means I can do it again—this time, with the aid of bigger, rapidly spreading flames.

"Cymbre?" I shout over the monster's screeches and Lysander's roars. "Cymbre!"

There's no answer. She must be hurt somewhere, at the mercy of the monster and the blaze. Before I deal with the Shade, I need to get her away from the fire.

Meredy and I jump from the burning wagon together, our boots crunching as they touch down on the rocky mountainside. She offers me my sword, and I give her a nod of thanks.

"You have to run. Find a cave or somewhere you can hide, just in case . . ." My words are lost to a fit of coughing.

"What about you?" she demands, eyes narrowed against the smoke. "It's my job to protect you, remember?"

"I have to find Cymbre. Then I'm going to stop this Shade."

"Odessa—"

A burst of noise from the wagon cuts her off as the last of its canvas top collapses, sending up a shower of sparks that fleck our hair and arms, sharp as bee stings.

"There's no time to argue," I growl, edging farther away from the blaze. "Just go!"

Meredy calls out to Lysander—who's still in battle from the sound of things—as I dash to the front of the wagon, sweat already beading on my brow. The horses have fled, their tethers torn and trampled. Master Cymbre slumps across the driver's seat, firelight dancing along a deep gash down the side of her face.

At least her pulse is still strong.

"Master Cymbre." I gently shake her shoulders. "You have to hide. Our potions are gone, and I've got one nasty Shade to shove into a fire." I shake her harder, and when that does nothing, I realize

I'm going to have to carry her out of harm's way. I hang my sword at my side and slide my hands carefully under Cymbre's back.

With any luck, Lysander will force the Shade into the flames while I'm struggling to lift a woman who weighs more than me.

But the Shade must have tired of the bear—or worse. The monster plucks me off the ground, forcing me to drop Master Cymbre. An arm, skeletal but strong, snaps off my belt as I reach for my sword, then lifts me toward its mouth as it unhinges its jaw. Even with my heart sticking in my throat, I manage to kick the Shade in the spot where its eye should be, hoping to make it stagger backward toward the fire. But all my kick does is make the monster gnash its teeth in what appears to be excitement.

Icy breath blasts against my legs.

The last time I came face to face with a Shade, I remember my blood spilling out like buckets of paint. I remember that, after the initial gut-wrenching agony, I didn't feel much at all. Only this time, there's no Danial to heal my wounds.

The first scream tears from my throat as the Shade sinks its teeth into my leg.

And drops me with a piercing wail.

I land facedown, spitting out a mouthful of dirt and fallen leaves. I guess I taste worse than I look. As I scramble away from the monster, dragging myself toward my blade along the rocky ground by my elbows, a bright-orange glow washes over me.

The Shade claws at itself, tugging on a burning arrow lodged in the softest part of its chest. But it's too late. It's already engulfed in flames.

Several paces back from the wagon, looking immensely pleased with herself, is Meredy. She drops her bow at Lysander's feet and rushes to my side. "You're lucky I had Lysander carrying my things instead of storing them in the wagon. Are you hurt?"

"No. Not bad, anyway." But my head spins when I touch my aching lower leg, and my hand comes away slick with blood. "Check on Master Cymbre."

Frowning, Meredy hurries to where Cymbre fell. I catch my breath, watching the Shade melt into ash.

There's something odd about the way it appeared on this particular mountain, when there are dozens of trails like this one leading into Elsinor, and the only people who know our chosen path to Abethell Castle are back in Grenwyr.

It's as if the monster knew exactly where we'd be tonight.

I peer into the shadowy forest surrounding the wagon trail. But other than the lonely call of an owl, I don't see or hear anything. There's no sign of Vane or anyone else.

The Shade's skeletal body hisses and pops. Or maybe that's the wagon, blazing with all our spare clothes and rations inside. Rubbing the pin on my tunic, I stare into the fire and wonder if I did my duty as Serpent when I didn't make the kill. I didn't even help.

"Where'd you learn to shoot like that?" I ask as Meredy drags an unconscious Master Cymbre off the trail. I try to stand, but the stabbing pain in my leg forces me to stay down, and I crawl toward the woods until I can no longer feel waves of heat on my back. Lysander joins me, grumbling deep in his chest.

"In Lorness," Meredy says at last. She props Master Cymbre against a tree, then rests with her hands on her knees to catch her breath. "I learned from my teacher, so I could survive in the wild if Lysander was ever too sick or hurt to hunt for us."

"I'm surprised, is all."

Meredy's smile is bright like the moon. "The world's full of surprises. You'd know that if you just looked around once in a while. Like Valoria. Did you even know she's an artist? She drew me the best picture I've ever seen."

Somehow, she still manages to irritate me moments after saving my life. "I'm aware of her talents, seeing as she was my friend first. What's the picture of?"

"We need to get out of these woods soon," she mutters, apparently ignoring my question.

She's right, though. The blaze is spreading, catching on dry leaves and twigs and blackening the ground between us and the charred wagon.

There's no sign that a Shade was ever here, thanks to this Serpent and her questionably loyal protector.

"Can you walk if you lean on me?" Meredy extends a hand and I take hold of her. "Have you ever considered that . . . maybe raising the dead isn't worth the risk?" she asks quietly. "That it causes more suffering than healing?"

All the time, I want to say. Ever since Evander died. Since she asked me to raise Firiel.

Before I can reply, I hear a faint voice drifting on the night wind. "Anyone out there?" It sounds like a man's deep tone.

I put a finger to my lips, looking around, then point to a lone torch bobbing up the mountainside from slightly east of the direction we were headed in before the attack.

Lysander growls as the torch bobs nearer. Meredy puts a hand between his furry shoulders, calming him within a few heartbeats. We wait in silence until the light of the wagon fire lifts the cloak of darkness from the haggard face of a man some years our senior. He has a bow strapped to his back and an axe hanging from his belt, but his eyes are kind.

Meredy and I exchange a glance, and she nods. If we're wrong, I can take him, even with my leg a bloody mess.

"Over here!" I shout, revealing our location.

Meredy waves a hand, echoing my call.

It takes only a moment for him to navigate around the spreading fire. When he sees the condition we're in, he says, "Don't worry. I'm here to help," and hurries to check Master Cymbre's pulse. He passes me his torch so he can lift Cymbre into his arms.

"Is the bear friendly?" he grunts, eyeing Lysander. Not even Meredy's calming influence keeps Lysander completely quiet with a stranger so close, and I think back to what she said about him not liking most people.

Meredy gives a terse smile. "Mostly."

"I saw the fire from my cabin," he adds. "Not many folk pass through these parts, so I thought I'd better come check . . ." His voice dies away as he gets a look at the gold pin on my chest. He offers me a crude bow. "Can't remember the last time there was a necromancer in my woods." Shifting his gaze to Meredy, he adds,

"Or a beast master. Now let's get your friend here to a healer. Abethell Castle's the place you'll want, just down that hill. And there's plenty of time to tell me what happened here along the way."

We hurry past the fire into the black night while I describe the Shade attack as quickly as I can. It's too fresh in my mind for me to want to dwell on it for longer than is necessary.

The hunter merely grunts in response.

"What?" Meredy snaps.

"There were footprints in the woods near here. All from the same set of boots, by the look of it," the man says thoughtfully. "I figured whoever attacked you fled the scene after they set your wagon ablaze. Thought I might have to use this." He taps his axe hilt.

Meredy's eyes meet mine, searching.

It's Vane. It has to be. Somehow, he knew our path, and he brought his pet Shade with him to stop us.

XXIII

Abethell Castle is really more of a squat fortress built into the stone of the mountain on which it rests, overlooking a valley far below.

By night, it appeared crouched like a wary beast guarding against our approach. I shivered as we were ushered through a dark side entrance. But by morning, waking in a guest chamber filled with sunlight, it doesn't seem much different from the palace in Grenwyr. And it has a better view.

Throwing off the blankets, I use the washbasin on the far wall to scrub off the blood, dirt, and soot I was too tired to deal with last night. Baroness Abethell was determined to attend to our every comfort, summoning a healer who deserved to be paid his weight in gold for making my leg good as new, and offering us three rooms on the top floor of the castle.

I wish I had fresh clothes to change into, but since everything from the wagon burned, I throw on last night's mud-and-blood-stained uniform of black trousers and a tunic. At least I still have my cloak with Valoria's drawing tucked in the pocket. I take a quick look at it before heading into the hallway, my stomach rumbling. The baroness seems like the type to put out a lavish breakfast spread, and I plan to eat my fill before we journey deeper into Elsinor.

I stride down the corridor, turn a corner, and walk right into Meredy, her forehead banging against mine. We break apart, rubbing our heads, and I hastily look away to hide a grin.

Meredy clears her throat. "You should've asked me for a change of clothes. I brought a few extras. They're not much, but at least they're clean."

"Oh." I take in her simple tunic, the color of Lysander's fur, and her deerskin trousers, which are a damn sight nicer than last night's battle clothes. She's lucky she has a bear to carry all her things like a giant pack mule. I wonder if they managed to house him in the stables and how they kept him from eating the horses.

"You saved my life," I blurt. "That's twice now, if you count keeping me prisoner."

"Just doing my job." Meredy rubs the scar on her cheek, like she does when she's nervous or lost in thought.

Suppressing a grin, I mutter, "Thanks, my humble savior."

I start down the stairs toward the noise of what I hope is a dining room, pausing for Meredy to follow.

"It's not your fault you couldn't stop the Shade, you know." She reaches my side and keeps pace with me, stealing a sideways glance when she thinks I'm not looking. "It kept going after you," she adds. "You had no hope of killing it. It was like you were its only target, and—"

I stop cold in the middle of a glittering tiled hallway. "The key to killing them is taking them by surprise." I finish the thought for her.

Meredy nods, then waves at someone over my shoulder.

"Good morning!" a handsome woman in a fine gown calls, sweeping toward us. The baroness. "And thank you again, on behalf of all of Elsinor, for slaying our monster." Her weary gray eyes meet mine. "I've had the cooks pack you plenty of breakfast, so I hope you're hungry." She tosses her long, dark braid over her shoulder and checks the fastenings of her cloak. "Everything's waiting in the carriage. This way, please!"

Meredy takes a step forward, but I hold her back with a hand on her arm.

"Where are we going?" I ask, careful to keep my voice pleasant.

Baroness Abethell flashes a dazzling smile. "On a tour of our valley, my dear Master Odessa." Her smile dims slightly as she adds, "Master Cymbre declined to join us. She may need a second visit from the healer, but for now, she's enjoying breakfast in her chamber."

"I'm afraid we don't have time for a tour," I say slowly, forcing myself to smile back. "I don't mean to sound ungrateful. You've been more than generous. But we're here to find the Shade that's been attacking Elsinor, as you know."

And after that, we're needed back in Grenwyr City, where Jax and Simeon are probably overwhelmed with restless Dead in the wake of news about the king's disappearance spreading. At least it doesn't seem like anyone here has heard what befell our leader, and if they haven't, I don't want to be the one to share it.

"I insist," the baroness says a moment later, her voice still cheerful. "You deserve to see what your brave actions have protected, master necromancer."

I glance down at the pin on my tunic. "Killing that Shade had nothing to do with bravery, and everything to do with survival, Lady Abethell." With a glance at Meredy, I add, "It was my guard who killed the monster, not me, so you should be thanking her."

"And a tour sounds like a lovely way to do that," Meredy says, covering the awkward moment.

The worried look she gives me as we follow the baroness to the carriage house is the only way I know she doesn't like this waste of time any more than I do.

Two hours and four sticky buns later, though, I have to admit, the tour around the valley isn't so bad. There are pastures where sheep wander aimlessly like little white clouds, a small lake, and a wide green field where four weather mages stand side by side, dressed in slick, shimmering robes that remind me of fish scales as they cast a rainbow of light on their surroundings. Moving as one, the mages draw water from a passing cloud and shower the leafy green crops around them. It's an incredible sight.

Meredy points out a baby calf, a tangle of ripe blackberry bushes, and a distant figure taking a naked dip in a pond, no doubt thinking himself unnoticed. We laugh as we spot a miniature horse chasing a donkey around a paddock, and it's clear the tension has eased between us.

It feels strange to be laughing at all with King Wylding presumably still missing, but it's not like we can leave the castle until Master Cymbre sees the healer again. Still, I fidget on the hard carriage seat as I think of how quickly a Shade could devastate this sleepy valley.

As quickly as the raven flies, as Her Majesty would say.

"We've been busy preparing for the big harvest," the baroness says pleasantly from the opposite seat. "With our high number of gray-eyed citizens, Elsinor trains more weather mages than any other province."

"Fascinating," I murmur. Louder, I ask, "Do you know who the Shade used to be? The one we killed last night?" The baroness frowns, but I press, "Were any of your Dead reported missing recently?"

"Not to my knowledge." Her smile is back in place, though her tone is cooler. "I'm sorry. It's just that we've had so much death recently. So much destruction. I'd prefer to focus on happier things."

"But where are the frightened villagers, the mourners?" Meredy asks quietly. "Where are the people mending fences?"

The baroness locks eyes with Meredy, evidently thinking how to respond. I don't know why it should take so long unless she's not telling us the truth, and I'm about to politely point that out when the carriage driver calls, "Lady Abethell! The signal fire!"

I lean out the window and follow the baroness's gaze to a flickering flame at the top of the next mountain.

"What—?" I start to ask.

"A Shade attack in the next valley," the baroness answers tensely, all her pleasant mannerisms gone. "We'll head there right away. My guard will have seen the flare and know to meet us."

The carriage veers wildly onto a new path, making Meredy slide into me. I steady her with an arm around her waist, but quickly pull away when a sudden heat pulses through me.

"Are you sure the Shade is in the next valley?" Meredy asks a moment later, sounding out of breath. When the baroness asks what she means, Meredy points out the window to another mountain.

Another signal fire glares from an outpost on high.

And on the mountain beyond that, so faint it could be a trick of the noon sun, another fire shines a plea for aid.

As the carriage rushes down the wide dirt path, I look out the windows on either side, and a heavy weight settles in my stomach.

There's a signal fire lit on every mountain around us.

I wrap my fingers around the comforting hilt of my blade and whisper a prayer to Vaia as Meredy mutters something under her breath, perhaps summoning Lysander. But nothing prepares either of us for the grisly sight in the next valley.

For carnage and chaos unlike anything I've ever seen.

This isn't a village in need of an army. This is a massacre in need of a cleanup crew.

The second the carriage halts, I throw open the door and scramble out. My boots slide in someone's blood, and I lean against the carriage to steady myself as I struggle to make sense of what I'm seeing.

Hollowed-out buildings still burning. A smashed signpost. A stray horse shaking under the eaves of an empty blacksmith's forge. And the corpses. All the corpses. Men, women, and children strewn across each other, like they were cut down as they tried to flee. The Shade didn't even bother feasting on most of them. I think I see a few stray limbs, but I can't bring myself to look close enough to know for sure.

The smell hits me in a rush, threatening to bring me to my knees.

And I let it. I kneel in the putrid mix of blood and mud.

We're too late. Too late to help any of these people, and if the eerie wail rising into the clear sky is any indication, we're too late to help those in the other valleys as well. Vane has to have been here, forcing the monster's—or *monsters'*—every move with whatever power his unique Sight gives him. This feels calculated. Organized. No Shade would leave the Deadlands voluntarily, let alone wreak this much havoc without even eating its prey. And no Shade knows how to coordinate attacks on this scale.

Forcing another look at the wreckage, I promise myself I won't stop chasing the rogue necromancer's trail of victims until my hands are around his neck.

Meredy appears at my side and offers me a handkerchief. I dab my soaking face while she lets her own tears fall freely. It's only when she takes my hands that I feel I can properly breathe again. She guides me back into the carriage, where the smell is slightly more bearable, though my head spins.

Her touch is all that keeps me from losing my balance until I slide onto the empty seat.

The baroness remains outside, talking in low voices with what must be her entire guard of fifty armed men.

"Hadrien would have sent us with more help if he knew it was this bad," I manage to say at last. "Why didn't the baroness or someone else say how many Shades had been spotted?" Before Meredy can respond, I answer my own question. "They must not have known. This must be the first attack of this scale." As Meredy wipes her eyes with the back of her hand, I add softly, "I wonder who the Shades were. Who they used to be."

"At this point, I think the more important question is *where* they are now," she whispers. "It doesn't seem like anyone killed them."

Last night, after the surprise Shade attack, Meredy asked me if I ever considered whether raising the dead was worth the risk, and finally, I have my answer.

None of the Dead want to become Shades and hurt the loved ones who sacrifice so much to bring them back, but as Evander's parents proved, accidents happen. Accidents that could be prevented if the Dead stayed where they belong. If I quit doing the one thing I've trained most of my life to do.

The thought catches me by surprise. It's something Lyda might say. I shake my head to clear it.

Gradually, villagers emerge from behind the shells of homes and shops, wide-eyed and deathly pale. Some are spattered with blood, and all look lost. Even the few Dead in their long shrouds are clearly shaken, leaning against their living relatives for support.

"We'll make room in the castle for them all," the baroness declares to her guards. Even from a distance, there's no mistaking the shock in her voice. She clearly had no idea how much destruction Shades could cause, or she'd have spent her time arming her soldiers with liquid fire instead of taking us on a valley tour. The earlier attacks reported to the king must have been like the Shade attacks of years past, monsters picking off livestock and the occasional late-night tavern-goer from the shadows.

We emerge from the carriage to join the survivors, the sounds of someone weeping filling the air. It's one of the Dead, I realize, as a living man pushes away someone beneath a shroud, then points down the road.

"I'm sorry," the man says, shaking his head as the shrouded figure clings to his arm. "Don't you understand?" His voice breaks, and something inside me cracks at the overwhelming sadness of the sound. "You could be the next to turn. One slip of your mask, and . . ."

"You'd become a monster," someone else calls.

"I never knew the Dead were capable of *this*," a dark-haired woman stammers.

"They're not!" I shout. Almost every head turns my way. Even the man arguing with his shrouded relative falls silent. "The Dead can become Shades, but most *never do*. We're careful, and so are they. They wear layers to hide their skin. We're following the same rules we always have. This was no mere accident on the part of the Dead or their kin, mind. Some madman decided to break our rules, and this"—I make a sweeping gesture—"is the result. It doesn't mean the Dead should be feared or blamed."

I say it as much to defend the shrouded figures around me as to prove to the voice in my head that we *are* better off with the Dead here.

"But this *is* our fault, in a way," a woman murmurs, one of the Dead. "Maybe it's best we leave. I don't want to hurt anyone."

"All the Dead should get out of Elsinor!" someone yells.

I search for the speaker so I can glare at him, but I can't tell who said it. Not with several echoes of the sentiment passing among the survivors, and even among the baroness's guards. The farmers and tradesman who make up the heart of Karthia have always looked upon the Dead with respect bordering on awe. They've dreamed of saving up enough to have their own loved ones raised. But then, most of them have never seen a Shade before today.

"And what about the king?" another voice demands.

"Maybe," a young blue-eyed girl says as she hugs her mother's knee, "the Dead king will turn bad, too."

"Maybe," Baroness Abethell agrees softly, her face suddenly looking ten years older, lined with guilt and worry and the same uncertainty that's plaguing me.

"May he reign eternal!" someone cries, sounding defiant. But no one takes up the familiar refrain.

I hang my head. Partly because I can't see a point in arguing with people who have just lost everything. Partly because I can't stand the sight of the Dead trudging away from their ruined village with nowhere to go, not one of them uttering a protest for fear that they might hurt their families if they stay. And partly because a little voice in the back of my mind shares the blue-eyed girl's worry, and I can't seem to silence it.

After a while, the weather mages from the next valley arrive, their gray eyes misting over as they draw more rain from the blue sky's passing clouds. Their movements are like a dancer's, practiced and elegant, each gesture of their hands wringing a little more water from the wisps of clouds above.

Watching them work reminds me of Kasmira, and I hope she's somewhere safe. Out at sea, perhaps.

A few of the more isolated buildings have already stopped burning, but others hiss as rainwater splashes their fiery insides.

The guards comb through the cooling rubble, rounding up more survivors.

Even Meredy finds a purpose, calming the frightened horse from the forge and climbing on its back, riding past the border of the village to search for others in need of help.

I join the baroness at the top of a raised platform that looks like a poorly constructed stage, and together we watch a flock of dark figures ascend the nearest mountain.

The Dead are gliding away toward the horizon, and I'm powerless to stop them.

"Evander," I murmur to my quiet room near the top of Abethell Castle, "I can't sleep." There's no hallucination sitting beside me on the bed, not since I've given up the potion. But I can't seem to shake these conversations. I know he's gone, yet here I am.

"Do you remember the time we snuck into the Deadlands together without Master Cymbre? Chasing after that young Dead baron who'd just become a Shade, because we thought we could change him back with a vial of honey?" I shake my head at the memory. "We were lucky that rock you threw distracted him. Lucky to get out of there with our lives."

I gaze out the room's arched windows at a dark valley that should be flickering with light. With life. Where are Elsinor's exiled Dead now?

"Here's what I've been wondering since the massacre, Van. What if the Dead turn into Shades when we look at them, or when they've been in our world too long, because they were never meant to leave the Deadlands at all?" The words make me a traitor to the sapphire pins on my chest, Evander's and mine both. But now that I've said it aloud, I can't stop myself. "What if I can't find Vane? What if he loses control of his Shades?"

Or worse. "What if our magic is the weapon that brings Karthia to its knees?"

I can practically hear Evander saying it now, carefully weighing each word. "What I do—what we do—brings hope."

Nodding along with his voice in my head, I say, "Our magic is *love* triumphing over death."

But there's no denying our magic can be deadly.

All around me, the sobs of several villages' worth of survivors seep through the floors and echo in the hallways. The survivors are restless in rooms beneath me and around me, and perhaps some of the sick feeling in the pit of my stomach belongs to them, is for them, because I know the ache of loss thanks to Evander.

I hug my knees to my chest and wish all my imagining could conjure the weight of Evander's arms around me one last time. "I forgive you for being gone," I whisper. "I just wish I could forgive myself."

For not saving him. For not saving the people of Elsinor. For allowing Meredy to come here and risk her life, too.

I wipe my soaking face on my sleeve. "She reminds me of you," I whisper into the dark. "That used to make me miserable. But lately, it's made me happy. I promise I'll keep her safe, Van—not that she needs protecting. Honestly, she's saved me a time or two. I just think you'd like to know someone has her back, since . . . you're not here anymore."

I sit straight up on the bed, kicking one of the pillows across the room. Why did it have to be Evander?

It should've been me who was decimated by that Shade.

XXIV

I pull on my boots and slink through the castle, headed for a
stretch of bare earth washed in moonlight: the guards' training
grounds.

I may not be able to save anyone, living or Dead. But beating
stuffed dummies with a wooden practice sword? No man or beast
in Karthia can stop me from making the straw fly. Except maybe
the one sitting on a hay bale beneath the archery target, her chin in
her hands and her bow in her lap, watching me approach.

"Let me guess," Meredy says mildly as I cross the flat ground
cleared for sparring. "You couldn't sleep either."

"Thinking about all the spirits the Deadlands gained today?" I
drop down beside her.

"Among other things." She looks so composed, even after the
day's tragedies: her eyes bright and dry, her long hair brushed and

shining, her clothes clean and unwrinkled. It makes me completely envy her composure.

I narrow my eyes at her, searching for some sign that she's troubled by what we saw. "Do you *ever* get mad? Really mad, like you need to hit something or you might explode?" Meredy frowns slightly as I add, "Or what about sad? Has anything ever hurt you so much, you couldn't hold it all in?"

Meredy grips the bow on her lap, but her expression doesn't change. "Yes. Of course. Just because you haven't been around me long enough to see me hurt or mad doesn't mean I don't feel everything as deeply as anyone else. Maybe I just have a different way of showing it. Not everyone needs to punch things when they're upset."

Her gaze is so intense, I want to look away, but I force myself to keep meeting her eyes. "I don't believe you. I think you care more about appearance than how you feel."

Meredy breaks our stare, glancing over her shoulder at the valley below. Every slight movement, from her restless shifting to wiping her palms on her skirt, sounds too loud in the otherwise silent night. The archery target looms over her, masking her face in shadow.

I can't sit here another moment. I steal the bow off Meredy's lap and pick up the quiver near her feet, selecting an arrow. Meredy turns back to me, a question in her gaze, but I let the thick silence wrap itself tighter around my throat.

"Do you even know how to shoot?" Meredy calls, heat rippling through her voice.

I don't so much as glance at her as I stride over to the line that marks where the archers should stand.

Hurrying over, Meredy snatches the bow out of my hand and grabs an arrow. I've never seen her glower at anyone quite like this before, and I have to squash a sudden urge to laugh. Best not to tempt her into aiming at me.

Meredy's lips remain pressed into a thin line as she takes aim and releases the bowstring.

"I'm angry that my brother's dead and I never really got to know him!" Her words ring through the still night as the arrow sails straight to the center circle of the painted target, but I'm too distracted to be properly impressed. My head spins at her sudden confession.

Meredy studies the target with a satisfied smirk, and as the proud archer's words echo in my mind, I realize there are a lot of things I want to shout into the night, too.

Clearing her throat, Meredy thrusts the bow at me. "Your turn. But don't you dare snap the string or try anything stupid. This is the only one I have."

I nod and take aim, resisting the urge to taunt her with a comment about my poor archery skills. I've only practiced with a bow a few times, years ago, with Simeon and Master Nicanor. I'd forgotten how much strength is needed to pull the string back and hold it, how much concentration is required to line up the arrow tip with the target.

The arrow flies wide. As I watch it, willing a breeze to correct its path, heated words tumble from my lips. "I hate that your mother tried to keep me from Evander!"

"Don't get me started on her." Meredy grabs the bow back, pressing her lips together like she's trying to keep from grinning at the sight of my arrow lying in the dirt.

She takes another perfect shot. "I was never what my mother wanted me to be, and I never will be." Her second arrow sticks beside the first.

Her face is as calm and proud as ever, while my heart's picking up speed and my blood is running hot.

I think of Evander as I aim my next shot and release the bowstring. Of King Wylding and the other missing Dead. I imagine my arrow gaining speed, catching fire, and plummeting straight into the heart of the rogue necromancer.

I think, *I'm sick of not being able to protect anyone I care about, no matter how hard I try.* But something stops me from saying it aloud.

The arrow hits the very bottom of the target, and a flicker of pride curves my lips.

"Not bad, Sparrow." Meredy's eyes seem to shine brighter than usual as she takes the bow back and assumes the archer's stance. "With some practice, you might be as good as Fir . . ." She falters, blinking hard. "Firiel." As though saying the name took her by surprise, she sinks slowly to her knees and sets her bow aside.

Her shoulders quake. She bites down on her trembling lower lip. And a sob escapes her, a desperate sound like an animal caught in a trap.

I half sit, half fall down beside her. I don't know what I expected to be hidden under Meredy's stiff smile and porcelain skin. Certainly not pain deep enough to destroy her from the inside, though perhaps I should have seen it all along. She's lost even more than I have.

Meredy's crying gets louder, drowning out the small night noises of birds and deer and the wind in the trees. It's the kind of cry that shakes her from head to toe, making her fingers curl and her whole body seem to shrink inward like she wants to disappear.

But I don't want her to. I wrap my arms around her, pulling her against me and holding her until her angry cries become soft, hiccupping sobs.

"I don't know how you do it," she murmurs.

"What?"

"Before I met you, it wasn't hard to be heartless."

I stroke her wine-red hair. It's not quite as silky as I'd imagined, but it's thick and smells faintly of vanilla and cedar chips and something I can't name, something that might just be Meredy, and I love the way it tangles around my fingers like it doesn't want to let me go.

"Odessa?" Meredy draws back, gazing blearily at me. Her face is splotchy and damp, her lower lip raw where she must have bitten it.

And yet, somehow, she looks more beautiful than ever.

"Odessa . . ." She puts a hand on my arm, and I realize I'm still holding her.

We break apart. I hastily turn my head, hoping the night air will cool my burning face.

I don't even turn back when Meredy says, "You didn't have to do that. I just—" She pauses, taking a deep breath. "I want to tell you what happened. I want to be strong like you and live with the memory instead of pretending it doesn't exist. We share Evander, and now I want to share Firiel with someone, too."

"All right," I whisper, tucking my hands in my lap.

"Firiel loved to explore the wilds, maybe more than Lysander and I did. She never trained as a mage, but she had greener eyes than mine. I used to tell her she'd make an excellent beast master." Fresh tears splash down Meredy's cheeks as she talks. "A few weeks ago, we went to visit her family's manor in southern Lorness. She asked me to wake up early with her one morning. Said she had something special to show me."

She pauses and sniffs, dabbing her nose with her shirtsleeve. I meet her eyes to show I'm listening, and she continues in a hoarse voice, "It was so foggy that morning, I could barely see the ground right in front of me. I told her we could go see whatever it was some other time, that it wasn't worth either of us tripping and breaking our necks, but she insisted."

Meredy lays a hand on her bow, her tears still falling steadily. "It was a fox's den full of newborn kits. I only saw them for a moment, because we heard men and horses and tried to run, but Firiel . . ."

I nod, eyeing the bow in her hands as gooseflesh spreads over my arms, dreading the words to come.

"There were hunters," Meredy says, swallowing a sob. "They must've seen us take off and thought we were deer. I don't know. Firiel was standing beside me one moment, cooing at the foxes, and the next, she was on the ground with an arrow through her." Meredy swallows hard again. "The men were really sorry, not that it mattered. I should've killed them on the spot, but I was too much of a coward to even do that. I watched her family prepare her for burial, dyed my hair, and then fled Lorness. I didn't want to be the person she loved anymore. The person who failed to save her."

"What could you possibly have done? No one is as quick as an arrow!" I wipe the tears from Meredy's cheeks with my thumbs as fast as I can. They're rough as bark against her dewy skin. "If there was a chance you could've saved her, you would have. Besides, there's no point being angry with yourself for something you can't change."

"Have you forgiven yourself for what happened to Evander?" Meredy dabs her eyes on her already-damp sleeve. "Or did you just get addicted to a potion so you wouldn't have to carry the guilt around?"

I open my mouth, but it takes a moment to find words. "That's not fair."

"Sure it is." Meredy frowns at me, and her tears finally stop. "You seem to think it's easy for me to forgive myself for not taking that arrow instead of Firiel, but you can't forgive yourself for not letting Evander go into that ravine first?"

I gasp. "How did you know—?"

"You talked a lot in your sleep during those first few days of potion withdrawal." Meredy scoots closer, extending a hand. "If you want me to even *try* to forgive myself, you have to do the same. Deal?"

I take her hand, but the simple shake turns into something more. I'm not sure who twines their fingers through the other's first, or how much time passes before both her hands are joined with mine, only that every slight movement makes my heart jump.

"Do you ever get the feeling," she whispers, her hands suddenly trembling in mine, "that if you make one wrong move, one stupid choice, the whole world will come crashing down around you?"

"All the time." I shiver in a strong gust of wind, which frees a scrap of old parchment from Meredy's cloak. I watch it flutter to the ground. "What's this?"

"Nothing," she says quickly, untangling our fingers to grab it.

I reach for it, too, so fast we almost bump heads. She catches one edge of the parchment while I grab another, stretching it into a flat sheet. If either of us pulls any harder, it'll tear. Naturally, I tug the parchment toward me, forcing Meredy to release it.

I turn it over, blinking at an ink likeness of myself in a familiar style, and my stomach does a flip. "Valoria gave you this."

"She did." Meredy leans over the parchment, raising her gaze from the drawing to me. "She has a way of seeing how things are meant to fit together."

"Must be those brown eyes of hers," I whisper.

Without thinking, I drop the parchment and reach for Meredy. She stiffens, then shivers as I press my palm to her cheek.

"We shouldn't. We can't," she whispers, more to herself than to me, as she touches my waist with both hands. Her fingers are feather-light, as though they'll vanish if I startle her the slightest bit. Her lips are red and inviting. She blinks a question at me, lowering the shield that always covers her face. I beckon her closer with a look.

I don't know what's gotten into me.

My lips burn at the betrayal of sharing breaths with her. But the small clouds of heat against my mouth make me shiver and set me on fire all at once.

As I close the remaining distance between us, pulled forward against my will by the invisible strings lashing us together, something moves at the corner of my sight. Startled to my senses, I jerk back before our lips can touch, gazing up in time to see a winged shadow crossing the moon, and whatever spell was cast here is broken.

"A messenger raven," Meredy murmurs, low and urgent, as if she's already putting what almost happened out of her mind. The bird's shape becomes clearer as it descends toward the castle. "It's frightened and in a hurry. We should—"

"Have a peek at its message. Just in case it's from Grenwyr," I finish, leaping to my feet. She tosses me a strange, unreadable look, and my head spins with the realization of what we almost did.

"I'm sorry, Evander," I mutter under my breath as we start to run. Because all I can think of are his sister's vivid green eyes, and the way she makes my blood run hot every time she opens her mouth. And when I try to remember what it was like to kiss Evander, I imagine kissing Meredy instead.

We race to the front of the castle, where the raven appears to be heading, with Meredy in the lead. I hold up my arm and let it fly to me, only wincing slightly as its claws graze my bare skin. Meredy breaks the ties around the letter strapped to the raven's leg with her fingernail, then leans in as she unfurls the parchment.

I draw back, careful not to get too close to her again.

My blood runs cold as I recognize Simeon's loopy scrawl. "More Dead are missing, including Her Majesty," I read aloud. "It happened right after you left. And no one's seen Hadrien for hours.

There's panic in the city. Don't return to Grenwyr, dear sister. Go to the coast, or better yet, take a ship and set sail. Love, Simeon."

Crumpling the parchment in my fist, I take a deep breath and fight a sudden urge to scream. I have to stop this, all the death and disappearances. And Vane is my one lead, whether he's the one who stole the Dead from the palace or not.

"Get Lysander," I say softly, trying to keep my voice from shaking with rage. "I'm going to wake Master Cymbre and show her this." I hold up the wrinkled letter. "We're going to the Deadlands now. All this fear and hurting has got to end, and there's only one person I know of who might be able to tell us something useful."

XXV

Master Cymbre's room is empty. A hint of spice and leather hangs in the air, a sure sign that she was here not too long ago. Yet all her things are gone: her sword, her boots, and the tiny book of poems she carries everywhere. The bed is neatly made, as perfect as though she never slept in it.

Meredy peers at something dropped behind a chair, then checks inside the wardrobe, her brows knitting together in concern. "There's no sign of a struggle."

Lysander watches from the doorway, unable to squeeze his bulk across the threshold.

"Right. I doubt rogue necromancers forcing her into the Deadlands would have made sure she had time to pack her favorite book and her weapon," I murmur, thinking aloud. Besides, when Master Nicanor was abducted, there was evidence of a fight at his house. The only other option here is that Cymbre went against the rules she taught me for most of my life—that she went into the Deadlands alone of her own free will.

A faint blue glow from the windows draws my attention. There's a gate to the Deadlands a brisk walk from the castle. Master Cymbre must have entered it to find Vane after hearing about the massacre. After promising me she'd rest.

I know that's what happened, because it's exactly the sort of thing *I* would do. It's what I did do, when I needed to prevent the Shade that killed Evander from taking any more lives. For better or worse, she brought me up to be just like her, risking everything to protect the people she loves.

"She's gone," I whisper. "She went to the Deadlands alone. To protect us. To protect all these people. But if Vane is there, she'll need our help. Who knows how many Shades he'll have with him?"

"We're going after her. Lysander can track her scent if we let him sniff her pillow." Meredy's eyes glitter in the candlelight, hard and determined. Some part of me wishes there was time to kiss her firmly set mouth, to finish what we started and see if it's something I'd want to do again. To see if she tastes like Evander, or if there's something distinct about Meredy that's making me crave her like this.

Sleeping in Jax's bed never made me feel this guilty, but maybe that's because with Jax, I didn't really think about it. About him. My time with him was always an escape from thoughts of Evander, like my potion addiction. What's happening with Meredy feels like a force all its own, as strong and perplexing as lightning.

I can't think about her this way, not now or *ever*, but especially not when Master Cymbre's in danger.

When someone's life depends on it.

Shoving Meredy firmly to the back of my mind, I turn to the small writing desk in the far corner of the room and pick up a quill and parchment from a tray. "Before we go, I'll tell Jax and Simeon where we're headed. Just in case."

A short while later, we breeze past several stunned guards and out the back gates of Abethell Castle, with Lysander bounding ahead.

"We have to go through a gate to the Deadlands," I murmur, glancing at Meredy through the inky darkness that's settled over the grounds. Clouds have rolled in since our earlier target practice, blotting out the stars.

I offer Meredy my hand, much as I'm afraid of what her touch might make me feel. "You'll have to hold on to me, because you can't—"

"See it," she finishes for me, taking my hand. "Evander trusted you. That means I trust you, too." As we jump into the gate, just a short leap off the ground, she mutters, "Besides, if you screw this up, I'll tell Lysander he can snack on you."

It takes Meredy a few moments to get her bearings inside the tunnel. Brushing dirt off her clothes, she keeps her head carefully turned to the lichen-covered wall, like she doesn't want me to see her face. Somehow, she commanded Lysander to leap through the gate after us without uttering a word, and now she keeps him by her side in the tunnel without the use of a chain. It seems she can't stop him from snarling and pacing around us, though.

I wonder if he's remembering the last time we were here.

Meredy takes my hand again as we hurry down the tunnel. Her fingers burn where they clutch mine, and I wish I could let go, but I don't want her getting lost. The Deadlands have ways of calling to anyone living, luring them into forgetting why they'd ever want to return to the other world. The world where they belong.

For Meredy, it'll probably be Firiel who appears to lure her into staying.

But no matter what we encounter, I'm going to keep Meredy alive. I can't lose her, not after how much trouble I went through to save her the first time. Not after we've finally started talking about Evander, sharing memories to keep him with us. Not after . . . well, everything she's become to me.

"Lysander's found something." Meredy squeezes my elbow, jarring me back to the present.

"Which way?" I demand, putting a hand on my sword.

The bear gazes straight ahead, at one of the Deadlands' many gardens. I take a step toward it, but Meredy holds me back, her hand turning cold in mine.

"She's nowhere near here," she says in a dreamy, distant voice not quite like her own. Her face is completely blank. A shiver runs through me as I realize Lysander's eyes are glowing a vivid green, identical to hers. Somehow, she's searching his thoughts in a way I've never seen before.

"Then we'd better start running," I murmur. Now that we're in the Deadlands, there could be Shades nearby. Or the very man I'd like to catch by surprise.

"No." To my relief, Meredy sounds more like herself. She meets my gaze, then nods to Lysander. "Riding will be much faster."

Every necromancer should see the Deadlands on the back of a grizzly, I decide as I settle myself on Lysander's warm bulk. The view is different somehow. Sharper, with every twisted tree and every moonflower seeming to jump out at me, vying for my attention.

Meredy sits in front of me, and at her urging, I wrap my arms around her waist.

My heart taps out its excitement against my ribs, and there's nothing I can do—save for letting go of Meredy's soft curves or tucking my nose into my shirt so I don't have to breathe her subtle vanilla scent that makes my head spin—to slow it down.

I just hope she can't feel the faint pounding against her back, or hear the slight quickening of my breath.

Lysander picks up speed, and I grip Meredy tighter. He seems to be following the meander of a dark and icy river. As the water rushes past in a blur, my thoughts turn to Master Cymbre.

The day she first came to see me at Death's convent, her face was less lined and her fiery hair had no trace of gray.

She wanted to be a mentor, not a mother, but I was ten years old and I didn't know the difference. We both learned a lot that first year, as she tried to pass on her knowledge of the Dead while I tried on her clothes and lip rouge and begged to sleep in her bed.

Wind chills the tips of my ears as Lysander carries us through a grove of trees that have dropped their silver leaves.

I asked Master Cymbre about the seasons in the Deadlands once. I think I was twelve. She couldn't explain why there weren't any, she said, any better than her mentor could when she'd asked the very same thing. But she still knew a lot more than I did, and I never stopped relying on her to answer my impossible questions.

Why the moon turns blood-red sometimes.

Why we can't look upon the Dead without them turning into Shades.

Why Simeon doesn't like kissing girls, only boys, but I like both.

Why love hurts when it's the thing we live for. The thing some people search their entire lives for. The thing some people die for.

Why I don't know where I belong.

"With me, chickadee," Master Cymbre would singsong when I asked her that, in the years before I started going by Sparrow.

She's never been my mother. She's always held a little something of herself back from me, just enough to remain as mysterious as Vaia, the Five-Faced God who created our world and then vanished long ago.

But she's all I have. All that's left of our trio, which once felt invincible.

"You're quiet back there," Meredy murmurs, gazing at me over her shoulder. "Everything all right?"

I nod, still lost in memories. Like the day Master Cymbre first took Evander and me into the Deadlands and explained the price of our magic. That while we could come here and have the freedom to bring spirits back to their bodies, *our* spirits would never rest here when we died. We'd just . . . disappear.

It seemed so unfair to ten-year-old me, I'd flopped down under a silvery tree and cried so hard I gave myself hiccups. Nothing we

got in return for raising the dead—invitations to all the palace parties, the fame, the heaps of gold for each person we brought back
to life—seemed to be a good exchange for our spirits.

"All magic has a price," Master Cymbre told me more than
once. "If it didn't, every blue-eyed person would raise all their loved
ones and Karthia would be overrun with Dead. If gray-eyed people
could change the path of a huge storm without giving themselves a
stroke, we'd never have to fear another dark cloud."

"Sounds like a perfect world," I'd grumbled.

But Master Cymbre had merely smiled. "You wouldn't think
it was perfect. There would be other problems. Karthia would be
crowded, restless, and miserable."

"What are you trying to say?" I demanded.

"I'm saying we make our own problems. As long as people
exist," she'd said, her steely blue eyes focused intently on mine,
"there will be trouble and discontent and rumblings of how things
could be better. There is no 'perfect.'"

Meredy gives me another worried look, and my face warms as I
realize I've been staring absently into the distance. Still, the heat in
my cheeks feels good compared to the cold breeze that's numbing
every bit of my exposed skin as Lysander bounds up the side of a
small mountain, his pace never lagging.

"What's the price of a beast master's magic?" I ask her, careful
to keep my voice low.

If Meredy's surprised by the question, she doesn't show it.
"When we exercise any amount of control over our beasts," she
murmurs, "we become like them for a little while. Feral. In posses-
sion of only our most basic instincts."

I think of how different she sounded as she searched her bear's mind earlier. "You didn't seem very beastly after you and Lysander did your silent-talking thing."

"That's because it was brief. Just a little magic. I wasn't trying to see through his eyes, or to fully possess him and force his limbs to move." Meredy's lips twist in a grim smile. "As you've seen, I'm quite capable of controlling my . . . less human urges."

"Like what?" I ask, trying to distract myself from thoughts of Master Cymbre fighting for her life, from horrible scenarios playing out in my mind like a shadow-puppet play on a wall. "Eating raw fish? Running naked through the Deadlands?"

Meredy doesn't answer.

It's hard to tell in the Deadlands' perpetual dimness, but her cheeks look redder than usual. I wish I could read her mind right now.

Instead, I'm left alone with my thoughts. I should've paid more attention to Master Cymbre after Master Nicanor's death. I was so caught up in trying to get revenge on the giant Shade and in grieving for Evander that I didn't notice how she must have been grieving, too. Maybe we could have mourned together.

Maybe if she'd thought I was willing to listen, trusted that I wasn't some potion addict trying to escape the past anymore, she would've told me what she was planning tonight. But I'd sided with the healer and insisted she rest. I should have known better.

She's too much like me to just sit on her hands and wait when something is wrong. She's doing this to protect me.

Lysander suddenly comes to a halt on a narrow stretch of beach beside a large dark lake, breathing hard. Meredy leans forward, wordlessly talking with him again. He stomps a huge paw and lowers his head.

There in the sand, right beneath Lysander's nose, are a few fiery red hairs streaked with gray.

I scramble off the bear's back and drop to my knees, sifting through the chilled sand for any other sign that Cymbre was here. For any reason to hope she's still alive. Meredy joins me, walking up and down the lake shore so many times I get dizzy watching her.

"Don't touch the water! Not even with your boot!" I warn her over the lump in my throat as Meredy's path veers closer to the water's edge. As she moves farther out of my reach.

There are a few spirits floating farther out in the lake, toward the middle. From shore, they look like mist or fallen clouds as they hover on the water's surface. They don't notice us, too busy forgetting who and what they were as the lake strips away their dearest memories. I don't want that to happen to Meredy, and all it would take is one accidental step into the water to make her forget something about herself.

"We should move on," I tell Meredy as she strides toward me again. "Can Lysander try to pick up Cymbre's scent again?"

Meredy shakes her head, her face pale. "The trail ends here."

I swallow hard as a wave of cold crashes over my head. "Does that mean . . . ?" I can't finish. I can't go through this again. Meredy steadies me with a hand on my shoulder, and after a moment, I find my voice again.

"There's no body. How can we be sure she's *dead* if there's no body?"

"Breathe," Meredy urges, squeezing my shoulder.

"Where's her sword, if she's really dead? She wouldn't have gone looking for the Shade-baiter if she didn't have her sword and her—"

"She's dead, I assure you. She made a nice meal for my hungry Shades," a harsh voice says, causing us to whirl toward the sound. "As will you both. Very soon."

XXVI

Even with his tall form hidden beneath a handsome cobalt cloak, his face obscured and his eyes shadowed by a painted silver mask, I'd recognize him anywhere thanks to his gravelly voice. Vane, the powerful rogue necromancer, strides briskly down the shore toward us.

I draw my sword and step in front of Meredy and her grizzly, the necromancer's words cutting into me like a dagger to the stomach, laying my insides open. Cymbre's dead. And all her stories, her hopes, her loves, her wisdom have died with her.

Lysander growls, low and menacing.

Several more cloaked figures form a half-circle around us, creeping closer by the moment. If we want to flee, we'll have to go through them. Or swim out into the lake, which is as good as a death sentence.

Vane holds a broadsword at his side. It's so much larger than mine, I don't know that I have a hope of matching him in strength. But I might be quicker. And perhaps smarter, too.

It isn't until I spot the five Shades waiting in the distance, in the field at the necromancers' backs, that my heart seizes and I don't know how we're going to make it out of here alive. But we have to try.

I raise my sword.

"Vane," another of the cloaked Shade-baiters—if that's what they are—mutters worriedly. "Don't forget to collect the Sparrow's pin as proof of her death." She locks eyes with me. "He could stiff us if we don't follow orders exactly as he gave them . . ."

"Who's *he*?" I glance briefly at the woman, whose dark curly hair spills out from her hood. "Tell me, and maybe I'll bring you to the dungeons instead of killing you."

"Silence!" Vane raises his free hand at the female Shade-baiter like he's about to strike her. Then he turns toward me, no doubt sensing where I'm standing. "You all kill the others. I want the satisfaction of slaying this one myself!"

He charges toward me, swinging his blade. I stop him midstrike with mine, metal screeching against metal as I try to push him back, my shoulders burning with the effort.

"Don't worry about the others," Meredy says tersely from somewhere behind me. "Lysander and I will keep them busy."

Lysander darts past me, his eyes glowing green again, charging up the beach and making the other necromancers scatter as he tries to eviscerate them with his claws.

Someone screams. A sword drops onto the sand, accompanied by a spray of blood, and I have a feeling someone's just learned not to point a blade at a bear.

"You're lucky he let you live this long," Vane growls.

Something tumbles from his cloak pocket as he slashes at me. I dance away from his blade, and as my mind makes sense of the tiny object on the sand, my heart lurches. Vane might as well have stabbed me when he dropped it.

Master Cymbre's ancient book of poems.

The one with my sticky jam fingerprints on the front page and a few of my tears in the middle. There's a page still carefully held by the braided silk bookmark I gave Cymbre on her birthday last year.

She's really gone.

She's gone, and I still need her. Just like Evander.

Vane lashes out again and again, never even breaking a sweat. Without his vision, his other senses are heightened, making him more than a match for me. My forehead grows slick, my mouth cotton-dry as I jump and dodge to stay a hairsbreadth away from his blade. Each time our swords clash, my body screams with the staggering force of his blows. I can't keep this up much longer—the realization that Master Cymbre's gone forever has made my blocks and jabs as clumsy as a beginner's.

There are Shades waiting beyond the shore, their skeletal bodies restless with the need to hunt, and I'm sure the only reason they aren't charging toward us is because they're waiting for Vane's order. It could come at any moment.

I barely deflect his next blow, which knocks the breath out of me and shatters the vials of honey and blood on my belt. I try to scoop some of the honey into my hand, but it oozes through my fingers, and tiny shards of glass slice my skin.

"Oh, did you need those?" Vane snarls as the vials crunch.

He throws me to the ground, ramming his shoulder into my chest. I get a brief glimpse of Meredy as I go down, standing mere paces away near the water's edge, her eyes glazed in concentration as she controls her grizzly like a puppeteer. I hope she snaps out of that daze before Vane comes for her.

Pain blossoms through my middle as I writhe on the sand, my sword lying just out of reach, everything hurting too much for my body to obey my commands to roll away. My neck is exposed, ready for Vane's blade to come swiftly down and cleave my head from my shoulders.

He raises his sword again. I force myself to gaze into the slits of his mask, hoping I'll make Master Cymbre proud by witnessing my own death. By not letting Vane win entirely, because I'm not afraid. It's exactly what Cymbre must have done earlier, on this very spot. I won't disappoint her.

Fury sings through my veins as I greet my coming death.

His sword slices through the air but swings wide as it flies out of his hand. Finally, I manage to draw a shuddering breath that clears my head a little. But the pain in my chest is still white-hot as I roll across the sand to dodge the errant blade.

Vane crashes to the ground beside me, a dagger sticking out from between his ribs. That explains his poor aim with the sword.

Running over to admire her handiwork, Meredy gives a satisfied nod. "Finish him, Odessa," she growls, looking past me and raising an arm. I follow her gaze in time to see Lysander raise that same arm, his claws slashing the face of an already-wounded man.

Beside me, Vane groans, drawing my attention.

"I think your dagger might've done the job," I tell Meredy, but she's not listening, once again focused on fighting through Lysander.

Still breathing hard, I wrap my bloody, sticky hand around the hilt of the dagger in Vane's ribs and shove it in a little deeper. My stomach does a flip as his scream fills my ears, but I hold on tight to the blade in case he's less injured than he's letting on.

"Silly girl," he coughs. Blood flecks the narrow mouth opening of his mask, like it flecked my lips the day Evander died and I nearly lost my life. "I would've made quick work of you before the Shades cleaned up your remains. Now you'll have to feel their every bite."

I glance toward the horizon. Sure enough, the Shades are opening their cavernous mouths and scraping their bony fingers against the hard ground—impatient to come for us when their master gives the order.

Still, we can't leave yet. Not without knowing who paid these people to create more monsters the world didn't need.

"I can either dig this dagger in deeper and scramble your insides or give you a swift end if you answer my questions," I whisper, not sure it's a promise I can make. His end seems to be coming swiftly with or without my help. I rip off his mask, flinging it into the sand, wanting to study his face for lies as we talk. "Now tell me, how were you controlling these Shades?"

He spits blood in my face.

I wiggle the dagger just a little, and once he stops screaming, he starts talking in a ragged voice. "Magic. I taught myself. My eyes may be weak, but there's nothing wrong with my Sight. I see differently than you, so my powers are different. I thought you'd noticed last time we met, when I didn't have a mask in the way."

I gape at him. "So you can . . . control Shades, like a beast master controls an animal?"

Vane nods stiffly.

I make a hasty note to tell Valoria, if I ever see her again. Maybe there are others with powers we don't understand or even know about. And perhaps, like Vane, there are others who have mastered their abilities alone in the shadows.

In the distance, Lysander roars. I hope he's running down the other Shade-baiters without any trouble, but Meredy must be worried, as she edges away from us and draws another dagger. Still in her dreamlike state, she runs farther up the beach.

"What were you planning to do"—I rip my gaze from her and quickly return my attention to Vane as the Shades beyond the shore moan and grumble—"with all those monsters?"

He laughs, though it's more like a splutter. "Why should I tell you? I'm dying, and you're as good as dead. Soon . . ." He tilts his head in the direction of his companions' shouts farther up the beach, where the other Shade-baiters are trying their luck against Lysander—and suddenly, I understand. He's preventing his Shades from attacking to buy his companions time to escape, time they wouldn't have if they were still around after the monsters finished with me.

"Tell me what you were planning!" I demand again. Even with Vane stalling on behalf of the others, it won't be long before he's gone and we're all Shade food.

He shakes his head, still laughing.

I punch him in the chest, just to stop the sickly sound ringing in my ears. "Fine. Allow me to guess, then. First, you kidnapped Dead nobles from the palace and pulled off their shrouds to turn them into Shades. Then you fed people to them, like Master Nicanor, to make them stronger. Then you kidnapped His Majesty, probably to make another Shade. You've been killing necromancers and creating Shades, building an army from our Dead—but why?"

Vane's breathing is ragged as he chokes out, "If you're so clever, girl, you tell me."

I remember the horrified faces of the villagers who survived the massacre in Elsinor. I remember their Dead, marching away to an uncertain future, and it dawns on me. "You were trying to make people fear the Dead. By turning them into Shades, you reminded the living of the danger that surrounds them at all times. But there has to be more to it than that."

Vane goes suddenly still beneath me, and my heart stops for a moment. I slap his cold face so hard that the sound ripples across the lake.

He's lost to a fit of bloody coughing. At last, he says, "There's nothing you can do that'll make me talk."

It takes a moment to find my voice again, I'm shaking so hard all over. "Who is he? The man who hired you? A duke—one from the southern provinces?" After all, there have been some with their eyes on King Wylding's throne for decades.

Vane says nothing, but offers me a strained smirk.

I grab the hilt of the dagger and drive it in deeper, eliciting more screams. Every Karthian's life depends on knowing who's really behind these attacks. "Tell me his name, and I'll make the pain stop!"

Still Vane doesn't answer, due to agony or his twisted code of morals, I can't tell. "I'll find your family, or whoever or whatever it is you love. I'll kill them, every last one, if you don't give me the name of the man who hired you right now."

It's an empty threat, but he doesn't need to know that. I must sound wild in my desperation, as he cowers slightly in the wake of my words.

"I do care about the living people of Karthia. Same with my partners." Vane makes a wheezing sound, struggling for breath, but continues, "And I was promised a seat on his court when he takes the throne. When the living rule and decide the future."

The living *people of Karthia*. The words remind me of something Hadrien said once, as he held me close to the beat of a drum. Hadrien, who has enough money to hire a host of men like Vane. Hadrien, who was the last person seen with King Wylding according to Meredy. Hadrien, who Simeon said no one had seen for hours at the time he'd penned his letter to me. Hadrien, who I left with Her Majesty and my friends, thinking they would watch over each other. Hadrien, who is next in line for the throne.

Suddenly, I see what I couldn't before.

Head spinning, I drop my gaze to the sand. Vane's blood-spattered hand twitches, and beneath the grime I notice a smattering of bruises, dark against his white knuckles.

"How did you get those marks on your hands?" I demand, but as I expected, Vane can't or won't answer. "You punched Prince Hadrien, didn't you? To demand more rewards when you finished his—his murder crusade. Is that right?"

The last time I saw him, mere days ago in the throne room, Hadrien's face was bruised just beneath his eye. Still, I want to hear Vane say it aloud. To hear Hadrien's name spoken by someone who, in his final moments, has no reason to lie.

"Death be damned—say his name!"

But Vane is still and silent again. I shake his shoulders. He doesn't move, his body limp beneath my hands.

He's gone; his spirit has vanished, leaving behind the shell of a mage who could have done some good with his unusual power—protecting necromancers during their travels to the Deadlands, for one. But instead, he was loyal to Hadrien to the end.

And now, no longer under their master's control, his Shades are free to hunt.

I hurriedly grab Vane's silver mask and cloak, careful to avoid touching the part that's wet with blood. They're a reminder that Karthia's enemies can be slain. That *I* can slay them, even the traitorous prince who was once, perhaps, my friend.

The lake becomes a blur as I sink forward in the sand beside the Shade-baiter's body. I thought Hadrien loved me. I swear I heard caring in his voice that day in the throne room, but he sent me here to have me killed, away from my friends, from help.

I stagger to my feet. The world, *my* world, is falling apart, and I'm probably much too late to stop it—but I have to try. Even if I don't know who or what to trust anymore.

A Shade howls in the distance, fighting with its companions as they feast on the body of the rogue necromancer who managed to flee farthest.

Gazing up the beach, I realize *all* the other Shade-baiters are either dead or gone. I don't see Meredy, but Lysander's chomping on one of the mangled corpses without a care, meaning she must be alive and unharmed nearby.

The spirits of the Deadlands haven't yet lured her to taste their fruit or wade in their lakes, though they might, and I have no honey. We need to get out of here before the Shades run out of other bones to crunch.

I hurry to where Master Cymbre's book is half-buried in the sand. My heart soars pitifully as I tuck the leather-bound poems into my front pocket for safekeeping, as though touching the battered pages will bring me closer to Cymbre. I pat the book, trying to tell my foolish heart it's of no use.

A Shade howls again, and another one answers with a gleeful, lilting noise.

Shaking my head to clear it, I pick up my sword and call to Meredy, "We need to go!"

There's a gate on the lake's western shore. It won't take long to reach, just a sprint down the beach, following the curve of the narrow stretch of sand.

"Oh good. There you are," I say shakily as Meredy reappears beside me. I need her steady presence to help me focus as I lead us out of here. "Get Lysander. Hurry."

But she doesn't seem to hear me or even the Shades' hunting cries as they start to close in, bounding on all fours like hounds instead of the humans they once were. With a vacant expression, she kneels by Vane and pulls the dagger from his flesh. She brings it to her lips and licks the gooey crimson mess from the flat of the blade.

"What are you doing?" I try to suppress a shudder.

She glances up, her eyes still blank, and wipes her mouth with the back of her hand, smearing blood all over her face.

I reach for the dagger. She holds it out of reach, snarling like a feral dog. Then I remember: the effects of her magic. She was using Lysander like a puppet to hunt the other Shade-baiters, and now she's become like a beast herself.

Vaia only knows for how long.

Lysander bounds toward me, whining softly and looking from me to the Shades. They're coming toward us, swift gray shadows we can't outrun.

But perhaps Lysander can.

Waiting until Meredy is distracted by her dagger again, I bash her on the temple. "I'm doing this for her own good," I mutter to a growling Lysander. Then I throw Meredy's limp form over the bear's back. This time, it's not Meredy commanding him to give me a ride, I realize as he lowers himself so I can climb on behind her. He's trying to help me escape along with his master. That, or he knows he needs me to find the gate out of here.

The Shades spray sand everywhere as their skeletal feet hit the shore.

Lysander takes off in the direction I point. "Stay out of the water!" I yell as I hang on to his back with one hand and steady

Meredy with the other, keeping Vane's cloak and mask tucked securely under one arm.

The spirits in the lake are so far gone, they don't even notice our passing as we race along the shore, steps ahead of our pursuers.

The water becomes a blur as Lysander pushes himself to run harder.

The Shades' rattling breaths ring in my ears.

Without Vane's power compelling them, the monsters won't leave the Deadlands. If we can just get to the gate, we'll be safe. They might try to go after the spirits in the lake instead, but there's no time to worry or feel guilty about that now.

The blue glow washes over Lysander's fur, over Meredy's pale face. Her eyes flutter open, widening with horror at the sight of whatever's right behind me, whatever's breathing frost down my neck.

Lysander jumps into the gate. Our hushed breaths fill the dark tunnel.

XXVII

By the time we're through the gate, our feet steady on the cold, firm ground of our own world, Meredy is herself again—groggy and paler than usual, but not about to chase down any of the nearby squirrels or rabbits for an early meal.

Swathed in gray predawn light, we make our way straight to Abethell Castle's stables, not bothering to stop back in our rooms, leaving Lysander waiting at the entrance. His hired thugs all dead or wounded, we might've ruined Hadrien's plans for now, but we need to return to Grenwyr at once to learn what he's planning next and where he's hidden the king.

If we still have a king, and he isn't already a monster.

Taking a deep breath, I shove the thought to the back of my mind, where it'll have to stay for now. Buried, along with my grief for Master Cymbre. The one person I need most right now, who can never again tell me what to do or rush to my aid.

I'm on my own. I have to figure out a way to stop these attacks myself. And if I mess up, no one will swoop in to save me this time.

"I'm sorry you had to see me like that," Meredy murmurs as she chooses a chestnut horse and slips into its stall. She spits. "I can still taste his blood."

I'm halfway through saddling a white horse when a shadow blocks the torchlight, forcing me to pause and turn. Baroness Abethell, in a long robe and slippers, stands at the stall door, watching me with a frown. She must have entered the row of stalls from the far side, as there's no way she could have marched past Lysander.

"There's no time to explain," I mutter as I tighten the horse's girth and adjust the stirrups. "We'll pay you back for the horses when we're able."

"Consider the horses another gift from the people of Elsinor," the baroness says. "You killed a Shade for us, after all. No one in the castle will forget that anytime soon. But are you sure you have to leave like this?"

I blink at her.

"Why not stay for a nice breakfast before you go on your way? The cooks will have it ready in just a few hours."

The baroness's forced pleasantness reminds me of the day she took us on a tour of the surrounding valleys. Yesterday, I realize. Everything's a blur without sleep. Still, there's something off about the overly hospitable baroness, and I doubt my feelings would change even after a long nap.

"Why don't you want us to leave?" I demand as I ready my horse.

But the baroness is staring at Meredy, and when she finally shifts her gaze to me, she looks just as stunned. "Is that *blood* on your faces, dears?" she stammers. "I can call a healer . . ."

"We're leaving. Now," I grit out, touching the hilt of my sword. I'm willing to bet I look as feral as Meredy did, with my blood-shot eyes and tangled hair. "There aren't any more Shades coming for your people right now, if that's what you're worried about. But there will be if you don't let us get back to Grenwyr to find and stop a madman."

"A madman? What—?"

"Tell me why you don't want us to leave!" I snap, cutting her off. The baroness sucks in a breath and pales.

"You'd better answer her," Meredy snarls, and Lysander echoes her with a distant growl. "If you're interested in getting out of here in one piece. The bear is hungry."

The baroness braces herself against the stall door, and the horse I'm saddling whinnies happily. Baroness Abethell strokes the horse's soft nose with a trembling hand as she says quietly, "I was just following Prince Hadrien's orders. I can show you his letter. He asked me to keep you delayed and entertained in Abethell until he sent for you. And not to breathe a word about it to anyone. Not even my guards." She frowns as she gazes from me to Meredy and back. "Has something happened? Is he in some kind of trouble?"

"You have no idea," Meredy murmurs.

"Am I in trouble, too?" The baroness glances between us, still pale. "Is this about the Shade attacks . . . ?"

"Kind of." I push open the stall door, leading my horse into the wide aisle with Meredy's. The baroness makes no move to stop me.

"There's no time to explain now, but you're not in any immediate danger. We just need to hurry. Prince Hadrien . . ." I swallow hard, the name sticking in my throat. "The prince urgently needs us back in Grenwyr. We received a raven in the dead of night ordering our return."

"Safe journey, then," Baroness Abethell says softly, looking uncertain but like she'll be glad to see the back of Lysander.

As Meredy and I ride out of Elsinor, back up the mountain path where charred remnants of our wagon still litter the ground, my eyes are on the grizzly scouting the road ahead. But my thoughts are with Hadrien.

I picture the bruise on his face where Vane punched him and wish I could give him a few more bruises. Scenes of the Shade attacks in Elsinor—attacks that Hadrien ordered—flash mercilessly through my mind, death and misery on the grandest scale I've ever seen.

Then I remember the way his eyes lit up whenever he spotted me at the palace. The way he seemed so protective of Valoria and his younger siblings. The way he looked up to King Wylding as though he were Vaia the Five-Faced God himself. Was it all an act?

"I've been so stupid," I mutter, mostly to myself, though Meredy turns in her saddle to glance at me. "I should've taken you at your word when you told me your suspicions in the wagon instead of trying to pick a fight with you."

Meredy narrows her eyes and says nothing, evidently lost in thought.

"But why all this murder? Why destroy his family? Why hurt the people of Karthia if he wants to rule them? And why hurt—?"

I stop myself before I can add *me*. Whatever I thought he felt for me, it must have been part of his grand illusion.

"I wonder if anyone can ever truly know another person," Meredy says softly, her eyes lingering on me as she trusts her horse to stick to the path. "Or if we all keep a few rooms' worth of secrets locked away in our minds."

I'm tempted to ask what secrets Meredy keeps, but I'm too exhausted to hear them. I wonder if I'm keeping any of my own. Yet all thoughts seem to lead back to Hadrien, making me too sick to eat despite my stomach growling.

We ride in silence for hours.

"You were right about something else," I say a while later, as we descend the mountain. The late afternoon light makes our shadows leap and dance along the path ahead of us, like phantoms leading a parade of the living. "I *am* selfish."

Meredy halts her horse until mine catches up, frowning as she watches me.

"I took Master Cymbre for granted. I thought she'd always be there to clean up my messes, like that was her job or something. Like she was untouchable." I take a breath. Just saying her name makes my whole body ache with the loss. "I didn't even pay enough attention to you when you came to me for help with Firiel. I should've taken time to warn you about what was happening in the Deadlands, and because I didn't, you nearly died."

I drop my gaze. "I was hurt, and I forgot about everyone else who was hurting, too. Cymbre, and you, and Lyda—"

"Shut up." Meredy leans toward me in the saddle, tucking back a loose strand of my hair. "You can't take on the blame for any deaths Hadrien caused. This was out of your control, like you'd have me believe Firiel's death was out of mine."

I nod, choked by a sudden rush of tears. I flick the horse's reins and urge her to resume the steep downward walk, Meredy's fingers grazing my cheek as I drift away. My hands shake, reminding me of my potion withdrawal. But I don't want potions anymore. I don't want to be numb. I want to feel angry, want my blood to run so hot that when I find Hadrien, I can kill him without mourning yet another lost life.

I want to grieve for my friends, so that their deaths will have meant something.

Tears slide down my cheeks as I hold their faces in my mind. Evander. Nicanor. Cymbre. The people of Elsinor. And perhaps even King Wylding, if we're too late.

Please, by Vaia's grace, don't let us be too late.

One day blurs into the next as we cross Grenwyr's lush farmland on our way back to Grenwyr City. Meredy forces us to stop for a few hours' rest, which I agree to only because I can't tell which end of my horse is the head. I wake up curled against Meredy's back, and we push our still-exhausted horses to gallop the rest of the way to the city.

Early morning sunlight warms Meredy's hair, turning it from its usual deep purple-red to a fiery shade. From behind, I could almost mistake her for Master Cymbre, but when my horse draws level with hers, the scar on her cheek and the determined look in her eyes—even her smile—are all Meredy. Not Cymbre, not Evander. *Just* Meredy.

"You don't have to do this, you know," I murmur as we cross into the oddly quiet heart of Grenwyr City at last. "This isn't your fight."

Meredy smiles, a warrior's sharp smile, and I'm flooded with gratitude that I've got such a brave girl beside me. "But it is. I'm helping you get justice for Evander. Besides, this is every Karthian's fight now. I know I wasn't myself in the Deadlands after working my magic with Lysander, but I still heard most of what the masked necromancer said before he died. Hadrien has a lot to answer for."

"Thank you." I clutch the horse's reins harder, resisting a sudden urge to reach for her, to steal a moment with her calming touch. I wonder if she knows how important she is to me. I want to tell her, but instead what leaves my mouth as we crest another hill is, "It feels like we've come a long way in just a few days."

Meredy opens her mouth, but as the palace comes into view, the determination in her eyes is swiftly replaced with fear.

I follow her gaze, struggling to make sense of the scene unfolding on the grassy slope below the palace. It looks as though all of Grenwyr City has gathered there, a sea of dark and light hair, scarves and dresses and fishermen's caps all blurring together.

That explains why the city seemed so quiet.

Above the people of Grenwyr, closer to the palace, sits a metal cage large enough to hold ten men or more. It's mostly covered by a sheet, but I glimpse a few pairs of boots and the bottom edges of the bars that form the cage. The sight makes my skin crawl.

And beside the large cage, looking handsome as ever in a tailored green doublet as he gazes down at the crowd, is Hadrien. I'd know his saunter and blond hair anywhere. Several men and women in archer's uniforms stand behind him, holding bows.

"Meredy," I say softly. "I need you and Lysander to go find Valoria, Jax, and Simeon. Warn them about Hadrien, if they don't already know." With shaking fingers, I unfasten Evander's sapphire pin from my tunic, the last piece of him I have to hold on to. "And take this. For luck."

Meredy closes her fist around the pin. Her gaze softens, telling me the gift needs no explanation. "Are you sure about Valoria?" She sticks the pin gently below her beast master's emeralds, blinking mist from her eyes. "What if she's been helping Hadrien with . . . whatever this is?" She gestures to the distant crowd on the hill.

I shake my head. "There's no way." Of course, I would have said the same thing about Hadrien just two days ago. "But be careful. Vaia knows I'm no great judge of character."

After a pause, Meredy says, "And assuming I *can* trust her?"

"Get her and the others out of the city, if they're willing," I murmur, wrapping Vane's blood-crusted cloak around my shoulders and pulling up the hood. "Otherwise, make them hide somewhere for now. You and Lysander must join them." I check that my cloak is concealing my sword completely. "Hadrien's only one man, even if he's a mad one, so I need to do this alone. Besides, I've got the perfect disguise."

Meredy's eyes widen as I put on Vane's silver mask. I'm sure I look like a nightmare. A nightmare who can barely see out of these tiny eye holes.

"I'll warn them, but then I'm coming right back for you," she says softly. "And before you try to argue, I'll save you the trouble.

You won't change my mind. Now tell me what you're going to do in that awful costume."

It takes me a moment to form the words. I can't believe I'm about to say this, but then, I can't see another way. I just know I've got to stop whatever's happening up on that hill.

"Kill Hadrien," I answer as I dismount from my horse.

"Odessa." Meredy slides off her horse's back and moves to my side, putting a hand on my arm. She doesn't tell me to be careful. She doesn't need to. The plea is there in her eyes, along with something else I can't name.

"You're nothing like I expected," I murmur from beneath the mask. It's already too warm against my skin. "You're nothing like, well, *him*. Evander."

Meredy purses her lips. Her expression is harder to read than ever as she pulls the mask from my face, running a finger along my jaw. "Is that a bad thing?"

"No," I insist, my mouth suddenly dry. "What I meant is, I'm scared. More scared than I've ever been. But . . ." But with her fingertips lingering on my cheek, even though I know what's waiting on that hill, I feel ready to fight.

"That makes two of us." She drops her hand to my shoulder. "You unsettle me."

"Me? Not the madman on the hill?" That earns a shaky smile from her.

In one swift motion, she closes the space between us and kisses me, wrapping her arms around my neck, and I melt into it, parting her lips with my tongue. Her hands grip my waist, pulling me closer, and I slide my fingers through her silky hair. Maybe it's too soon, but it doesn't feel that way anymore, not when she's so gentle and sure. She tastes of salt and a hint of strawberries, and I hunger for more. The way she muddles my thoughts with a single brush of her lips, making the whole mad world disappear and every part of me achingly, perfectly, wonderfully *alive*, is all the encouragement I need to survive.

Up on the palace hill, a nervous murmur rises from the crowd, loud enough to startle us apart. Meredy puts a hand to her lips, and I shiver as I realize we're doing the thing I swore I wouldn't do. Betraying Evander.

"This was a mistake," Meredy stammers as I slip my mask back on. "Evander. Firiel . . ."

"Agreed," I choke out, to stop her from saying more. Hearing the other girl's name on Meredy's lips stings, when it never has before. "It's already forgotten."

I don't want the last thing I ever see to be her guilt-stricken face. I don't want to wonder whether this would have happened if she'd come home when Evander was still alive.

Heart thumping like crazy, I hurry toward the crowd on the hill and force myself not to look back.

XXVIII

As I weave through the sea of Karthians on the hill, jabbed by a hundred elbows and coughed on by at least three people who probably have the black fever, I try not to think about that kiss.

About the way she pulled off my mask. About the way she tasted. About her startled, "This was a mistake," as she thought of Evander, or Firiel, or both. She's right, of course, but she's the one who started it.

It was only a kiss. A really good kiss, but still. It didn't have to mean anything.

By the time I break free of the crowd, I'm sweating under the bloodstained cloak. Thankfully it's a blue so dark that the stains aren't obvious, but I'm painfully aware of where each patch of dried blood on the cloth brushes against me.

"What kept you, Vane?" Hadrien asks, sounding far more irritable than I've ever heard him. He's paced a circle around the cage, worn his boot prints into the ground in his agitation. "I was start-ing to think something happened to you, and I was about to move forward without your particular brand of help." He scowls. "I *hate* being kept waiting."

I move to his side, not saying a word, tucking my shaking hands into the folds of the cloak. He seems to be awaiting some sort of explanation, but if I make a single sound, my disguise is ruined.

"Never mind." Hadrien sighs. He takes a deep breath and seems to brighten. "You're here now. Let's get started!" He claps his hands together, his brown eyes shining with manic glee as he spins to face the crowd.

I touch the hilt of Meredy's borrowed dagger in a sheath on my belt. A faint ringing echoes in my ears as I realize how much I'm dreading this. Dreading the murder of this killer, a man whose darkness was buried so deep beneath a mask of sunshine, I could've kissed him and never tasted a hint of shadow. I start trying to pull out the dagger, a difficult task while keeping it hidden beneath my cloak, when a familiar face catches my eye.

Lyda Crowther and several other nobles stand behind Hadrien's group of archers, all watching the restless crowd with solemn, almost bored expressions. Like they know exactly what's about to happen. But how could Lyda support Hadrien's twisted desire to make more Shades, when she never fully recovered from seeing her husband become one?

"Ladies and gentlemen of Grenwyr City," Hadrien shouts in a booming voice, spreading his arms to the crowd and drawing my attention away from Lyda. "Welcome! I, Prince Hadrien Wylding, have summoned you all here today for a demonstration of the greatest importance."

Softer, to one of the guards, he snaps, "Drop the cover."

As the sheet is whisked away from the cage, nearly everyone in the crowd gasps. Six shrouded Dead are cowering inside, gags tied over their masks to muffle their shouts. Two of them wear tall golden crowns set with five gems each, for Vaia's five beautiful sets of eyes: a glittering sapphire and emerald, a smoky quartz crystal, polished jasper, and turquoise.

The king and queen.

"Now listen up!" Hadrien yells to make himself heard over the shouts of the people. A few citizens tentatively step forward, and the guards take aim with their bows. Something tightens in my chest at the sight of Karthians facing senseless murder, but Hadrien holds up a hand to still the archers' volley.

"Necromancers have been allowing the Dead to rule over Karthia for far too long. Have you ever wondered why the Dead have to be slain and brought back every few years? Why they have to wear those shrouds?" Hadrien pauses for effect. "It's all to keep them from turning into the monsters they are inside."

The crowd is nearly silent now. I clench my fists at my sides, shaking with a hatred I've never felt toward anyone but the Shade that killed Evander. I don't know what Master Cymbre would do right now, but since she can't give me a better plan, I'm going to shove my dagger so deep into Hadrien's chest that he collapses on the spot.

"The Dead become monsters because it's nature's way of telling us they should *never* be brought back to the land of the living."

Hadrien's eyes flash in triumph as he says it, though I don't see anyone in the crowd nodding in agreement. "The necromancers' magic is a dark magic. A corruption of the natural order. The Dead belong in the Deadlands. And Karthia belongs to the *living*!"

Silence blankets the crowd. Many people's mouths hang open, while others turn away, heading back down the hill to their homes and their jobs.

"You don't believe me?" Hadrien shouts at them. "Then allow me to show you the monsters that have been walking among us for far too long!"

He nods to one of the guards, who removes the king's gag.

"Hadrien," King Wylding says in a low voice.

It takes every ounce of control I have not to reveal myself. To run to the cage, to press my face against the bars and promise the king I'll get him out of this somehow. I fumble to get a grip on my dagger without anyone noticing.

"Please, don't do this," the king continues in a shaky version of his usual rasp. "If you want me dead, if you really want me gone forever, then kill me in private. Burn my bones so my spirit has no home. But don't make me a Shade right here, not where I could hurt my people. Their lives matter far more than mine."

"You don't care about their lives," Hadrien snarls. "If you cared, you'd have stayed dead!"

"You think so?" the king says, anger warming his voice. "I thought you were smarter than this, Hadrien. But since you seem to need a reminder: I *don't* enjoy being run through with a sword every few years. I *don't* like being pulled from the peace of the Deadlands to this demanding, exhausting, messy life!" The king grips the bars of the cage with his gloved hands. "But I come back to Karthia because I have a duty to my people. No one knows them like I do. No one loves this land like I do. You think you can rule better than me after a mere eighteen years in the world?"

As the king and Hadrien growl at each other, I finally pull my dagger free of its sheath. It's hard to tell through the narrow slits of my mask whether anyone spotted me, but no one's coming after me, so I think I'm safe. I make my way to Hadrien's side, steeling myself for what I'm about to do.

The time for questions is over. I don't want to hear another word from him. He's not the prince I thought he was.

Hadrien turns his back on the king and shouts something else to the crowd. I'm too focused on moving with him to pick out the words. I keep close to his side, with just enough room to hold the blade between us. As I'm about to thrust the dagger into his ribs, a guard pushes me out of the way.

I stumble back a few paces, winding up beside the cage.

"See the monster who was making your laws and watching over you?" Hadrien thunders.

"Hadrien, no!" the king cries.

Two more guards reach between the bars, ripping off the king's shroud.

For a moment, I can see a faint impression of the handsome warrior King Wylding was in life. Though he's shrunken in stature, though his shaggy dark hair is brittle and his skin is waxy, pulled tightly over his too-thin face and limbs, his brown eyes are as bright and alive as Hadrien's. Then the change begins. His mouth grows wider, his teeth sharpening. His bright eyes shrink back into his skull until they're nothing but sightless black pits. His remaining flesh seems to wither before me, turning gray and stretching even tighter over his skeletal frame that grows taller, wider, suggesting great strength.

He throws back his head and howls, scratching the cage floor with his bony fingers, and it's all I can do to stay standing.

His eternal reign is over.

The other Dead in the cage writhe, either in pain or fear. I can't be sure. I drop my gaze, sickened by the monster wearing the king's crown. The cries rippling through the crowd make what I've just witnessed seem even worse.

"The king loved his people, Prince Hadrien!" a merchant shouts from near the front of the crowd. "He fed soup to the poor and brought gifts to new mothers and wrote poems for the harvest festival! How could you do this to him? To us?"

It's everything I wish I could say. Instead, I press my lips together to keep from screaming and concentrate on getting close to Hadrien again. I don't want the guards to see the knife slide into his ribs until it's too late for anyone to stop me or a healer to intervene. If I can attack soon, there's still a chance I can save the queen.

The caged Shade howls, then crunches down on something. Many people scream. The king-monster must be feeding on the other Dead trapped in there with it.

"Remove the rest of their shrouds," Hadrien calls to one of the guards. "And start passing out torches to the living."

Raising his voice, he shouts at the retreating crowd, "You see? That monster was your king! This is what the Dead all become, if given the chance. But we can fight them, my friends! Together.

With *me* on the throne, a *living* king. We'll close Death's convents and forbid anyone else from becoming a necromancer! We'll reopen the temples of Change and finally *thrive*!"

There are too many guards at Hadrien's side now. For the moment, I'm forced to clutch my dagger and glare at him from several paces away.

"We'll fight them with fire!" a woman calls from somewhere behind me. Lyda. "Take a torch and pass the rest along! The guards will help you light them. You see? The living are more powerful than the Dead!"

Her words are like a blow to the stomach, sending a wave of nausea through me. I wonder if Evander's mother knows that by supporting Hadrien's insanity, she helped to murder her own son. I don't really want to hear the answer.

If I make it out of this, I never want to see her again.

"Take a torch! Hurry!" Hadrien shouts.

The crowd has stopped retreating, many of them staring at the Shade wearing the king's crown as it presses against the bars of the cage, straining to get free.

"We can burn these monsters out of existence and take back our city! All you have to do is listen to me." Hadrien's teeth are stark white against his tan skin. "We can get rid of *all* the Dead before they become Shades and hurt those we love! It's time to take Karthia back from the cold hands of the Dead!"

"Why should we trust you?" yells a girl no older than nine. She clutches three dolls made of gray rags like they're weapons. "King Wylding was my friend!"

"King Wylding let your friends and neighbors die of the black fever," Hadrien retorts, his eyes flashing. "I tried working on a cure once, and do you know what your monster of a king did? Threw all my research away. *Burned* it! Years of studying and perfecting a life-saving potion, all gone." His voice breaks as he shouts, "The Dead hold us back with their fears! My sister Valoria has created inventions, inventions that could make Karthia a better and safer place to live, yet she's forced to hide them because of the laws of people whose time in Karthia should have ended long ago!"

I've made it to Hadrien's side again. No one is in my way. No one is stopping me from doing what I need to do. I can't bear to look behind me at what's in the cage. I just need to act. Now.

"Goodbye, Hadrien," I whisper as I jab the dagger toward him.

With a cry, he leaps aside as the blade nicks him in the ribs. But I know in a glance I didn't hit quite the right spot. The blade tore through his shirt and made a gash in his pale skin, deep enough to draw blood, but not enough to kill. I chase after him, heart pounding and mouth bone-dry, raising my dagger for a second attack.

But in an instant, two guards are on top of me. They rip off my mask and pin my arms too tightly behind my back, forcing me to drop my dagger.

"Sparrow, my love," Hadrien murmurs as I struggle against his guards. I kick both of them in the shins a few times, but they don't loosen their grip. "You were supposed to die in Elsinor."

He runs a finger slowly along my cheek, and I spit at him.

"Now, there's no need for that," he says coolly as another guard clamps a hand over my mouth. I glare at Hadrien, hoping he can feel the hatred pouring out of me from my eyes alone. "I should have known better than to underestimate you." He leans in, brushing his nose against mine, and all I can do is gag behind the guard's callused hand. "I really do admire your strength, my Sparrow, even if it's proving to be a colossal thorn in my side."

The sincerity in his voice makes me shudder. Not because he admires me in his twisted way, but because if not for Evander, there was a time when I could have liked the prince in return. I *did* like him, at least as a friend. But now I understand there's nothing but rot and weakness at his core. Nothing worth saving.

"I had a feeling it wasn't really Vane under there. He was usually trying to tell me what to do, not just quietly observing," Hadrien continues, still much too close to my face. "But I'll admit you fooled me for a moment, Sparrow."

Over Hadrien's shoulder, the glow of hundreds of lit torches is getting stronger by the moment, like a second sun rising.

As one of the guards snaps a pair of shackles around my wrists, I catch a glimpse of the crowd, and I'm relieved to see that at least some of them have fled. But not all. Not nearly enough. I hope Meredy didn't come back for me after all, but that she found my friends and she's taking them somewhere safe—if there is any such place anymore.

"Now, I'm going to have the guard remove his hand so you can tell me where Vane is," Hadrien says smoothly. "Nod if you understand."

I simply glare at him. It's all I can do with my hands, and now my feet, bound in heavy iron cuffs.

Still, the guard drops his hand. I utter every curse word I can think of, ones I picked up from the masters and a few that I've only heard in the Ashes. Words that feel gritty on my tongue and stick in my throat, though I choke them out anyway and hurl them at Hadrien.

The prince's face isn't so handsome anymore. He's frowning, his fists clenched at his sides like mine were when I had to listen to all the filth he spewed at the crowd.

"I was wrong about you, Odessa," he says at last, the words devoid of any emotion. "You aren't my Serpent after all. And although you haven't said so, I assume Vane is dead if you're wearing his mask." He looks me straight in the face and smiles. "Perhaps we're even, as my men are putting your friends Jax and Simeon to death as we speak."

He turns, gesturing to a guard. The older man drops a familiar sword in the grass at our feet, followed by several small daggers perfect for tucking up a sleeve or in a boot. Jax's blades. Jax, whose lips are dry and rough like his hands. Jax, who held me through the worst days of my new life without Evander.

Hadrien might as well have thrust the daggers into me, because the sight of them alone sends a wave of pain through my chest. Breathing hurts. Everything hurts.

The guard tosses something else. It's tiny, difficult to see in the blurry world of light and shadow dancing before my eyes. "I might actually keep that. It looks expensive. Kingly, even," Hadrien murmurs as the small shiny object lands near the daggers.

I don't need to blink away my tears to know he's got Simeon's ring. The one he still wears on a frayed cord around his neck, just like he did on the day the nuns found him, a frightened child wandering the Ashes. Simeon, the only person who can make me laugh on my worst days. Simeon, who's been my brother since the moment we met.

The noise of the crowd dies away. My knees buckle. If not for the guards, I'd fall to the ground. I want to sink through layers of earth to someplace where this pain can't find me. Where I can pretend everyone I love is waiting for me in the next room.

"Where's Valoria?" I demand. Surely he wouldn't kill his own sister?

"She's keeping the men of the dungeon company," Hadrien drawls unconcernedly. "And she'll stay there until she decides to support me, or she'll swing from the noose. But since *you're* here, you might as well witness the beginning of my reign."

He grabs my chin, forcing me to look toward the cage.

I don't fight him.

Three of the six Dead in the cage are now Shades, thrusting their rotting arms through the iron bars in an attempt to grasp at the distant crowd. The rest must have been eaten by the monsters. Six black shrouds and two gleaming crowns lie on the cage floor, forgotten.

Jax and Simeon are dead or dying.

Valoria's in a dungeon with thieves and murderers, if she's even still alive.

There's no one left for me to save.

Except—Meredy. If she can stay out of harm's way long enough, maybe I can escape and find her. The thought is all that keeps me standing.

"Now, let's see what a fine group of Karthians like yourselves can do to the monsters that are threatening to overrun your homes!" Hadrien roars at the crowd. "Burn them. Burn all the Dead, and purge our beloved Karthia of the necromancers' corruption!" He turns back to the cage. "I hope you're watching, Sparrow," he says softly, shifting his gaze from me to the nearby guards. "Release the Shades!"

The cage springs open.

I can't tell the Shades' shrill cries apart from the crowd's shrieks.

"Run!" I scream before a guard silences me again.

People scatter in all directions. The few foolish enough to hold their ground are slain where they stand. Some throw torches at the three Shades, while others drop theirs, setting the palace hill ablaze.

"Don't worry," Hadrien whispers in my ear, breath hot. "I have a weather mage ready to douse the fire. And I have archers standing by with flaming arrows, if the monsters prove to be too much for my people. But they're stronger than they think." He half smiles, a gesture that would be handsome if I didn't know how black his spirit was. "I had to have a backup plan, you see, in case Vane didn't come through." Winking, he adds, "I didn't *completely* underestimate you."

I have so much more I want to shout at him, but the hand over my mouth is pressed uncomfortably tight. Hoping to startle the guard into letting go, I push my tongue against the salty skin of his palm, but he doesn't even flinch.

As the people's screams get louder and tiny fires erupt all over the sloping hills leading up to the palace, Lyda and a few other living nobles join Hadrien beside the empty cage. They coolly survey the panicked fighting and the trail of carnage left by the three gray shadows as they dart among the people.

Lyda puts a hand on Hadrien's arm, not quite looking at me as she asks, "What are you going to do with her, Majesty?"

Her. She doesn't even have the courage to use my name.

"I'm glad you asked," Hadrien says, holding my gaze but talking to Lyda. "I want you to kill her, Baroness Crowther. She may have the strength of Vaia, but with her hands and feet bound, she's no more threat to anyone than a rabbit in a hunter's snare. Even *you* can't fail." Frowning slightly, he adds, "Given your history with her, I trust you'll see that it's done swiftly. She deserves a warrior's death, after all."

Lyda blanches, her blue eyes glistening, but she nods to one of the guards.

The clamor of terrified people fades as I'm struck in the back of the head.

XXIX

Everything is pitch-dark. I can't see. I try to reach up, to feel what's wrong with my eyes, but my hands are still shackled. I open my mouth to call for help just as Lyda speaks softly from somewhere nearby.

"I can't do it." She takes a deep breath. "I can't kill you, Sparrow, any more than I could bring myself to kill Evander when Hadrien asked it of me to prove my loyalty."

It sounds like she's crying.

The noise should probably fill me with dread, but I don't feel anything.

Jax and Simeon are probably dead by now. Valoria's trapped. Vaia only knows where Meredy is. And now the Dead I worked so hard to raise, to protect, are being made into monsters and hunted down by Hadrien and his followers just to terrify the people of Karthia into choosing him as their leader.

If I let myself feel any of the pain, any of the losses, right now, I'm afraid it'll break me open and what sanity I have left will slip away.

And if the Dead don't have me to fight for them, they'll have no one.

"What's happening?" I cough, swallowing to wet my parched throat. Lyda's finally stopped crying. "Why can't I see? What have you done?"

"I blinded you while you were unconscious. A few drops of potion in each eye. And now I'm taking you to the Deadlands." I picture her frosty blue eyes narrowing as she adds in a crisp voice, "It'll only be a matter of time before a Shade finds you and does what I can't."

And now I understand. Without my sight, I can't find my way out of the ever-shifting Deadlands. And with my hands bound, I can't fight any monsters that come near.

Lyda's well-manicured fingernails dig into my arms as she starts to drag me. I try to kick her, relieved to find my feet are no longer shackled like my hands, but I only lash at air. Whatever gate she's pulling me toward, she's doing it alone, or someone would no doubt be holding my legs.

"Why, Lyda?" I ask as she sets me down a short while later. "I know you fear the Dead, but this . . ."

There are cold cobblestones beneath my head, and the occasional scream echoes in the distance. We must be on the outskirts of Grenwyr City, barely removed from the crowd and the rampaging Shades.

I'm amazed Hadrien hasn't had his archers kill them by now.

I thought he only wanted to scare people into following him, not murder them before they have a chance to make up their minds. But then, Hadrien wouldn't be doing any of this if he truly cared about his people.

"Sometimes," Lyda says softly, drawing my attention back to her, "we have to sacrifice those we love for a greater good."

"You think *Hadrien* is even remotely good?"

"Maybe not. But it's time we had a living king. It can only lead to a better Karthia." Lyda's breathing hard from the effort of dragging me. "After what happened to my husband, I knew living among the Dead was impossible. Death is an ending, not a new beginning. That's why I begged and pleaded with you and Evander for years to stop your foolish necromancer training—but you wouldn't listen. You became part of the problem, and neither of you cared how much it hurt me. The necromancers had to be stopped. It doesn't matter that one was my son. Or that one is you. It's for the greater good of Karthia."

"And you think all this death is going to bring *peace* somehow?"

"Yes." She groans as she pulls me upward onto cool, damp earth, and I know we're inside a tunnel to the Deadlands now. "With Hadrien on the throne and the Dead back in the Deadlands, my daughters can live in a world where they won't have to fear monsters."

I laugh, though there's no joy in the sound. "You realize you're about to murder me, right? That makes you as wicked as a Shade, even if you're not willing to get your hands dirty." I wish I could see her face as I taunt her. It's so much more satisfying that way. "If it's a world without monsters you want, you should start by falling on your own sword."

Lyda's breathing becomes more and more ragged as she pulls me by the back of my shirt down a long tunnel to the Deadlands. This is probably the hardest day's work a delicate lady like her has ever had to do. Maybe she's even breaking a sweat.

She doesn't say another word. My back aches, sore and scratched and probably bleeding from being pulled over sharp stones and twigs. Finally, she releases me, and my head falls on a soft bed of flowers.

I must be in one of the Deadlands' fields or gardens.

Something sharp slices across my arm above the shackles. It's a shallow cut, but it still hurts enough that I have to bite down on my lip to keep from crying out. I don't need to ask why Lyda did that. I've done it enough times myself.

She wants to be sure the Shades will find me.

"Goodbye, Sparrow," she murmurs, pressing a light kiss to my forehead. "I'm sorry. I did care for you once, you know, back when I still hoped I could change your mind."

"So that's it, then?" I shout after Lyda's retreating footsteps. I can't believe I ever looked to her as a mother of sorts, a silver-tongued snake in a fancy dress. Cymbre was my real mother. A sword-wielding, foul-mouthed, plain-trousers-wearing *real* mother. "You're just going to leave me like this?"

Of course she is. She's no better than Hadrien, and just as much of a coward.

The wind rustles through the Deadlands' giant blossoms like

a song, lulling me to sleep. This is when I'd reach for the honey on my necromancer's belt, if I were wearing it.

But my sword is gone. My friends are gone, or as good as gone. There's nothing left to tie me to the land of the living.

Nothing, nothing, nothing, the flowers sing.

I might as well stay here and breathe in the chill, utterly scentless air until my own end. I've been fighting so much lately. All my cuts and bruises, the screams of the dying, the sights and smells of so much carnage. It's a lot for anyone to bear. I deserve a good long rest in a place where everything is beautiful, a place where the cold dulls all other senses.

I close my sightless eyes and curl up on my side.

After a while, I can't feel the warmth of fresh blood trickling down my arm anymore. I'm as light as a blade of grass, ready to float away.

Evander drifts in and out of my thoughts. Sometimes he offers me his hand from the other side of a deep ravine, and at others, he turns his back on me. Almost like he's two different people. I wonder which Evander is real, and which is the one I conjured during my potion-fueled hallucinations.

A hand closes firmly over my shoulder. I guess this is the real Evander, come to take me to wherever he is now.

He grips me by both shoulders, shaking me so hard my teeth bang together.

Gasping, I sit up, inhaling the Deadlands' crisp air.

Another pair of cold but solid hands grabs hold of mine, pulling up to my feet.

"What's happening?" I rasp over the sound of my beating heart.

No one answers. I can't tell how many pairs of cold hands are on my back, are gripping my arms, are marching me through the field. They're spirits, I'm sure of that much. But I can't imagine where they're taking me. Maybe they want to feed me to the Shades that have been terrifying them all into hiding at the farthest corners of the Deadlands.

As I stumble down a hill, quickly steadied by their many hands, I say the first spirit's name that comes to mind. "Firiel?"

Long, icy fingers trail through my hair, then touch my cheek as if to say, *Yes.*

"Meredy, she could be in danger. If—if you help me find my way out of here, I can try to save her from the terrible thing that's happening in Karthia."

As I think of Meredy, a knot forms in my throat. I wish I could see her again. But even if I do make my way out of here, I don't know how long I'll last in the Shade-ravaged Grenwyr City when I can't see a thing.

The spirits steer me to the left, and my shoulders tense at the sound of running water.

There's a bridge here, I realize, as the wooden planks groan under my feet.

A moment later, I feel a familiar tugging around my navel, drawing me toward a nearby gate. Lyda must have forgotten why they call me the Sparrow. And so, for a moment there, did I. I don't need to rely completely on my sight when I'm in the Deadlands.

The spirits support me as I stagger toward the gate, too dizzy to run, and the pull grows stronger until I know without needing to look that we're standing in the gate's glow.

The spirits must be repaying me for all the times I've taken many of them home to their bodies. Protecting me, like I've always tried to protect them. Or else they know I don't belong here. That I belong in Karthia, with the sun and the birds and the wide, sparkling sea. With the hopes and failures and laughter of the living.

I want to cry and smile at the same time. "Thank you," I murmur. "I had no idea you'd come to . . ."

My voice trails off. The touch of the cold hands vanishes as suddenly as it arrived. The spirits must be gliding away. All but one, it seems, as someone gives me a firm push toward the gate and home beyond.

In the distance, the flowers of the Deadlands rustle their soft petals and sing.

Stay, stay, stay.

I hesitate, one foot in the gate.

If I go back to Karthia, everything around me will be out of my control. The killings. The monsters. The twisted dreams of a mad prince.

Except there's one thing I can control. What I do about it.

I step my other foot in the gate, humming to drown out the Deadlands' song, and begin the long walk through the tunnel.

Things will never be perfect, as Master Cymbre tried to teach me. Life will be hard and painful as long as I cling to it, but there's beauty in it, too. It used to be easy to find, whenever I looked in

Evander's eyes. And now I've seen it in Meredy's. And it's *mine* to fight for.

I'll think of every lost life with every breath I take, always.

Yet as long as I'm alive, I have to keep going. One step after another through this tunnel until I'm back in Grenwyr City to rejoin the battle, a little more broken than before.

For Evander. For my friends and the Dead and the helpless. For me.

All I can do is keep fighting.

I fall out of the gate feet-first, toppling over onto cobblestones that are cold and slick with what I hope is rain.

I push myself up using my elbows and stagger to my feet, all the while straining my ears for any sign of the crowd from the hill. Or any of Grenwyr City's citizens, for that matter. The scents of death surround me, but I don't hear anything, not a whisper or a scream. I hold my bound hands out, trying to feel the walls of any buildings before I hit them, my stomach churning over the stench I can't seem to escape no matter which way I turn.

I hurry down what must be an alleyway, a place where the air is cooler and, mercifully, cleaner. Maybe this is a safe spot to catch my breath. But the moment I forget to test the ground in front of me with my toes before taking a step, I trip over the still-warm body of someone large, likely a man, and crash down hard. He's not breathing.

Gasping for breath, I crawl away. There's no way I'm going to find my friends, or the frantic people of Grenwyr, if I can't even walk a few paces without falling.

Still, I made a promise to myself in the Deadlands. I have to get up. I have to keep going.

A gust of warm, fishy breath stops me as I retrace my steps through the alley. I raise my hands to shield my face as a beast growls, and something furry wallops me right in the middle. It knocks me backward, but mercifully, not off my feet again.

"Good boy, Lysander!" Meredy calls. "Odessa, where in Vaia's name have you been?"

I slump against the bear's familiar bulk and laugh until my chest aches.

"We've been looking for you everywhere," Meredy breathes, much closer now. "Oh, no. What's wrong? Danial, get over here!"

A moment later, a slender hand—wearing several rings, by the feel of it—covers my sightless eyes. Danial, preparing to heal me.

"Your mother did this," I murmur to Meredy.

"What?" There's shock and desperation in her voice. I try to soften my approach, but the words still come out in a breathless rush.

"You know how she always resented Evander and me for becoming necromancers? Well, she's one of Hadrien's biggest supporters." My voice burns with bitterness. "He ordered her to kill me, so she took my sight and left me bleeding in the Deadlands."

There's a long, heart-pounding silence, then: "I don't want to believe it, but . . ." Meredy sighs. "I know you wouldn't lie. And after everything I've seen in the past few days, not much could shock me. How'd you get out, blind and bound like this?"

I smile at the memory. "Your Firiel. She and some other spirits helped me to a gate."

Meredy clasps my hands in hers. "I'm sorry," she says fiercely. "I'm so, so sorry."

I squeeze her hands, wanting to repay her for all the times she's steadied me.

"She's not my mother now," Meredy adds, her whisper turning harsh. "She's *nothing* to me. But Firiel, she—helped you?"

I nod, and Meredy makes a noise between a laugh and a sigh. "She was always so kind. I'm glad to hear death hasn't changed her."

Sudden warmth pricks my eyelids. As Danial draws his hand back from my face, his light hazel eyes fill my view. I grin, leaning in to kiss his pale cheeks one after the other, and spot Meredy beside him.

Her blouse and deerskin trousers are torn in a few places, and there's blood on one of her sleeves, but it doesn't appear to be hers. Danial's sturdy white healer's uniform is torn, too, his kohl eyeliner smudged, and his scraped knee is crusted with bits of dirt and grass.

"You should probably heal yourself," I whisper to him as we pull apart.

"If only that would work." Danial grins, his hands shaking slightly. "Welcome back, Sparrow."

"Where's—?" I start to ask, but Meredy interrupts.

"Valoria's out of the dungeon and still in one piece," she says quickly, anticipating my question. "One of Hadrien's guards tried to kill me on the way there, but after I stabbed him . . ." She lets the words hang in the air, grinning wearily, and perhaps a little proudly. "He told me where the princess was. And that's where I found Danial, protecting our Valoria from the unruliest prisoners."

"We were in the middle of lunch when Hadrien ordered the guards to seize her," Danial explains, his eyes glinting with a fierceness I've never seen in him. "Apparently protesting a wrongful imprisonment earns you a spot in the dungeons these days. That, or they didn't appreciate me trying to stab them with my steak knife while they were leading Valoria away."

I gaze past Meredy to the mouth of the alley, where muted gray afternoon light covers the city, half expecting to see Valoria dashing toward us. There are far fewer bodies on the ground than I imagined, and the sight of the calm street gives me hope. "Where's the princess now?"

Meredy exchanges a glance with Lysander, who delicately pokes a claw into the shackles around my wrists. As they spring open, she gives a fleeting smile. "Last we saw Valoria," she says, somber once again, "she was heading for the harbor. She heard a rumor that Jax and Simeon were drowned there."

"We were with her for a while, looking for you on the way." Danial reaches to heal the cut on my arm, and I'm relieved it's not as deep as I thought. His light touch warms my skin as the cut pulls itself shut, leaving only a faint white scar that should fade within days.

"We got separated when one of the Shades chased the crowd across Market Square," Danial adds, distracted. He gazes off into the distance as he whispers, "If we make it through this, if he's still alive, I'm going to ask Simeon to marry me."

I give him a long look. "What if Si still wants to be a necromancer after this?"

Danial smiles, grimly determined. "Then I'll learn how to be the warrior he needs, so I can protect him. So I can be strong even when he's in the Deadlands."

"I hate to interrupt, but—there are fires all over the city," Meredy says urgently, kneeling beside us. "One of the Shades is dead, but two others are still roaming around, terrifying everyone and feeding on anyone they can grab." She laughs bitterly. "I heard some of Hadrien's shouts from inside the palace. His archers aren't controlling the monsters as well as he'd planned. He's worried all the deaths will keep him from winning over his new subjects."

"Then you've got to go after Valoria. *Now*. Make sure she stays safe." I grip Meredy's arms, grateful as always for her steadying presence. "Karthia will need her when this is all over. After I kill Hadrien."

Her green eyes widen. "You tried that once before. It didn't work out so well, remember?" She points to the shackles on the ground.

"I'll be more careful this time."

She leans closer, her breath damp against my lips, reminding me of our earlier kiss. "Not good enough. I don't think you know the meaning of that word."

My heart threatens to beat out of my chest as I meet her gaze. "Maybe my version of careful just looks different from everyone else's. Don't go getting yourself killed either, all right?"

Beside us, Danial clears his throat, ushering us back to our senses. "Remember Valoria?" he murmurs softly. "That princess we need to find?"

My face is hot as I turn to him. "Danial, will you go with Meredy to the harbor?" I sound stupidly breathless and hope that he doesn't notice.

Danial nods, tying his long raven hair back from his face. He leans over the dead man I tripped on when I first stumbled into the alley and rifles through his belongings. When he straightens, he's clutching a handsome dagger. "This time, I want to try stabbing them with something bigger than a steak knife."

I bite my lip, taking a moment to study him as I get to my feet. I never knew there was a fighter hiding beneath Danial's pristine healer's robes and gentle smile. I clearly wasn't looking hard enough.

"Where'd you learn how to wield one of those?" Meredy asks him, fighting back a grin that surfaces despite the weary look in her eyes. "They teach you how to kill people during your healer's training?"

"It's just healing in reverse," Danial says quickly. It's the kind of joke Simeon would make, and perhaps he realizes it, because as soon as he utters the words, his face falls. "Actually," he murmurs to his boots, "I didn't know I could handle any kind of weapon until today. I always thought I'd be the one in need of rescuing in a fight. But . . ." He shrugs. "When someone I knew was in danger, instinct took over. And it turns out my instincts are almost as good at hurting people as they are curing them."

I wrap my arms around him, stealing his breath. "You're stronger than you think, Danial. I'll come find you and Meredy after . . ."

"Hadrien," Meredy finishes. "He's locked himself in the throne room with some of his guards, last we heard. He didn't want to take any chances until the Shades were all gone." She rolls her eyes, then grows solemn again. "I'm sending Lysander with you, so you won't have to fight him alone."

"Are you sure that's a good idea?" I take both her hands, remembering what happened after she possessed Lysander during our fight against the Shade-baiters.

She squeezes my fingers. "Good idea or not, you can't talk me out of it. I can split my attention between my body and Lysander's," Meredy says confidently. Her voice wavers slightly as she adds, "At least, I think I can . . . I've only tried it once before, and that was over a year ago."

There's no way I'm letting her experiment at a time like this. "Meredy—"

"If it's too much, I'll pop out of Lysander's mind like *that*." She snaps her fingers and raises her head, looking determined. Her eyes linger on my face. "Do you trust me?"

"Of course." I sigh. She's too stubborn, too much like me once she's made up her mind. "Just be careful. I need you." Cringing at how that sounded, I hurry to add, "I mean, I need you to have your wits about you for whatever happens next."

Mustering a grin, Meredy nudges my shoulder with hers. "Surely you forget who you're dealing with, master necromancer. I'm the youngest beast master in almost a century."

"I could never forget anything about you, *Master Crowther*." I grin back. "Even if I wanted to."

I drop her hands and stride out of the alley, looking for anything I can use as a weapon. I feel exposed without my sword and can't rely on Lysander alone—especially if we get separated.

I break into a run, Lysander easily keeping pace with me. Meredy and Danial are already out of sight, no doubt on their way toward the harbor.

"You're better than a sword anyway," I tell the grizzly. "Just look for something sharp I can grab as backup, all right?"

He snarls, his eyes glowing a familiar shade of green.

"That's the spirit," I mutter, patting his massive shaggy head. "Now let's go overthrow the king."

But instead, Lysander stops in his tracks. He growls again, deeper, the bone-chilling sound I've come to think of as a warning signal. I follow his glowing eyes up the narrow road leading out of the city and spot what's filled him with such rage.

A Shade stumbles toward us, scenting the air, a victim half-dangling out of its cavernous mouth.

XXX

The Shade snarls at us as it chokes down the last of its meal, boots and all. There's no way to tell if it was once King Wylding, but in my mind it was, which makes it more difficult to pick up a jagged piece of wood from the road and take a swing at its skeletal face.

It's a new Shade, so it's clumsier than the one that killed Evander, but it's already grown strong feeding on Grenwyr's citizens today. It effortlessly dodges my attack, lashing out with a rotting gray arm and grabbing the other end of the wooden beam.

I grip my end of the beam with both hands, but playing tug-of-war with the Shade is like playing against several grown men. Gritting my teeth, I struggle to hang on, my fingernails tearing, until Lysander breaks the Shade's hold with a swipe of his deadly claws.

"Thanks," I murmur, reminding myself that it's really Meredy in there.

As Lysander roars in the Shade's face, I look around at the empty buildings of Merchant Square, hoping to spot a flicker of flame I can drive the monster toward. But everything is soaked thanks to Hadrien's weather mage.

I take another hasty look around as the Shade tosses Lysander across the road. The bear groans but staggers upright almost at once.

There's a fountain at the center of this square. The pretty teal and gold mosaic tiles around it glisten with overflowing water. Since Shades rely on scent to hunt, it shouldn't be able to find us if we're submerged. It'll smell something else in the air and move on.

"Into the fountain!" I shout at Lysander.

The bear turns, bounding toward the fountain with the Shade on his heels.

Bracing myself for the cold, I climb over the edge and take a huge breath before dunking my head underwater. This would never work in the Deadlands, where the water would strip my memories away before I could say *Karthia*. But maybe here, in the land of the living, my quick thinking could save us.

The cold stings at first, forcing itself up my nose and under my eyelids.

Lysander crashes into the water as the breath I've been holding starts to burn.

Howling, the Shade plunges its bony arm into the fountain, and I squirm to keep it from grabbing my leg.

Too late, I realize that the fountain, deep as it is, may not entirely cover Lysander. The bear does his best to flatten himself against the bottom as the Shade hisses and spits, trying to catch a piece of our flesh.

Any moment now, I'm going to have to come up for air. Then we'll really be in trouble.

Forcing my eyes to stay open in the clear water, I nearly touch noses with Lysander. Lysander's glowing green eyes hold mine. We don't have time to waste on this Shade, not with each second meaning Meredy might lose control of her senses.

My head is spinning. My body's getting lighter.

My lungs are on fire.

Blinking an apology at Lysander, I push myself off the fountain floor and emerge into the brisk afternoon air, gasping and shaking.

The Shade is nowhere to be seen.

"Palace," I say to Lysander through chattering teeth. "And Meredy, if you can hear me, get out of Lysander's head. I can manage him on my own from here."

The bear lumbers out of the fountain after me, growling, his eyes flashing an unearthly green. He slides on the tiles as he shakes himself off, soaking me with a fresh wave of icy water. Then he darts out of Merchant Square, leading the uphill climb to the palace, his glowing green eyes assuring me it's really Meredy still in control.

I run after him, my clothes clinging to me like a second skin. I pause only once, not for breath but to search the pockets of a fallen guard I dimly recognize from the palace.

Unexpected tears prick my eyes as I slide a dagger from her belt. I wish she had a sword, the weapon I've trained with for years, but this will have to do. I squeeze her hand, shuddering as my gaze settles on the spot where a Shade took a bite out of her.

Lysander growls from somewhere up ahead, and I take off running, dagger in hand.

The back entrance to the palace is surprisingly empty. I expected guards with flaming arrows stationed in every nook, at every door and window, yet there's no one near parading past the sad iron cage. There's no one standing with a weapon at the ready, taking aim at a soaking wet girl and her bear who look like the sea just spit them out.

Maybe everyone is hiding until this storm blows over, I decide as we navigate the vacant corridors leading to the throne room. If I were one of the Dead, I surely wouldn't want to be seen by anyone living right now, not knowing how they'd taken Hadrien's little "demonstration." Knowing the king I'd followed all my life was gone.

I rub my chilled arms as Lysander rounds a bend, taking us down another deserted hallway where we have to step over potted trees and flowering shrubs that have fallen across our path. The silence is somehow more unsettling than the screams and clashes of battle.

As we near the throne room, someone coughs. The sound startles me into alertness, and I hold my dagger at the ready. Peering around a corner, I count ten guards stationed outside the throne room's only entrance and exit.

Of course Hadrien's in there, the arrogant boy who thinks himself a king. But *king* is more than just a title, and while he can call himself whatever he pleases, he'll never rule the hearts or minds of Karthia.

"Now, Lysander," I whisper as one of the guards bends over to inspect a cut on his leg.

Glowing eyes narrowed, the bear charges around the corner, sending the newly hired guards into a frenzy. I don't know what promises they made to Hadrien, but while they draw their swords and bows, not one of them looks prepared to fight a grizzly.

I dart through the chaos toward the throne room. Lysander's bulk knocks me sideways, into a soldier who swings his sword at me. I drop to the ground, slashing the backs of his knees with my dagger, and crawl as fast as I can toward the throne room doors.

Something pierces my leg. The soldier I cut looms over me, his face white and livid, the tip of his blade stuck in my calf. "Where do you think you're going?" he sneers.

I try to jerk away, but the blade pins me in place. The slightest movement sends fresh waves of pain through my leg.

The soldier shakes his head, pulling the sword from my leg and raising it like he's about to end my life, right here on this worn old floor.

But before he has a chance, Lysander knocks him back into a bloody pile of his fellow guards. The bear roars, rising up on his hind legs in a sort of victory dance. "Doing okay in there, Meredy?" I whisper.

Lysander's eyes flicker as he settles back down, shifting from green to brown, then back to glowing green.

I shiver. Could Meredy be losing control? Or worse, what if she's hurt? Hopefully, she's keeping her promise and leaving Lysander's mind to focus on whatever she and Danial are facing now.

As Lysander saunters toward the throne room, I hiss, "Meredy, if you're still in there, *go*. Take care of yourself. That's an order!"

Then I charge after the bear.

"What's the news from the city—?" Hadrien's question dies on his tongue as he catches sight of Lysander and me. "Sparrow." He blinks at me from atop the throne, perhaps wondering if he's seeing a spirit walking among the living.

Four more guards charge toward us, but Lysander quickly sets to work disarming them.

I raise my dagger, noting the absence of the usual longsword at Hadrien's side. His blade rests in its scabbard on a table well out of reach of the throne, almost like it's on display, or at least like he doesn't feel he needs it here. King Wylding's jeweled crown looks especially fine on the handsome prince, making his shadow on the floor taller, more imposing.

But I'm not afraid.

Hadrien frowns at the water I'm dripping on the room's glossy floor. "Did Lyda try to drown you?" he asks quietly, not bothering to rise as I climb the steps to where he sits. "She couldn't even handle this one simple task. You were as good as dead when I handed you over!" He shakes his head, disgust evident in his tone.

I clutch the dagger so hard my knuckles ache in protest. I'm almost to the throne. Almost close enough to knock the crown right off his overinflated head.

But as I gaze from my blade, still slick with the guard's blood, to Hadrien's neck, my stomach churns. There's been so much death today already. More than anyone should have to witness in a country that's not at war. But then, I guess that's what this is.

Hadrien rises from the throne, gazing past me at Lysander and the guards. Remembering the way Lysander's eyes had returned to their usual amber brown, I wish I could see what's happening, but I won't turn my back on Hadrien for an instant.

"Take off the crown," I say firmly as his eyes return to mine. Finally, we're face-to-face, standing on the narrow platform that holds the throne. "If you come with me peacefully, I'll tell Valoria not to have you hanged. We can get you your own dungeon cell, where you'll never have to gaze upon any of the Dead again . . ."

Hadrien lunges for my dagger. I drop the blade and grab his wrist with both hands, twisting it as hard as I can. The resulting crack raises gooseflesh on my arms.

He screams several names at me as we both scramble to retrieve my fallen dagger. I reach it first, my fingers closing around the hilt and the fingers of his good hand closing over mine. He spits a curse, releasing his grip as though my skin burned him.

Lysander growls low and long like thunder, drawing my gaze for the briefest moment. Like a sheepdog, he's herded all the guards into a far corner of the room, unimpressed by their blades and their taunts.

Sensing my distraction, Hadrien wraps his good hand around my neck, snarling as I struggle to pry him off.

"It doesn't—" I splutter as his fingers squeeze the breath out of me. I strike with the dagger one-handed, still trying to pry him off with the other, but my aim is terrible as stars dance before my eyes.

The dagger sinks into his shoulder, which only makes him choke me harder.

"It doesn't have to be like this," I gasp. "No one has to die."

Hadrien shakes his head, smiling almost sadly as he tightens his grip, crushing my throat. I dig my jagged fingernails into his hand, to no effect. "Only one of us will walk out of this room alive, Sparrow. So think of what's best for Karthia. Think of what our people need. You, or me." Gazing calmly into my eyes despite the blood oozing from his shoulder, he adds, "I trust you'll choose what's right."

Finally, I manage to shove the dagger just beneath his ribs despite my lungs screaming for breath. "Fine," I growl, plunging the blade deep into him before he has time to react. Finishing what I started back on the hillside. "Me."

My heart thuds in my ears and time seems to slow, Hadrien suspended on the end of my blade. Every monster can be beaten. Of course, he hardly looks monstrous now. He looks like a pale, scared boy who has no idea how many lives he's ruined.

He collapses at the base of the throne, gasping for breath, trying vainly to stop the life from leaking out of him.

Swallowing hard as I'm reminded of Evander's final moments, I kneel beside him.

"If you'd been the least bit afraid of me, you might've had a chance. You might've bothered to fetch your blade before I made it all the way to the throne," I whisper.

His eyes are glassy as he nods. "You . . . you're unkillable." He tries, I think, to smile.

"No. Just lucky."

He raises a bloodied hand to my face. I bite back my revulsion, allowing the hesitant touch to my cheek. "I wish I were strong like you, Sparrow," he murmurs. "Like it or not . . . you're the one who will change things around here. But you're going to regret this someday, I promise."

His hand falls from my face. As his body blurs beneath my gaze, I press my fingers to his neck, clumsily feeling for a pulse. His heartbeat slows to nothing.

The reign of Karthia's mad king has ended after just one day. Yet for some reason, I don't feel any better.

Evander. Jax. Simeon. Master Cymbre. Master Nicanor. I whisper their names as I stand over Hadrien's body. He may be gone, but in case his spirit is lingering, I want him to hear everything he took from me.

I want to hate him more than I do. I just don't have enough anger left.

Lysander's fishy breath washes over me, and I brush the tears from my face.

"Time to go, is it?" I ask thickly.

The bear growls in answer, his unearthly green eyes flashing.

Rubbing my sore neck, I take a last look at the still-warm husk of the beloved brother I've taken from Valoria. The handsome prince who always asked me to dance. The prince who loved his siblings. And who, in some twisted way, loved his people.

I gently close his empty brown eyes, glad I can't see the future he glimpsed with them. "Goodbye," I whisper one last time, snatching the crown from his head.

I set it on the seat of the vacant throne, where it can wait for the new queen to claim it. A queen who didn't choose to murder or scheme to get here.

Lysander whines, pawing the throne. Past him, I notice for the first time a group of dead or unconscious guards scattered around the base of the steps.

His eyes are brown again, not glowing green.

Meredy.

Even if she's not hurt, even if she merely kept her word and left the grizzly's mind, I have to find her. Just to be sure. "Come on!" I tell the bear.

I rush out the doors, wincing from the pain in my lower leg where the guard stabbed me, and collide with a finely dressed woman when I round the corner.

Lyda Crowther gasps, swaying from the impact. "How did you—?"

"Lysander!" I shout, hoping the grizzly will still obey me without Meredy's influence.

I shove Lyda against the wall. She tries to break free from my grip on her arms, kicking and scratching me with her sharp nails, but I manage to twist her arms behind her back as Lysander dashes to my side.

"You take a swing at me again, and the bear will eat you," I growl, dabbing at one of the deeper scratches on my forearm.

Lysander raises a paw, eliciting a shrill noise from Lyda, but all he does is press her against the wall so I can search for something to bind her hands.

"Too bad I don't have those shackles you used on me," I mutter as I tie her wrists together with strips of cloth from my already-ruined tunic. It'll have to do, at least for the few minutes it takes to reach our destination.

I steer her down the hall by her shoulders, giving Lysander a nod of thanks. His eyes are still brown, and my heart beats faster with the need to get to Meredy.

"Where are you taking me?" Lyda asks quietly.

I don't answer. She'll figure it out soon enough on her own, when we descend the dark steps to the dungeon.

XXXI

It's not hard to find the crowd this time. Judging by the sight and sound of things, one of the Shades has found them before me. A column of smoke rises over the buildings facing the harbor, dark against the pale gray sky, and Lysander and I run through the empty streets toward the beacon of ash.

I search for Meredy each time we pass a body in the road. My stomach sinks further when Lysander stops to sniff the air and whines near the alley where we saw her last.

I've lost enough, *more* than enough for any lifetime, in just a few months. And somehow, cold and wet and tired as I am, I have to be ready to fight whatever awaits me deeper in the city. I have to protect whatever life Grenwyr has left. And I can't lose hope.

As we approach a dense cluster of buildings where fishermen live and sell their wares, the voices and shouts that began as faint murmurs on the palace hill grow louder. I stride through the alley between two pale stone buildings and find myself at the back of a crowd. A hundred people or more have formed a circle around the fire that guided me here. Hadrien's weather mage must have fled or been killed, or he'd have doused these flames by now.

Tears flow freely down some of the gathered faces. But their shouts, I realize, are calls of triumph. There are even a few smiles reflected in the dwindling blaze.

"Was that a Shade?" I ask a grim-faced woman in the uniform of a palace chambermaid, pointing to the pile of rubble slowly burning down to nothing.

"Two of them," the woman answers, nodding.

"Did Prince Hadrien's guards kill—?"

The woman cuts me off with a wave and a glare. "Them? They ran away after one of the monsters ate their captain. *We*"—she nods to a ragged-looking assortment of Grenwyr's fishermen, merchants, and farmers—"were the only ones who didn't flee or hide. We trapped the last two monsters here and threw torches at them. They were outnumbered. Didn't know who to grab or which way to turn."

I take a deep breath and slowly exhale, gazing around. Some people are dispersing from the crowd, calling loved ones' names. A few boys start moving the bodies of the fallen into neat rows where their families can identify them. And a tall willowy girl raises her arms to the sky in a sort of elegant dance, squeezing rain from the heavy clouds to put out the remaining flickers of fire around us with magic worthy of a master weather mage's robes.

Maybe I shouldn't worry so much about this city and its people. It turns out Karthia can take care of itself, just like Hadrien thought.

Someone taps me on the shoulder. Before I can turn around, a familiar voice says, "Thank Vaia you're all right! Meredy said you were headed to the palace alone to confront Hadrien. I was so worried for you, I nearly threw up. Also—hello."

"Valoria!"

As I turn to face the princess, time seems to slow. Everything around us fades into the distance. Studying her soot-blackened face, her matted blond hair and crooked glasses, I wonder if she's ready to hear that she's now queen. To hear what I had to do. But there are other pressing matters. Too many of them.

"Have you seen Meredy and Danial?" I blurt. "Are you hurt? Are they?"

I can't bring myself to ask about Jax and Simeon.

"I'm fine, thanks to the quick thinking of the good people of Grenwyr." Valoria tries to rub some of the ash off her face, but she just smears it around. "But . . . your trip to the palace . . ." She frowns, searching my eyes. "What happened up there? Where's Hadrien?"

A heavy weight fills my stomach as I hear the ache in her voice. "I'm sorry, Valoria. But he gave me a terrible choice," I explain slowly, hoping she can sense my regret. "He had his hand around my neck, and he said one of us had to die. To think of what was best for Karthia. So . . . I chose."

She stops me with a look. "After everything he did . . . I'm just glad I didn't have to do it myself." She bows her head, then takes my hands.

For a moment, we're joined in silence.

Necromancer and queen.

Friends, after everything.

"But . . . I can't be *queen*," she says at last. "I never thought I'd—I don't know the first thing about leading. I hardly left my tower until I met you." Her cheeks redden as she continues, "And the Dead—those who are left—they're terrified of what Hadrien's brought out in people. I don't think they'd welcome a living ruler. I want to cure the sick and study our magic, but . . . I don't want the crown if it's going to make me set in my ways and completely unaware of the plight of everyone who needs me. Or one who frightens and bullies people into giving me more power."

I gently poke Valoria in the shoulder. "Enough. You're not *him*. And you're not King Wylding, either." I squeeze her hand, earning a reluctant smile. "You're exactly what Karthia needs. Even if no one realizes it yet. You have to believe it first, and others will follow. You'll see, my queen."

"I'm not that brave." She shakes her head. "I'm not you."

"That's a good thing, because I'm not brave at all. I couldn't have survived this long without Evander, Master Cymbre, Meredy, Lysander . . ."

My voice trails away as my heart leaps into my throat. The bear is gone, vanished from my side as I spoke with Valoria.

"Don't worry, Sparrow," I faintly hear Valoria saying. "You'll never have to fight alone."

I frantically look around for Lysander. A creature as large as a grizzly should be easy to spot, even in a massive crowd.

I shake my head to clear it. Lysander still hasn't appeared, but Valoria's smiling, pointing to something past the fishmongers' stalls.

Several familiar figures hurry toward us.

Jax reaches me first, lifting me off my feet and spinning me around until I'm dizzy. I bury my face against his shoulder, assured by the scent of his evergreen soap that it's really him and not my mind playing a cruel trick.

Simeon quickly shoves Jax aside, squeezing the breath out of me in a rib-cracking hug.

Danial waves from over Simeon's shoulder, looking tired but no worse off than the last time I saw him. "Hurt yourself again I see, Sparrow," he calls. "I'll heal your leg, if these two will let me borrow you for a little while."

"Not a chance. Not yet," Simeon murmurs to Danial, quickly refocusing on me. "What happened?" he whispers, pushing back his soggy bangs to better look at me. "You're as soaked as we are, and we took a dip in the harbor!"

"You—what?" I stammer, realizing that both he and Jax are as damp and frigid-looking as I feel. But I don't care if my whole body goes numb with cold right now, because my heart is soaring. "I was hiding from a Shade. Why were you in the harbor?"

"Hadrien ordered his guards to drown us. I guess so no one would find our bodies," Jax says, slipping an arm around my shoulders so I'm pinned between him and Simeon. Just like old times. "The bastard. But it took ten of his men to do it."

"It was more like five," Simeon counters, grinning slyly.

"However many there were, they did a pretty good job," Kasmira says, joining Danial with several of her crew in tow. "But I thought these two had brighter futures than serving as fish food." She winks, tossing her many dark braids over her shoulder. "The crew and I dredged them up as soon as the guards had their backs turned. Hid them on the *Paradise*, and that's where the princess here found them."

"You saved my friends," I mutter, beaming at Kasmira. "If there's anything I can do to repay you . . . anything, just name it."

She arches a perfect brow. "Before today, I might've asked you for a raising. But my dead are going to stay that way, I've decided." Her cool gray eyes dart to the mess in the streets, then focus on my face again. "I wouldn't mind a taste of royal gold, though, if we're talking rewards."

"Consider it done," Valoria says firmly, gazing at each of us in turn: Jax, Simeon, and me in the middle. She holds out a hand to Kasmira. "And from now on, consider yourselves free to come and go from these waters as you please."

Kasmira grins at her crew, then gives Valoria a long, thoughtful look. "That's almost a better reward than the gold, Highness."

"Actually—" Valoria's cheeks redden as she boldly declares, "it's Majesty now, but I prefer just Valoria."

Kasmira blinks. "All right, Valoria." She bows, and the other smugglers follow her lead.

I raise my voice. "Has anyone seen Meredy?"

I still have to find her, and while everyone around me looks relieved to see each other again, I can't breathe easy until I know where she is. That she's safe.

Danial frowns. "She ran off right before I found Valoria and the others . . ." He grimaces. "I wasn't fast enough, and she disappeared on me. Before that, she was acting strange. Erratic."

Maybe she's still nearby. Even if she was in a feral state when she ran off, it may not last long. I'd better find her before someone else does. Someone who might not understand why she's growling at them like a bear.

"We were looking for her when we found you," Valoria adds in a small voice. "We thought she might've been drawn to the crowd."

Jax nudges my shoulder, startling me. "Look." He points to an oddly shaped shadow moving toward us through the late-afternoon gloom. My muscles tense as I wonder if another Shade got loose somehow.

But as Jax reaches for one of his blades, I shake my head. It's not a Shade, but a large creature dragging a smaller one by the back of her cloak.

Lysander, and—

"Meredy!"

For the second time since leaving the palace, I forget everything happening around me. The steely water of the harbor at my back. The city already starting to heal.

Meredy looks so small and pale when Lysander drops her at my feet. I kneel beside her in the ash and dirt, pressing a hand to her cheek. "Meredy?" When she says nothing, staring at me blankly, a knife of panic plunges into my chest.

"Can a beast master's magic make them forget their humanity for good?" I ask Valoria over my shoulder.

"I have no idea," she says, her eyes glistening.

As I cradle Meredy in my arms, racking my brain for something that might help her return to herself, she pulls my face to hers and kisses me.

I kiss her back. Lightly, and then not so lightly, rubbing my thumb over the scar on her cheek the way she often does. She tastes different from before, like the wilderness, like new beginnings, like surrender. I run my hands up and down her back, over her hips, then slide my fingers through her hair.

And her heart beats against mine like it remembers.

She kisses me with a wolf's hunger, hard and needy, breathing fire into my mouth. Her body bends and presses against mine, finding new ways for us to fit together as we trade kisses like bites of something sweet that only make us ravenous for more. I don't ever want this to stop, because I've found a part of me I didn't know was missing.

Someone gasps, breaking the spell. Meredy. She buries her face in my hair and whispers, "What are we doing?"

"You tell me." Drawing back to give her space, I force myself to smile. "Welcome back, Master Crowther."

I risk a look at my friends. They're all gazing tactfully away. All except Valoria, who, glancing from me to Meredy, grins her approval.

Then she turns to Jax and starts a conversation that makes him laugh, his voice deep and rich. It's a sound I haven't heard since Evander left us. A sound that makes me smile, if only for a moment.

I help Meredy to her feet, gazing around once again at all the destruction. Smashed windows and broken buildings, bits of ash, lives in tatters. Only now I see the hope among the rubble, glittering in Valoria's keen eyes, in Danial's selfless hands healing the wounded, in the voice of the girl beside me as she whispers, "I wish Evander could see this. How we fought, and won. But I'd bet my mother's fortune he already knew we would."

Hand in hand, Meredy and I hurry to the shop fronts where Simeon and several children are sweeping up glass. One of the Dead, a slender woman with hardly any voice, hands us spare brooms and works quietly beside us.

It's time. For change. To clean up all evidence of destruction, but not to forget the cause. It's time to rebuild all that was set ablaze. And maybe, in the days to come, everything that rises from the ashes will be better than before.

XXXII

The palace courtyard is more crowded tonight than I've ever seen it. Standing around bonfires and feasting tables, commoners mix with nobles while Valoria's younger siblings mingle with weather mages, beast masters, and healers from all over the province. And among them all, at every fireside, at every table, holding glasses of the finest elderflower wine and plates piled high with the tastiest dishes, are most of Grenwyr's remaining Dead.

I watch the merrymaking from an alcove at the back of the courtyard, near the garden where, not too long ago, I sank to my knees and mourned the death of who I had once been.

In the distance, Jax and Danial escort Valoria around as she talks to all the guests as their queen for the first time, though she hasn't yet had her coronation. And nearby, Simeon leads a group of children in a dance. One he's making up as he goes along.

Tonight and from now on, there will be new dances, new

recipes, and even new fashions on display, because this is the first Festival of Change in over two hundred years. It's a celebration of everything new and will be the first of many under Valoria's rule, she says.

Catching Simeon's eye, I wink and raise my glass to him.

Time is a funny thing, I realize as I take a sip. I thought Evander and I had so much more than what we were given.

And that's what we all want, really, from the newest child in Karthia to the Dead who have stayed around to witness many generations of their family: more time.

Just a few paces away, a shrouded female figure tries to embrace a hesitant, tearful boy about my age, perhaps her son or brother. She must be one of the Dead who has chosen to return to the Deadlands tonight, who's using the party to prepare herself for moving on to whatever comes next.

After all, this festival is a night for celebrating their lives before Simeon, Jax, and I lead them through a glowing blue gate.

"Oh, come now! There's no room for tears here! This is a party!" Valoria pushes up her glasses, glancing worriedly between the boy and the Dead woman.

The boy throws his arms around the shrouded figure at last, and I smile. I'm surprised Valoria's brown eyes haven't spotted what I can see already: that in between the boy's grief and the Dead woman's quiet sobs is love.

And nothing, not time or distance or the Deadlands themselves, can change that. Or even make it fade.

I'm no stranger to sadness. I still cry for Evander in the long weeks since he's been gone. I can't smell fresh-cut grass or leather without thinking of him. Of what we had. And what I lost. But I only cry because his love is still with me, a familiar ache in my chest. I'll carry it with me, always, something no one can ever erase.

"So?" Valoria waves a hand in front of my face, making me jump. I don't know when she got so close. "What do you think?"

She spins around, and it's clear she means her new trousers and strange, stiff long-sleeved jacket, with its high collar, pointed shoulders, and gleaming brass buttons. It's a far cry from her usual party gowns, and when I say so, she flashes a wicked grin worthy of Jax. "I know it's not fancy. But it's what I plan to wear to my coronation."

"It's just . . ." I gaze around at the massive crowd of living and Dead partygoers as I search for words. "I've never seen anything like it. Is it one of your inventions?"

Valoria's eyes shine. "Not exactly. I found an image in one of the old books I saved, and I had a tailor recreate it." She smooths the jacket and stands taller with pride. "I believe it's what the master inventors used to wear. It's hard to be sure, seeing as I've only found evidence that three of them ever existed, but—"

"You mean four," I cut in, tapping her on the shoulder and grinning.

"Four, then." Valoria's face turns pink. "And how are you enjoying the festivities?" She waves to someone across the courtyard, then returns her keen gaze to me. "There weren't any writings on the Festival of Change that survived, at least not that I've found. So all this"—she spreads her arms to indicate the biggest feast I've ever witnessed—"was my design. If the Dead like this way of leaving our world, we'll do it again next year, too, for any that weren't ready this time."

I shake my head. "When do you find time to sleep? Don't you have the Festival of Evergreens to organize before next week? Not to mention your coronation before that."

"You know us Wyldings." Valoria laughs. "We love a good party." The light in her face dims as she adds, "But all good things must end, yes?" She gazes to our left, where Jax is organizing shrouded figures into a group for their departure to the Deadlands. "Looks like they're preparing for the grand farewell."

The Dead have eaten their fill, and it's almost time for me and my friends to guide them through the nearest gate. But before they go, their loved ones are presenting them each with a gift to take on the journey, to remind them of the world they're leaving. A ruby-studded hair comb. A worn storybook. A toy raccoon.

Valoria thought about suggesting that the Dead give their living relatives each a gift as well, until Simeon pointed out that their presence in our world is a gift. They've all been here to shape Karthia, for better or worse, long after they should have earned their rest.

Valoria leads everyone in raising a glass, making a toast in honor of the fallen. As my eyes mist over, someone taps my shoulder.

"I've been looking for you everywhere," Meredy murmurs in my ear. "You seem to have a habit of disappearing on me at parties . . ." She slips her hand into mine.

I quickly pull away, grabbing a miniature berry tart from a passing tray as my insides ache with guilt.

Meredy frowns. "Something's bothering you."

I don't meet her searching gaze. Instead, I shove the tart in my mouth and feign interest in the ceremony as more families step forward with gifts for their Dead, and my thoughts wander back a few hours.

Earlier in the evening, before the food came out, Valoria had people write down secrets on slips of paper and burn them in what she called the Fire of Letting Go. It didn't make me feel any better to watch the words go up in flames.

I'm ready to retire.

Everyone else is making a place for themselves in this new Karthia, changing along with it. Valoria is a queen now, with inventions to dream up and festivals to plan, and new laws to write to protect the living and the Dead. Jax and Simeon are still partners, ready to decide with Valoria what their new role as necromancers will be. Danial is training with the queen's guard, having found a talent with blades. And Meredy . . . she has her pick of security jobs anywhere in the country with Lysander, but she seems set on staying in Grenwyr. Near me.

Trouble is, I can't picture myself here anymore. Evander's not an easy partner to replace in any sense, and I'm not sure I ever want to return to the Deadlands after I guide our Dead safely home tonight. I'm hanging up my necromancer's belt for good.

So tonight, once the festival is over, I'm booking myself passage on the *Paradise*. Kasmira told me she's setting sail for uncharted waters at dawn, and I'll be on board.

I guess that means I'm changing, too. Evander's dream has become mine, and I'm ready to learn what lies beyond the walls we put up to shut out the rest of the world for so long.

But first, I owe a goodbye to Meredy, who's still standing by my side after everything. "You're right. Something is bothering me." I nod to the garden archway. "Walk with me for a little while?"

She grabs a glass of amber liquid from a servant and drains half before responding. "There's . . . something I need to tell you, too, come to think of it."

She leans in, her face alarmingly close to mine, and I take a step back. There's a wildness in her eyes that makes my heart beat double, and I realize I'm not ready to hear what's about to spill from her lips. Especially not when all I want to say is goodbye.

Turning, I flag down the nearest tray of berry tarts, plucking the entire platter from the hands of a startled serving boy. "Thanks!" I call as I present it to Meredy, who looks paler than she did a moment ago.

"You have to try these, they're excellent." I grin to cover the hollowness of my words, and shove the tray at Meredy.

But her attention has roamed elsewhere, lost in the heart of the crowd.

All around us, people are finally letting their Dead go. Listening to them, I should understand the language of farewell. I should be able to say a proper goodbye to Valoria, Jax, and Simeon—to Meredy—rather than slipping away in the dead of night. But maybe I don't understand farewells because that's not what they're really saying—their murmurs and embraces seem to mean, "See you later."

And that's just what I'll say to Karthia and everyone I've come to love here.

But for now, it's time for one last job. Time to lead the Dead home.

XXXIII

The palace is too quiet this late at night, even with the many preparations being made for Valoria's coronation. I put a borrowed bag of Jax's on my bed, one he'll never realize I snuck from his disaster of a room, and stare hard at it as I try to figure out what to pack.

There isn't much time. Kasmira isn't expecting me, so she won't wait, and judging by the deep indigo of the starry sky and the utter silence around me, I've only got a few hours to slip away unnoticed before the pale gray of predawn wakes the first palace inhabitants.

I toss Master Cymbre's book into my bag. It's the only place where she recorded her thoughts, leaving little imprints of herself across the pages, and I like that I can take her with me wherever I go next.

But I can't take the rest of my friends along, so that leaves my sword, some clothes, and a bunch of jewelry I probably won't need.

I pull a teardrop-shaped emerald pendant apart from the rest. It's cold and heavy and sharp against my skin, a perfect farewell gift for Meredy. But how would she react? She'd probably dismiss the gesture as romantic, and I can't tell her she's wrong when *I* don't even know what it means.

I toss it back in the bag.

A lump forms in my throat as I steal down the darkened hall to the guest room where Meredy is staying with Lysander while her sister Elibeth is busy helping repair the Crowther manor and other homes in Noble Park destroyed by Shades.

All is quiet outside Meredy's door. No trace of light glows from underneath. Not even an occasional grumbling snore from Lysander.

I press my cheek to the cold wood for a moment and close my eyes. It's hard to believe I once thought her a brat. That I was so befuddled by calming potions, I couldn't see her for the warrior she is. I'm going to miss her steadying touch when I'm at sea, feeling off-balance around so much that's new. Squaring my shoulders, I stride quickly away, before thoughts of her can call me back, before she senses the presence outside her door and wakes.

Slipping through an exit not often used, I sling my bag over my shoulder and start off into the night, off to explore the great unknown like Evander always dreamed.

The banners of the *Paradise* billow in a nighttime breeze, beckoning me toward the harbor. I take a misstep and knock over someone's potted shrub, grinning guiltily because I must still be slightly tipsy from the Festival of Change. After fighting for our lives, we all needed another celebration more than we realized.

A glimmer of moonlight on sleek feathers catches my eye. I turn, gazing up the hill to my right, back toward the palace.

There, pecking the last blackberries of the season from a row of neatly tended bushes under cover of darkness, is a pet peacock with a suspiciously crooked wing.

I raise a hand in greeting. The bird stretches out its long neck and squawks in return. I haven't broken it after all, only changed it in my moment of carelessness, for better or worse, like Karthia was changed by the actions of a madman.

"I'm really sorry," I whisper. But sensing movement on the distant ship, I realize there's no time left for regrets or apologies. The crew is preparing to set sail.

As I run toward my new beginning in the harbor, the salty night wind combing my hair, I realize there are some changes I don't regret. Ones I'm glad for, even, like Valoria's inventions—some of them, anyway.

By the time I step on board the *Paradise*, the sky holds a faint trace of gray.

"You sure you want this?" Kasmira asks, looking me over with mild concern after I explain my intentions and press a hefty payment into her hands. "You've been through a lot, Sparrow. More than most people endure in a lifetime. All I'm saying is . . . this is a big decision, and I won't turn my boat around for anyone." She smiles and squeezes my shoulder. "Not even my favorite people in the world."

"I'm sure."

I follow Kasmira to the sleeping quarters, where I stow my bag in the tiny room I'll be calling home for Vaia knows how long. I sit on the narrow bed, resting my chin on my hands, trying not to think about anything more than why there are several extra bags shoved in the corner next to a table and water jug.

It looks like my hard-earned money bought me a bed in the storage room.

When the sky has lightened a few more shades, Kasmira raps on the door, beckoning me to the main deck in time to watch the ship pulling away from shore. As I reach the rail, my stomach does a flip. I stare at the sea below, unsure whether I want to watch Karthia retreating into the distance as we glide toward open water through the early morning mist.

"Are you sure you're in the right place?" a familiar voice asks. "Because we're not turning this ship around just because a high-born lady forgot her hairbrush. Or so I've been told."

I whirl around.

I must be hallucinating again, some long-ranging side effect of all those calming potions, because she looks different than I remember. Maybe it's the plain trousers and black blouse beneath her fur-trimmed cloak, or the kohl thickly lining her eyes. Maybe it's her glowing skin, or the way her smile isn't so tightly controlled, or that her wine-red hair is half in a braid, half down, falling in waves around her shoulders.

But when she cautiously reaches out to touch my arm and it makes my mouth go dry, I know it's really her—the person I was trying most to escape, stuck on this too-small boat with me.

I open my mouth to shout to Kasmira at the opposite rail, to demand that she turn the boat around. She catches my gaze and winks, and that's when I'm certain there will be no turning back. This is really happening.

"Where's Lysander?" I stammer, glancing around the deck.

"Making sure Kasmira doesn't take any of his things," Meredy murmurs.

"*His* things?"

She gives me a hesitant grin. "Bones, mostly. I packed a lot of tasty grizzly food to make sure he won't gnaw on anyone here if the fish are scarce."

I turn slightly away from her, deciding I need to gaze at Karthia's familiar rocky cliffs for as long as I can. "When were you planning on telling me you were leaving?" I blurt out. Some of the crew turn to stare, and the back of my neck burns.

"You're one to talk!" Meredy gives me another strange look, like she did earlier at the festival. "*I* tried to tell you, at the party. You were in such an odd mood, though, that in the end I thought it would be easier to say nothing."

I think of the emerald pendant I almost left her, and nod. Then I frown as a ridiculous and unpleasant idea occurs.

"Were you following me? Is that why you're here?"

Meredy draws herself up, her eyes flashing. She pulls out a tattered leather-bound book from inside her cloak and thrusts it at me. "*This* is why I'm here. And for your information, I came here straight after the party. *You* weren't on board yet. Just so we're clear on who's following who."

As I flip open the book, she adds, "That was my father's. I kept it all these years because it's the one thing my brother and I had in common." She taps the open page. "These are all my father's notes on Karthia's provinces. His personal maps." She flips toward the middle of the book, where the pages are blank except for a few water stains. "And these were waiting to be filled in by Elibeth or Evander—or me."

Shaking, I lean harder against the rail, but that only makes me feel like I might fall overboard at any moment. I straighten. "Why now, though? Why this voyage?"

Meredy arches a brow. "I don't know of any other ships leaving Karthian seas anytime soon, do you?" Retreating behind her mask of coolness, she adds, "Besides, it seemed the smartest thing to do, given . . . recent circumstances." She pauses, narrowing her eyes at me. "Now. What are *you* doing here?"

I shake my head. "Believe it or not, the same as you." When she frowns, I add, "I thought I'd fulfill Evander's dreams since he'll never have the chance."

Meredy sighs. "Well, since we're both here, we'll just have to make the best of things, no?"

I watch her lips for a moment before I concede, "Sure, Master Crowther," nudging her playfully.

A wave crashes against the shore we're leaving behind. The only place I've ever known. I wonder when I'll see it again, and what else will change before then. Already, Valoria has reopened the temples of Change and spoken with her advisors about starting a mage school. A place to help people understand their magic—its dangers and its gifts.

"You'll find your way back here sooner than you think, Sparrow," Meredy murmurs, as if sensing my thoughts.

I open my mouth to say I hope so, but the words won't come out. Even if I did return soon, what would Jax, Simeon, and Danial say about my leaving? Worst of all is picturing the betrayal on Valoria's face. I'm not sure I want to come back to Karthia soon, if ever. The only thing I'm sure I want right now is to be alone so I can clear my head, but that's plainly not going to happen.

"Storm's coming," Kasmira says.

I glance over my shoulder. Behind us, our captain searches the dawn skies with her gray-eyed Sight, checking whether she'll need to work her magic. "Hope you're both ready for an interesting first day's sailing."

"Oh, it's already interesting," Meredy whispers, almost making me smile.

If I close my eyes, listening to the gulls' cries and breathing the salt air, I can pretend for a moment that nothing's changed. But when I open them, there's a beautiful girl by my side with adventure in her eyes, and a new world shimmers on the horizon.

And at long last, I'm ready to greet it.

ACKNOWLEDGMENTS

So many brilliant people played a role in bringing Odessa's story to life—and, in doing so, played an important role in mine as well:

First and foremost: Lucy Carson, the champion agent every author dreams of and deserves. The one who believes in me even when I don't. I am beyond fortunate to benefit from your guidance, wit, and wisdom. I'd trust you to have my back in the dangerous Deadlands—even if neither of us knows how to wield a sword!

Equally vital to this story was Jessica Almon, editor extraordinaire and now wonderful friend. From the moment we first spoke on the phone, your love for Odessa and her world was so clear, I knew I had to work with you. The care that you put into editing with me gave me renewed confidence and joy in my writing, and I will forever be thankful for that. Thank you also for always staying true to my voice and vision as we worked to polish each scene.

Extra-big thanks to Julie Rosenberg for stepping in to help bring this story to publication and to continue the adventures in book two. Odessa and her friends are in excellent hands with you, and I'm so lucky and thrilled to have you on Team Reign!

My wonderful publicist, Elyse Marshall, and the rest of the fierce folks at Razorbill—Ben Schrank, Alex Sanchez, Casey McIntyre, and so many others: Thank you so much for all your hard work in making this book a reality, for truly making me feel like a valued member of the team, and for publishing lots of my favorite stories! Here's to taking risks and making good art.

Many thanks to Toby and Pete, Maggie Edkins, and Kristin Boyle for creating and designing the book cover of my dreams. And thanks to Eric Ford for the beautiful interior!

Lenore Dukes, thank you for patiently spending so much time brainstorming and talking through the idea for *Reign* with me on the phone when it was in its fledgling stages; this story wouldn't be the same without your thoughtful influence.

Martina Boone and Jodi Meadows, two super-talented authors and marvelous friends. Thank you for talking out this idea with me late one night at our hotel room in New Jersey, back when *Reign* was just scribbles in a notebook, and for giving me new ways to think about villains.

My amazing CPs and beta readers: the one and only KT, the talented Eve Castellan, world's best pen pal Kat Kennedy, the phenomenal Mana from *The Book Voyagers*, Brittany (of *Book Rambles* fame), sweet Becky G from *Life of a BookNerd Addict*, darling Nori from *ReadWriteLove28*, super-smart editor Carolee Noury, Natalie B., Christine Pellegrini, Rachel Simon, Emily Skrutskie, Rachel Stevenson, and Amber Hendricks. I'm so grateful for your insights as readers, but even more so for your friendship, whether we only chat occasionally or we text every day.

Jessica Spotswood and Wendy Higgins, thank you so much for your support for this story and for your friendship!

Jo Painter, one of my favorite artists. Thank you for your support and for working with me to bring these characters to life so beautifully.

My dear, creative friends Gwen Cole, Erin Cashman, Erin Manning, Erin McQuaig, Chelsea Bobulski, Ami Allen-Vath,

Teresa Yea, Heidi Lang, Kati Bartkowski, Rachel Pudelek, Brian Schwarz, Joe Sparks, M Evan Matyas, Christina Gustin, Anna Schafer, Laura Weymouth, Karina from *AfirePages*, Lauren from *Live, Love, Read*, and the inimitable ladies of 16 to Read. Thank you for your friendship, your ability to make me laugh, your willingness to let me vent, and just generally inspiring me with your awesomeness.

My family: Mom and Dad, my sister Lindsey, Nana and Papa, Team Williams, Ben and Galena, and the rest of the Peters family. Also my in-laws, Marilyn and Joe Lauscher. I'm so thankful to have you all in my life.

Chris, you get your own paragraph. Epic. Thank you for giving this book its title, for listening to my favorite scenes out loud so many times, for always seeing me as I am and accepting me, and for pushing me to dream bigger.

Every marginalized person who has spoken out and who continues to speak out against injustice and in doing so encourages our society to grow and change in the right ways: We need your voices now more than ever.

Lastly, to everyone reading this, whether you helped bring this book to life in any way or you've just arrived in Karthia for the first time: Thank you for going on this journey with me. Much love to you all.

DATE DUE

FEB 2 3 2018	
MAR – 5 2018	

PRINTED IN U.S.A.